W9-AKB-654

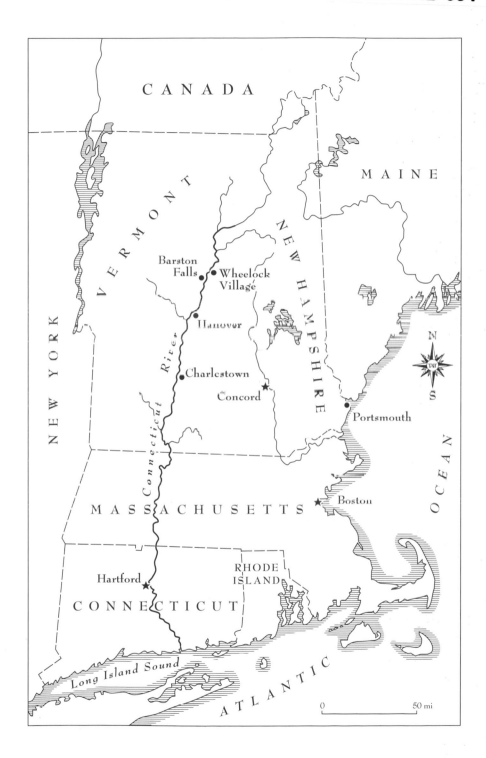

Old Sam's Thunder

Some Responses to

Old Sam's Thunder

"**. . . a literary masterpiece.** If *Old Sam's Thunder* doesn't become a classic, I will be very surprised. This book will hold its own with the best . . . one of the finest works of historical fiction that I have ever read. "

— **Floyd Ramsey,** author of
Shrouded Memories

"**A thunderous story, masterfully told!**

"Sure to thrill all readers, whether or not they've ever set foot in the Connecticut River valley or on the Dartmouth College campus. Fourth of July preparations have never been more touching, humorous or suspenseful. Just when you think you know what's going to happen next, the chicanery takes a surprising turn.

"This tale left me so elated that I then had to read Jack Noon's first book about this mythical town, *The Big Fish of Barston Falls*. I just hope he doesn't keep me waiting long for the next one!"

— **Tom Burack**

"It is the many wonderful stories of the founders and early settlers of New England that make its history and folklore so rich. *Old Sam's Thunder* celebrates both America's independence and the independent mindedness of the 19th century residents of New England — and in particular the people of the Upper Connecticut River valley."

— **John Mudge,** author of
The White Mountains: Names,
Places and Legends

"If you ask how I like my history, I like it the way Jack Noon writes it: strong story, rich characters, and spiced with dry, wry Yankee humor.

"Jack Noon's work fills an important educational niche, especially for young people, by bringing New England history to life. The life he gives it through his strong characters makes it entertaining as well as educational. And that's a lot to say about a book."

— **Rebecca Rule,** author of
The Best Revenge

"Another great yarn from the fictional town of Barston Falls. Jack Noon's forte is combining the imagined with the historical.

"In *The Big Fish of Barston Falls* he gave us a regional version of Hemingway's *The Old Man and the Sea*, describing in detail community life along the upper Connecticut River during the early 1800s. The cast of characters and the time period in *Old Sam's Thunder* are much the same. The story, however, focuses not on fishing, but on family, town, and nation. Especially recommended for fans of July 4th ceremonies."

— **Prof. Jere Daniell**
Dartmouth College

"While reading Jack Noon's new book, *Old Sam's Thunder*, I noted this weird feeling that I was living the story right here in Haverhill Corner, New Hampshire, where I live. Every detail is *now*, even though the story took place in 1826. The rivers, the mountains, the people and the history are accurate and exciting. Noon's stuff is that real! I'm even poking around our nearby Ladd Street Cemetery, because I have a distinct feeling that Old Sam Barston is buried right here.

"Jack Noon says it's fiction, but I'm not convinced."

— **Bernie Marvin**
Publisher, *Northcountry News-Independent*

Also by Jack Noon

The Big Fish of Barston Falls
The Squam Lakes and Their Loons
The Bassing of New Hampshire

Writing as M.J. Beagle

Sit Free or Die
The New Hampshire Primer

Cover and Illustrations
Walt Cudnohufsky

Maps
Alex Tait

Old Sam's Thunder

by Jack Noon

Moose Country Press

1998

Moose Country Press
Warner, N.H.

© 1998 – Jack Noon
All Rights Reserved– No part of this book may be repro-
duced in any form or by any electronic or mechanical means,
including information storage and retrieval systems, without
permission in writing from the publisher, except by a re-
viewer who may quote brief passages in a review.

ISBN 0-9642213-6-5

Library of Congress Cataloging-in-Publication Data

Noon, Jack, 1946–
    Old Sam's thunder / by Jack Noon.
        p.   cm.
    ISBN 0-9642213-6-5 (alk. paper).
    1. New England – History – Fiction.
    2. Vermont – History – 1775-1865 – Fiction.
    3. New Hampshire – History – Fiction. I. Title.
PS3564.0489043 1998
813'.54 – dc21   98-6203
                                                           CIP

10 9 8 7 6 5 4 3 2 1

Printed in the United States of America

To my sister,
Laura Jennings

Author's Foreword

For a few years early in nineteenth century America, patriotic celebrations enjoyed a special vitality. Americans had twice tussled with Britain, claimed victory both times, and were proud of their independence and of their growing nation.

During this era the few cannons in the New Hampshire and Vermont portion of the Connecticut River valley were greatly prized as noisemakers for Fourth of July celebrations. In the muster-day, militia tradition of the time, the artillery company in each regiment most typically had the lone cannon among the half dozen or more towns whose companies made up the regiment. Often the militia's cannons were jealously guarded. Other cannons were rare, and for the towns' Independence Day celebrations there weren't nearly enough to meet demand. In addition amateurs of artillery, loaded with alcohol and ignorance, would occasionally overcharge a cannon and blow it up; thus reduce by one the number both of available cannons and of amateur artillerists.

The upper valley cannons claimed glorious traditions. One or two had supposedly helped defend forts along the Connecticut back in the days of the French and Indian wars. Others, as far too many long-standing accounts had it throughout New Hampshire and Vermont, were the very ones General Stark had captured at the battle of Bennington.

In early July of 1807 or 1808 night-riding citizens of Keene stole Walpole's cannon and were taken to court. The judge ruled that the cannon, supplied decades earlier by the king, belonged to no particular town and dismissed the case. Walpole, entering into the proper spirit of cannon-grabbing, stole it back on the next Fourth of July. Later on, Westminster and then Alstead and possibly Westmoreland joined in and temporarily held this same cannon during its swiftly rotating ownership. Thereafter, in several places up and down the valley where there were vulnerable cannons, this light-hearted and light-fingered activity, mostly nocturnal, assumed a town rivalry status much like today's high school athletics. As nearly as I can tell, at least a carryover of this tradition endured well into the twentieth century. Some mis-intentioned selectmen in Lyme brought the last vestiges to an end, without asking anyone's permission, during a World War II scrap metal drive. They were unknowingly getting even for their townsman, Kimball, a cannon casualty July 4th, 1851, in Hanover on the Dartmouth College green; victim of his failure to swab the cannon's bore between firing and reloading.

In *Old Sam's Thunder* the Vermont township of Barston and New Hampshire township of Wheelock are fictional, as are their inhabitants. However, all other details of this time just before the fiftieth anniversary of independence are based either on facts or on oral traditions later written down. Names of Dartmouth students, teachers, and buildings of the town and college are accurate. Sewall Tenney was in fact the bell ringer and did live in room 10 on the third floor of "The College." The college museum down the hall from his room had included a flamingo, penguin, "robe of an Owyhee priest," and many other treasures before a cannon fired inside the building obliterated the museum walls, and the surviving trophies began to wander. A traditional claim, too perfect to risk demolishing with close research, identifies Benjamin Pierce, older brother of the president-to-be, as ringleader for this particular cannon-blast episode (there were others at Dartmouth) and continues the legend with his separation from college and later career as artillery officer. The stuffed zebra, a cherished member of the college for more than a century, had been given to Dartmouth by "King" Derby, who started the China trade. Charlestown did in fact have a cannon, perhaps the same one that had originally defended Fort No. 4 from the French and Indians. The Hanover and Norwich cannon rivalry had been one of the valley's strongest, but 1826 found the buildings of Norwich's American Literary Scientific and Military Academy (precursor to Norwich University, now located in Northfield, Vermont) temporarily abandoned and the rivalry dormant; not actively useful for this novel. The old cannon kept "in a ... shed ... south of the Tontine" was the one, according to one tradition, which had been captured at Bennington and which Dartmouth boys decades earlier had allegedly stolen from Windsor or Norwich. Another tradition claimed it as a ship's gun sent to Hanover as a trophy of the Revolution.

In time, the state militias disbanded, and shattered cannons weren't replaced. Nagging, busybody sentiments for civilization and temperance and common sense eventually prevailed. The bores of surviving cannons were filled with concrete or their priming holes were spiked, and mere firecrackers replaced cannon blasts. More people managed to survive the Fourth of July celebrations, but the day without the crash and thunder and echo — and danger — of cannon fire had lost some of its sparkle.

Jack Noon
Sutton, New Hampshire
July 4th, 1998

Old Sam's
Thunder

I

Barston, Vermont
October, 1825

The wheels of the slowly moving wagon rattled over occasional rocks and holes. The light shocks jostled Old Sam Barston, who slouched in the wagon seat, scarcely aware that he held the reins.

Hayfields lay off to both sides of the road. They had yielded cuttings in late May and early August and would now pasture some of the many merino sheep in the valley until the hard freezes of November. To Old Sam's right the fields sprawled down to the edge of the Connecticut River. To his left they rose gradually out of the riverbottom land and ended at a long stone wall. Beyond the stone wall sheep pastures alternated with more stone walls all the way up to low hills of woods interspersed with ledges.

Old Sam gazed ahead over the backs of several hundred grazing sheep at the swath of autumn foliage along the banks of Mill Brook. His eyes followed the colors down to the marsh where the brook flowed into the Connecticut, and then they swept across the stippled expanse of red, yellow, and orange beyond the river in New Hampshire. Only a few pines interrupted the bright colors between the river and the continuous belt of spruce and fir along the slopes of Hackmatack Ridge, Catamount Ridge, and Mt. Wheelock.

The mid-afternoon sun on the scene across the river made little impression on Old Sam, however, for he was lost in thought about events sixty years past.

At the brook the thudding of shod hooves and the light rumble of wheel rims on the bridge planking roused Old Sam. Past the bridge and off to the left John Parker sat on the porch of the North Barston store, which had belonged to his father, Eli. Old Sam merely nodded to him and kept on his way up towards the cemetery.

Old Sam stopped the wagon by the cemetery gate. As he reached under his seat for his jug, he stared at the gravestones. Some were slate. Others were marble. A few were fieldstones. Here and there among the stones were sunken rectangles in the sod. Some, marked at neither the head nor the foot, were pathetically short. Old Sam gazed at the cemetery between drinks, occasionally shaking his head. At last he pushed the corncob stopper back into the jug, put it under the seat, and painfully climbed down from the wagon.

Leaning heavily on a walking stick, Old Sam passed through the gate and hobbled over to a corner of the cemetery. Four white pines, about as tall as Old Sam, grew just inside the hewn stone of the cemetery walls. Two clumps of lilacs there stood several feet taller than the pines. Old Sam halted between a pair of marble stones beside the lilacs and the pines, touching one stone and then the other.

"Eli and Molly," Old Sam said. "Thought I'd say goodby this time. I ain't likely to get up here again."

Old Sam let his walking stick fall to the ground as he stood with a hand grasping each stone. After a while he brushed the back of his hand across his eyes, shook his head at the four small stones between him and the corner, and with difficulty picked up his walking stick. Slowly he pulled off a few lilac leaves and pine needles and put them into his pocket.

As he sat again in the wagon seat, panting from the effort of climbing back up, he reached for the jug once more.

"All dead," he said between drinks. "Everybody from the early days dead and gone but me. Ain't another soul left."

He put the jug away and then stared at the cemetery for a long time. Finally the mare shook her head in the harness and nickered.

"Sure, Brownie," Old Sam said. "I ain't forgot you. We'll go back down to the Falls. It's just that Eli and Molly are gone, and I'll never see 'em again. And I might not get up here any more. But we'll go. There's more to visit before the day is done."

He turned the mare and urged her forward with the reins. As the wagon rolled back across the bridge over Mill Brook, Old Sam noticed thunderheads building on the horizon.

"Too late in the season for a thunderstorm," he said.

*****

Two hours later the wagon crossed Tannery Brook and skirted the village of Barston Falls. Old Sam guided the mare up a slight incline onto the east side of Barston Hill and stopped by the cemetery there. He gazed for a moment over to the east; saw clearly many of the buildings of Barston Falls, the canal through the center of the village, the fast water beyond it in the Connecticut, the big bay and eddy off to his right, the looming mass of Rattlesnake Hill over in New Hampshire rising abruptly from the river. He sighed as he remembered the time before there was a village. One family of Barstons and one family of Parkers had been the township's only inhabitants. The scene there at Barston Falls had certainly changed since those days.

Old Sam turned his head and admired the hewn capstones atop the rock walls of the cemetery. Yes, that had been good work his brother Israel had caused to have done.

Those walls would stand for eternity, or close enough to eternity so that it wouldn't make any difference. He remembered back to the days when he and others had raised the gate pillars. Everybody had grumbled about having to set them so deep, but the effort had been worth it. He doubted they'd budged even a mite in all those years. He frowned at the wagon ruts passing between the pillars.

A fine state of affairs when men are so weak and prissy they can't carry a coffin on their shoulders from the house parlor of the deceased up to the grave! When they have to stoop to usin' a horse and that special wagon to help 'em avoid doin' their proper duty!

A curse would be on the whole village if they treated his coffin like that. The wheel ruts ran up towards the receiving vault, dug into the slope of the hill; its oak door facing east towards New Hampshire. That vault had been a chore to build from hewn stone, and of all the men who had worked on it only Old Sam was still alive. It didn't seem possible. The others had all been young, strong men, and now they were gone. Gravestones spread out across the slope between the two side walls of the cemetery. There was no back wall because people in the village had never been able to agree on just how big the cemetery should be. They had argued back and forth and had finally resolved the dispute by agreeing to decide about it later. That had been decades ago. Now no one seemed to care if there were a back wall or not. As the generations pushed forward, the gravestones might go all the way up to the top of Barston Hill — or at least as far up as the digging stayed decent. So many headstones, Old Sam thought. So many people dead and buried there over the years, and he could remember before there had even been a cemetery. It made him feel old.

"Well, I guess I should visit the graves," he said. "Can't set here the rest of the day."

As he was climbing down from the wagon, the mare lurched ahead a step to begin cropping at the last of the season's green grass. Old Sam sprawled hard onto the ground. Dazed, he sat up slowly.

"Course you don't care, Brownie," Old Sam groaned. "Could of broke my neck and you wouldn't care just so long as you get your grass. Lucky you ain't my horse, Brownie, or I'd teach you better manners with a chain or a crowbar. Might just do it anyways."

The mare paid no attention; continued to pull at the grass. Old Sam felt shaken to the marrow and took quite a while regaining his feet. When at last he did begin to wander among the gravestones, it was with his cane in one hand and the jug in the other. On one side of the cemetery he stopped by a score or more of stones bearing the Barston name.

"Isaac . . . Caleb . . . Israel . . ." he said slowly, nodding at the graves of three of his four brothers where they lay by their wives and by those of their children who had died young. His memories of the many burial days mingled together so that he had no clear recollection of any of them, though he was certain he had been at each one. Well, there was nothing more he had to remember other than that the people were all dead and gone. Nothing else mattered.

Old Sam wandered down to the one stone in the cemetery he had set there with his own hand so many years earlier. How long had it been now? He was still so shaken from his fall that he couldn't think clearly enough to remember. Amanda Barston, the only wife he'd ever had. She'd always been healthy until her last year; until the onset of the cruel, wasting disease that had taken her life. None of the six children she had borne had died in childhood; all had lived to grow up and marry. That was a comfort, Old Sam thought, but it wasn't a comfort that not even one of them had stayed in the Connecticut River valley. All had left for the west. Ohio was one of the places. He couldn't remember the names of where else they had disappeared to. Why, if it hadn't been for the many descendants of his brothers, Old Sam would be alone in Barston Falls. He wondered if his own children were doing well; wondered if he would ever see any of them again.

"I miss you, Mandy," Old Sam said. "I miss you and the old days and the times we had together." He clenched his cane under the arm carrying the jug, reached into his pocket, and scattered a lilac leaf and a few pine needles onto her grave. "That's from Molly and Eli."

The wind gusted in on Old Sam as he was standing by his wife's grave. He glanced above and, shaking his head in disbelief, saw the black storm clouds and the not so distant flickers of lightning; heard the low rumble of thunder. He nodded at his wife's headstone and worked his way over towards the far edge of the cemetery to the grave he always visited last.

He stopped by a stone separated from the others, a slate marker Old Sam had paid to have erected two years earlier. It bore the lone word, "Malik." A bouquet of asters, wilted but not yet dried, lay in front of the stone.

"Sue must of left 'em," Old Sam murmured and took a drink. Then he splashed rum onto the ground beside the asters. "Here you go, Malik. We always did like to drink rum together. Just a taste now, you ornery old Abenaki. The rest is for me."

Old Sam felt the first drops of rain. He turned his pocket inside out and dumped the remaining lilac leaves and pine needles onto the rum-wetted ground.

"And that's from Eli and Molly."

The rain came more quickly, and Old Sam hurried on towards the receiving vault by the cemetery gate. He rummaged for a moment beneath the stones by one side of the vault door and came up with a key just as a downpour commenced. As quickly as he could, he freed the padlock on the vault door from its hasp, pushed against shrieking hinges, and then ducked inside as the rain drummed on his jug and his cane.

The receiving vault had been given to the village of Barston Falls by Israel Barston, Old Sam's youngest brother. Israel had insisted on a vault large enough to hold a dozen coffins through the months when the ground was too hard to dig graves. So far the precaution of size had been unwarranted. While Israel had still been alive, Old Sam used to tease him mercilessly about the size of the vault, saying that Israel should partition half of it off, put a new iron heating stove in it, and rent the space to a family. He had also suggested using it for storing beef carcasses or as a root cellar. Israel, conditioned as he was by a lifetime of Old Sam's teasing, had countered with similar suggestions for the vats at Old Sam's tannery.

As soon as Old Sam had regained his breath, he pulled the door open as wide as it would go and glanced around him in the poor light. Lumps of dirt, fallen through gaps between the ceiling stones, lay across the hewn stone floor. Three shovels and a pair of rusted crowbars leaned into the corner to the left of the door. Otherwise the vault was empty. Old Sam made the comment aloud which he had made every time he'd been in the vault before — the comment about "dead air" — and out of habit laughed at it once again.

Old Sam peered through the curtain of rain as the storm settled over the village. Lightning flashed. Thunder roared back and forth between Barston Hill and Rattlesnake Hill, directly across the Connecticut; each peal echoing and re-echoing until it had rumbled down to nothing. Old Sam thrilled at the crashes and reverberations, smiling at each new report, echo, and re-echo and laughing to himself at the novelty of a thunderstorm in October. Then his face clouded, and he shook his head slowly from side to side.

"Bunch of old biddies," he said and spat out into the rain in disgust. "Even with the anniversary comin' right up they can't see plain as day that the village needs a cannon. Vote it down every year. Skinflints. Bunch of useless biddies — prob'ly hidin' under their beds right now at the thunder, every worthless one of 'em."

He thought of the past several March town meetings. At each one Old Sam had made the motion that the town buy a cannon for celebrating the Fourth of July, recovering drowned bodies from the river, keeping the militia in training, and "other uses." Old Sam had particularly wanted one in time for the coming fiftieth anniversary of independence from England. That would be a day to make some noise, he had said, and what better noise-maker was there than a cannon? With Barston Hill and Rattlesnake Hill facing each other across the Connecticut right at the village, Old Sam had assured the voters that they'd get five times the noise for the powder used. Other villages had cannons already. It was high time that Barston Falls had one too. Some people had been nearly as enthusiastic as Old Sam, but a majority in the village had voted against using town funds for buying a cannon. They had cited more pressing needs, and the two cannons Old Sam had known about — which had been for sale way down in Boston — had gone elsewhere. Then, particularly galling to Old Sam, the state of New Hampshire had given a cannon to Wheelock Village — right across the river and up a couple of miles. The state of New Hampshire, with its tradition of privateering down along its coast, had cannons to give away. Vermont had none that could be had by any means. And perhaps some of the cannons that were being given away were the very ones that Vermonters had taken from Ticonderoga and, with Henry Knox, had hauled to Boston to use in the siege which finally drove the British away. Vermont had a moral right to cannons, but was as cannon-poor as a state could be. New Hampshire could give them away. It didn't seem fair. And besides, he reflected, Wheelock Village didn't have any decent hills for echoes. It lay between a couple of brooks which flowed into the Connecticut. There was enough slope to the land for a little water power, but nothing that could fling back a proper echo. Wheelock Village didn't deserve a cannon. Barston Falls needed one — cried out for one — and did without simply because Barston Falls was in Vermont rather than in New Hampshire and because a bunch of weak-kneed, skinflint biddies had decided they didn't want to spend a few dollars of the town's money for a cannon. Cheap, ignorant cusses! Fifty years of independence and all they could think about was their pocketbooks! He wondered what their idea of a celebration would be. Pony rides? A tea party with cookies?

A pain crept into Old Sam's chest, gradually doubling him up and forcing him down onto his knees. He labored hard to breathe.

"It ain't time yet, God. You know that. Take me when I'm out fishin' some day, and I'll come right along. But give me a little more time. Please give me a little more time."

Old Sam stayed down on his knees as the storm played itself out. Gradually the pain in his chest eased and finally disappeared. Old Sam crawled outside the vault and raised his eyes to the breaking clouds in the east.

"Thank you," he said.

An afterthought of thunder rumbled and thudded over the village, rolling back and forth between the hills.

"Thank you, sir!" Old Sam roared out. He tottered to his feet and went to retrieve his cane and jug; never even thought about closing the vault door.

The mare stood in her traces, soaked and shivering. Old Sam put the jug and his walking stick into the wagon. As he started to climb up onto the wagon, he spoke to the horse.

"You dump me this time, Brownie, and I'll whale on you 'til you turn to butter. And if I can't do a proper job, I'll hire a young man to do it — hire him by the day! Now behave."

Old Sam felt another twinge in his chest as he settled into the seat. He ignored it and brushed at the mud on his knees.

"Now pull a little, and you'll warm right up. We'll likely find you some grain when we get back to Jared's."

Old Sam drove the wagon up along the road used by freight wagons bound up and down the river when they didn't happen to have any business in the village. The road was west of another which ran parallel to the canal around the falls. It was on enough of a rise in the sweep of the land up onto Barston Hill to give Old Sam a good view of the village. The sun came out as he drove. The horse began to steam.

"Well, Brownie, you might live after all," Old Sam said. "Can't be helped."

At the junction with Tannery Road the mare wanted to turn right and go back to her stall in Jared Barston's barn.

"No. I ain't done with you yet," Old Sam said. "It won't take long, but there's one more place."

He turned left and kept going until he got to the tannery, which he owned and had worked in for years when he'd been younger. He stopped, but had little interest in the tannery. Instead he gazed across the road from it — up the slope at the cliffs on the north side of Barston Hill. His eyes fixed on a tremendous white boulder at the foot of the cliffs — a white boulder with dark bands running through it. It had been several years since he had last been up to the boulder, and he didn't think he would ever get up to it again. His father had been buried there in 1759 after dying of wounds suffered in the attack on the Indian village of St. Francis with Major Rogers. Old Sam and his mother and his brothers had later settled on the land where his father was buried. Old Sam's deranged brother, James — a suicide so many years ago — was buried at the boulder. The third and final grave there was that of his mother, who had wanted to lie for eternity beside her husband and son. There had been no more graves there by the boulder after that mainly because the digging was so hard and the access so difficult. The town-designated cemetery, on land Israel had donated around on the east side of Barston Hill, was easier to get to.

"Well, that about covers it for dead folks, Brownie," Old Sam said. "Guess I'm just a relic of the early days — about the last relic left in the whole valley. My turn 'll likely come before too long, but I've got a few more fish to catch, and I'd sure like to stick around long enough to see the village get a cannon and use it at the anniversary. Yes sir. That would be one thing worth stickin' around for. But with so many skinflint misers in town and with Vermont so cannon-poor, I don't know as there's much chance. Likely I won't live 'til the anniversary anyways."

Old Sam at last turned the horse and headed home — down Tannery Road to the cluster of six brick homes that Old Sam and various other members of the Barston clan lived in. Old Sam stopped the wagon by the home of Jared Barston, his grand-nephew. Benjie, one of Jared's sons, saw him there and came out to talk.

"We was just settin' down to supper, Grampy Sam," Benjie said. "Interested?"

"Don't feel up to it tonight, Benjie. I think I just want to go to bed. Had quite a day today. If you can help me home, I'll just go to bed."

"You look wicked tired, Grampy Sam," Benjie said. "Brownie behave herself today?"

"Mostly she did," Old Sam said. "She got a little chill in the storm, but I think she warmed all right after that. I don't imagine she'd mind eatin' somethin' now."

"No. She never minded that. I'll see to her."

Even with Benjie's help, Old Sam got down from the wagon with difficulty. He leaned hard on Benjie as he crossed the road to his own house. Benjie put him to bed with some bread and a jug of water within reach in case he later changed his mind about eating.

After Benjie left, Old Sam felt a few more twinges in his chest. He lay back, exhausted, and thought about the graves he had visited during the day. So many friends and relatives had died. Some of them had been gone for a long time already. No one he had known as a boy or as a young man was still alive. And Benjie — who had been a baby just the day before yesterday it seemed — why, he must be sixteen. It hardly seemed possible.

"Well, maybe it is time for me to die," he said just before he closed his eyes to go to sleep.

II

Aaron Reckford opened his toothless mouth and squalled, twitching his tiny fists in accompaniment. His face purpled as his wailing intensified. After a while his crying confounded his breathing. He choked and gasped and had worn himself down to mere whimpering by the time his mother arrived.

Annie Reckford looked exhausted. Sweat beaded on her forehead and plastered down wisps of hair which had come undone since its hasty, morning brushing and pinning. Her hands were red and puckered; her arms wet to the elbows. She snatched Aaron from the cradle, held him with his head over her shoulder, and patted his back. She yawned and interrupted the patting to rub her eyes. Then she rubbed Aaron's back until he stopped whimpering.

"There, there, Aaron," she said. "Couldn't of been so bad as all that."

She laid him back in his cradle and glanced over her shoulder at him as she headed back towards the washtub, the washboard, and a tremendous pile of dirty clothes.

Amos Reckford opened his toothless mouth and squalled. Annie halted, returned to the room, and muttered as she lifted him from his cradle. She tried to comfort him to silence, but he kept howling anyway — a slow staccato wavering with the pats on his back.

"Your brother went and woke you, did he?" Annie said. "Can't see why the both of you can't cry at the same time, sleep at the same time, and eat at the same time. Make about half so much trouble for me if you did."

Just as Amos began to weary of crying, Aaron started in again. Annie hugged them each to a shoulder as she walked back and forth through the house. When at last both of the boys had worn themselves out, had finally stopped crying, and had given Annie hope that, for once, they might take naps at the same time, Joe Reckford walked in through the door.

"Past noon time, Annie," he said. "It don't look like you got much of a start on the washin' this mornin'. Dinner ready yet?"

Annie's glazed eyes suddenly came alive. Her glances jerked from the mud clinging to her husband's shoes to the trail of dirt behind him.

"No!" she snapped. "It ain't ready! It ain't even thought about yet, and you, Joe Reckford, might just once wipe your feet before you come into this house! I ain't so idle that I need you to make more broom work every time you come in!"

"But I did wipe 'em," Joe said. "I wiped 'em good at the door. It's just the clay from the brickyard sticks on so. It don't all come off when I wipe my feet."

"No," Annie said. "And it don't none of it come off when you don't wipe your feet. Sticks on hard outdoors, of course, even if you wipe and wipe and wipe, but just you set foot in the door, and off it falls just like it was magic! Why if you could just once, Joe Reckford . . ."

The twins commenced a duet of misery, trying to outdo each other in their efforts. Annie thrust one of the boys into Joe's arms.

"Here, you take Amos, and see if you can't do anythin' with him. If you could see, Joe Reckford, how much work it is to take care of a pair of twins day and night, then you might . . . No. If you could take care of 'em just for a day or two by yourself, I don't imagine you'd get very far makin' bricks! There ain't time for washin' clothes! There ain't time for fixin' meals! And all of it has got to get done, but there just ain't time for it! If you could know that, then you might wipe your feet once in a while and not come home for dinner screamin' about where's your food!"

"But I do wipe my feet," Joe said. "It's the clay, Annie. And I ain't come in screamin' about dinner. I just asked you was it ready. If I'm runnin' a brickyard and come home for dinner instead of takin' food to eat there, then I can't wait too long. I got men workin' for me, and I got to . . ."

"All right. All right," Annie said. "I didn't have time to make anythin' for your dinner. But there's bread, and there's that meat from supper last night. That should get you through the afternoon. Here. Give Amos back, and go eat. You got to go back to your brickyard, so don't waste time."

"But I want to eat with you, Annie."

"I can't right now, but you go and get started. I'll feed the twins and eat with you when I get done . . . if you're still around then."

Joe was still eating when Annie at last came in and sat down across the table from him.

"Where's Sue?" Joe asked. "Ain't she been in for dinner?"

"If I ain't had time to make you a dinner, you think I had time to make her one?"

"But she didn't come for dinner yesterday or the day before neither," Joe said. "She shouldn't be missin' dinner like that."

"Well, I ain't got time to run after her so's to put food in her mouth. If she don't have sense enough at sixteen-years-old even to eat, then maybe you should have a talk with her — if you can find her. After all, she is your daughter."

"She's your daughter too, Annie," Joe said.

"Stepdaughter," Annie said. "I can't take any of the blame for how she was raised before I got hold of her. You can't stick me with that, Joe. She's a trial now for certain, and I ain't the one to blame for it."

"But you two used to get along so good — before the twins come along, I mean. Think she's jealous of 'em, Annie?"

"I might think that if she was the same girl she was when I met the both of you — three years ago, was it? She was so shy and needed a ma so bad. But now she just ain't the same girl. She don't need a ma near so much as she needs a good sound spankin' from her pa. It's a scandal, Joe, how she carries on in the village. Be a scandal if a boy carried on the same way, and it's a double scandal that she's a girl actin' like that."

"Hold on, Annie," Joe said. "George says you was the same way when you was a girl — that you was more like a brother to him than a sister sometimes — runnin' around just like Sue is now."

"No, Joe! Not the same! When did I ever come to the supper table with the drools of chewin' tobacco dried in streaks down my chin? Or reekin' so awful from pipe smoke — the same pipe pokin' out of her pocket all the time? Never is when, and you can ask George about that. She drinks, Joe. And she sneaks out in the middle of the night and goes the devil knows where. She'll get her come-uppance some day unless you can make her stop. Mark my words on that!"

"Oh, she'll grow out of it, Annie."

"She's sixteen already, Joe. It's time to outgrow it right now. Why, there's girls married at her age, and here she is raisin' the devil all the time just like she was a twelve-year-old boy. That stink in church last Sunday. Don't tell me she wasn't right in the thick of that. And the stink would of been twice as bad next Sunday if Charlie Porter hadn't of found that fish tied up under the pulpit. And how about all the snakes in the pews that Sunday last June? Ask her about that sometime. And the flock of chickens they found in the hall last town meetin' day?

"Oh, when I was a girl I might of liked showin' boys that I was stronger than them and beatin' 'em at their own games, but there was nothin' that would of got me in trouble if I'd of got caught. I can't say the same for Sue. Some day she'll go too far and get caught, and she and the boys 'll be in a lot of trouble. And folks in town 'll all be mad at us for not keepin' her out of mischief. You got to talk to her, Joe, in a way that 'll make her listen."

"Well, maybe I should talk to . . ."

"There ain't a 'maybe' in it anyplace, Joe Reckford, and you know it!"

"It's just that she was so miserable lonely all the years I was tryin' to raise her by myself. You remember how she was, Annie. And it took her a long time to get to like Barston Falls, too. I guess when she got friends and started havin' fun, she got wilder, but I just didn't have the heart to clamp down on her then. You remember how unhappy she was, don't you Annie?"

"Oh, course I do, Joe," Annie said in a quieter voice. "She jumped at her own shadow and couldn't hardly talk to anybody. Malik was the only friend she had there for a while, when she started fishin' with him, and then I guess Old Sam. Just the two of 'em 'til she caught the big fish with Malik. I don't s'pose there was a soul in New Hampshire or Vermont that didn't know her after that."

"You was awful good to her, Annie, before she caught that . . ."

"Oh, I was only after her pa," Annie said, as the frown lines in her forehead smoothed for the first time in hours. "Seems it worked. No, it was just Malik and Old Sam before she got everybody's attention with that fish."

"Speakin' of him — Old Sam I mean — he had another spell just yesterday. Steve Danforth told me."

"In his chest?" Annie asked. "Bad as before?"

"Worse, Steve said. I don't see how he can take many more of 'em. They always claimed Old Sam was tough as a sackful of axeheads, but he's a sick man now, Annie. He's lost so much weight in the last year or so I don't know as how he'll make it through this winter."

Annie shook her head and spoke quietly, scarcely more than a whisper.

"Old Sam . . . He's the last one left now, Joe, of all the early settlers. He was awful good to me when I was a little girl growin' up in the village — teasin' me about bein' pretty when I was just as plain as a barn plank and carryin' on sayin' that if only I was ten years older, he'd marry me in a second. He made me feel important; made me feel good."

"He was the same way with Sue," Joe said. "Awful good to her when she was so lonely."

"Old Sam was always so big and so friendly," Annie said. "And he went out of his way to spend time with all the youngsters in the village — loved to laugh and make us laugh. Skinny as can be now, of course, and I don't see him smilin' much these days, come to think of it."

"He knows he's dyin'," Joe said. "That ain't somethin' a man can smile at much — knowin' that maybe the next week or the next day he might be dead."

"And don't forget how he got you set up with the brick-yard, Joe. You owe him for givin' you a livin' you can raise a family on."

"I ain't ever goin' to forget that, Annie. Old Sam's always been an awful good man. Buildin' up the village with his brothers and keepin' an eye out to help the folks that live here. It just won't be the same when he's gone."

"Might have him over to supper sometime," Annie said. "We can thank him right to his face — thank him before it's too late."

"Jared says Old Sam ain't goin' out anyplace lately. Claims he's afraid he'll drop dead in somebody else's house. Jared says Old Sam told him he wants to be out fishin' for trout when his time comes, but since it's gettin' too cold for trout fishin', the next best thing is to die at home."

"Well, we should do somethin' for him," Annie said.

"Yes, we should," Joe said, rising to his feet. "But here now I'm chatterin' away the afternoon when I need to be up workin' in the brickyard. Got to go now."

Annie followed him towards the door.

"And Joe," she said. "You talk with Sue when you see her. She won't listen to me. She laughs and tells me what she thinks I want to hear and then goes right off and does whatever she wants. I can't do a thing with her. She could be helpin' here a lot with the twins, but she don't want no part of it. Talk to her, Joe — tonight after supper at the latest."

"Oh, all right," he said as the door shut behind him.

Annie swept the floor by Joe's place at the table and brushed the accumulation of dirt into the fireplace. She cleared the dishes from the table and then went to peek in at the twins.

III

"Won't that pig never get drunk, Benjie?"

"Sure he will, Sue," Benjie Barston said. "I just hope it's sometime tonight. Pass the jug over, would you?"

In the moonlight Sue tilted the jug back against her tightly closed lips, dribbled rum down her chin, and passed the jug to Tom. Tom sealed the jug mouth with the edge of his palm as he made a show of drinking and then passed the jug along to Foss. Foss allowed the merest taste of rum into his mouth before he gave the jug to Benjie. Only Benjie took an actual swallow. Then, just as soon as he could breathe again, he soaked yet another loaf of bread with rum and fed it to the pig.

The pig, if the truth be known, was drunker than any pig in the township of Barston had ever been before, yet that wasn't good enough for the four sixteen-year-olds, who kept feeding him the strange bread. He was moderately confused at the lateness of the feeding hour. However, in the manner of inebriated pigs, he didn't give the matter much thought. He glanced unsteadily at the four people in the moonlight and at the horse and carriage on the other side of a small fire; kept eating the soggy loaves as they were set before him and didn't have a care in the world. Half a dozen loaves of bread earlier the pig had ceased to be concerned about the strong smell of death and decay surrounding the tannery. Now he smelled nothing but rum fumes.

"How much rum we got left?" Foss asked.

"Three or four more jugs," Benjie said. "We got plenty

of rum, but we ain't got but two more loaves of bread. If the pig ain't drunk by then, I don't know what we'll do."

"Have to hold him down and pour it down his throat," Sue said.

"It ain't all that big of a pig," Tom said. "And we been slammin' the rum right to him. Seems like we should of got some results by now. There ain't somethin' special about rum and pigs we don't know, is there?"

"Course there ain't," Sue said. "It's just goin' to take time."

"Well, we can't let it take the rest of the night," Benjie said. "We figured the pig and the rig need to be in the square at least a couple hours before dawn on account of there's folks gettin' up right after that."

"I say we should get started on the horse and on the deacon's rig," Foss said. "It don't take the four of us to get the pig drunk."

"All right," Benjie said. "We can heat up the pitch and get goin' on that. Just remember to keep the pitch off of your hands, so you won't have to explain it tomorrow."

"Just warm and sticky," Sue said. "You put it on too hot, and that horse 'll run off and smash the rig all to flinders."

"Melt the pitch right down," Tom said. "Slap it on hot over the deacon's rig, and it'll cool down enough for the horse by the time the rig's ready. If it ain't hot enough, the feathers won't stick."

"Well, go to it," Benjie said. "I'll give the pig the rest of the bread, and if he ain't drunk by then, I guess we will have to pour it down his throat. We got a lot to do, so let's go to it. And don't forget to put on the gloves."

The four youngsters bustled around in the moonlight. They built up the fire so they could better see what they were doing and so they could heat the pitch-pot. They moved Deacon Russell's horse and carriage into the better light and discussed how they should best use the pitch when it was hot enough.

Deacon Russell was sleeping soundly at the time, under the delusion that his carriage was in his carriage shed and that his mare was in her stall. With care and luck the four youngsters had eased the horse and carriage away from the barn adjoining the deacon's house without awakening him, had harnessed the horse and hitched her to the carriage when they were safely away, and had taken turns leading the mare and riding in the carriage all the way up Tannery Road to the tannery itself. Though the tannery was often busy during the day, at night it was deserted. Over the years it had been in operation, the tannery stench had discouraged anyone from building a home nearby. Thus there was no one but the four youngsters themselves — and the pig and the mare — to see the flames of their fire and to hear their voices. For over two weeks they had planned for this night, sneaking materials to their secret storage in an old tannery vat long unused because of an unmendable leak in its bottom. Now all of the stolen materials came out: the harvest from Deacon Russell's clothesline ten days earlier, a pitch-pot borrowed from Jared Barston's warehouse at the lower end of the canal through the village, four goose-down comforters whose earlier owners had left them out to air just a little too long, a pilfered hearth broom, an assortment of gloves, a generous supply of rum.

Deacon Uriah Russell, a former lawyer whose aspirations of becoming a judge had never been realized, was on the diaconate of the Congregational Church. He was a narrow-minded, sanctimonious man of sour disposition — a disposition not likely to be improved by what he and many others in Barston Falls would see in the town square the next morning. When Sue, Benjie, Foss, and Tom had begun casting about for candidates to work their most ambitious prank on, there had been no need to search further after Deacon Russell's name had been mentioned. He was their man. Their only concerns then had been that some refinement of their prank might not be thought of until after the prank had been accomplished; that they might later regret not having been thorough enough; that through some stupidity they might be caught.

Benjie joined the others just as the broom spread the first of the pitch onto the side of the carriage. Foss Richardson threw a handful of feathers from a butchered comforter against the pitch.

"No, no," Benjie said. "We ain't got all that many feathers, and we don't want to leave 'em all over the ground. Press 'em into the pitch a handful at a time so that more of 'em stick. That's what we got the gloves for."

Benjie fed more wood onto the fire and stood watching with satisfaction as the plastering of feathers slowly covered the side of the carriage. He and Sue cut open the rest of the down comforters. Then Benjie went to check on the pig and, after a while, returned deeply satisfied.

"Pig can't even stand up now," he said, as he put more wood onto the fire.

"Good," Sue said. "Let's do the spokes too and then turn the other side of the wagon to the light. We still got a lot to do."

When the four agreed that the side of the carriage was done, they walked the horse around so that the other side of the carriage faced the fire. Tom Beasley recommended painting with the pitch broom. Foss followed him closely, pressing on the last of the feathers from the second comforter. Sue and Benjie took the deacon's stolen clothes over to the pig, struggled with them for a while, and then brought the clothes back.

"Too dark," Benjie said. "Leave off here for a little and help us get the pig over in the light."

One to a leg, they dragged and carried the pig over by the fire. Instead of proper squeals of protest, all the pig could manage were blubbering caricatures. When the four of them let go of his legs, he lay on his side like a sack of sand, feathers clinging to the leg Foss had held.

"That's better," Sue said. "Now you can go back to your pitch and feathers. Here, Benjie, we got to get him over on his back."

Together Sue and Benjie wrestled a pair of the deacon's britches onto the pig; then one of the deacon's linen shirts. The topcoat, not the sort of thing to be washed and hung out on a clothesline, had been stolen elsewhere, but was enough like the deacon's own coat to satisfy all four of the youngsters. When it was on the pig, Benjie and Sue were quite satisfied with the effect.

"The pig don't have the deacon's crooked teeth," Benjie said, "but I guess he'll do. We could waste an awful lot of time searchin' for a pig ugly as the deacon."

"He does look better 'n the deacon wearin' those clothes," Sue said.

At last Deacon Russell's carriage was fully fledged and ready for its passenger. Sue studied the deflated carcasses of four down comforters strewn around the fire.

"You didn't save many feathers for the horse," she said.

"No," Foss said. "We should of got another one or maybe a whole feather bed from someplace. We ain't got enough to do the mare all over, but we can decorate her here and there. Might look better like that anyways."

"How's the pitch, Tom?" Benjie asked.

"Still wicked hot."

"Let's get the pig up then and do the horse after."

The mare looked over her shoulder, puzzled at the activity. It was strange enough to be led off and harnessed in the middle of the night, but now the youngsters were loading a pig — barefoot and hatless, but otherwise fully clothed

— into the carriage. They struggled and swore and raised the limp pig with difficulty. The mare shook her head at the great stupidity of it all, little suspecting that her own turn was next.

"Think he'll stay in the seat?" Foss asked.

"He's drunk enough so he won't move around much," Sue said, "but maybe we should tie him just to make sure. There might be some trouble when the rum wears off."

"We'll tie him for when we're movin' the carriage down to the square," Benjie said. "I think it'll look better down there, though, if he ain't tied right in the seat. Look more natural. If we get some more rum into him down in the square, he ain't goin' to move for hours I bet."

"Help me tie him, Benjie," Tom said. "Sue and Foss can get started on the horse if the pitch is cool enough now."

Foss wielded the pitch broom where Sue told him to. Sue gleaned feathers from the four comforters and stuck them to the pitch. Thus Deacon Russell's mare sprouted a foot-wide collar of feathers; boasted a stripe of feathers down the middle of her back and two stripes on each side. The mane and tail hung stiff with pitch and feathers. Benjie and Tom finished tying the pig and watched with admiration as Sue used the last of the feathers to cover the mare's hooves and get as far up the legs as she could.

Finally the project was complete, and it came time to move the horse, the pig, and the carriage down to the village square. First, however, the four youngsters built up the fire and began burning the evidence of their activity. The remains of the four comforters smoldered for a while before they flamed, the stench from the burning feathers temporarily masking the putridity of the tannery. The pitch-covered broom flared brightly as it burned. The deacon's underwear and stockings, snatched from the clothesline along with the shirt and britches, were consumed by the burning pitch of the broom. Benjie hid the pitch-pot back in the old tannery vat along with all but one of the remaining jugs of rum. They flung their gloves onto the flames last of all and then used the firelight to scrutinize one another for evidence of feathers or pitch. Wherever they found pitch, they rubbed it off with a rag soaked in rum. Finally they burned the rag.

Then in a slow parade and speaking only in hushed whispers, the four led the horse the length of Tannery Road: past the six brick homes of Old Sam, of Benjie and his family, and of various Barston family relatives; across the canal on Tannery Bridge, right to where the road ended. They turned right down towards the village square. The carriage creaked. The slow hooves of the mare struck the ground, nearly silent compared to the clatter they'd made crossing the bridge. The feathered apparition of horse and carriage carried its well-dressed passenger past quiet buildings. Here and there on the outskirts of the village dogs barked, but none were close enough to the four youngsters to give them any concern or make them pause.

They tied the mare at the watering trough in front of the Eagle Hotel. Benjie went in to the stable next door and stole enough oats to keep her busy and quiet for the following quarter hour. Then the rum jug was set next to the pig, and the four of them backed off to the edge of the square, where they admired what they could see of the horse and carriage and pig in the light of the obscured moon.

"The pig's still tied," Sue whispered.

"Let's leave him that way." Benjie said. "We're away safe, and there ain't a sign of pitch or feathers on us. Let's leave it like that."

"Sounds good to me," Tom said.

"Remember what we said," Foss added. "Everybody get up tomorrow the same time you usually do. And no braggin' to nobody but each other. We don't know nothin' about the deacon's carriage and horse or even whose pig it was that got stole. Nothin'."

"That's right," Benjie said. "Now everybody get on home. I'll go back up and make sure about the fire."

The four separated. Benjie checked the fire back up by the tannery; pushed the last remnants of the comforters onto the flames. There'd be nothing but ashes and a few scattered feathers by dawn. Satisfied, Benjie at last went home. He climbed the familiar branches of the ash tree and leaped to the window of his bedroom on the second floor.

It was a struggle for Benjie a short while later when the sun rose, but he forced himself out of bed and managed to look awake at breakfast.

IV

Seth Barston arose slowly, more slowly than usual on this particular morning because of the rain. He had a reputation as the laziest man in the village and lived up to it, rising a full hour later even than Old Sam, his great-uncle, who lived in the house next door. It was after ten o'clock by the time he had dressed and gone downstairs. His breakfast was on the table, but there was no sign of Sarah.

"Useless excuse for a wife," he muttered as he eased himself into his chair and stared at the plate she had left for him.

Fried pork. Fried eggs. A chunk of bread. Two hours earlier, when the pork and the eggs had been warm, it would have made a fine breakfast. Now, however, the congealed masses of fat were just something to put into his stomach. He ate. When it came time to wipe up the fat with the bread, Seth was surprised. Usually the bread cleaned off the fat no matter how long the breakfast had sat cold. This morning, however, the rawness of the day had fused the fat to the plate so hard that Seth had to scrape it off with his spoon.

Seth yawned and belched. He tipped back in his chair and put his feet on the table wondering what he should do for the rest of the morning. There was never very much work at the upper warehouse, even on days when the weather was good. It would be unlikely that any river traffic would move in the cold rain. The polemen for the flatboats would be holed up somewhere waiting for the rain to end. The upper warehouse could take care of itself, at least for the morning.

"Might as well go see what's happenin' with Steve," Seth said at last.

Ten minutes later, bundled up against the rain, Seth was on his way down to Steve Danforth's store in the village square.

*****

Danforth's store was a natural gathering place. On the east side of the village square, its central location put it in the routes of people going about their business. Many villagers stopped there daily, whether they needed to buy anything from Steve Danforth or not.

Steve loved to talk; loved to be with people. Talking was as natural to him as breathing. Although anyone caught alone in conversation with him for an hour or two was always glad to get away, in shorter doses or in a group it was fine to be with Steve. People looked forward to it, in fact. Steve's garrulity extended to everyone: villagers, travelers, traders, complete strangers. As a result, he was always among the first to know current village gossip or the latest news from up and down the Connecticut River valley. Villagers who had heard only the bare bones of a rumor would hurry over to Danforth's store to flesh it out. Rarely would they be disappointed. If Steve didn't know the details of a story, someone else would soon be coming to the store who did.

Seth hunched his shoulders against the rain. It was a cold, raw day. It wouldn't surprise him too much, he reflected, to see a few snowflakes fall with the drizzle. He thought ahead to Steve's store and to the iron heating stove there. Likely there'd be a group already gathered around it. Cold and rain always drew them, just as it was drawing him. There wouldn't be as many as on a day of cold rain during mud season, when villagers were heartily sick of winter and sought diversion more actively than at any other time of the year. Sometimes it was hard even to find a place to sit then. That was what kept getting Steve re-elected time and again as selectman — having people gather at his store for several weeks right up to town meeting day. Naturally they talked politics and issues then. Steve was adept at pointing out all sides of an issue — since he was certain to have heard them all — and reasoning out a consensus without offending anyone, other than a few with temperaments similar to Deacon Russell's. Steve Danforth had a reputation for common sense and level-headedness, even if it was agreed that he talked too much. He'd been a selectman for twelve years and moderator of the town meeting for ten.

Rain began to fall hard as Seth walked into the square. Three people bolted up the steps of the Eagle Hotel and disappeared through the door. Seth kept on without altering his pace. His hat and the shoulders of his coat soaked through, and he could feel the first trickles of water run down his neck and back. He hunched his shoulders further and at last got to Steve's store.

Seth glanced at the men surrounding the stove as he shook the rain from his hat. They smoked their pipes silently, not trying to compete with Jane Warren's strident voice directing Steve to measure out and wrap half a dozen things she wanted. George Ballard was there with his brother-in-law, Joe Reckford; Seth's brother Jared, who ran the lower warehouse; Mark Hosmer, who had once worked for Jared, but who was now in the logging business; Charlie Porter, a teamster. Steve tallied Jane Warren's purchases, wrote the amount down in his day book, and gave her one of the squares of canvas he kept by the door. Thrown over her head and shoulders, it would keep her dry enough as she crossed the square in the rain. Sometime during the next few days she would get around to drying it and returning it. All the men in the store were grateful for the canvas, without which they would have been captives in the store with her — unable to talk their man-talk or smoke their pipes in peace; unable, perhaps, to get a word in edgewise the way she and Steve both talked.

Seth lighted his pipe as the door closed behind Jane Warren and sat with the men on one of the benches by the stove. Steve bustled over to join them after he had watched Jane walk halfway across the square.

"Deacon's rig is for sale, if you want it, Seth," Steve said. "Might be a horse for sale later on too, if he can't figure how to get the feathers off. A man might find himself a deal if he knew how to get feathers and pitch off."

"There ain't a good way for the horse," Charlie Porter said. "If it was me and the price was low enough, I'd buy the mare and not do a thing. Let her shed 'em off in the spring. If it was summer and I couldn't stand the notion of a nag with feathers, I might try to shave her, but then the flies 'd bother her so. And besides she'd look just about as silly with bald patches like that as with feathers. Know what he wants for her?"

"Too much, likely," Mark Hosmer said. "Old skinflint. She never was that good of a mare to start with. He'll have to pretty much give her away, if he wants to get rid of her."

"I'd buy her if the price was good," Charlie said. "She's young enough so a man might get some work out of her, but she needs to have the feed put right to her, she needs to be worked steady — every day — to toughen her up, and she needs to be harnessed with a good team that knows what it's up to. I could train her up to help haul one of my rigs — put her on a pung this winter. And if folks down below was wonderin' about the feathers, it wouldn't be no skin off of me to tell 'em it was the mare that belonged to Deacon Russell."

"That's right," George Ballard said. "And maybe the deacon don't realize that. If he sells the mare or the rig now the way they are, he'll keep folks talkin' about him. That's why if it was my horse, I'd keep her out of sight or sell her far away or maybe just shoot her and have done with it. I wouldn't want to put her out where even more folks could have a look at her."

"How about the carriage?" Steve asked. "Know any good ways to get the feathers off of that?"

"If anybody does," Jared Barston said, "and can do it without wreckin' the carriage, the deacon 'll pay five dollars — worth it to him. And if you know who might of had a hand in featherin' the mare and the carriage, he'll give you ten dollars."

"Oh he must of had a conniption fit!" Seth said. "That old pinch-penny. Ten dollars!"

"You can count on that," Steve said. "He was good and mad. Been in every day since, I think. What's that — five days now? Comes in every day to see if there's any word, but so far there ain't been."

"Some suspicions, I s'pose?" Joe Reckford asked.

"A few," Steve said. "But if anybody knows, then they don't want to tell, or maybe it was too careful a joke for anybody ever to find out. Somebody was pretty smart about it, that's for sure."

"Well, I know just who it sounds like," Charlie said. "Might even put money on it if I was a bettin' man."

"Who's that?" George Ballard asked.

"Old Sam," Charlie said. "Who else?"

The men laughed.

"Oh, that's the truth," Mark said. "I wouldn't put it past him, even old and crippled like that. Some of the stories about him when he was young get you laughin' so that you just want to push folks out of the way 'til you get your air back. That sounds just exactly like Old Sam Barston's work."

"Think maybe we should turn him in, Jared, and get the ten dollars?" Seth said.

"Sure," Jared said. "Grampy Sam 'd love that. And he'd help us spend the ten dollars on rum and drink it up."

"Yes he would," Seth said. "And it'd be good for him. When Grampy Sam heard about the feathers all over the deacon's horse and rig and about my pig drunk and dressed up in the deacon's clothes, he just had to see 'em. And when I brought him down, he just laughed and laughed. I ain't seen him laugh like that prob'ly for two years anyways."

"He ain't been too happy lately," Mark said. "Ain't like him. And he's got so skinny over the last year. Wasn't all that long ago when he was a big, heavy man and full of fun, but he just ain't been himself for quite a while now."

"He's at the end of his life, and he knows it," Jared said. "That's what's made him so sad lately."

"It's too bad he can't enjoy things right to the end," Joe Reckford said. "He's an awful good man. I owe him a lot more 'n just money for settin' me up with the brickyard. He's always done a lot to help other folks, and he's done a lot for the village, too."

"Him and his brothers," Seth said. "Israel and Caleb and Isaac and crazy James. All of 'em ten foot tall and could lift a ton with each hand."

"Built it twice," Jared said. "First with wood and then with brick after the fire."

"Anyways, it seems like we might try and do somethin' for him to thank him — do somethin' while he's still alive and can enjoy it," Joe said.

"Well, there's that cannon he's always after," Charlie said. "I s'pose I'll vote for that this time around, and I'll speak up for it too."

"I asked him about that," Seth said, "and he just don't seem to care about it the way he used to. He told me he don't think he'll live 'til town meetin' day, for one thing, and told me he knows he won't be around for the next Fourth of July. It's almost like he wants to die now."

The men puffed on their pipes in silence for a moment. Mark Hosmer blew a cloud of smoke towards the stove and then jabbed his pipe stem towards Steve.

"Tell me, Mr. Moderator," he said. "Ain't there some way we could have meetin' day earlier this year? It'd give Old Sam the meetin' to look forward to, and after we vote him his cannon, then he'll want to stick around 'til the Fourth of July. I sure don't want him dyin' on us just 'cause he wants to die. Seems like we need to do somethin' special for him right now."

"No," Steve said. "Town meetin' is always set on that same Tuesday in March, and we can't have it earlier. But what we can do if there's good enough reason is to have a special town meetin'. We can have one of those any time."

"This is special," Joe said. "How do we go about havin' a special town meetin'?"

"By petition," Steve said. "You write up a petition and then have two-thirds of the voters on the checklist sign it. Then you give the petition to the selectmen, and they set the date with the moderator."

"We'll do it," Charlie Porter said. "We owe it to Old Sam to get him his cannon. How soon can we have the meetin'?"

"The rule says we got to post the warnin' for at least a week before the meetin'," Steve said. "So you get me two-thirds of the voters to sign the petition, and about a week later, if the selectmen decide it's a proper petition with valid signatures, we can have the special meetin'."

"Sounds pretty reasonable to me," Charlie said. "Everybody think it's a good idea?"

He looked around as the men nodded.

"Well then, if Mr. Moderator would get us some paper

and ink and a pen, I think we might work up a petition here pretty quick."

"Seth, you and Jared 'll tell Old Sam about this for us?" Joe Reckford asked. "Might make a difference to him right away if you could tell him we're doin' it for him."

Seth nodded to Jared.

"Yes sir," Seth said. "This might be just about what Old Grampy Sam needs. We'll tell him today."

V

Deacon Russell was outraged. He had been outraged the whole time the five men had been at his house, but such was his self-control (he congratulated himself) that probably none of them had realized it. He had been the voice of restraint and calm rationality in explaining to them why he wouldn't sign their petition for a special town meeting. Now, with the men gone, he gave vent to his anger — calling his wife as witness.

"Blatant extortion, Beulah," he said. "Nothing less than blatant extortion to force their will on the town. Do you suppose any of the timid souls of the village would dare to stand up to them all in a group like that? Dare to refuse to sign their petition? It's intimidation, and I for one won't stand for it. Oh, they'll get their special town meeting — no doubt about that in my mind — but getting the meeting and passing their resolution will be two separate matters. They'll find that out in short order. The law is written to protect the majority from such tactics, and I'll see to it that there is no miscarriage. Count on it."

"You held your temper well, Uriah," Beulah said.

"I could not lower myself to have sharp words with them, Beulah. Sharp words would have served no purpose. Far better to have my full say at their special town meeting and let the voters of this town have their say afterwards. I'll not stand by idly and see town funds misused — squandered."

"You thought that Seth Barston might have been one of the ones who vandalized your carriage and horse," Beulah said. "Perhaps the others who were just with him, as well?"

"I'll never prove it, Beulah, but that is my suspicion. After all, it was Seth Barston's pig in the carriage. He keeps his pigs penned right next to his house, the smell notwithstanding, and it stands to reason in my mind that if someone else had taken his pig from him in the middle of the night, that the noise of its squeals would have awakened him. That does not appear to have been the case, so I do suspect him strongly. He is an idle and shiftless man, and if he hadn't come by his house and his livelihood by the simple means of being in the Barston family, I doubt he'd have much more than a hovel over his head today. He will avoid honest work as if it were the tooth-ache, but when it comes to deviltry and vandalism and destruction of property, he will expend any amount of effort. He is just that type."

"Yes, although his wife . . ."

"A saint to put up with him like that. A virtual crime that she ever married a man so slovenly. She deserves far better."

"What will you do about the special town meeting?" Beulah asked.

"Oh, I shall repeat the same arguments I usually do whenever Sam Barston has brought the matter up at past town meetings, and I shall have a few additional points to make concerning the manner of securing signatures for the petition for the meeting itself. I shall prepare myself well for this meeting. Unless I am mistaken, a week must elapse between the time the selectmen review the validity of the signatures and the meeting itself. That time should be more than sufficient to build a solid, common-sense case against the resolution. I shall make you proud of me, Beulah, and I shall save the town from needless expenditure of its funds."

"I am always proud of you, Uriah," Beulah said. "But I shall look forward especially to the meeting."

"I shall too, Beulah, but I must first give the matter much thought. And I will go confirm with Steve Danforth that a week must elapse before such a meeting may take place. Perhaps I should do that now."

Beulah Russell watched from the window as Uriah went out to the road. She smiled and then began to think about what she could cook for supper that might especially please him.

*****

Ellen Hosmer sat in one of the back seats of the town hall and kept at her knitting. She had gotten a good start on a sock for her husband, Mark, in the short time since Steve Danforth had called the meeting to order. Steve had read out the warning notice that had been posted a week before at half a dozen places around the township: "To see if the voters of this town shall approve, at special town meeting, the appropriation of town funds for the purchase of a cannon to be used by the militia, for Fourth of July celebrations, and for the recovery of bodies from the river. This cannon shall be purchased in honor of Sam Barston in acknowledgement of his many services to the town during his lifetime; shall be purchased in time to be used July 4, 1826." Ellen's needles had continued clicking as she had listened to an assortment of testimonials about Old Sam Barston. She thought it a shame that his health had been so poor lately that he couldn't be at the special town meeting and hear all the nice things people were saying about him. Ellen had heard short speeches from Charlie Porter and Joe Reckford, among others. The men were beginning to repeat themselves, and she wished that they'd get on with the vote. There was no arguing about how much Old Sam had done for the town, but the speeches seemed wasted without Old Sam there. At last Steve Danforth called a halt to them.

"In the interests of keepin' this meetin' movin' towards the business at hand," Steve said, "I suggest we cut off our speeches of appreciation to Old Sam. If he was here, course I'd let 'em go on for as long as anybody had anythin' to say. But since he ain't, let me remind you again of the motion under discussion: 'To see if the voters of this town shall approve the appropriation of town funds for the purchase of a cannon.' Nobody's goin' to argue about how much Sam Barston has done for this town. The motion under discussion is whether or not we should use town funds to buy a cannon in his honor. Further discussion on that motion? Charlie Porter."

"I want a cannon for the town," Charlie said. "I think it'd make us proud to have one."

"Thank you, Charlie. George Ballard."

"We owe it to Old Sam," George said. "It's a good use of town funds since without Old Sam and his brothers there wouldn't even be a town."

"Thank you, George. Deacon Russell."

Uriah Russell rose slowly to his feet. When he didn't begin speaking immediately, people turned to look at him. Ellen Hosmer left off her knitting.

"Just a host of questions, Mr. Moderator," he said at last. "I don't expect answers for them, but they are the sorts of questions I think the voters of this town should be asking themselves before they decide how they will vote on the issue.

"Granted, that Old Sam Barston has done a lot for this town, and he should be honored in some manner. However, is the expenditure of town funds for a cannon the best way? One might attach George Washington's name to this suggested cannon purchase in hopes of painting the proposal with respectability. At issue is the expenditure of town funds for a cannon. I ask the voters if they would be in favor of the measure if Old Sam Barston's name weren't attached to it, remembering that a vote against the purchase of a cannon does not constitute a vote against Old Sam.

"I ask the voters to consider if at any time during the discussion of this warning item they have heard a dollar amount assigned to the purchase of a cannon. Are we voting blindly, not knowing whether we are voting to spend five dollars or five thousand? How much will it cost? I, for one, would not agree to purchase a farm if I didn't know the price of that farm.

"The successful passage of this measure will raise taxes, but in a different way. Many members of this community, in lieu of paying their taxes in money, work off the amount by putting in days on fixing the public highways, supplying lumber for town building projects, or hewing stone blocks and timbers for bridges. Joe Reckford, for instance, gives us equivalent value in bricks. This is a fine arrangement, for it meets the needs of the town. However, this cannon measure requires the expenditure of cash money — not lumber or bricks or bushels of grain or road work — and will require the collection of cash money from us in taxes. Do we have it? Can we afford it?

"If we spend town funds on a cannon — an item whose sole function is to make noise — then we will not have that money — however much it might be — for the things that will materially improve the well being of the town: new churches, new schools, new bridges, roads, public buildings, and the like. I maintain that the cannon is merely an expensive and useless toy. It is the sort of thing that a town accepts as a gift from a private citizen or group of citizens, but which I, for one, cannot justify spending public funds on.

"I think we are premature on this matter, Mr. Moderator. I think that this issue should not be brought up for a vote yet. Mind you that I am not making this as a formal motion, but I think we would be far better served if a committee of citizens were to look into the availability of a cannon, discover a firm purchase price for one, and then report back to us on how much expense we would be facing if we were to purchase it for the town. That would be the time to have such a meeting as this. I cannot vote for the matter as it stands, simply because I don't know how much money we are being asked to spend.

"I would remind the voters from North Barston, too, that there has yet to be word of where the cannon would be kept. They are being asked to spend their own money in taxes so that the town might have a cannon, yet with the assumption that the cannon would be kept here in the village. I don't see what benefits of entertainment they could expect to get from it. I doubt they could even hear it in North Barston from here. And yet they are expected, by this proposal, to spend as much tax money on it as anyone here in the village. Perhaps later they will be taxed annually along with the rest of us to pay for the powder used in the cannon, though there has so far been no word of what arrangement we might be expected to make for the powder. It hardly seems fair to me to tax people in North Barston for Barston Falls' cannon.

"In summary, Mr. Moderator and the voters of this town, I believe there are far better uses for our town funds. I think this proposal to purchase a cannon is rushed, ill-conceived, poorly planned, and unfair to people who live outside the immediate village. The minimum statutory period of one week passed between the posting of the warning and this special meeting. Had the members of the town had more time to think about and discuss this proposal, I believe that some of the questions I have just raised might have been dealt with far better than they have been so far — which is not at all. Thank you."

Deacon Russell sat down.

"Thank you, Deacon Russell," Steve said. "Further discussion? Yes, Seth Barston."

"I just want to point out that cannons ain't easy to come by," Seth said. "When you find one for sale, you got to buy it right then or somebody else will. When Grampy Sam found that pair of cannons down in Boston and we spent a lot of time talkin' about 'em here, they got snapped up pretty quick."

"More?" Steve asked. "Deacon Russell again."

"I will remind this meeting that the record will show a majority at that time very wisely voted against spending town funds for a cannon and that if someone else hadn't bought the two cannons, the town of Barston wouldn't have either."

"Further discussion?" Steve asked, scanning the room without seeing any further hands raised.

"Motion to vote," Joe Reckford said.

Steve Danforth acknowledged the motion and its second, asked for discussion, and took a voice vote on the motion.

"Ayes clearly have it on the motion to vote, so now we will vote on the warnin' item: 'To see if the voters of this town shall approve the appropriation of town funds for the purchase of a cannon.' All those . . ."

"Procedural question, Mr. Moderator!" Deacon Russell interrupted loudly.

"Yes, Deacon Russell. What's on your mind?"

"I move that the voting be by secret ballot," Deacon Russell said. "I so move because of special circumstances I think the voters should be aware of. May I speak my mind, Mr. Moderator?"

"Of course," Steve said.

"I, and perhaps others as well, objected to the manner in which the signatures on the petition for this special meeting were gathered. A group of the petition's supporters solicited the signatures together in such a manner as to leave themselves open to the charge of intimidation. I don't believe so many would have signed if the petition had simply been posted in a public place and had left the citizens free to sign or not to sign as they wished. In the interests of fairness, I think that the voting should be by ballot so that no one might know how anyone else chooses to vote. Perhaps only those in favor of intimidation might object to the fairness of a secret ballot?"

"I second the deacon's motion for a secret ballot," John Parker said.

The vote for the secret ballot was unanimous, though the last few hands came up slowly and seemingly in response to the glares of those voters whose hands were already raised. There was some delay in getting sufficient paper cut into small squares, getting quills and ink, and trooping the voters one at a time to a corner of the room where each could write "yes" or "no" on his ballot and then leave it folded on the table in front of Steve Danforth. Steve shuffled the ballots for a moment and then appointed three people to count them under the public eye.

The measure failed to pass. Steve Danforth revealed no personal bias as he announced the results.

"Let the record show that the voters of this town present at this special town meetin', by a vote of forty-seven to twenty-two, decided not to use town funds for the purchase of a cannon. Motion for adjournment?"

Seth Barston leaned over to speak to Jared as Steve continued through his procedure for a formal end to the meeting.

"This news ain't goin' to do Grampy Sam much good."

"No. He won't like it a bit, but I guess we better tell him in the mornin'."

People were already talking and standing up to leave as Steve Danforth announced that the meeting was adjourned. Most paused where they were as he continued speaking.

"For those of you willin' to spend town money on a cannon, I hope you'll be willin' to spend some of your own. And for anyone else as well let me announce that I'm collectin' donations for buyin' a cannon for the village of Barston Falls in honor of Old Sam Barston. I . . ."

A short cheer interrupted him.

"I expect you know my bookkeepin', and I promise I'll keep careful records of who gives how much. If you want to know what the tally is any time, just come to my store and ask. Be best if you could give hard coin — those as want to give — and I'd like to get us a cannon soon as we can. I'll announce right now that next Fourth of July is Old Sam Barston day, and I want him to hear a little cannon thunder."

The meeting broke up into a confusion of many greetings and conversations among people who hadn't seen one another for a while.

VI

Old Sam shuffled into the cold of his back parlor and shut the door behind him. Sunlight glared through the frost patterns on the panes of the three southwest windows. For a moment he stared at the three windows as his rapid and shallow exhalations rose toward the ceiling and disappeared. Then he went to the chair turned toward the lone window of the southeast wall, settled heavily into it, and peered through the frost crystals.

Past the corner of Seth's house next door and out across the village, smoke rose in straight columns from every chimney he could see. Just beyond the mills he glimpsed part of the great eddy, now iced over, below the falls. The eddy always kept from freezing until the normal cold of January had settled into the Connecticut River valley. In mild winters it never froze, but this new year had come in anything but mild, and the wheeling rafts of ice had caught a week or so earlier.

Old Sam scraped at the frost with his fingernails and tried to keep from breathing directly onto the glass. He grumbled and thought about the window table upstairs, where his old brass spyglass lay gathering dust; grumbled anew at the thought of the climb. It had been a long time since he'd seen the upstairs of his own home. And here it was already into the third week of January, and he had yet to set foot outdoors in 1826.

A chill settled through him as he sat and stared out the window, but he continued to sit. His breathing slowed to nearly nothing. He caught himself wondering about death: not feeling the cold, no pain or stiffness in his joints or muscles, breathing stilled forever, the inevitable decay. The long shadow of Barston Hill crept further up the side of Rattlesnake Hill over across the river. There was still sunlight on the upper slopes, but its brightness seemed diminished. The deep blue of the sky earlier in the day had faded to a pale white.

"Is dyin' like that, God?" Old Sam whispered. "The light goes? The cold and dark just come on?"

Since the beginning of the new year Old Sam had spent the end of each sunny afternoon watching the rise of shadows up the side of Rattlesnake Hill; had ignored the cold in the back parlor until he had seen the last of the sunlight on top of the hill. Then he had returned to his rocking chair by the iron stove in the room where he spent all the rest of his waking and sleeping hours, except for times when he used the chamber pot in his old dining room. On this day, however, he didn't want to stay to watch the shadows reach the top of the hill. There was the writing to get back to before his hand chilled too much to hold the quill pen and before Benjie got back from school. His gaze lingered on Rattlesnake Hill for a moment. Then he got to his feet with difficulty and went out of the back parlor and up along the hallway to the winter room.

The warmth felt good as he shut the door behind him. He sat in his rocking chair beside the stove, and immediately its wool padding began draining the chill from his back and thighs and buttocks. It was a good winter room, he thought. It was only the sameness of it day after day which fed his discontent. He rocked in the chair and for a moment shut his eyes as the sameness began to irritate him again: the windows permanently shrouded with blankets to keep out the cold with only about a third of one window uncovered; his writing desk just beneath the partly uncovered window; old canvas and rugs hiding the floorboards everywhere but right near the stove so that the drafts wouldn't sneak up from the cellar; his bed along one wall and Benjie's along another wall; the woodbox now with only a few sticks left from the armloads Benjie had dumped into it in the morning; the pitcher and basin on the small table where they always were; the water bucket beneath the stovepipe between the stove and the bricked-off part of the old fireplace; the dishes from the dinner Elizabeth — Jared's wife — had brought to him at mid day sitting just where they always sat to remind Benjie to carry them home when he went to bring back their supper from across the road. If he thought about it enough, Old Sam was certain he could dredge up every dreary detail of the room with his eyes shut.

Old Sam opened his eyes. His rocking ceased as he glanced over at the only window panes in the room not shrouded with blankets.

"Still enough light for a little," he said. "Benjie should be along by the time I need a candle. He can do the stove too."

The chair rocked again as he gazed at the stove. *Ugly thing* he thought. *They claim a stove warms much better than a fireplace. I know that's a fact, but heat ain't the only thing. I surely miss seein' a fire. Always was somethin' to watch. Wonder what Mandy would of thought if she could see me with a stove here and the fireplace all bricked over. Likely have a conniption fit if she couldn't have a fireplace to cook in.* He rubbed his hands together; probed the bony fleshlessness of his wrists. *Have a conniption fit if she could see how skinny I am now.*

"You ain't goin' to let me live to see leaves on the trees again, are you God?" he said aloud. "And I don't s'pose there'll be any more trout for me, will there? Here I am just waitin' to die, and there you are just takin' your time. Well, if you keep puttin' it off, a sack of shucks 'll be worth more 'n my old carcass. I'm near ready right now, and you just keep me waitin'."

His hands fussed under his shirt for a while before he brought out a wad of paper, unfolded it, and tipped the creased pages toward the poor light from the window. He squinted to decipher the shaky scrawl of his own writing.

Yes. Bury me next to Mandy, but they'll do that anyways. Pine coffin. And no ride in their fancy bone wagon. Carry me over to the graveyard from here. Likely that won't kill 'em. It's a bargain with me so skinny. If the pine's dry, that shouldn't be any great chore. Save me in the vault 'til the ground's soft enough and then pick a sunny day to bury me. Bad enough for folks to stand around in a graveyard without gettin' rained on too.

The rest of the writing was notes about matters he still had to decide. He glanced over at the writing desk, but made no motion to get up. It was thinking that he needed to do. There was no point in picking up his pen until he'd thought of something to write. Again he tried to decide about the rum. A few years earlier the decision would have been easy, but now people just didn't drink as much rum as they had in the old days. A day without rum then was about as common as a day without food. Now there were people who never drank any rum at all, and somehow religion had gotten mixed up with it. The thought of a rum keg in a graveyard would have worked well — had worked well — back in the years when his brothers had been buried: something to make a burial day special and remembered years later with the fondness of a barn raising. But these days skinning a live calf in church during Sunday meeting probably would cause less of an uproar. He'd have to think about it more. And there was a headstone to decide about too. A century hence he wanted someone looking at his tombstone to realize that it wasn't just another dead man there. There should be something special about it, and he didn't know what. Old Sam wondered too about deciding what words should be read over his grave. It didn't seem right just to have a sour-faced minister do dust-to-dust, but unless Old Sam decided what should be done instead, then the sour-faced minister would be there for sure. There was property to decide about too. Who should own his house after he died? Who should get the tannery? Or the acreage he owned in Barston and across the river in Wheelock? Should he deed it to his children out west in hopes that one of them might come back and settle in the village? Should he give it to his brothers' children and grandchildren instead? That was something that had to be decided too. There'd be an awful mess if he didn't do anything about it.

He lowered the papers to his lap. Sometimes they seemed so important. Other times he was sure that none of the arrangements mattered at all. When he was dead, he was dead. Why should he care if he got buried in the graveyard or if they threw his carcass into the river; if his coffin got carried on shoulders or in a freight wagon? What difference would it make if he had a tombstone or not? And whatever words were said over his grave wouldn't be anything he'd be bothered to hear, whatever they might be. If he didn't write a will, perhaps that would get all of his scattered children back to Barston Falls to fight over their shares. Otherwise they might just decide to have whatever was due to them sent out west; might sell the property from afar if they had clear ownership of it.

He rocked slowly in the chair, thinking of himself as a half-crippled and all-but-decaying old man alone in the big house. This was not the old age he had envisioned for himself years before. He'd always counted on Mandy to be with him, for one thing. There'd always been children and grandchildren in the vision as well, either living with Mandy and him — there was certainly enough room in the big house — or else close enough so that he'd see them every day. Who'd have thought that they'd be scattered to the ends of the earth, out in Ohio and such places, and that it would be such a long time between their letters?

Old Sam sighed and shook his head. It was hard to be old and to know that the longer he kept living the more broken down he would become. It would have been far easier if he had died on the same day Mandy had been buried. The leaden emptiness of depression bore down on his chest so that his pulse slowed and he scarcely breathed. What was the point in going on day after day, tethered to this joyless room by winter and old age? All his friends from the days when he'd been young and full of strength and fun were long since in their graves. His children and grandchildren were hundreds of miles away, and he didn't expect to see any of them again. In Barston Falls he was a bother to several of his brothers' descendants because they felt it was their duty to keep track of him. So far, however, he had managed not to be too great a burden on any of them. By going next door or across the road, he could have wintered with grandsons of his brother, Israel. Two widowed nieces and a nephew lived in the three other brick houses of the Barston family enclave on Tannery Road and had themselves offered him winter quarters, but he had turned them down as well. The need for him to spend that winter in his own home, if only to prove that he could still do it and didn't have to plague relatives with his needs, had overwhelmed all common sense objections. Well, perhaps he was more than a moderate burden to Jared's family. Living right across the road, they had taken on the chore of feeding him. Perhaps it would have been easier for them if he had lived in their home. Benjie had somehow been coerced into sleeping in the room with him every night to keep an eye on him, though Old Sam didn't know what good it would do. If his time came to die, there wouldn't be much that the boy could do to keep the life in him. Perhaps it would be a comfort not to die alone, but it would be a comfort bought at the expense of a youngster who had far better things to do than to watch an old man die. He wondered how he would have felt in Benjie's position.

The rocking chair creaked into its rhythm of waiting. Night would come on, and day would break again the next morning. The timeless cycles would continue at their own paces, indifferent to an old man from whom the life was fading. Then one day, it didn't really matter when, the old man would be gone. Old Sam sat and rocked and thought.

VII

Benjie rattled through the door; pulled it carelessly behind him so that it banged hard and the latch didn't catch. The door stood open a foot. Cold air from the hall surged in as Benjie glanced into the woodbox on his way by it. From two paces away he tossed his books onto Old Sam's writing desk. One of them slid off the desk and fell open and face down on the floor, but Benjie didn't give it a thought. He took the remaining sticks from the woodbox and dumped them into the stove.

"Cold out, Benjie?"

"No, Grampy Sam. It ain't near as bad as last week."

Benjie banged the door of the stove shut and then, striding back out into the hall, slammed the door to the room with another crash. Once again the latch didn't catch, and the door stood open a foot. A few moments later Benjie wrestled a double armload of wood through the gap between the door and the doorframe: knocking the door all the way back against the wall, gouging the frame with one of the chunks of firewood, and nearly losing his grip on the load as he came. He dropped the wood with a crash into the woodbox and then went out for more. This time he made no effort to close the door. By the time he had carried in the fourth load, the room was nearly as cold as the hall. Benjie dropped the wood into the woodbox. Two of the chunks toppled onto the floor, but Benjie let them lie where they had fallen. He pulled the door to the hall shut with a bang that again failed to latch it; pulled it again and then a third time. On the fourth attempt he took the time to latch it. Then he moved over to the stove to warm his hands.

"Have a good day at school, Benjie?"

"No. I didn't," Benjie said. He stood rubbing his hands. "Well, I better use the light while I got it. Be back in a little, Grampy Sam."

Benjie grabbed the dirty dishes on his way out of the room and disappeared, again with a crash that left the door ajar. Old Sam listened to him clump a few steps down the hallway and go out the front door. Then the room was silent again except for the hissing and shifting of the wood in the stove. Old Sam sighed, heaved himself out of his rocking chair, and walked over the trail of nearly melted snow Benjie had tracked in. He latched the door.

Tough on the boy gettin' stuck as a nursemaid, Old Sam thought. *But I guess you can't ever yoke a strong, young ox with a weak, old one and expect either one of 'em 'll be happy about it.*

Old Sam went over to his writing desk and sat down. He pushed Benjie's books aside, glanced at the one on the floor, left it there as requiring too much effort to retrieve, and pulled the paper from his shirt again. For a moment he smoothed it to flatten the folds and thought again about his gravestone, trying to picture in his mind how it might look, but then letting his thoughts slip morbidly away from the design of the stone and whether it would be slate or marble to an image of himself dead and buried beneath that stone. His eyes shifted from the paper to the few panes of the window not covered with battened blankets. There was no view outside for him, and he had no desire to scrape at the frosted glass. The fading translucence of the panes made Old Sam think that if Benjie didn't get back soon and light a candle, the boy might make quite a chore of it later fumbling around in the dark.

"Come to that now, has it?" he muttered suddenly. "Just provin' that I have made a nursemaid out of that boy. Sunk down so low that now I even wait for him to come and light a candle for me?"

Old Sam took the candle from his writing desk and carried it over to the stove. Awkwardly he opened the stove door, hunched over and picked up a two-foot-long splinter of dry pine from the hearth of the bricked-up fireplace, lighted the pine, and got the candle going. He failed in several attempts to blow out the flames on the burning stick, waved it unsuccessfully through the air for a moment, and finally dropped it into the water bucket behind the stove. As he was letting go of the pine, he tipped the candle and dribbled hot tallow across the backs of his fingers; recoiled at the sensation, but didn't let go of the candle. Then carefully he carried the candle upright and set it down on his writing desk. In a glow of triumph he steadied himself with one hand on the chair and picked Benjie's book up off the floor. After he sat down, he examined the book in the candle-light. It had the look of old wounds; had likely been abused long before Benjie had gotten his hands on it.

"Rhetorical Exercises," he said and began thumbing through the book. He stopped at one passage and read aloud, "Patriotism of 1775 — Patrick Henry." *Over half a century ago — think of that. And even then I was over thirty years old.* "Mr. President," Old Sam continued, "it is natural for man to indulge in the illusions of hope. We are apt to shut our eyes against a painful truth . . ."

Old Sam shut the book and shook his head. *You missed fire on that one, Patrick. Life is over for me. I know it. And that sure ain't shuttin' my eyes about things. Where's the hope? Back half a century ago. That's where.*

Some imperfection in the candle caused the wick to sputter for a moment before the flame returned to normal. For some reason, however, it had filled the room with smoke.

Benjie's footsteps crashed up through the hall. The door opened, and the footsteps stopped dead.

"You all right, Grampy Sam?" Benjie thrust down the basket he was carrying, leapt over to the stove, and slammed the door. "Left the stove door open, is all," he said as he went over to stand by his great-great uncle.

"Ha!" Old Sam said. "What do you s'pose my worthless old carcass 'll do next, Benjie?"

"Ain't anythin' to worry about, Grampy Sam. It'll air right out. Just seein' all that smoke scared me for a little. No harm done, but you got to make sure you shut the door."

"No harm this time, boy, but you best take me out and shoot me or stuff me through a hole in the ice if you can find one. If you let me have a next time, I might burn the house down with us in it. Yes. You best take me out and shoot me right away."

"Too much trouble, Grampy Sam," Benjie grinned. "Much rather just take my chances of the house burnin' down."

"Sit down, Benjie," Old Sam said. "I know it ain't easy livin' with . . ."

"Ma sent over supper," Benjie said and went to retrieve the basket from the floor. He set the basket down next to the candle and began laying out its contents on Old Sam's writing desk. "Stew," he said. "Ma claims it ain't too bad."

They started eating. After the smoke had thinned, Benjie shut the door to the hallway and came back to finish his supper. Old Sam gazed at the boy and after a few mouthfuls of food set down his spoon.

"What I was tryin' to say earlier, Benjie, is that I know it ain't easy for you livin' with an old man like me. I ain't exactly a droolin' old fool yet, but that might come sometime too. Never thought it'd get to where I can't take care of myself, but here I am anyway, and you're the one that's got stuck. I know it's a nuisance for you and that there are other things you'd rather be doin', but I expect that before this winter is over I'll stop bein' a bother to you and to everyone else."

"What are you talkin' about, Grampy Sam? You're goin' to be around for years yet. Just see if you ain't out fishin' next spring just like always. Sure, maybe you're slowin' down a little bit, but that's all. If it means I got to go with you every time you go fishin', then maybe I'll finally figure out how come you catch so many trout."

"But on account of me, Benjie, you can't even live at home. You're stuck over here."

"Ain't like home was a hundred miles away, Grampy Sam."

"But still . . ."

"I like it better over here anyways. It's nice sleepin' in a room with a stove and no drafts. Cookin' ain't a chore on account of Ma does it all. I only have to carry it."

"But you have to haul in all my wood and water too."

"And on account of that I don't have to haul 'em at home. Believe me, Grampy, there ain't any more work for me livin' here than at home. And there ain't any whinin' little brothers and sisters. I like it better over here."

"Maybe I'll believe you, and maybe I won't, Benjie. Just answer me a question or two about when you came in this afternoon. It was botherin' you then to have to take care of me, wasn't it? You had other things you wanted to do, and you had to come right back here to take care of me. Don't lie to me, Benjie. You were pretty well disgusted with it. I could see that clear enough. Throwin' books around. Bangin' into doorframes. Slammin' every door you touched. Just tell me, Benjie."

"Well, I guess I might of been hurryin' too much on account of wantin' to use the daylight. And you're right that I was good and disgusted, Grampy Sam, but it sure wasn't with you. It's that teacher we got this year — Teacher Tenney. He tricked me, Grampy Sam, and it don't seem right that somebody like that who don't look too sturdy to start with can kick so hard. Look at this here, Grampy Sam."

Benjie rolled up the cuff of his pantleg and swung his foot up onto the desk next to the bread to show the bruise and the swelling in the candlelight.

"Boots, Grampy Sam. Big heavy ones."

Old Sam stretched out his hand between the bread and Benjie's foot and glanced at the shin.

"Quite a bruise, Benjie. He must of fetched you a pretty good whack. How'd he happen to do that?"

"Tricked me is how. He was readin' right along to us, walkin' back and forth with a book in his hands, and wouldn't you s'pose that when a man is readin' like that he can't keep track of other things goin' on in the room? Well, what I figure now that I didn't figure then is that he knew the words by heart and that he wasn't readin' from the book at all — just holdin' it up and pretendin' he was readin' and lookin' all over the room at the same time. That's how he come to notice me kind of tappin' at Willie Adams with my foot — couldn't call it kickin' at all. It was just to tease him, and I was sure that Teacher Tenney couldn't see it because he was busy readin' from the book. Well, I sure was wrong because the next thing I know he was walkin' and still readin' right over towards me. He went by, and next he turned and walked back, and then he really hauled back and kicked me one. I was sure my leg was broke, and Willie Adams thought it was just about the funniest thing ever. I'll get him for it sometime, but it won't be in school."

"Sounds like havin' a Dartmouth College boy teachin' you this winter is a little different. That teacher you had last year . . ."

"That's just another trick," Benjie said. "We did anythin' we wanted with the one last winter, and then the one we got this winter looks so much like him — and he's livin' with Deacon Russell just like the one last year — that he tricked us to thinkin' we could do anythin' we want with him too. Only we can't. He's got those wicked boots, and the switch he's got is more like a club than a switch. School ain't fun the way it was last year. Not much you can do but set still and work."

"Careful who you tell that to, Benjie, or they'll go back down to Hanover and hire another Dartmouth boy for next winter too."

"Oh I ain't worried about that," Benjie said. "We had a Dartmouth teacher the winter before last. He was all Greek and Latin and preachery, and we sure gave him a run, just like we done for that wreck of a teacher we had last winter. If we don't get a good one after Teacher Tenney, well I ain't plannin' to go to school forever. I can read good enough and do sums and differences enough to get by. Ain't much more anybody needs than that. This winter might be my last schoolin' anyways. I been thinkin' it might be time for me to get out and see some of the world. Charlie Porter knows I can handle horses, so if he'll hire me next winter, I might drive a pung for him. Pung drivers get to go all over. It's a nice smooth ride — not like a freight wagon — and I'd earn money doin' it."

"What 'll you do after school is done this winter, Benjie?"

"Well, me and Tom and Foss sometime want to have our own flatboat and work the river all the way from Fifteen Mile Falls down to Middletown, but prob'ly this ain't the year to start. We want to grow a little bigger for one thing on account of all the fights that flatboat men get into, and for another thing we ain't got a flatboat yet. So I'll prob'ly help Pa and Uncle Seth in the warehouses and on the canal again this summer. But sometime I want to work on the river."

Old Sam nodded.

"Yes, Benjie. Spend a few years on the river when you're

young and strong. That gives you friends and memories for a lifetime. Well . . . my memories have lasted longer than all my friends, but that won't happen to everybody."

"I want to hear all the stories from your river days, Grampy Sam. I know some of 'em already, but I want to hear 'em all."

"Well, not tonight, Benjie. I'm too old and tired tonight. I'll be older tomorrow, of course, but maybe I won't be so tired. I think I'm goin' to head off to bed pretty quick here now."

"But it ain't hardly but supper time now."

"When you get old as me, you can feel tired just as soon as you get out of bed in the mornin'."

"You feelin' all right, Grampy Sam?"

"Just tired and feelin' like I lived too long."

"Well, eat some more," Benjie said. "It'll help you sleep better. You don't hardly eat a thing these days, and Ma's kind of blamin' me for it."

"Don't have the hunger for it, boy."

They sat in near silence as Benjie finished eating. From time to time he would glance up at Old Sam. When he was done, he announced that he was going over to visit his family across the road.

"If you leave the candle burnin', Grampy Sam, I can come in quieter. I don't expect I'll be over there very long, but I don't want to trip over things when I do come back."

Benjie put the dishes and the empty pot into the basket and carried it out of the room. By some miracle the boy latched the door on his way out.

Old Sam felt the aches and twinges even as he sat still at the desk. He shook his head and let out a sigh. As he lifted himself to his feet and tottered over to his own bed, he cast grotesque shadows onto the walls of the room. He sat on the side of his bed and worked off his shoes and britches and shirt. The time probably wasn't too far off, he reflected as he crawled between his blankets, when he'd need help getting dressed and undressed. With luck he'd be dead before it came to that. He lay back in weariness with his head turned toward the lone candle and felt twinges in his chest. Perhaps he would die in his sleep that night, he thought. Well, it really didn't make any difference.

Benjie was a good boy. He would remember to put a stick of dry wood and a stick of green wood into the stove to hold the fire overnight. He wished he could give the boy a better time. Benjie had been so eager to hear again the stories of Old Sam's days on the river on the chance that there might be something in the telling that he hadn't heard before about the masting and logging upriver, the mast drives and the log drives down the Connecticut, the dangers, the fights, the recounting of memories Old Sam had of incidents long past about people who now were all dead — all but for Old Sam himself. Not so long ago Old Sam would have teased Benjie mercilessly about getting kicked in school by the teacher. Now he didn't have the energy, and he couldn't even remember the teacher's name — the Dartmouth boy that was living with Deacon Russell. A few months back Old Sam would have talked far into the night about the early days as he drank whiskey or rum, and Benjie would have been the first to make excuses about needing his rest. He thought of the boy's protests that it would be years before he'd die and that the two of them might be out catching trout again. For a moment a fragment of a laugh interrupted the rhythm of his breathing. *No. If he's thinkin' about drivin' a pung for Charlie Porter next winter, he knows I'll be gone before then. He thinks there's a little chance that I might be around this summer, so he'll stay in the village, but after that he figures he'll be free, and he'll be off drivin' a pung or workin' on the river. The only time he'll have to visit will be to stop by my grave every now and then. He knows.*

It had been a good life, he thought as he gazed at the candle. There were a few regrets now, right at the end: that he'd outlived Mandy and all of his friends from the early days, that his own children didn't live anywhere nearby and never would, that he was being a burden to some of his relatives, and that nagging pains in his muscles and joints seemed to be part of every day now. Well, some day soon the candle would have burned down to nothing. Perhaps he'd be gone before the candle was.

He turned his head toward the wall and closed his eyes. Later he heard Benjie rattling around with the stove, but he didn't remember anything after that.

VIII

By the light of two candles Sewall Tenney sat writing in his room on the first floor of Deacon Russell's house. The deacon and his wife had long since gone to bed. Only the ticking of Sewall's watch on the writing table, the occasional shifting of wood in the stove at his back, and the scratching of the quill pen broke the stillness of the house.

Because of the stove and the ready accessibility of fire wood out in the deacon's shed, Sewall had taken to working late into the night ever since he'd begun teaching in Barston Falls. In the mornings he would sleep practically until the deacon's wife had breakfast on the table — a complete reversal of his habits at Dartmouth College.

He finished the work he'd set himself to do in preparation for his teaching the next day. It didn't amount to much: reading and writing; sums and differences. Presenting that material as a teacher was a far cry from being a student under Professors Adams and Chamberlain and Haddock and wading through the unending Greek in Dalzel's book, the Latin of *Taciti Historia*, the conic sections and spheric geometry and trigonometry, chemistry, Paley's work on natural theology and moral and political philosophy, and then the compositions and declamations. The main challenges of teaching in the schoolhouse at Barston Falls seemed to consist of keeping discipline and of getting a good fire going in the huge heater stove in time for it to keep his students from shivering through the early hours of the school day. The teaching itself was very easy. The stove had been a problem earlier because the wood for it was round and green — cut late in the fall, he supposed, and stacked out beside the schoolhouse. He had handled the situation well, however. Rather than going around to various people in the village and making a pest of himself whining about green firewood and a classroom as cold as the outdoors, he had encouraged his students to do the whining for him. Soon enough there had been dry wood on top of the stacks of green wood, and heat in the school-house had made teaching possible. He'd had a problem with discipline early and guessed that the troublemakers had been used to teachers who hadn't controlled them. He smiled as he thought back on the day just past. Yes, he'd certainly gotten Benjie Barston's attention. If he reminded the boy a few more times, he doubted he'd have any more whispering, poking, or other fooling around from him. The kick had made an impression on the other troublemakers. He expected everyone would be attentive in class the next day.

Sewall dipped his pen into the inkwell again and then scratched down a few figures. The cost for a year's tuition at Dartmouth, for room and board, and for such expenses as firewood and candles had risen even higher than the outrageous sum of a hundred dollars. That was a great deal of money. He'd had to work hard and skimp for several years to save enough to pay for his preparation — particu-larly in Latin and Greek — at Moor's School in Hanover and then to pay for his first two years at Dartmouth. He'd been working whenever he could to save enough money to get him through to graduation — a year from this com-ing August if all went well. Sewall, at twenty-five, had only a handful of classmates older than he. "Baby Alph" Crosby, the youngest boy in the class, was nearly a full decade younger, but then Baby Alph obviously didn't have to pay his own way. Sewall's own family in Chester, New Hamp-shire, was not rich; couldn't possibly have paid for him. Nor had they managed to pay for his brother, Thomas, who nonetheless had been graduated from Dartmouth the previous August. Now Thomas was twenty-seven years old and teaching at Moor's School so that he could save enough money to go to seminary. Sewall was comforted that he was far from being the only Dartmouth student from a poor family. Many of his Dartmouth classmates, almost all of them from New Hampshire or Vermont, had to struggle to earn tuition money. Most taught school during their seven-week winter vacation, which began early in January every year; scheduled specifically so that Dartmouth students could teach in New Hampshire and Vermont schools and earn money to help pay their college expenses. Some of them would continue teaching for as many as five weeks beyond the end of the vacation. The college, itself in a time of financial difficulties, accommodated them all with special arrangements. Sewall Tenney himself would return right at the end of vacation. The twentieth of February would be his last day of teaching; the last day of earning money to take back to Dartmouth. He had special reason to be back for the recommencing of the course of studies.

President Bennett Tyler of Dartmouth, in his own formal way, had teased him about making certain to return from his teaching work on time. He had called Sewall "the one indispensable student at this college, the one without whom the entire curriculum would be crippled." The reference was to Sewall's responsibility as the Dartmouth bellringer, a job for which he was given, without charge, a watch and the room on the third floor of The College — the middle room on the east side — with the bell rope hanging down through the ceiling. It was a continual, nagging responsibility to ring the bell on time: to set students into motion towards morning prayers in chapel, recitations, lectures, and indeed all events at Dartmouth. Ringing the bell for chapel was a particular headache for him because he always had to get up, without delay, at the first hint of daylight. Chapel was held every day just as early as President Tyler could see by natural light to read the Bible. Sewall had recurring dreams about oversleeping; of irate professors and tutors or the president himself waking him roughly when the morning was well-advanced. He could never relax and was continually hauling out his watch at all hours to see what time it was.

Getting away from his bellringing responsibilities had been a welcome relief, but Sewall missed his friends and was homesick for Dartmouth College. Bell rope or not, he loved living in room 10 on the third floor of The College. Twenty-seven students out of a total of one hundred seventy-four lived in The College, the only Dartmouth-owned building of note aside from the chapel and New Commons. New Commons stood just to the northwest of The College and housed students. Although its original function had been to feed students, New Commons had ceased serving its legendarily poor food a decade earlier. Unending complaints about the alleged food had led Dartmouth to cease providing meals and to allow all students to make whatever eating arrangements they wanted. The boys rooming in New Commons (and in the privately owned Brown Hall next door) claimed that on rainy days they could still smell the ghosts of the carrion and corpses served as food to earlier Dartmouth classes. Many students arranged to take their board in various village homes, but some — Sewall included — cooked in their own rooms.

All lectures and recitations took place in the building known, somewhat confusingly, as The College. It held the meager Dartmouth library along with what was left of the college museum. The third floor, where Sewall lived, was known as Bedbug Alley and was the envy of all the Dartmouth students who took their lodgings downstairs in the same building, in Brown Hall or New Commons, in Hanover private homes, or in the huge and rambling brick building, known as the Tontine, in the middle of the village. Sewall had himself lived upstairs in the Tontine during his freshman year, above the shops and businesses of all varieties which took up the first floor. For his sophomore year he had lived in Mr. Wright's home with three other members of the class of 1827: Charlie Little of Boscawen and Edwin Jennison of Walpole — two fellow New Hampshire boys — and Jim Alvord of Greenfield, down the river in Massachusetts. Those three this year were continually in his room in Bedbug Alley whenever they had free time. Often he let them ring the bell. Three other classmates lived in Bedbug Alley and frequently cooked meals with Sewall — all four of them thinking to save the expense of meals at village boarding houses. Sam Smith from Francestown lived two doors down in room 12. Levi Bartlett lived down by the end of Bedbug Alley in room 2. He was from Haverhill, across the river from Barston Falls and north two towns. It was Levi who had told him about the teaching position in Barston Falls. Next to Levi, in room 1, lived Jonathan Worcester. Since he was from Salem, Massachusetts, Jonathan was teased constantly about being first cousin to Elias Hasket Derby Esquire Salem Massachusetts, a stuffed denizen of the shattered museum appearing periodically on the chapel roof, astride the college well, or at the lecture platforms of the four class recitation rooms. To visit Levi and Jonathan, Sewall had merely to walk through the fractured walls of the museum to the end of the hall. There were forty-two juniors at Dartmouth that year. Sewall knew them all, but he was closest to the six who were either living in Bedbug Alley with him this year or else who had lived with him at Mr. Wright's the year before. Charlie Little and Jonathan Worcester were his best friends, and the three of them had decided to live together for their senior year at Mrs. Gates' house, where Charlie was living that year. Sewall could scarcely bear the thought that he would be graduated from Dartmouth in just a little more than a year and a half. He was sad and nostalgic about it already, brought home clearly to him by being away on his teaching absence. He and his friends, he knew, would be strong parts of one another's lives until they died — whether they saw one another daily or but once in ten years.

Sewall interrupted his musings to put more wood into the stove. It was wonderful having so much wood and being able to keep the room continually warm as long as he stayed up and kept putting in the logs. At Dartmouth the firewood situation was impossible. Whenever he bought wood from the farmers who hauled it in daily on wagons or sledges, he had to carry it all the way up to the third floor of The College. There was no leaving it outdoors, even marked with his name on a sign, or it disappeared overnight. If he went out to try to find windfalls to haul back from the already well-gleaned countryside, it meant many long trips without much wood to show for his exertions. It would have been full-time work in itself. It was far easier to buy wood, but most students had little money to spare and kept their eyes open for wood they didn't have to buy. Every student room in The College had a newly installed stove, and each stove had to be fed wood constantly in the colder months if the room's occupants were to have any comfort. A stick of wood "borrowed" from the stack in any room whose occupants were temporarily absent would soon enough burn down to ashes and be completely untraceable as evidence. Firewood thieves generally had to be caught in the act of stealing to be proven guilty. The exception had come when Levi Bartlett had bored into a stick of firewood, filled the hole with black powder, plugged it, and set it on top of the pile in his room. A pair of sophomores down on the second floor soon thereafter had requested a new stove from Dartmouth because theirs had "fallen apart." They'd had to pay for its replacement. Later, however, Levi's own stove had "fallen apart," and he himself had had to buy a new one. All the Bedbug Alley boys had a mutual firewood truce and hauled — and burned — their own wood, but there was no trusting the boys downstairs either on the first or second floors. It was a luxury for Sewall now in Barston Falls to have a nearly unlimited supply of dry wood out in the deacon's shed and not to have to haul it up any flights of stairs.

As far as Sewall could tell, Deacon Russell had been the low bidder to the selectmen for providing room and board for a teacher. The deacon was well-to-do and certainly didn't need the money; indeed, had probably bid low purposely for the prestige, such as it was, of having a Dartmouth College boy living in his house. The deacon was a clever, intelligent man and had clearly yearned for conversation with Sewall, but his bearing and that of his wife had always been so close to sanctimony as to put Sewall off. There had been the start of a religious revival at Dartmouth and in Hanover during the fall of Sewall's sophomore year. It had prospered; was still going on. A temperance enthusiasm had soon joined it. That too was doing well. Sewall had avoided both of these unyielding movements as being too extreme, had thought them confined to Hanover, and had been surprised to realize that Deacon Russell preached God at him with practically every breath and that he regarded alcohol as both poison and sin. Though Sewall was religious himself and had been thinking of going eventually to seminary, he didn't particularly like the deacon or his wife. Immediately after supper each night he would retire to his room ostensibly to work and study, but actually to avoid having to bear their company and their opinions. He had enjoyed rum occasionally at Dartmouth and missed having it here in Barston Falls, but realized that the mere presence of alcohol in the house would have been anathema to both Deacon Russell and his wife. Sewall hadn't drunk anything but water since he'd arrived in Barston Falls. It didn't seem likely that the situation would change before he left.

Sewall wrote a letter to his parents in Chester and then another to his brother, Thomas, who was a preceptor at Moor's School in Hanover. His watch said that it was close to eleven o'clock by the time he had finished. He would have stayed up later if he'd had work or other letters, but he had none and was tired besides. He blew out one of the candles, put two more sticks of wood into the stove, shoveled a few ashes in on top of them, and left two more sticks on the floor in front of the stove, where he could reach them during the night or first thing in the morning.

The room was always cold in the morning, and Sewall had no hope of warming it before it was time to go to the schoolhouse. At best he would simply hold the fire in the stove with green wood or with an ash cover to save him from having to kindle a fire anew when school was over. Sewall moved the chair over to beside his bed. From its peg on the wall he took down his black frock coat and laid it over the back of the chair. It was his Dartmouth uniform coat, and he was inordinately proud of it. Dartmouth students the spring before had taken the initiative of bringing a school uniform into existence, perhaps with an inspiration from rumors of the Yale students, who had five years previously determined on a uniform for themselves, but more likely in envious response to the very good looking military uniforms which the boys in the A.L.S. & M. Academy across the river in Norwich had worn. The Dartmouth coat had a sprigged diamond about three inches long and three inches wide embroidered onto the left breast. On the left sleeve there were three embroidered half-diamonds, signifying that Sewall was a member of the junior class. Seniors had four half-diamonds; sophomores two; freshmen one. The coat was to be worn with black or white pantaloons, stockings, vest, and cravat. Sewall used the coat indoors at Deacon Russell's house as a robe to fling on first thing in the morning to fend off the cold; on the coldest nights as a supplement to his blankets.

Sewall took off his boots and stockings, laid his britches and shirt over his coat on the chair, and knelt down to say his prayers. Then he blew out the remaining candle and crawled into bed. He fell asleep with visions of Bedbug Alley and of his friends creeping into his dreams.

IX

Sue Reckford trudged up the stairs in the Reckford home. For the time being the house was quiet and would be until either the twins awoke or her stepmother returned from Danforth's store. The twins would awaken first, she guessed. Annie rarely went to the village square these days just to do errands. She often spent hours there talking in the store and visiting friends and leaving Sue at home to take care of the twins. Usually there was sweeping or cooking or washing to do as well, and Annie would expect it to be done by the time she returned. Just then, in fact, water for washing clothes was heating on the stove.

Sue sneaked silently into the twins' room. Annie greased the hinges on the door at least once a week and had insisted on having rugs on the floor. Even the rocking chair was on a rug. Well, the boys were both still asleep. That was a blessing because they could be a trial indeed when they were awake and wanted to be fed and Annie wasn't there. Sue slouched down into the rocking chair, knowing it would be quite a while before the water would be ready for washing that pile of the twins' diaper cloths.

Life had certainly changed for her and for her father in the three and a half years since the day they'd arrived in Barston Falls. She had felt far closer to him then, when they'd only had each other. In the years before they'd come to the village, they had moved constantly. Joe Reckford would work for a few months, and then they'd leave for someplace new. Sue had inherited an almost morbid shyness from her father. Neither of them had ever been able to talk easily with strangers; seemed generally to avoid the possibility of new acquaintances and had lived a jointly withdrawn existence. Never in their wandering years had they been in a place long enough so that they could think of it as home. Sue had learned it was pointless to make any plans that ignored the certainty that she and her father would soon be wandering again. Even after their first six weeks in Barston Falls, neither of them had known well anyone in the village; had known nothing of the gossip or goings on. Then, almost by accident, she and Malik — an old Abenaki Indian — had gradually developed a friendship while they'd both been fishing. They had formed a fishing partnership, and Sue had gotten to know Old Sam, who was a friend of Malik's from many years before.

Then her old world had suddenly turned upside down, and she'd been overjoyed at the difference. She and Malik had caught a huge fish together, an exploit that had been written about in newspapers throughout the Connecticut River valley. Seemingly everyone in the village had known her after that, and her loneliness had come to an abrupt end, or so she had supposed. At about that same time Annie Ballard, the blacksmith's sister, had dragged her father out of his isolation and into an active and successful — and very short — courtship. Sue had liked Annie so much then and didn't think it possible that she could have been happier. Her father was settling into the village for the rest of his life and had bought a new house. Old Sam Barston had helped him get set up in the brick business in an abandoned brickyard which had once belonged to his brother, Israel Barston, and in which every single one of the many thousands of bricks in the village had been made. Sue had close friends her own age for the first time in her life: Benjie, Foss, and Tom.

Sue's happiness, however, hadn't been complete. After the surge of joy had settled down, she found that some elements of her former unhappiness remained. She was still an overly large and plain-looking girl. Though she knew other girls in the village by name and could have conversations with them readily, she was close to none of them; really didn't have much in common with them. With the boys she was more successful, but only because she could out-do them at their own games and diversions. Until only recently she had towered over Benjie, Foss, and Tom and had been certain she was stronger than any of them. She continued to wear britches, as she had all her life, rather than dresses. She chewed tobacco with the boys, carried a pipe in her britches pocket as they did to smoke wherever they could find privacy and a flame, drank at least token swallows of rum or whiskey with them whenever they could get it, and sneaked out at night with them so she could be part of whatever deviltry they had conjured up for their entertainment and for the embarrassment of a particular person or group in the village. The boys thought of her simply as one of their gang and sometimes when she was with them would even talk among themselves about how pretty Mary White and Betsy Mattoon were — talk about them as if she weren't even there or if she too were a boy who could appreciate young, female beauty. Her hair for many years had been cropped short, but for over a year now she'd been letting it grow. She hoped that as it lengthened it might take some of the attention away from her plain looks.

Her life at home hadn't been what she'd expected after her father and Annie had married. She had thought that Annie's presence would at once compensate for all the girl friends she had never had and for the mother she couldn't remember. However, it hadn't worked out like that. Certainly Annie was friendly, but the difference in their ages kept her from being a close friend, and Sue had felt awkward right from the start as a stepdaughter. Also Sue wasn't nearly as close to her father as she had been before. He had been so constantly busy at the brickyard that he didn't spend as much time at home as he once had. In addition, he and Annie often spent time alone together going on walks or talking. Occasionally they included her with them, but most of the time Sue had the distinct impression of being left out. Before Annie had married her father, Sue had taken care of him: cooking and cleaning and washing clothes and so forth. As Joe's wife, Annie started doing all those things, and Sue had felt useless. Then the twins had arrived and had instantly taken over the entire household. Neither Annie nor Joe had seemed to have any time left for Sue after that, and she had felt neglected. The final difference that Sue had noted was that now her father no longer talked with her about her long-dead mother. Reluctant to dredge up painful memories, it had taken him years to begin talking to Sue about her. When he finally had, Sue appreciated it and felt that it had drawn them closer. However, ever since he had married Annie, Joe Reckford seemed to have forgotten about his first wife. Annie had apparently stolen even the memory of Sue's mother from him.

Sue ran her hands through her hair. It seemed a great deal longer than it had been only a month earlier. She wondered if . . . She got out of the rocking chair and tip-toed over to the cradles. Both boys were still sound asleep.

Quietly Sue left the room, turned down the hallway past her own room, and opened the door to her father and Annie's bedroom. Probably she shouldn't go in, but it was the only room in the house with a looking glass. It couldn't do any harm just to have a look. Besides, Annie probably wouldn't be back for quite a while yet.

Sue studied herself in the mirror. *No, same as ever: too big and too plain. Nose is too wide, and so ain't my face. Better when I smile, but still it's just a big, strong, tomboy face, twice as big as Betsy Mattoon's. The boys are right. She is pretty . . . only thing I can change is my hair.* She bunched her hair behind and then tried to see how it would look if she piled it on top of her head. She hummed softly as she turned to see one side of her head and then the other. *Well, there is kind of a shine to my hair that don't look too bad.* Without thinking, she took up Annie's brush and arranged her hair this way and that to see if she could discover the way it looked best. A couple of Annie's hairpins did just manage to hold it in place, the first time it had been long enough for her to do that. She smiled at herself and thought that perhaps she looked pretty good. On a sudden impulse she kicked off her shoes and quickly shed her britches and shirt. Then she took down Annie's best dress from the peg where it was hanging and pulled it on over her head. She straightened the shoulders of the dress, touched her hair once or twice with the brush, and smiled as she turned her head left and right without taking her eyes off the image in the mirror.

A glimpse of movement made her whirl towards the door. Annie stood there staring at her.

"Oh, there you are, Sue. What on earth are you . . .?"

"I didn't mean to put your dress on, Annie," Sue said, purpling with embarrassment as she thrust the hair brush behind her back. "I was just . . ."

"Of course you meant to put my dress on, Sue," Annie snapped. "It wouldn't put itself on you, and while you was foolin' around up here with my things, you as good as let the fire go out under the wash water. I think that you . . ."

Annie stopped abruptly and cocked her head toward the thin wails of the twins. She sighed and spoke more quietly.

"Now Sue, I think you should just take the dress off and put it back where you found it. Get your own clothes back on, and come see me in the twins' room after that."

Annie disappeared from the doorway. Sue felt so humiliated that tears started in the corners of her eyes. She brushed at them with the backs of her hands and then with her sleeve after she'd put her own shirt back on.

Annie was sitting in the rocking chair, the front of her dress undone and a son at each breast.

"Sue, you know you shouldn't be in my room goin' through my things. You know — I hope you know — that ain't right. You should ask me if you want somethin'."

"It wasn't the kind of thing I could ask, Annie."

"What's that mean?"

"It's only because that's the only lookin' glass, and I wanted to see if my hair was long enough yet so I could do things with it. I never meant at first to put on your dress, but I wanted to see how I looked in it."

"So that was it."

"Yes, Annie."

Annie shifted her sons slightly in her arms and then rocked back in the chair and gazed at Sue.

"Sixteen now, ain't it?" Annie said. "Sometimes it's hard to remember. We started off all right together, I think, but I ain't had time for you since before the twins came. You been growin' and changin', of course, and I ain't paid attention to it. I guess I ain't much of a mother to you, Sue."

"But you ain't my mother, Annie. You're my step-mother."

"I surely know that, Sue, and that makes it a lot harder for me. If I was your real mother, you think I'd put up with your tobacco and drinkin' and sneakin' out of this house at night? I see a time comin' when that'll mean bad trouble for you, if it ain't already. That's somethin' I been leavin' to your pa just on account of I am your stepmother and not your real one, but maybe it'd be better if I didn't leave it to him. Maybe I should keep right after you, but I just ain't got the time — not with the twins to look out for every hour of the day and night. And I think maybe you're old enough so I shouldn't have to track you down every day just to get some dinner in you.

"Lately I was thinkin' that it might of been hard on you when I married your pa on account of you was used to keepin' house for him and not sharin' him with any other woman. But let me tell you somethin' that maybe it's time you got used to: just as soon as I married your pa, I became the woman of whatever house he lives in. You used to be, but you ain't any more. If that's somethin' that you don't like, it's too bad, but that's the way it is. You can fight me about things, or we can get along. It's all up to you. You got anythin' to say about it, Sue?"

"No."

"Well you think about things. I surely don't understand what's got into you these days. When your pa and I got married, you didn't like it that there wasn't much work left for you around the house, and right now you don't like it when there is work here for you to do. With the twins there's plenty for the both of us. You can like doin' it or you can hate doin' it, but you will do it. Now, why don't you go down and see if the water's hot enough yet for the washin'? And get right on it if it is. I'll be down when I'm through here. And you stay out of our room unless you ask first."

Sue, eyes downcast, left the room. Annie shook her head slowly.

"No tellin' how that girl's goin' to turn out," she muttered.

The twins quickly took her thoughts away from Sue, however.

"Won't you two little pigs never stop? If you had teeth, I'd think about stuffin' the both of you in a sack and dumpin' you in the river. And I s'pose if you was triplets, I'd jump in the river myself."

She leaned further back in the rocking chair, rubbing their backs.

X

Still clenching the glowing iron with the tongs, George Ballard thrust it into the plunge tub beside his forge, kept it underwater until the steam had subsided, and then held out the newly darkened piece as he turned towards Charlie Porter.

"This about what you got in mind for a strut, Charlie?"

"That's it," Charlie said, glancing over the two-foot-long iron rod with a wrapped eye at each end. "If you can bend the two eyes out some so they'll lay flat against the runners and the bed and make sure that the eyes are big enough so that a bolt like the one I'm leavin' with you 'll fit 'em, then that's what I want a dozen of."

"All right. Should make a mighty rugged pung."

"That's what I'm aimin' to have," Charlie said. "I want the ruggedest pung in Vermont or New Hampshire. Can't have the runners foldin' over when I load on a little weight."

"No chance they will with a dozen iron struts bolted on to 'em. So, a dozen struts like this with the eyes bent out a little more and then what about that big ring bolt and iron plates you're talkin' about for a block and tackle anchor point? You sure you need somethin' that rugged?"

"Well you help me figure it, George. I'll be haulin' some pretty heavy iron in that pung, and I got to have a ring bolt that won't pull out or bend when I'm loadin'. So what do you think?"

"You don't need but one iron plate to spread the strain over the plankin'. Just one on the outside of the pung box up front for the threaded end and nut to fetch up against. Don't need one on the inside too for the ring."

"Oh. Course that's right," Charlie said.

"You just goin' to use timbers for a loadin' ramp?"

"I was thinkin' maybe to have the back end flop down on hinges and use that for a ramp. Sometimes timbers shift around when you don't want 'em to. I need a good steady ramp that I can use rollers with. I think with rollers and a big block and tackle that I can load just about anythin' into that pung. What do you think about that?"

"You'll need good heavy hinges — prob'ly four or six instead of two. And just to make sure the back end is rugged enough for a ramp, maybe I should get some iron in there so it ain't just the wood that's takin' all the weight."

"Good," Charlie said. "The back end ramp is the full height of the pung box — about six and a half foot. Longer the better as far as loadin' with the rollers goes. So I guess it could use some extra strength in it.

"Now I was thinkin' to leave the plankin' off the top of the pung box and just put a good canvas there to keep out the weather. I think the pung 'll be plenty heavy already without that extra plankin'. Thought maybe to have iron bows over the top so the snow and rain 'll run off better 'n just havin' it flat."

"Oh, I can do that in iron if you want," said George. "If you want to pay me for it, I can, but you don't need the strength just to hold up canvas. Cheaper for you to steam and bend some wood. That's what I'd tell you to do."

"All right. You just talked yourself out of that work."

"Well, bring the pung over maybe sometime next week so's I can have a look. The struts 'll keep me busy for a little after I run out of my other work, but then I'll need to see your pung so we can figure out the rest of the iron for it."

George set the strut down onto a tub of sand and hung his tongs back on a rack within easy reach of his anvil and forge. A dozen other sets of tongs hung there with them — all of them in different shapes and sizes.

"'Bout dinner time, ain't it, Charlie?"

"Feels like it to me," Charlie said.

"I'll call it a mornin' then."

George took off his heavy, leather apron and hung it from a wall hook.

"Haulin' stoves, you said?"

"Mostly stoves," Charlie said. "But really anythin' else that's heavy and needs haulin' in the winter. Iron for you from Franconia, for one thing. Freight wagons just ain't quite rugged enough for a lot of the things folks need hauled these days. Winter's the time to haul weight on account of a pung 'll carry a lot more than anythin' with wheels. A wheel 'll break twenty times for every pung runner you can break. And with all the call for stoves and hollow ware these days, seems like a rugged pung is just what I need to get that business. Course you can get stoves on flatboats in the summer and haul 'em that way, but still you got to haul 'em from the manufactory to the river and then from the river to wherever they're goin' to get used. Easier to load 'em on a pung once at Franconia, drive 'em where they're s'posed to go, and unload 'em once. Smoother ride in the winter too, of course."

"Oh," George said. "Reminds me, Charlie. I was wonderin' the other day if they ever might make any cannons over at Franconia. Seems like you could ask 'em next time you might be over there for stoves if . . ."

"Asked 'em quite a while back," Charlie said. "They ain't set up for it. There ain't a way we can buy a new cannon. Got to find an old one."

"Too bad," George said. "Seems like Steve's got money enough for Old Sam's cannon, if only we could buy one someplace. And Seth and Jared went clear down to Portsmouth and Boston to see if they couldn't find one down there, and they couldn't. The militia don't have but a few, and they're pretty tight with 'em. What towns have 'em don't want to get rid of 'em, and can't say as I blame 'em, but it seems like there's got to be some way we can get a cannon for Old Sam. Steve, of course, sees a lot of folks from up and down the river and asks 'em . . ."

"Talks a lot, don't he?" Charlie said. "Not the sort of a man that can ever keep a secret, is he?"

"No. I don't s'pose . . ." George paused. "Anyways, Steve says he's been askin' all around, and there ain't a cannon to be 'begged, borrowed, or bought' from anyplace. That's what he says. He talks to folks from all over when they stop at the store, but of course you haul freight a lot of places too. Steve's right, ain't he, Charlie? You ain't seen any different anyplace, have you?"

"I prob'ly see about the same things that Steve hears," Charlie said. "I s'pose that travelin' around so much I do know where to find most of the cannons. And there ain't one anyplace I know of that we can buy. Steve's right about that. I don't expect either that anybody's goin' to give us one no matter how hard we beg. Whether we can find one to borrow or not, I guess that depends on just exactly what you mean by 'borrow.'"

George fussed with the remnants of charcoal burning in his forge. He put two sticks of wood on top of the coals and then shoveled an inch of ashes on top of the wood from an ash bucket.

"There. That should hold it 'til I can eat a decent dinner. You know with a pung that rugged, Charlie, you could haul most anythin', and with that ramp and rollers and a block and tackle you could likely load just about anythin' onto it."

"Well, there's more and more call for stoves and other heavy things these days," Charlie said.

"You're in a good business then," George said. "Be plenty of call for your pung once you get it set up the way you want. You know, there's other work I got to do, but I might just set it aside for a little, and I think I can get to those struts this afternoon and finish 'em off maybe sometime tomorrow. If you ain't doin' anythin', why don't you bring the pung around tomorrow mornin' so's we can see exactly what else I need to make for iron. I think it might be a good thing if we got you set up quick as we can with that pung. Likely there's some poor old grandmother someplace freezin' to death on account of there's nobody to haul a stove to her from the Franconia works. I'll take it on as my Christian duty to get the ironwork for your pung done before I do any other projects. How's that sound, Charlie?"

"Sounds good to me, if you ain't busy with somethin' else."

"I am busy with somethin' else, but I think I'll work on this and get it done. I got to see if that pung's goin' to work the way you want or not. You know, Charlie, if you ever need any help movin' somethin' heavy that ain't a stove with this rig, just let me know. I can think of a couple other men with a little bit of heft to 'em that might want to help too and that can keep quiet about it if there's a need."

"Course I ain't got the ghost of a notion what you're suggestin', George."

"I know you ain't. That's why, right here not much more 'n a month away from the end of winter, you're riggin' up a pung rugged enough to haul the Barston Boulder in so's you can get some poor old lady her stove in time to keep her warm for the summer."

"That might be," Charlie said. "But the pung ain't for just this winter. I was hopin' that your ironwork might of improved and that the pung might last for more 'n just a month."

"That's what keeps me in business: men like you that ain't afraid to take a chance." George paused. "And I think you're right about Steve. He's so used to talkin' to everybody all the hours of the day that he prob'ly is the kind of man that you tell somethin' to when you want everybody to know it just as quick as they can. Likely he ain't the kind of man that you could tell a secret to and have it stay a secret."

"No. He ain't," Charlie said.

"Well, if there's ever a time when we might have a secret, maybe we shouldn't tell it to him."

"That might be a good idea, George."

"And you'll bring around your pung tomorrow mornin'?"

"First thing."

XI

The two Barston brothers sat next to the stove in the small room boarded off from the rest of the warehouse. A pair of candle lanterns burned on a nearby table. Two additional candles, stuck into bottles, helped light the room. Snow the brothers had tracked in was melting to slush-puddles on the dirty and deeply-scarred planking of the floor. Both of the men glanced occasionally through the window of the small room out towards the warehouse's huge double doors, which they had left slightly ajar.

"So, you really think they might of left some behind down in Norwich, Seth?"

"Stands to reason, if they ever had 'em to start with. Old Pewt marched the boys all the way down the river to Middletown, and they sure didn't drag 'em to Connecticut when they marched."

"But you think they had 'em at the Academy to start with?"

"Don't it make sense to you that they did, Jared? After all, the 'M' in A.L.S. & M. was for 'military.' Stands to reason that they had some cannons, and stands to reason that they couldn't take 'em along when Old Pewt moved the Academy — marched the boys — from Norwich down to Middletown. All we got to do is find one and sneak it back up here, and Grampy Sam 'll have his cannon for the Fourth of July."

"But if the cannons was just lyin' around out there by the Academy with the Dartmouth boys right across the river, then don't you think . . ."

"That's how come we got to talk to Benjie's teacher to-night," Seth said. "Like as not he can tell us. And if there are some down there, just left around, it don't seem like it'd be much trouble to get one of 'em back up here. Sewall, you say?"

"That's it," Jared said. "Sewall Tenney from Chester — that's New Hampshire and not Chester, Vermont. He ain't such a boy as we had teachin' last winter. Must be about twenty-five, and he won't let Benjie and the other boys walk all over him. Got a pair of boots so he can do some walkin' himself, so Benjie says, and a good thick cane to help him keep attention. If I had my way, I'd see if we couldn't get him to come back again next year. I think Benjie might even learn somethin' this winter. I hope he does because it might be the last schoolin' he gets."

"Benjie's teacher ain't quite so sour as the one that lived with the deacon last winter, is he?"

"I guess not, Seth. Not from what Benjie says, but the way that one let the boys treat him last winter, he had every reason to be sour."

"So how are we goin' to ease into talkin' about cannons with Benjie's teacher, Jared? We don't want him to get suspicious if later on somebody happens to borrow a cannon across the river from him."

"Oh, I s'pose we'll get around to it one way or another. We need a cannon, and if there ain't one for us at the old A.L.S. & M. Academy, then I don't know where else we can go. I thought we might find one down at the coast, but of course there wasn't a thing. What we need is another good war. That'd get the cannons trotted out and movin' around. And we could just . . ."

Jared stopped talking abruptly as he saw a light through the window.

"In here!" Jared yelled, as he got up and opened the door.

Sewall Tenney entered with a lantern in hand and stamped the snow from his feet. He set his lantern down on the table beside the two others and blew out its flame.

"I wasn't sure I had Benjie's message right," Sewall said. "It didn't seem as if anyone would be in the warehouse in the late evening, but since he's beyond playing tricks on me now, I knew I should come. Is there a particular reason for meeting here rather than elsewhere?"

"No particular reason," Jared said. "Except the house is so noisy with my children, and I wanted a chance to talk to you about Benjie where we could have some peace and quiet. Just seemed easier to talk to you down here than up at the house. I hope you don't mind."

"Not at all," Sewall said.

"Well, I'm Jared, his pa. And this is Seth, my brother."

"Yes. I've seen you in the village. And I am Sewall. It's a rather formal name, but I hope you won't judge me just by that. I'm not as formal as my name might seem to indicate."

"Good teacher is what I hear," Jared said. "You got Benjie's attention this winter, and I think he's learnin' somethin'. Last winter I don't think he learned a thing because he was too busy tryin' to make life miserable for the teacher we had."

"He was pretty successful at it," Seth said.

"He's a well-behaved boy now," Sewall said. "Still not overly serious about his studies, but he behaves in school, and every now and then he tries hard."

"Well, I'm sure you're to thank for what progress he has made this winter," Jared said.

"Sounds a little like how I was in school," Seth said. "All except for the part about behavin' himself and tryin' hard every now and then. Tell me, Sewall, how it is livin' over with Deacon Russell and his wife."

"Oh, they're both very intelligent people," Sewall said. "There's no doubt about that."

"You like 'em?" Seth asked.

"Not so much a question of that," Sewall said. "It's more that we don't seem to share many things in common. Oh, I'm very likely headed for seminary after I am graduated from Dartmouth and have had a chance to save enough money, but I don't think I'll ever get to the stage of being so prayerful as the deacon and his wife. They strike me as a little stiff and tight, but it's probably because I am younger than they."

"They're both strong for temperance," Seth said.

"Yes, they are," Sewall said. "They both regard the drinking of strong spirits as a sin, and that was not my upbringing."

"You drink rum?" Seth asked as his eyebrows raised.

"I haven't yet while I've been teaching in the village, but I don't mind a little cider or beer or rum or whiskey every now and then down in Hanover."

"Would you mind a little whiskey right now?" Jared asked.

"I suppose that I wouldn't," Sewall said. "In fact, I'd like some. But . . ."

"Wait a minute," Jared said, "and I'll get some. And have a seat anyplace that's comfortable. There's no reason to stand."

Jared took one of the candle lanterns with him and disappeared through the door out into the rest of the warehouse. Sewall dragged a chair from one wall and sat down next to Seth.

"My brother and me was just wonderin'," Seth said. "We was talkin' about Hanover and Norwich, and we got to talkin' about Dartmouth College and the A.L.S. & M. Academy. And we just couldn't remember what the A.L.S. & M.

letters stand for, except that we got the 'M' for military. Wonderin' if maybe you could recall."

"Oh, that's easy," Sewall said. "It's American Literary, Scientific, and Military Academy. That's what it all stands for."

"You ever see much of it while it was there in Norwich? Before it moved down to Middletown, I mean."

"Can't say that I did," Sewall said. "They never liked us Dartmouth boys much, I'm afraid. If any of us got caught on their grounds over in Norwich, they'd grab us, and then they'd take our coats and tear them right up the back seam all the way to the collar. There were some hard feelings there, you may be sure. Unless we were actively looking for trouble, there was no reason for any of us from Dartmouth to pay the bridge toll and go over to Norwich."

Jared returned with an earthenware jug.

"It's whiskey," he said as he sat down. "No cups or mugs to go with it, so we'll make do without. Don't swallow too deep 'til you feel how cold it is 'cause it ain't a bit warmer than the rest of the warehouse, and you don't want to freeze your throat."

Sewall took the offered jug first and tipped it back for a small swallow and then several longer ones.

"So, you ain't temperance," Seth said as he took the jug. "Headed for the seminary some day, and you ain't temperance. Swallow the spirits right down."

"That's right," Sewall said with a long sigh. "Ephesians 5:18."

"What's that?" Jared asked.

"A favorite chapel verse," Sewall said. "Let's see . . . 'Do not get drunk with wine, for that is debauchery; but be filled with the spirit.' And we surely do like the spirits, but nothing that comes from the grape, 'for that is debauchery.'"

The jug circulated.

"He was tellin' me about the letters for the A.L.S. & M.," Seth said.

"American Literary, Scientific, and Military Academy," Sewall said.

"So that's what it is," Jared said. "I guess I might of known that once, but I must of forgot."

"Smart lookin' bunch of boys is what I heard," Seth said. "Uniforms and muskets and marchin' here and there. It's a great bunch for walkin', so I hear."

"That's right," Sewall said. "Captain Partridge is a great one for leading the boys out on long walks, and it's not many of them as can keep up with him. Marched the whole school right down to Middletown when they moved last year, as the story goes."

"What's to become of the buildin's and equipment they left behind in Norwich?" Jared asked.

"I couldn't tell you what they're being used for just at this moment," Sewall said. "There's talk of setting up a preparatory school there for the Academy, but so far nothing has come of the talk. As far as I know, the Academy is locked up — has been ever since they marched down to Middletown."

"They leave any guns behind when they marched down to Middletown?" Seth asked. "Any guns or cannons?"

"I couldn't tell you for certain," Sewall said as he paused to tip back the jug again. "I believe they must have taken whatever muskets they had with them, but I don't know about any cannons. The only cannons I know about are the ones Dartmouth College has. A few stories there I could tell if I had the time, but I'm here to talk about Benjie and not about cannons at Dartmouth College."

Seth and Jared both leaned towards Sewall.

"You say Benjie's behavin' himself in school?" Jared asked.

"Yes. Now he is."

"And he could work harder at studyin'?" Jared continued.

"Yes. That's right."

"Well, that's all I really needed to know about Benjie," Jared said. "The rest of it was maybe just havin' a chance to set and talk with you. Winter is a time when a lot of the people in the village pretty much stick to themselves, and I know in the past we sometimes ain't been very neighborly to the teachers we hire. By the time spring comes and people are feelin' friendlier, of course school is over and the teacher is gone. I don't expect that you've had much of a chance to just set and talk and have a good time."

"It's true I haven't had . . ."

"Not livin' with the deacon and his wife in that temperance home," Seth said. "Now what about them Dartmouth College cannons? Just how many are there?"

"Well, there's really only one that counts," Sewall said. "That's the old iron one in a shed just south of the Tontine — the Tontine's a big building in the middle of Hanover where a lot of students live on the upper floors. It's just south of the Dartmouth Hotel, if perhaps you know where that is. I lived in the Tontine myself two years ago. That cannon gets borrowed at night a few times a year and gets used and would likely be borrowed a bit more frequently if it were to have a carriage. It's quite a weight to drag."

"What are the other cannons?" Seth asked. "And how come they don't count?"

"There's a big brass cannon that the militia owns," Sewall continued. "It's kept at a little distance from Dartmouth, so it isn't as convenient to get at as the one by the Tontine. It's the one that the state gave to the militia just a few years ago after their old one blew up on the Fourth of July."

"Just how many others are there?" Jared asked. "Seems like a gold mine of cannons for one town to have, when other towns ain't got any at all. How'd they happen to get 'em?"

"Well, there's just one more that I know about. Brass. It's quite small, perhaps three and a half feet long. The president of Dartmouth — President Tyler — showed it to me one day and told me strictly that it was my responsibility to keep it hidden and that he'd hold me accountable if the cannon came out again and wrought any more damage. I'm not quite certain where that one came from. The militia's cannon, of course, was given by the state of New Hampshire. The old iron one has been around for a long time. There's a rumor, at least, that the iron one was stolen many years ago from the town of Windsor by Dartmouth boys, but whether that's true or not I really have no idea."

"And if the boys from the A.L.S. & M. Academy had cannons too, then that's quite a collection of cannons to have right at one place in the river," Seth said.

"I couldn't tell you for certain if they had any cannons over there or not," Sewall said. "Seems as though they should have had some, but the only times I was over by their grounds, I don't recall seeing any. The bridge toll, to tell you the truth, kept me pretty much on the New Hampshire side of the river. When I was over in Norwich, I stayed outside the picket fence, of course, since I didn't want to have my coat ripped up the back. No. I can't remember any cannons on their grounds. And I can never recall hearing any booming of cannons — their cannons, that is — from across the river. If the A.L.S. & M. Academy had any cannons of their own, then they certainly didn't use them much."

"Did they steal the iron cannon from town?" Jared asked. "That what you meant — from near the . . . what's the name of that buildin'?"

"The Tontine," Sewall said. "Yes. It was taken over to Norwich one night last year and fired off and left where it had been fired. That was two or three months before they went to Middletown. There was no proving that it was the Academy boys, but everybody knew that it was."

"Now how about that little cannon?" Seth said. "How come you're the one that's s'posed to keep it hid?"

"Oh, that's because of my responsibility as the Dartmouth bellringer," Sewall said. "Dartmouth gives me my lodging in room 10 on the third floor of The College in exchange for ringing the bell. The rope comes right down through a hole in the ceiling of my room, and I'm the one that has to make certain the bell gets rung every time it's supposed to be rung. I know about the little cannon because President Tyler showed it to me when he was showing me the clappers."

"What clappers?" Jared asked.

"There's a supply of extras for the bell," Sewall said. "It happens several times a year that someone's idea of a prank is to steal the clapper from the bell so that it can't ring for chapel the next morning. When that happens, I have to go up the ladder into the attic and then up into the tower and ring the bell for chapel with a sledgehammer. Then later in the day, when I'm free and there's sufficient light, I have to replace the clapper. When I get it mounted in the bell, I'm supposed to paint it with a mixture of grease, carbon black, and printer's ink from a bucket President Tyler gave me. Then every time the clapper disappears, he looks at every student's hands. Catches a lot of them that way. The cannon is up there being stored under the eaves just because there doesn't seem to be any other good place for it. The president is so strict about keeping it a secret that I wouldn't dare tell any of my classmates about it. They all know the stories, of course, but none of them realizes that the little cannon is right up there in the attic."

"What stories?" Seth asked.

"It might have been fifteen years ago. It might have been twenty-five. No one seems to know. But at any rate in the course of some spirited high jinks — everybody guesses there was rum involved with it somewhere — one group of students locked another group of students out of The College and put a solid barricade behind the door so that it couldn't be forced. Soon enough the group outside disappeared, and when they came back, they had a cannon. They charged it with powder and loaded it up with rocks or turf and then just blew the door right down. Quite a scandal about it. I don't know if it was the little brass cannon they used or the old iron one or some other, but it was quite effective. President Tyler is under the impression that it was the little brass cannon, but he has no way of knowing for certain."

"I can see how that might make a president of Dartmouth College a little cannon-shy," Jared said.

"But that wasn't the worst of it," Sewall said. "That was nothing compared to what came later."

Seth's face lighted up immediately. "Worse than loadin' a cannon and touchin' it off point-blank at a buildin'?"

"Oh yes," Sewall said. "Much worse. There was an interior wall in The College that the students didn't like and rather than just take it down with crowbars or sledgehammers, they decided that the work could best be done with a cannon."

"No!" Seth said, approaching ecstasy. "From inside?"

"There was an appealing flare of the dramatic to it," Sewall said. "And it was certainly effective. They risked destroying the whole building when they did it, but the end result has been an improvement. It was up on the third floor, where I live. We call it Bedbug Alley up there. Well, the building was built so that no one could walk end-to-end on either the second or the third floor. The second floor had a library blocking the passage, and the third floor had a museum of curiosities. Anyone who lived at one end of the second or third floor who wanted to visit a friend at the other end had to go down the stairs to the first floor and then up the stairs again at the other end. So they decided that the walls had to go. They might have planned to remove walls on both floors, but they began on the third floor, and there was only one cannon blast. It completely shattered the walls of the museum and destroyed a number of the curiosities as well. The building rocked from end to end, or so the story goes, but through some miracle remained standing. When the smoke cleared, the passageway through the museum was there, just as it has been ever since. Of course President Tyler is quick to add that shortly after the smoke cleared, the ringleaders of the cannonading project were separated from Dartmouth and on their way home. It happened, I guess, when John Wheelock was still the president of Dartmouth."

"Think of that!" Seth said. "Blowin' out a wall from inside with a cannon!"

"Now I've tried to decide what cannon was used for blowing in the door and destroying the walls of the museum, but I can't be certain. I guess the small brass cannon would have been sufficient for blowing in the door, but the brass cannon seems far too small for the destruction wrought on the walls of the museum. If the old iron cannon were used on the third floor, however, there remains the question of how the students ever raised it up there. It is so enormously heavy that it doesn't seem possible students could have carried it up one of the stairways — hardly logical that the stairs could have supported the weight. I would love to find one of the ringleaders some day and ask him about what cannon they used then and perhaps thank him for the convenience of the passageway in the middle of Bedbug Alley."

"If I was the president of Dartmouth College, I'd be scared to death of cannons," Jared said. "But didn't they fix the walls?"

"No, they never did," Sewall said. "The school's finances have always been poor. If something is broken and there's not a pressing need to fix it, then it generally stays broken. Dartmouth's students don't have any money to speak of either. That's how I happen to be here now teaching in the village and why I was glad to get the position in spite of its inconvenience and why already I'm twenty-five years old. I'll have to work my way through seminary too when I go, and I may be close to thirty by the time I'm through."

"They fix the door?" Seth asked.

"Yes. They fixed the door, but as far as I can tell all they did with the walls of the museum was sweep them up and throw them away. It was really a shame about the curiosities in the museum. Quite a few have disappeared, I imagine. A lot of them decorate the rooms in Bedbug Alley. My friend Levi uses the robe of an Owyhee priest for a bed covering and has a Pinguin sitting on a little shelf on his wall."

"Pinguin," Seth said. "What's that?"

"It's a bird, all black and white, from almost at the South Pole. It's a heavy-bodied bird with small wings so that it has to move them as fast as a hummingbird's in order to fly. I'd love to see a live one some day, but I don't want to have to go to the South Pole for it. Oh, there are a lot of other things that somebody at Dartmouth should take better care of. There's a Flamingo, a great tall gangling bird that's all pink, and an egg from an Osterich that's nearly as big as somebody's head and a lot of skins and heads of animals and birds you can't even imagine. Elias Hasket Derby Esquire Salem Massachusetts is the most famous. Have you heard anything about him up here?"

"No," Jared said. "Who's he?"

"He's a Zebra. Stuffed."

"What's a Zebra?" Seth asked.

"Like a horse, but with just black and white stripes all over his body. From Africa."

"No!" Seth said. "I'd like to see that! All the way from Africa! Must of been quite a job to stuff him."

"Must have been," Sewall said. "Well, Elias Hasket Derby Esquire Salem Massachusetts likes to go wandering. He sometimes greets us from the chapel pulpit in the morning or grazes on the chapel roof. He's been known to go drink from the college well. He likes to get to places where it takes a good deal of effort to retrieve him."

Jared's laughter ended in a snort. Seth kept on chuckling.

"Anybody down there ever been known to study?" Jared asked. "Somewhere along the line I got the idea that it was mostly ministers and doctors and lawyers and teachers that came out of there, and that Dartmouth College was to blame for the new notions of temperance and religion that seem to be workin' their way up through the valley. Guess I was mistaken. Sounds like the kind of place where Benjie might fit right in. I think that boy might show you a thing or two."

"Oh there's studying," Sewall said. "I think most of us are pretty serious when it comes to studying, but we certainly need a little diversion every now and then. There are a few boys that tend to take a little too much diversion, particularly at Captain Symmes' tavern, but their numbers are few, and most of them won't last until graduation. There are others too, like Alpheus Crosby, or Baby Alph as we call him, who are entirely too serious. Baby Alph is extremely young, the youngest in the class, and he comes from a fairly serious-minded family. He is an enthusiast for religion and temperance and just as gullible an infant as one can imagine. He has been the victim of numbers of practical jokes, and some of my other classmates consider him so distantly aware of the world around him that they wonder if he has ever noticed that pranks are being played on him. There's a fair amount of prank-playing back and forth among the students and some directed at the faculty or the townspeople."

"What kind of pranks?" Seth asked.

"Well, snakes or frogs find their ways into chamber pots now and then and seem quite eager to leave when the chamber pots are in use. A few skunks get locked into recitation halls. Sometimes the firebuckets that are supposed to be kept full of water in each room get tied up onto the tops of doors, where they tip when the door is opened. As I've said, the bell clapper occasionally disappears. And the bellringer from last year cautioned me to keep my watch always with me so that someone won't set it ahead or back as a trick. One bellringer several years ago evidently had his watch changed and rang the bell for chapel — six minutes of ringing — at two o'clock in the morning. Probably the most consistent pranks, in the warmer months at least, involve the cows that the townspeople pasture on the Dartmouth Green, which they consider a common. As you can imagine, there are frequent disappointments among students crossing the green in the dark when they step into the places where the cows have been. It is not a good feeling, believe me, and generates a fair amount of ill will. As a result, some nights the entire herd from the Green finds its way down into the cellar of The College or perhaps into Chapel. A few years back all the cows were discovered one morning four miles up the river in Vermont, driven up during the night and forced to swim across, or so the story goes. Those seem to be the main sorts of pranks."

"Reminds me of some of the things our great-uncle used to do when he was young," Jared said. "Or maybe somethin' that Benjie would fit right into. I used to get complaints about such things from teachers he had in past years, but I guess you've shut him down for this year."

"I think perhaps I have. He's told me this might be his last year of schooling. What is he planning to do with his life? Do you know?"

"He talks about workin' on the river," Jared said. "He'd like to travel up and down the Connecticut on flatboats for a few years. If he gets his fill of that or when he marries and settles down, I expect he'll come back to the village and work in the warehouses or on the canal or else take up some kind of tradin'. He'd like to make his livin' fishin' and huntin', but I think he's beginnin' to realize that ain't possible. If he learns enough readin' and writin' and cipherin' from his schoolin' so that he can keep records of his tradin' and write down accounts, that should serve him good enough for his life ahead."

"He has that already," Sewall said, "though he could improve some. I don't expect he'll ever be a scholar or have any need for more learning."

"No," Seth said. "That don't seem to run in the Barston family."

Sewall pulled his watch from his pocket and looked at it.

"How much longer does school run in the village this year?" Jared asked.

"My last day of teaching will be on the twentieth," Sewall said. "That's just ten more days. I'll need the next day for traveling, and I have to start ringing the bells again on the morning of February twenty-second."

"By all accounts you did a good job teachin' here this winter," Jared said. "I want to thank you for it. If you think you might want to teach back here another winter, I think the village 'd hire you in a second."

"Thank you," Sewall said. "I may very well need to teach somewhere so that I can save money for seminary, but it's too early yet for me to think about next winter.

"Now I'm afraid I should get back to Deacon Russell's."

"Sure," Seth said. "Take another drink on your way out. I liked hearin' your stories. It'd be nice to talk to you again some evenin' before you go back to Dartmouth."

"Good," Sewall said, as he stood up. "I'd like that, whiskey or no whiskey."

Seth and Jared both smiled.

"We'll have whiskey," Jared said.

Sewall drank again from the jug, lighted his lantern with one of the candles stuck into a bottle, and left smiling into the night.

Seth and Jared took turns at the jug in silence. Then Jared got up, went outside, and quickly returned.

"He's gone, Seth. When?"

"Sooner the better," Seth said. "If we get down there in the next week, then the boys 'll still be away on vacation. We don't want to have 'em catch us lookin' too hard at their cannons after they get back. The Tontine. We'll have a look at that one. Then we got to go look around in Bedbug Alley and up in that attic."

"Good," Jared said. "I want to get a look at that Pinguin."

"Pinguin?" Seth said. "That ain't but a bird. Me, I got to see that Zebra!"

XII

Sue and Annie, carrying the well-bundled twins, paused on the bridge over the canal. The ice seepings into the drained canal during the past several months looked like the cumulative, congealed gutterings of many candles. Here and there along the canal walls of hewn stone large dirtied areas showed where workmen had patched deficient chinking with clay to keep the water within the canal during the coming season. Trickles from melting snow had left a scattering of clean bands on the dirtied stone.

Sue spat a dark amber streak onto the bottom of the canal, next to a rotted boot.

"I wish you wouldn't chew when you're carryin' one of the boys," said Annie.

"Don't worry about it," Sue said. "Aaron ain't likely to jump in front while I'm holdin' him."

"Well, I don't like it."

The two stood without speaking further. Annie fussed with the blanket wrapped around Amos and with the straps of her pack. Sue spat again and without looking at Annie walked across the bridge and continued up Tannery Road. Annie followed along and quickly caught up with her. Then the two walked in silence up the road to the cluster of six brick homes that belonged to the Barstons or their relatives. As they turned onto the pathway to the last house on the left — Old Sam's — Sue spat her tobacco into the snow and wiped her mouth with the back of her free hand. Still without having spoken to Annie since the canal bridge, Sue began knocking on the door.

"Likely he don't hear us," Annie said after a while. "We should go right in."

Sue didn't say anything, but opened the door and stepped inside into the hallway ahead of Annie. She could scarcely see once she was inside, but managed to poke along down to the door of the winter room, where she knocked again.

"Come in," Old Sam said.

"Come to see you," Sue said as she passed through the doorway.

The air of the room was stale and overly warm. It smelled of unwashed bodies and old tobacco smoke along with what might have been a hint of decay. Sue could barely see, but realized that Old Sam was sitting in his rocking chair next to the stove.

"It's wicked bright out," Sue continued. "I can't hardly see you 'til my eyes get used to it in here."

"Well . . . it's Sue and Annie and the little fellers," Old Sam said. His voice was flat and old with a stale quality to it like the air of the room.

"We wanted to show you the twins," Annie said. "They're gettin' to be big boys now."

"I see they are," Old Sam said. He set the chair into a barely perceptible rocking motion.

"I brought you some little sweet cakes," Annie said. "They're the kind you like, and I thought you and Benjie might find a use for 'em."

"Oh, that's nice," Old Sam said. "I don't eat much now, but Benjie will like them."

"You got to have some of 'em, Old Sam," Annie said. "I made 'em for the both of you."

"Yes," Old Sam said. "I'll try one now."

Annie handed Amos to Sue, shed her pack, and delved into it. She put one of the cakes into Old Sam's hand. He took a bite.

"Yes. That's nice. I remember these," Old Sam said.

Annie's eyes grew accustomed to the dimness of the room. She glanced at the blanket-shrouded windows, the disheveled blankets on the two beds, the thick patches of dust on the desk by the only uncovered window panes — dust brushed away inadvertently in the places where either Benjie or Old Sam had rested his arms, the litter of bark fragments and balls of dust across the rugs, a scattering of ashes in front of the door of the stove. Then she saw the spider webs in the corners and where the ceiling met the walls. Her hands itched for a broom and a dust rag and a quarter hour to set the room in order. With a start she glimpsed the gray fuzz floating in the water bucket behind the stove — a drowned mouse.

"Got a mouse in your fire bucket," she said.

"Oh, I know," Old Sam said. "I been meanin' to have Benjie take it out one of these days, but I just don't seem to remember about it when he's here."

"Where is he today?"

"Ain't a schoolday, so he's likely off with his friends someplace. I can't say where. Says there's only a week of school left."

"That's right," Sue said. "Just a week."

"How are you?" Annie asked. "We ain't seen you for quite a while."

"I got a lot of aches and pains, and I expect one of these days I'll wake up dead, but it ain't happened yet. I go to bed, and I keep wakin' up alive in the mornin'. They give me good food from across, so not eatin' and gettin' so skinny is my own fault. My pall bearers might not think there's anythin' in the coffin, so maybe I'll have a window built in so's they can check. I think I'm a man that's just lived too long."

"Now hush," Annie said. "I don't want to hear that kind of talk. You just been cooped up too much in here this winter. You're good for a long time yet, and I won't hear any trash about pall bearers. I want you to think about your trout fishin' as soon as the snow goes. And I want you to think about you and me again. Truth is, Old Sam, that Joe is still awful jealous on account of I've loved you a lot longer than him. You think it over now, but if you're willin' to help me raise a couple of twins, I'll run away with you come spring."

Old Sam laughed in a hoarse cackle.

"Oh Annie," he said. "I don't have to think that over. You know that. You set a day, and we'll do it."

"Good," Annie said. "I'm glad that's decided. Been botherin' me for a long time that I went and settled for Joe Reckford when I could of maybe caught you if only I'd of tried a little harder."

"Let that be a lesson to you then," Old Sam said and again managed a short cackle. "You always was a pretty girl, but you never knew it, so you acted like somebody not too proud of her looks. You could of had anybody you wanted, Annie."

"That's what you always said, Old Sam. And it surely made a difference to me when I was growin' up. I'll always remember how good you was to me."

Old Sam took more bites of the small cake. Crumbs caught in the stubble of his chin whiskers, but neither Annie nor Sue said anything about them.

"Well, you always had some grit in you, Annie. Funny how Sue reminded me of you so much, and now you're married to her pa. It agrees with you, Annie. I think you're even prettier now with the twins than before. If I was only about fifty years younger, surely I'd chase after you, and we'd run away come spring. Now let me see the boys. Can't remember the names, Annie. You got to remind me again."

"This one is Amos," Annie said as she took one of the boys from Sue and put him into Old Sam's lap.

"Scrawny little cuss, ain't he?" Old Sam said. "Just like you and Joe. Must weigh twice as much as any other boy his age in Vermont except his brother."

"And this one is Aaron," Annie said as she put him next to his brother.

Old Sam's arms and his twisted and wrinkled hands circled the boys.

"Amos and Aaron. Well ain't that somethin'?" Old Sam said. "Who'd ever of thought it, Annie, that you'd have two boys so quick?"

"I was big as a barn, Old Sam, but it surely was a surprise when the first one was born and I thought I was all done and then the other come so quick. I was scared they might keep right on comin' 'til I wound up with a whole litter."

"Must keep you and Sue busy," Old Sam said.

"Yes," Sue said.

"And you, Sue. I hope you know that if it was sixty years younger I was and not fifty, that it'd be you I'd be chasin' after and not Annie. Both of you remind me so much of Mandy that sometimes now I get to confusin' the three of you."

"We'll go fishin' in the spring again, Grampy Sam," Sue said. "I'll take you."

"That might be, Sue, and I hope it is, but I think maybe my time's just about up. If I ain't around come spring, you go fishin' without me, and you remember me every time you catch a good trout and remember old Malik every time you catch anythin' else. The two of us 'll be right there with you."

Annie took both boys back from Old Sam, and the conversation ended for a moment as the twins commenced fussing. Annie swayed, gently jostling them in her arms, and then spoke over the sounds of their whimpering.

"Well, Old Sam," Annie said. "The main reason I'm here today wasn't to give you the little cakes or to set a date for runnin' away with you. What I mainly come for is to tell you to be ready when town meetin' day comes around 'cause I'm takin' you to town meetin' dinner this year."

"Well, I just don't know, Annie, if . . .'"

"You don't have to know," Annie said. "You don't have to know any more 'n what I just told you. I'm a hard woman, Old Sam, and I ain't about to take no for an answer. You just be ready for me to take you to town meetin' dinner when the day comes. You ain't been out of here in weeks, have you?"

"No. Not since before the new year."

"High time then. You just be ready when I come."

"Well, all right," Old Sam said. "If I'm still alive then, I'll go with you, Annie. But I ain't makin' any promises about whether I'll be alive or not."

"Oh, you got years left to you yet," Annie said. "All you need is the right woman to lead you around by your ear. Settin' in the same room week after week makes anybody think that there ain't anythin' else after a time. We got to get you out of here more. Soon as it warms up a little, you get Benjie to uncover the windows and get you some good bright light in here right through the day. And if it turns good and warm, have him get the windows open. The whole place could use some fresh air. You remember now, Old Sam, that for town meetin' day I'm your woman, and we're goin' to the town hall together. I want you shaved and washed and in clean clothes when we go, too. You understand me?"

"Just exactly like Mandy," Old Sam said. "There ain't rest and peace for an old man this side of the grave. Annie, I bet you think that just because you're a good lookin' woman that you can come right into my own house and order me around. You expect that I'll go to town meetin' with you and that I'll be shaved and washed and in clean clothes just the way you ordered me to, don't you?"

"That's right," Annie said.

"Well, I ain't washin' and shavin' and wearin' clean clothes. Three things like that is just too long a list."

"You got enough time for it between now and meetin'."

"A bath in winter ain't healthy. I'll take a chill, and then it'll turn to pneumonia — I just know it. A bath 'd kill me."

"Not right next to a good hot stove, it won't. I ain't expectin' you to go and swim in the river, you know."

"Well, I might go to town meetin' dinner with you, but I ain't makin' promises about the other things."

The twins' fussing escalated into thin crying.

"Don't worry about it any more today," Annie said. "I'll come back some other day, and we'll talk about it. But for now I want you to start thinkin' about things that are outside of this room. Winter can't last much longer, and after that you'll be out and around again and kickin' up your heels just like any animal that's penned up in a barn all winter — or just like a bear comin' out into the spring."

"Yes," Old Sam said. "You all come back when you can, and we'll talk some more. But I ain't shavin' 'til I see if I got a good chance of livin' to town meetin' day. Otherwise, if I die, it's just a waste of time. Same for that bath."

"We'll talk about it next time," Annie said.

Annie handed Aaron to Sue; rubbed and patted Amos with her free hand and then retrieved her empty pack. The boys soon settled down. Annie and Sue said goodby to Old Sam and left, squinting into the brightness as they moved down Old Sam's steps and out into Tannery Road.

"You're awful quiet, Sue," Annie said, as she worked the packstraps over one shoulder. "Hardly said a word in there."

"Didn't know what to say. Annie?"

"What is it?"

"You was good in there with him. Benjie says Grampy Sam don't laugh any more, and you made him laugh with your teasin'. And he liked it about town meetin'."

"He was good to me when I was growin' up in the village. I'll always remember that. I love that wonderful old man."

"So don't I, Annie."

Annie stopped walking and stared at Sue for a long moment.

"We should think of some nice things to do for him, Sue. If you want to help me take him to town meetin' dinner, I know he'll like that, but you do it only if you want to. You think about it. And if there's a time next week when you can help me take the twins back there to show him, let me know. He liked seein' the babies."

"Yes, he did, Annie. And next time can I be the one to cook him somethin'?"

"Course you can, Sue."

Sue and Annie carried the twins down Tannery Road on their way back to the canal bridge and then home. They walked slowly, talking about Old Sam.

XIII

Seth Barston and Jared Barston walked down the snow-dusted steps of the Union House in Hanover and moved north along the street on the firmly packed snow. A slight lateral hitch in their gaits betrayed the fact that they had spent the past two hours of the afternoon drinking rum in the tavern.

"Well, that Symmes don't seem to like the Dartmouth boys all that much," Seth said.

"Likes the temperance folks even less than that," Jared said. "But of course that's his business to sell spirits."

"So what can we do now 'til it gets dark enough to sneak into The College?" Seth asked. He stopped walking, and his brother halted beside him.

"Ha! Guess we'll put you on a little temperance reform right off. It ain't been but a couple of hours since we planned it all out over across the river. Can't you remember what we decided over there by the A.L.S. & M.?"

"I don't know that we decided anythin', Jared. Oh, we decided there ain't any cannons over there by the A.L.S. & M., and we decided to come over here and have some rum."

"Well that's good, Seth. I guess I'm goin' to make a little money hirin' you out to churches so they can show you off at temperance meetin's. You're just the kind of example they're always lookin' for. Show you off all around and then stand back so's I don't get trampled by all the folks comin' up to sign the pledge. Yes sir. We could make some money off of you."

"But we didn't decide . . ."

"The Tontine! Remember, Seth?"

"That's right. Course. Sewall said there was that iron cannon in a shed someplace to the south of it."

"Now see how good you can think when you let two minutes go by without drinkin' spirits? Just think how smart you'd be if you never drank 'em at all."

"Prob'ly smart enough to feel stupid for bein' so thirsty," Seth said.

"That's got to be the Tontine," Jared said with a nod of his head. "The big brick one up and across. So maybe we'll cross here and go poke around some and see if we can't find that little cannon shed. You remember anythin' more that he said except it was in a shed south of the Tontine?"

"That's all he did say about it, Jared. I know that for sure."

"And if you can't believe a good anti-temperance man out practicin' his anti-temperance, who can you believe?"

"Now you got it," Seth said.

The two crossed the packed snow of Main Street, which was marked thoroughly by the runners of sleighs and pungs, the hooves of horses, the boots of men and women, and the dark scatterings of horse manure. Once across, they wandered all through the area south of the massive brick building known as the Tontine. They kept moving among several nondescript, locked sheds, trying to decide.

"One of them," Seth said. "We can't tell for sure unless we get into 'em, but then that don't make a difference anyways on account of we don't have but that light sleigh with Brownie pullin' it, and we couldn't do a thing with the old iron cannon even if it was out layin' in the snow just waitin' for somebody to take it. Now's the time to grab it, and we ain't set to. When the boys get back from their vacation, it's goin' to be an awful lot harder."

"I guess we'll just have to think about it," Jared said. "Won't do to bust padlocks and have a look. Not today it won't. Seems like everybody's lookin' at us now already."

"Prob'ly this is the first time two such handsome men as us was ever in Hanover. You got to expect 'em to stare, Jared."

"Course that's it, Seth," Jared said. "Now I s'pose we should see to Brownie. Got to get her fed if we're goin' to use her tonight. Dartmouth Hotel still sound like the best way to you?"

"Oh, it is. Hate to spend the money if we ain't stayin' but part of the night, but we can't just set out in the cold waitin', and it seems like a way to take care of Brownie so's she'll be worth somethin' later on."

"We'll spend the money and make the most of it," Jared said. "Spend it and get our money's worth. Besides it's all for Grampy Sam, and this might just be a night we'll remember for a long time."

The brothers walked back to their sleigh behind the Union House and rode in it the short distance up Main Street to the Dartmouth Hotel. Seth studied the Tontine as they passed it.

"Two upper floors must be rooms for the Dartmouth boys," he said. "That's somethin' to remember if we're ever back here to get the iron cannon. They could prob'ly raise quite an alarm if they discovered somebody tryin' to steal their cannon."

"Might be easier to steal a hornet's nest," Jared said.

"There's ways to do just about anythin' if you put your mind to it. We just ain't got the right idea yet."

They stopped the sleigh in front of the Dartmouth Hotel, a three story wooden building topped with a flat roof and a balustrade. Three chimneys poked through the roof. Jared tied the horse, and the two brothers went into the hotel through a covered entryway. A mousey-looking man came to greet them from behind a desk in the dimly lighted room.

"Elam Markham at your service, gentlemen."

"We need lodgin' and could stand to have supper," Jared said. "And some oats and shelter for our horse. Oats — not hay."

"Certainly, gentlemen. That's easily done."

"And we got to get away pretty early in the mornin'," Seth said. "Be best if we was to pay you now, and if you put us someplace where we won't wake up the whole world when we go. You got stoves in the sleepin' quarters?"

"Not in all . . ."

"We want to be warm," Seth said. "Be nice to have a stove and some wood."

"Surely we can accommodate you," Markham said.

"Good," Jared said. "I want to take care of the mare right off, and then maybe you can find us some rum."

"All right," Markham said. "Just a moment."

The innkeeper opened a side door.

"Rosina!" he called and then turned back toward the brothers. "I'll go with one of you now about the horse. And my wife will show the other of you what we have available for lodging."

Jared went out with Markham to take care of Brownie. As Seth waited for the innkeeper's wife to appear, he thought about Bedbug Alley and what the night might bring.

XIV

The lanterns cast double shadows on the walls of the stairwell as Seth and Jared creaked their way upstairs.

"Colder in here than outside," Seth whispered. "Almost as cold as the room of the hotel. I think that wood he sold us was growin' someplace yesterday mornin'."

"These steps don't look any too rugged," Jared said. "Wouldn't likely hold a cannon if the boys hauled one upstairs."

"Might of pulled it up through a window."

The brothers stopped on the landing at the head of the stairs. Seth set down the sack he was carrying and shifted his lantern to his other hand. He gazed first at the floor and then lifted the lantern to shoulder height to study the battered walls.

"They don't keep the buildin' up very good," Seth said. "Look at the dirt on the floor. There ain't been mud to track in since early December. This is last year's dirt. Busted boards right in the wall, too, and looks like they was even throwin' knives at it."

"Maybe axes too. Nice dry boards — just the thing for kindlin' a fire in a stove. And look how they carved up the wall with names and things."

"They shouldn't let 'em do that," Seth said. "Think maybe we need to talk to Sewall about it? Think maybe we need to march out right now and find the president of Dartmouth College and show him?"

"I think we ain't goin' to say a thing," Jared said. "Just grind our teeth and try not to think about what bad housekeepers the Dartmouth boys are. Now let's go. It's one more up to Bedbug Alley."

The flight of stairs from the second to the third floor had one tread cracked along its entire length.

"I should think they'd fix that so folks sneakin' up here in the middle of the night won't fall through and break their necks," Seth said. "Careful of that one on the way out."

"Welcome to Bedbug Alley," Jared said at the top of the stairs. "We made it up here after all."

Seth didn't pause. Lantern in one hand and sack in the other, he headed down the hall directly towards the middle of the building. Jared followed him, but lingered at what had once been a board wall ending the hall and lifted his lantern to look at its remains: some boards with jagged, splintered ends; others crudely chopped off. Jared stepped through the rough opening, which was about four feet tall, three feet wide, and a foot above the floor.

"I found him, Jared," Seth whispered. The sack he'd been carrying lay on the floor. He held his lantern high with one hand and with the other embraced the neck of the zebra. "Ain't it the handsomest thing you ever saw? And all the way from Africa!"

"Well that's just amazin'," Jared said, raising his own lantern next to the creature. Never thought there could be such a thing — stripes all over it just like Sewall said! Oh my!"

"And there's writin' here," Seth said, as he turned a tag hung from one of the zebra's ears to the light. "'Elias Hasket Derby Esquire Salem Massachusetts.'"

"That's the right name," Jared said. "Looks like we got the right Zebra."

"This might just be the only Zebra in the whole United States of America," Seth said. "Maybe the only one there's ever been! Think of that!"

"But there's other things here too, Seth," Jared said. "Look. Here's that Big Pink Bird Sewall was tellin' us about."

Seth glanced for a brief instant at the big pink bird, scarcely acknowledging its existence. Then he stroked the zebra, circled it twice with his lantern, and kept rubbing it and talking to it almost as if it were a live horse.

Jared wandered through the confines of the small room, exposing everything in it to the scrutiny of his lantern light. There had been at one time shelves on most of the available wall space, but the cannon blast Sewall Tenney had mentioned had obliterated many of the shelves, leaving only fragments. The shelves which had escaped the blast were piled high with random assortments of rocks, bones, antlers, skins, feathers, and broken bits of things he couldn't identify. All of it looked filthy; seemed as if the mice and moths had been regular tenants during warmer months and had been voracious consumers of various items of cloth and hide. It was nothing more than a rubbish heap, Jared thought. On the floor against one wall were three empty cages made of boards and willow sticks. Their bottoms were thick with what Jared recognized as chicken manure, and a small dish of ice lay in each cage among the chicken droppings.

"Looks like a hen house up here now, Seth. The Zebra needs to keep better company."

Jared studied the hole in the wall opposite to the one through which he had entered the room. It was larger than the first. He stuck his lantern through it and saw that the damage had extended out into the hallway beyond.

"Looks like they shot the cannon this way, Seth. Likely made 'em all deaf — anybody that was up here when they touched her off. Don't seem like too smart a thing to do. Think of all the things on the shelves in here that they must of blasted to little pieces. Seems like a terrible waste."

"Sure does," Seth said without taking his eyes off the zebra. "They could of hit the Zebra."

"Well, leave that thing alone for a little. We got to find the way up to the attic. I'll go look through this side of the buildin', and you go back and check the rooms the way we come in."

Jared left through the hole in the wall. When he returned five minutes later, Seth was still rubbing the zebra and talking to it.

"You didn't even check your side of the buildin', Seth, did you?"

"No."

"Well, never mind. I found a ladder that goes up to a trap door. And I found the Pinguin, too. Come and see it. Seth!"

What 'd you say?"

"You all right? Come on. I found a ladder to the attic, and I found the Pinguin."

Seth stooped to retrieve his sack and kept his eyes on the zebra even as he was stepping through the hole in the wall to follow Jared. He moved so slowly that Jared grabbed him by the arm to hurry him along. He led him into a room off the hallway."

"There!" Jared said, gesturing with his lantern. "The Pinguin!"

"So that's what a Pinguin is," Seth said, as he studied the odd looking bird, which was perched on a small shelf nailed none too neatly to the wall. "Funny lookin' thing, ain't it? Sewall was right. It does have awful small wings."

"Sewall was talkin' about a robe on the bed in the same room with the Pinguin, but I don't see it here," Jared said.

"Whoever it was likely took it with him when he went off for the vacation," Seth said. "Sometimes things that are just left layin' around get picked up by people you don't want to have 'em."

"Yes," Jared said. "I hear that happens every now and again. Now come with me, and we'll see what's up in the attic."

Jared led Seth out of the room and a few yards beyond to the end of the hallway. There was a setback in the hall, and a ladder against the wall at the back of this alcove rose to a trap door. The ladder was simply two round poles with board scraps nailed to them.

"Good cabinet makers at Dartmouth College, Seth. Ever see a ladder like that before?"

"Ugly," Seth said. "But if it works, I guess they don't need anythin' better."

Jared mounted the ladder first, trying to avoid banging his lantern into the rungs. The trap door had at one time been secured with a hasp, but only holes were left where the hasp, and undoubtedly its last padlock, had been torn off. Jared climbed to the trap door, put his neck and shoulder against it, and lifted. He stepped up one more rung and then another, carefully swung his lantern up into the attic and set it down on the floor, and then lifted the door all the way open.

"Hand me up that sack and then your lantern, Seth."

Moments later the brothers were gazing at the unbelievable clutter the small orbs of their candle lanterns revealed. At one time, perhaps, boxes lying amid broken furniture in under the eaves must have contained much of the debris, but the boxes had since erupted their contents out onto the floor. The curiosity of Dartmouth students over the years about the contents of the boxes and their reluctance to put things back once they had looked at them had given mice and red squirrels nearly unlimited materials for building nests and for chewing on. They had taken good advantage of their opportunities. The light stink in the cold of what Seth and Jared guessed was bat manure suggested a nearly unbearable stench in the attic during the heat of summer. The brothers stepped over debris as they started moving slowly down the length of the attic with their lanterns held high. The clutter seemed only to get worse.

"Good thing that Zebra wasn't up here, Seth," Jared said, "or we never would of found it. I can't see how the president of Dartmouth College could lose any sleep about the chance the students might find a cannon up here. I don't think anybody could find even a crowin' rooster in this attic."

"Like a hog pen," Seth said. "We ain't got but about six hours before dawn. I don't know as we can find it by then. How big do you recall Sewall said that cannon was? I don't remember it bein' more 'n a yard or so long."

"I think he said three or four feet," Jared said.

"So it might be in any of the boxes," Seth said. "Or it might be behind 'em or under any of the trash that's scattered around. That's goin' to take quite a while to look everyplace there is up here."

"No," Jared said. "We only got to look in one place. We only got to look right where the cannon is."

"Oh good, Jared. Well you go right ahead and look there first off and save the both of us a lot of bother," Seth said.

"We could go and ask the president of Dartmouth College," Jared said. "From what Sewall told us, he'd prob'ly be glad to get rid of that cannon. I would be if I was s'posed to be runnin' things at Dartmouth College."

"Oh, he'd be glad to see us now in the middle of the night. Likely he misses havin' all the Dartmouth boys at college. Prob'ly awful lonesome without 'em to blow holes in the walls and the doors with cannons and put cows in the cellar and do other things to keep him entertained. Lucky man that we don't know where he lives."

"So where do we start lookin' for the cannon?" Jared asked.

"If it's monstrous heavy, then it prob'ly ain't far from the trap door," Seth said. "If it's somethin' that you want to hide and want it to stay hid, then maybe you'd put it way back in one of the corners — or almost in a corner if you didn't want somebody to figure it out. Or maybe you'd just hide it in the bottom of one of the boxes and put things on top of it that people wouldn't want to go through."

"That makes it easy, then," Jared said. "If you can narrow it down like that, then all we got to do is look through everythin', and we'll find it."

"Talkin' ain't goin' to find it," Seth said. "Might as well start lookin'. Oh, Jared, there's the bell rope over there."

"Well, don't you touch it."

The brothers separated and began looking, each holding his lantern in one hand and rummaging through the boxes and the piles on the floor with the other. For the first hour they called each other's attention to various things they uncovered which had evidently come from the defunct muscum: half a dozen mounted fish of strange shapes and all on the verge of falling apart, large seashells, a horseshoe crab, a box of rocks — each with the imprint of a leaf or a fish or a shell in the solid rock, a small alligator with two of its legs gnawed off, a large chunk of rock that looked like a piece of stovewood, a globe covered with maps of the world, another box of rocks of all different colors, the head of a large and very strange looking bird stuffed and mounted on a board. They rummaged through many piles of clothing shredded by mice and squirrels and through similarly damaged shoes of such strange shapes, colors, and materials as to make them think that they must have come from all the countries of the world. After the first hour, however, the novelty of seeing strange things had worn off sufficiently so that they lapsed into silence, doggedly going through the boxes and the piles of debris one after another. They broke from their search briefly when Seth had to replace the candle in his lantern. Then immediately they got back to work.

They were into their third hour of searching when Jared found the cannon hidden in a piece of tin stovepipe shoved back under the eaves.

"A lot thicker than I thought it'd be and way too heavy," was Seth's assessment as the two of them dragged it out toward the middle of the floor. "And it's goin' to be mighty awkward if two of us together try to carry it down those stairs. If we rig the ropes to strap it on my back and you help me get it up and steady me goin' down the stairs, I'll see if I can't carry it. But I tell you, I sure ain't goin' down that Dartmouth College cabinetmaker's ladder — not with the rungs just nailed on like that. We'll lower it down through the trap door and then see if we can get it on my back. That sound about right to you, Jared?"

"Sounds better 'n if you have me carryin' it," Jared said. "But say now. I think the both of us are talkin' too loud, Seth. We got to talk quieter, especially when we're wrestlin' away the cannon. Don't want to attract anybody's notice. Somebody catches us now, we're goin' to have quite a time explainin' what we're doin' with a cannon, and I don't expect we'll go home with it. Got to keep quieter."

"All right," Seth said. "We'll whisper. Keep remindin' me any time I start talkin' too loud."

Jared dumped the contents of the sack Seth had carried: two large pieces of canvas and about fifty feet of hemp rope in three pieces.

"We'll rig a couple slings with two of the ropes," Seth said. "Put one on each end and lower it right down. That's fastest I guess."

Quickly they knotted a rope around each end of the cannon and then very slowly dragged it across the attic floor toward the trap door. When Jared complained about the noise, they worked a piece of canvas under the cannon and dragged it on that right over next to the trap door.

"Now we got to just ease it over the edge," Seth said. "And let it down slow. It's heavy, so brace yourself. You set, Jared?"

"All ready."

"Well, here goes then," Seth said.

They braced their feet and took good grips on their ropes as they nudged the cannon right to the edge of the trap door opening and began lowering it into the darkness.

The darkness itself was the problem. Because they'd left their lanterns back where they had begun dragging the cannon across the floor, they couldn't see the cannon after they had begun lowering it. For the rest of their lives Seth would claim that it was Jared's fault for letting his end of the rope down too low; Jared that Seth was to blame for holding his end too high. At any rate, the cannon slipped out of the knotted ropes. The brothers sprawled backwards onto the attic floor at the same time as an unbelievably loud crash sounded down below. Seth was slower getting up than Jared, who sprang to his feet, ran for his lantern, ran back to the trap door opening, and lay prone with his lantern hanging down through the opening as far as he could hold it.

"Well," said Jared as Seth eased slowly to his feet. "There's one flight of stairs you ain't got to carry the cannon down."

Seth stood over his brother, gazed down through the opening, and surveyed the damage down below.

"Ain't that interestin'?" Seth said. "Right on through the floor."

"Seth, I thought we was s'posed to whisper."

"That was the old plan," Seth said. "The new one is to grab the cannon and get out of here quick as we can."

Jared climbed down the ladder. Seth grabbed the ropes, the canvas, and his sack and dropped them through the opening. Then he climbed down the ladder himself with the second lantern. When his feet touched the floor, Jared's hand pressed against his back.

"Watch out for that hole," Jared said.

The two stooped to gather the things Seth had dropped. They quickly found the stairwell at that end of the building; rushed down it and hurried out into the hallway of the second floor. Their lanterns, held shoulder high, bracketed the amazed looks on their faces as their glances rose and fell to the holes in the ceiling and the floor.

"Right on through that floor too!" Seth said.

They hurried down the next flight of stairs and out into that hallway. There the cannon lay on a badly sagging area on the floor. Seth dropped his sack next to it and set down his lantern.

"Jared," he said. "You go out the window we pried open and poke around outside for a little. If it looks like anybody's comin', give a yell or a whistle or somethin'. If it looks clear, come on back and give me a hand here."

"All right," Jared said. He went down the hallway and took a turn off to the side.

Seth worked as quickly as he could, rolling the cannon onto the two pieces of canvas, tying the canvas so the cannon couldn't slide out, and finally rigging rope straps onto the whole package.

He was just finishing when Jared returned.

"It's all right outside," Jared said. "I don't see how come we didn't wake up the whole village with that crash, but I guess we didn't. Not a sign out there of anybody stirrin' around."

"Good," Seth said. "But let's get out of here quick anyways. Help me get this thing up on my back."

They struggled to raise the wrapped cannon; at last succeeded in getting it up onto Seth's back and getting Seth's arms through the straps.

"How's that feel?" Jared asked.

"Terrible," Seth said through clenched teeth. "Ropes cut into my shoulders just like a knife, but I guess I can stand it for a little. Heft some of the weight from behind me, and let's get out of here."

Jared stuffed the empty sack into his shirt and grabbed one lantern and then the other in one hand. The lanterns crashed together hard enough so that the candle in one of them was jolted loose and went out. Jared put his free hand under the canvas and lifted as best he could from his awkward position. He stayed half a step behind his brother as Seth staggered down the hall and turned off into the room where they had forced open a window to get in.

"Back right up to the window, Seth," Jared said. "Rest the weight on the sill, and work the straps off, and we'll dump it right out. Just don't let the straps carry you out with the cannon."

"Help me," Seth gasped.

The canvas-wrapped cannon splintered the sill board of the window on its way out. Seth leaned panting for a moment against the sill, but then swung his legs out the window and twisted around to ease himself down onto the ground. Jared handed down the lanterns, then was quickly out the window and standing next to his brother.

"Drag it," Seth said, rasping his breaths sharply. "I ain't goin' to carry it another foot. Drag it."

Jared knelt by the lone burning lantern and freed one end of each carrying strap.

"Want to rest?" he asked.

"Want to get out of here," Seth said. "Let's go."

The brothers heaved against the short ropes, and the cannon's resistance to being dragged kept them knocking into each other and tripping as they followed the footprints they had made several hours earlier. Jared carried the burning lantern; Seth the one that had gone out.

Brownie and the sleigh were around on one side of the knoll up behind The College. Both brothers were sweating hard by the time they'd finished dragging the cannon. Seth dropped the rope and his useless lantern, leaned heavily against the sleigh, and scarcely could get enough air into his lungs. Clouds of vapor rose from the brothers' breathing and from their bodies themselves.

"Got to rest," Seth gasped. "Can't lift it in 'til I rest."

"Rest then," Jared said. "I'm goin' back to shut that window just so nobody 'll see it wide open if they come pokin' around. Set and rest, Seth."

Jared left. Seth watched the progress of the dim lantern orb until it disappeared from his view and then regretted not having relighted his lantern before Jared had gone. His breathing gradually slowed, and he stopped sweating. As more time passed, a chill began to settle into his sweat-dampened clothes. He commenced stamping around in the snow, his eyes straining in vain for a glimpse of anything but darkness. He felt his way up to Brownie and rubbed her neck.

"Get himself lost, did he?" Seth said aloud. "Prob'ly the candle in the other lantern went out too and left the both of us in a terrible fix."

Seth continued to stamp in the snow to chase the chill away. After what seemed an eternity, he caught a glimpse of light. Finally Jared was close enough for Seth to see the sleigh again.

"Thought you'd got caught or lost," Seth said, glancing at the sack Jared carried over his shoulder. "Or maybe that your lantern went out and you was waitin' for daylight. What's in the sack?"

"Well, we got ourselves a cannon, but it ain't a very big cannon. So I got somethin' else to go along with it, seein' as how we ain't likely to get up into The College again."

"Well, what?"

"We got ourselves a Pinguin, Seth. Now let's get the cannon up and get out of here."

*****

By dawn the brothers were up past Lyme and nearly into Orford village. They agreed they had done well to get a cannon for Old Sam, but spoke about how much better it would be if they could get him a big cannon to go with the little brass one. Already they were guessing about the sheds south of the Tontine; which one held the old iron cannon; how someone might go about grabbing the cannon from right under the noses of the Dartmouth College boys.

XV

Old Sam slouched at his desk by the window with papers spread out in front of him, but he paid no attention to them. Instead he gazed out the window at meltwater falling from the roof and carving a narrow trench into the snow lying against the house.

Well, I made it to March. Made it to town meetin' day. Thought I'd be dead way back, but here I am still breathin'.

He leaned closer to the window.

"Bright out," he said aloud. "Must be warm today. Must be practically spring."

Almost without knowing what he was doing, he reached up and grabbed hold of the blanket covering the upper panes of the window. He tugged at it several times without effect, but then suddenly the wooden strapping at the top of the blanket pulled free from the window frame, and the blanket fell onto the desk. When Old Sam dragged it off, some papers fell to the floor, and his inkwell spilled across the desk.

Stupid. Should of just left it alone. Stupid. Stupid.

He got to his feet barely in time to avoid the dripping ink. Awkwardly he dragged a foot across the papers on the rug and managed to push them away from the dark spattering. Looking around for something to wipe up the ink with, he was frustrated when nothing came to mind.

"Hang it," he said. "Stupid! Stupid!"

He hobbled to the other three windows of the room, pulled down the blankets covering them, and left the blankets in heaps on the floor along with the wooden strapping and nails which had held them in place. The sudden brightness of the room made him squint, accentuating the scowl already on his face. He sat down hard in his rocking chair and rocked furiously as he kept glancing over at the ink dripping from the desk down onto the rug.

After a while the rocking slowed. The ink ceased dripping. Old Sam's scowl eased, and he began studying the newly brightened room.

Hog pen. I was goin' to die in here this winter, and I didn't. I should of. Don't know how Benjie could stand to be in here with me. Oh why didn't I just die and get it over with? Nothin' left but waitin' and pain. Why can't I just die?

The rocking slowed to nothing. The spilled ink and the papers on the floor were forgotten. A great sadness settled over Old Sam, the sadness of being old and alone; of facing days of emptiness and nights of fitful sleep and grinding depression; of knowing that life would only get worse than it was. He folded his arms across his chest and sank lower into the chair. The slow and persistent heartbeat throbbed in his temples and against the palm of his right hand.

It just keeps goin' and goin' and goin'.

Muffled voices came from out in the hallway. The door rattled, and Annie Reckford walked into the room. Sue was right behind her, but came in shyly. She wore a dress, the first time Old Sam had ever seen her wearing one, and stood a little behind Annie.

"It's close to dinner time, Old Sam, and they got everythin' they always do down at the town hall," Annie said as she glanced around the room. "See you finally got some light in here, but can't say it's an improvement. You might exercise Benjie with a broom sometime while you can still find the rugs."

Annie approached the rocking chair and put her hand on Old Sam's shoulder.

"Well, you're a fine one. We wanted you shaved, and you ain't shaved. We wanted you washed, and you ain't washed. And you ain't prob'ly been out of those clothes for weeks. Too late for it now, if you're goin' to get any dinner."

"I don't know as I want to go, Annie. Seems like a lot of bother just to . . ."

"None of that nonsense with me, Old Sam. We'll get you in your coat and take you the way you are. Sue's here to help, and you won't be a bit of bother unless you go out of your way to make trouble for us. I hope you ain't got that on your mind, Old Sam, 'cause we're a couple of hard women for you to try and say no to."

"Oh, all right!" Old Sam said. He rocked back in the chair and then used the forward momentum to help him to his feet.

"There's a lot of your friends askin' for you," Annie said. "And it's a nice mild day out too, Old Sam. You'll like it, and it'll do you good. You'll see."

"Just a lot of bother," Old Sam said.

"Will be if you keep talkin' like that, Old Sam, so you can stop that right now. Where's your coat?"

"On the bed," Old Sam said, nodding toward it.

"I'll get it," Sue said. She stepped over to the bed and began untangling an old woolen coat from its twisted wrapping of several blankets.

"Don't Sue look nice today, Old Sam?"

"Sure she does," Old Sam said, scarcely glancing at Sue; turning his back to her as she helped him on with his coat. "Find me my cane."

Annie found a cane and handed it to him after he'd finished buttoning his coat.

"You got a hat?" Annie asked.

"There's one around here someplace," Old Sam said.

Sue and Annie searched until the hat was found amid the clutter on a chair by Old Sam's bed. Old Sam walked with his cane. Annie took his free arm, and the three of them went out of the room, to the door at the end of the hallway, and then outside.

"Bright out here with the sun on the snow," Old Sam said as he paused on his doorstep. He squinted his eyes practically shut.

"When's the last time you was out of your house?" Annie asked.

"I ain't been out this year," Old Sam said. "I was thinkin' I'd get carried out. Carried out in a box."

"Not today, Old Sam," Annie said. "Today you got to walk."

Sue and Annie helped Old Sam down the steps and up into the sleigh. Then the three of them set out for the village square.

*****

Town meeting was always held in the meeting room on the second floor of the town hall. It generally began at seven-thirty in the morning and ran continuously until the dinner break at noon; finished remaining business in the afternoon. In that era Vermonters prided themselves on nearly a half century of universal manhood suffrage: voting rights for all resident men of age without any property-owning requirement. The concept of having women vote, if ever even considered, would have been puzzling to Vermont residents for they had no tradition of it anywhere in their backgrounds. Nonetheless, town meeting was an affair for the whole township — men and women alike. Though the villagers of Barston Falls and of the smaller community of North Barston had seen a fair amount of one another during the winter, many of the other residents of the township had been isolated on their farms since the first heavy snowfall and welcomed town meeting as a chance to see people and as a respite from their current activities of early lambing or sugaring. Many considered town meeting to be the official beginning of spring no matter how deep the snow might still be. Steve Danforth was generally acknowledged to be a moderator who kept meetings under control and made sure that anyone who wanted to speak could be heard by the gathering. Many women who took active interests in the affairs of the town, even though they didn't have the right to vote, liked to add their opinions and arguments to the discussions of various issues and listen to what others had to say. Many of them knitted as they sat in the meeting room.

The social highlight was the dinner served at mid day down on the first floor of the town hall. Each household in the township was supposed to contribute something to the meal, the best cooks taking great pains with their specialty dishes and then basking in the compliments of their neighbors. All families brought their own plates, mugs, and eating utensils. The food was laid out on long tables. People lined up, helped themselves, and then found eating space either upstairs, downstairs, or outside if the weather permitted. Barrels of cider were still rolled out at town meeting in 1826, though the recent influence of the temperance movement and the enthusiasm with which it had been embraced by many — though by no means all — of the residents kept the bungs tight in the whiskey and rum kegs during town meeting day. Indeed, warrant items dealing with the regulation of alcohol had begun to appear in each of the most recent town meetings and seemed to be gaining more supporters with each passing year. The dinner, by tradition, generally lasted until about two o'clock. Then Steve Danforth reconvened the meeting and finished the business items as they had appeared in the warning for town meeting, took up any new business for consideration, and finally adjourned. Many residents were reluctant to let go of the occasion and often could be found hours after adjournment lingering in the town square or in the hall itself as they socialized and caught up with the news and gossip of their neighbors.

The town square was cluttered with horses and sleighs when Annie, Sue, and Old Sam arrived. Town meeting day in 1826 came in a sleigh year rather than in a wagon year, and most people were glad of it. During a wagon year a study of spokes on wagon wheels revealed the depth of the mud the wagon owners had had to drive through to get to town meeting. Typically the seasonal warmth of the day meant much deeper mud for people on their ways home. In years of deep mud, people rode on horseback to get to town meeting, or else they walked. Some meeting days required both sleighs and wagons. Residents from the hills in the western part of the township would set out from home in sleighs and then with the disappearance of snow as they descended from the hills they would be forced to leave their sleighs and walk the rest of the way into the village or else find wagon rides with their lowland neighbors.

Annie left the sleigh by her brother's blacksmith shop at the north end of the square. She and Sue and Old Sam walked down to the town hall. A number of people were outside the town hall eating as they approached.

Old Sam was not pleased with the brightness of the day, his eyes so long accustomed to his shrouded room. It had been a long time, too, since he had walked as far as from the blacksmith shop to the town hall. In spite of the slow pace, he felt out of breath and a little light-headed. When people greeted him by the door of the town hall, he scarcely glanced at them; managed to nod in the direction of a few of them he recognized. His squinting eased as he entered the building, but the scowl remained on his face. He could see so little in the dimmer light inside that Annie had to lead him by his arm.

"You come over here, Old Sam, and sit down," Annie said as she led him to the two tables in the corner of the room set aside by common consent for the older residents of Barston so that they could sit down and eat and not have to worry about balancing plates and mugs. "You sit down here, and we'll get food for you and bring it back. Cider?"

Old Sam nodded and sat on the bench at the table, his back against the wall. It was a relief to him to sit down and to escape the bright light of outdoors. The two tables were about half filled with other people. He nodded or grunted responses to the greetings they made and to the questions they asked. After a while they left him alone and went back to talking among themselves.

Babies. What are they doin' here? Not a one of 'em could be even seventy years old. Prob'ly think they still got half a lifetime to live when they see a relic like me.

Old Sam's eyes began to adjust better to the indoor light. He gazed over at the line of people by the food tables. Some of them he recognized. Others he swore he had never seen before in his life. All of them seemed to be talking at once.

Noisy in here. Oh I shouldn't of come. I should of just stayed home and rested. I can't hardly hear myself think here. It's goin' to be a bad afternoon. I should of just stayed at home.

Annie brought him a plate of food; Sue a mug of cider.

"You havin' a good time, Old Sam?" Annie asked.

"No."

"Eat somethin' then, and you'll feel better," Annie said. "We'll go get some food ourselves. Might be a while because the line's long. They let me go to the front for your dinner, but we got to go to the end for our own."

Old Sam took several swallows of cider as he watched Annie and Sue return to the food tables. It wasn't good cider: too watery and hardly even a tingle to it. His eyes moved around the room, and he began to recognize more people. His attention lingered on a few of them, and he found himself wishing he were as young as they again.

Well, they got their lives to lead. They can't even guess how quick the years go by and how soon they'll be old and then dead and gone. Good luck to 'em.

He caught sight of Reverend Harper and Deacon Russell going around together as they did every town meeting: a dual and united font of Christian Duty spreading their good works in a flurry of smug self-righteousness as they gadded about greeting everybody and made a particular point of ministering to the Afflicted. Old Sam knew it wouldn't take them long to come over to the old folks' tables. Reverend Harper was the Methodist minister in the village. Deacon Russell represented the Congregational Church, whose own minister lived across the river in Wheelock and preached in both Barston and Wheelock each Sunday; who always attended Wheelock town meeting. Old Sam suspected that the reverend and the deacon stuck together on town meeting days out of the fear each had that he might be out-Christianed by the other. The two of them were probably more responsible than anyone else for the absence of rum and whiskey at town meeting and for the weakness of the cider. *A plague on both of them,* Old Sam thought. He watched their progress around the room and kept his eyes on them as they inevitably approached his table.

"Greetings to you, Sam Barston," Deacon Russell said. "I hope you're enjoying this town meeting day. It seems to agree with you."

"Yes, indeed," Reverend Harper added. "But certainly you are enjoying it today. Certainly you're looking fit and happy on this fine day."

Old Sam's pulse quickened as he leaned forward and stared into Reverend Harper's eyes.

"The Devil I do! Don't you lie to me. I look like an old

man with both feet in the grave and ready for the shovelin'. I look like an old man that's goin' to stink things up all around if you don't plant me pretty quick. Don't you lie to me, reverend, for it ain't good for your soul."

Old Sam leaned back against the wall, watching the consternation of the reverend and the deacon with considerable satisfaction.

"Just trying to pass the time of day," Deacon Russell said. "Just trying to help you through your time of trial."

"If you two vultures want to help me," Old Sam said, "then it's your Christian duty to run off and find me a pint of whiskey. That's what 'll help me through my time of trial. It's a mortal sin to have to drink watery cider on town meetin' day."

The deacon and the reverend quickly spotted other people they needed to speak to.

"I'll pray for your soul," Reverend Harper said as he retreated.

"Pray for your own, reverend," Old Sam said. "For lyin' to me and for makin' 'em lock up the rum and whiskey."

Prissy-mouthed vultures. To the devil with both of 'em. Yes sir. With both of 'em.

Old Sam relished the warm glow he felt in his chest. He noted, however, the shocked expressions on the faces of the others at the table with him.

"Well, they shouldn't ought to of lied to me now, should they?"

He got no answers from them.

Many citizens of Barston stopped by the old folks' table to give their greetings to Old Sam or the others sitting with him. Of the questions directed to Old Sam, most were along the lines of "How are you today?" or "How are you feeling, Old Sam?" He replied with a fair amount of variety: "Not so good . . . Bad . . . Just about dead . . . Old . . . Almost rotten . . . Burial's next week, and you're invited . . . Awful." Most people responded with the hope that he would feel better soon. Then they continued on their rounds of greeting people they hadn't seen for a while. Old Sam wished they'd all just leave him alone.

Old Sam looked around for Jared and Seth, his nephew Tom, his widowed nieces — Rebecca Kimball and Sally Parker. They all lived in the Barston family enclave of six brick houses. He didn't see any of them and guessed that they had gotten their food early and had gone upstairs to eat.

When Charlie Porter approached, Old Sam thought about answering the inevitable question with "Like a cat in a sack and on his way to the river," but Charlie tricked him by not asking how he felt.

"Who's this old crow bait?" Charlie said. "If it was shaved, then it might look a little like Old Sam Barston, but it ain't shaved. Well, I guess it's Old Sam after all. So it's true what they say. You do look like the devil, and I s'pose there's a reason for it."

Charlie snatched up the mug from in front of Old Sam and took a swallow from it. "So that's why," Charlie said, turned his back on Old Sam, and walked out the door of the town hall carrying Old Sam's mug with him.

Old Sam was a bit taken aback.

That little pirate just walked off with my cider.

Old Sam picked at the food on his plate and wondered when Annie and Sue might come back. A few minutes later he looked up and saw Charlie Porter back in front of him.

"Well, I certainly am sorry, Old Sam. I got outside and seemed to be carryin' your mug. I don't know what in the world I was thinkin' of. I guess I just get excited when it's town meetin' day and ain't myself. Here it is back. Hope you ain't missed it."

Charlie set the mug back down in front of Old Sam and then left. Old Sam glanced at his back for a moment and then returned to picking at his food. Some of it really was quite good, he thought. He just wished he had more of an appetite. He didn't know if he could finish all that was on his plate, and all his life he'd hated to waste food. He ate a few more bites and then took a big swallow of his cider.

Old Sam's coughing fit raised the concern of everyone at the table. It passed in a moment, however. "Must of just swallowed the wrong way," he said. "I'm all right now."

Whiskey. Well, thank you Charlie Porter. There's more good in you than in a whole mountain of Reverend Harpers and Deacon Russells. I surely thank you.

Old Sam drank more slowly after that.

Sue and Annie at last returned with their plates piled high. Seeing empty places still at the old folks' table, they sat down with Old Sam. Annie announced to everyone else at the table that she and Sue would move if someone else came who might need their seats. Annie began eating and then turned to Old Sam.

"You havin' a good time yet?" she asked.

"A little better," Old Sam said as he lifted his mug.

XVI

After dinner the noise and bustle in the room didn't seem nearly as oppressive to Old Sam. He had managed to finish the contents of his mug and all the food on his plate. A dull lethargy began to steal over him. Seth came over to talk, then Mark Hosmer. Joe Reckford appeared with a son in each arm, and Annie went off with him. Benjie, Foss, and Tom seemed quite confused when they stopped by and discovered Sue wearing a dress rather than her accustomed britches and shirt. The four of them went outside. Steve Danforth said hello. Then Ellen Hosmer set a piece of pie in front of Old Sam. He'd left it untouched for nearly ten minutes before he felt he could take a first bite, but he had eaten it all. He hadn't felt so full in months. Jared and Elizabeth came down the stairs with some of their children in tow and spent a few minutes with him. After that a whole host of people had come by one right after another. Old Sam was feeling so drowsy by then that he wasn't paying much attention to who they were.

The ringing of a cowbell quieted the droning chatter, and Steve Danforth shouted out, "Upstairs!" Then the throng, as loud as ever, eased toward the stairwell and began to thin as people clattered up the stairs to the meeting room.

Seth and Jared approached Old Sam.

"You goin' to afternoon meetin', Grampy Sam?" Seth asked.

"Course I am! Why do you s'pose I came here today?"

"If you need any help up the stairs, we'll haul you up," Jared said.

"Well I don't need . . . " Old Sam began in a bluster, but cut his words off sharply and then spoke in a quieter voice. "Truth is I ain't sure if I need help or not. I ain't been up a set of stairs yet this year."

"That's why we're askin'," Seth said.

"Well, I might," Old Sam said.

"Look, Grampy Sam," Jared said. "We got to get up there, so we'll just haul you up. Me and Seth 'll grab wrists, and all you got to do is set down and lean back. Hold on to our necks if you want. Less work to haul you up than to keep talkin' about it."

"But no fair knockin' our heads together," Seth said, "if there's somethin' you don't like about the ride."

"All right," Old Sam said. "But wait 'til everybody's out of this room, and then you set me down soon as we get to the top of the stairs. I don't want you carryin' me right into the meetin' room for everybody to gawk at."

"Fair enough," Seth said. "Think we want folks to see us carryin' you?"

Old Sam made them wait until everyone in the room had gone upstairs and until it seemed likely no one else would be coming in from outside. He carried his cane himself. Seth and Jared set him down at the head of the stairs, and the three of them went into the meeting room together.

The afternoon meeting had already begun. Most of the seats were taken, but there were still a couple rows of sparsely filled benches in the back set aside for the old or infirm. Old Sam insisted on sitting at the very back of the room so he could lean against the wall. His grand-nephews sat on either side of him.

Steve Danforth kept the meeting moving through the warrant items with his usual skill: cutting off any discussion that tended to wander from the topic at hand; running through the motions and seconds and discussions and votes. He led the townspeople through decisions on varmint bounties, on repairs or replacement of three bridges over small brooks in the township, on whether to create a new school district or to keep things the way they were, on the arrangements for routine road maintenance. He dispensed quickly with the habitual warrant item about having a bridge across the Connecticut to join Barston with Wheelock, pointing out as he had for several years in succession the expense of such an undertaking. In all fairness, he said, half the costs should be borne by Wheelock. Wheelock was nearly always uncooperative on proposed joint ventures and thusfar had never indicated a willingness to pay anything for a bridge. As he had the year before, Steve recorded a vote of sentiment that the town of Barston would encourage any private endeavor to build a toll bridge over the Connecticut. For the time being people would continue to use the ferry in the summer and the ice roads in the winter to get from one side of the river to the other. If they wanted to use a bridge, they could go either up or down the Connecticut to other towns: up to the one under construction and soon to be completed between Bradford and Piermont or further up to the one between Newbury and Haverhill; down to the one between Fairlee and Orford.

It seemed to Old Sam that years earlier he had sat through many of the same arguments he was now hearing. When he listened to people arguing on one side of an issue, he already knew what arguments would be used in response. He was certain he had heard some of the same points at least thirty years before, when many of the people now arguing were just children or perhaps had yet to be born. It made him feel very old. The thought of getting interested in any of the issues he was hearing discussed and perhaps of participating in the arguments himself never crossed his mind. The voting — the decisions — were for those in the town who had a future. He himself, with a future of perhaps only days or weeks, was simply a listener. His mind drifted back to those people who decades earlier had been wrought up over the same issues people were still talking about. Hi Palmer, for instance, was so obsessed with road improvements and bridges within the township that he could have been Eli Parker himself if he had slid back in time a few years. No. There was nothing new. Old Sam told himself that he had lived so long that he couldn't expect to hear anything at a town meeting he hadn't already heard before. With his reminiscences he distanced himself from the matters at hand and soon let his chin droop down onto his chest.

Seth's persistent elbow roused him.

"Startin' to snore, Grampy Sam," he whispered.

Old Sam grunted a response and sat up trying to blink away his feeling of disorientation.

Good we sat in the back. Old Sam listened hard to what Steve Danforth was saying

"No, Zeke. We already had our say on that issue, and we took our vote on it. It was defeated, and it ain't right to bring it up again under new business. Besides, the vote won't be much different from what it was this mornin'. The proper procedure for you is to find more supporters for your point of view and bring the issue back to us next town meetin'. See if you can't come up with some new arguments, too, because the sentiment seemed to be strongly against the proposal as it stood today. Thank you.

"Other items under new business? Yes."

"What about the cannon for the Fourth of July?" someone called out from up in front.

"I'll have a report on that after this meetin' is adjourned," Steve said. "The vote of the town at our special town meetin' was against the use of town funds for a cannon, so I don't propose to keep the issue in front of the town. It is now a private matter, and those who might be

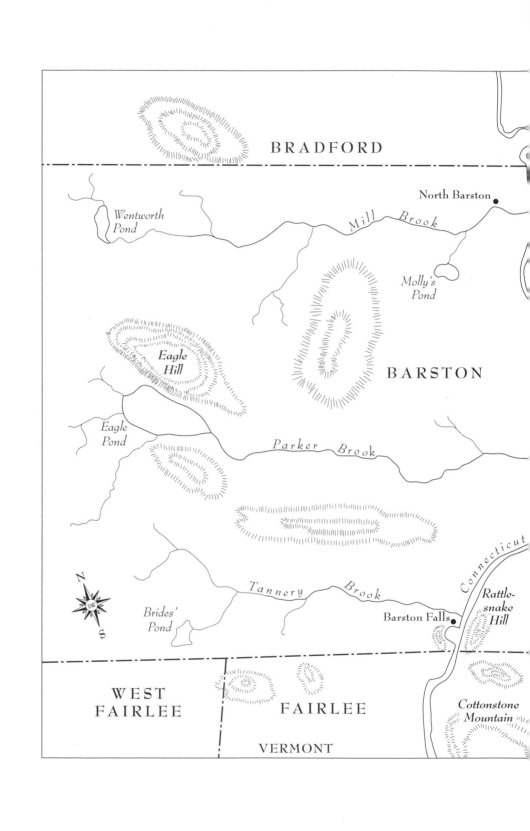

BRADFORD

North Barston •

Wentworth
Pond

Mill   Brook

Molly's
Pond

Eagle
Hill

BARSTON

Eagle
Pond

Parker   Brook

Connecticut

N
E
W
S

Tannery   Brook

Rattle-
snake
Hill

Brides'
Pond

Barston Falls •

WEST
FAIRLEE

FAIRLEE

Cottonstone
Mountain

VERMONT

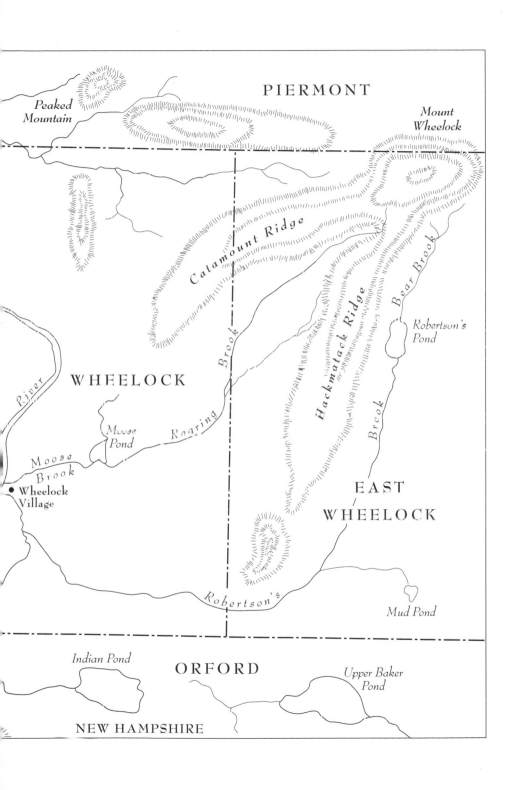

PIERMONT

Peaked Mountain

Mount Wheelock

Catamount Ridge

Hackmatack Ridge

Bear Brook

Robertson's Pond

WHEELOCK

River

Moose Pond

Roaring Brook

Brook

Moose Brook

• Wheelock Village

EAST WHEELOCK

Robertson's

Mud Pond

ORFORD

Indian Pond

Upper Baker Pond

NEW HAMPSHIRE

interested in it are welcome to stick around after our other business is completed. Other new business?"

There were several miscellaneous matters brought up, some serious; some frivolous. Nathan Thompson, having married within the previous year, was appointed hog reeve for the township — his attempt to decline the honor having been hooted down. There was a general exhortation from Robert Alstead for people to make certain that rubbish was cleaned up around their homes and to see that the mortar in their chimneys was tight, and, if not, to re-point it. He uttered a few dire predictions about fire if people didn't heed his words, and then he sat down. Ellen Hosmer wanted to plant elms along some of the smaller roads in the village, at no expense to the town. It was voted that she go ahead with the town's blessing, and a number of people offered to help her. The final item dealt with the seriousness of tampering with the ropes and cedar log floats maintained, since the previous year, at the river's edge below the Falls to rescue people from drowning. Several people cited instances in past years where a drowning victim could have been saved if such a rope and float had been available at the time. A fine of a hundred dollars was proposed for the crime of tampering with the ropes and floats. Some thought the amount was excessive. Some thought a fine was inappropriate and promised severe physical punishment in place of a fine, no matter what the law might call for. In the end an official fine of thirty dollars was voted for any activities which might render the rescue equipment unserviceable (a measure which included theft). There being no further business, Steve Danforth adjourned the meeting.

Even as people were leaving the meeting room, the same voice from up front called out again, "Now how about that cannon?"

Steve waited until those people who were leaving had cleared the room and until it was quiet enough for him to talk again.

"Well, about the cannon," Steve began, as the room gradually quieted. "We got ninety-six dollars towards it, which I think is more than enough for a cannon and powder and some barrels of rum to go with it, but the problem still is that there just don't seem to be any cannons out there for sale. Seth and Jared went all the way down to the coast, and they didn't find any down there, did you men?"

"No," Seth called out. "There wasn't any for sale in Boston or Portsmouth or in between, and it ain't likely there will be any time soon."

"So seems like we're stuck," Steve said. "I kept records of who gave money for the cannon, and I'll see to it that you all get your money back."

"Hang that," came the same voice. "We don't want our money back. We want a cannon for Old Sam Barston."

Old Sam craned his neck to see the speaker. He didn't recognize the man. He turned to both Seth and Jared asking who it was.

"David Stowell's his name," Jared said. "He's got a sawmill up Tannery Brook just below where the south branch flows out of Brides' Pond."

"Never saw him before in my life," Old Sam said. "Why's he want to get a cannon for me?"

"Everybody loves you, Grampy Sam," Seth said. "That's why. It must be the whiskers. Or maybe he's a temperance man, and he wants to do somethin' for somebody like you who's so strong in the movement."

"But I don't even know him."

"I guess that don't matter," Jared said.

"I surely don't know what to say," Steve Danforth continued. "We looked for a cannon and couldn't find one. Nobody seems to want to sell us one. We could have a committee to look further into the chances of buyin' a cannon, but I don't imagine they'd have much better luck than we've had already."

"Amend the notion of that committee, Mr. Moderator," Mark Hosmer said, doing his best to mimic Steve's voice. "I propose two motions. The first is that you take that ninety-six dollars and spend it on powder and rum. The second is that a committee of everybody forget about buyin' a cannon and start thinkin' about gettin' a cannon any way they see fit. And I suggest that they might just look across the river if they have any trouble locatin' a cannon that they might go and get any way they see fit."

"Second the motions!" came a chorus of voices.

"I guess we better not vote on this," Steve said. "I guess it's good that this ain't part of the proper town meetin'. If you're set and determined on this committee, seems like you might find a leader for it so that it's a committee and not a mob."

"There's only one man who's right for stealin' us a cannon," a voice Old Sam couldn't identify rang out. "Deacon Russell!"

Laughter roared through the meeting hall. Deacon Russell had been among those who had left at the end of the regular meeting.

"I'm takin' myself out of this discussion," Steve said. "I meant a leader who might keep lookin' for the chance of buyin' a cannon. I'll just remind you before I go that there's sometimes a fine line between good fun and outright stealin', and I'd caution you not to do anythin' that might be against the laws, wind you up in jail, or get the township of Barston on bad terms with our neighbors."

Steve stepped down from his speaker's platform and left the meeting hall. Laughter and buzzes of conversation continued to sound through the hall, but there was no attempt to organize the meeting after Steve had left. People stood up and themselves began to leave the meeting room a few at a time.

"Think of that, Grampy Sam!" Seth said. "There's actually people in this town that'd go out and steal a cannon from somebody else — folks that 'd go right over to Wheelock Village and take their cannon without askin'! Think of that!"

"Shockin'," Jared said. "Well, I sure won't have anythin' to do with that committee."

"What's wrong with it?" Old Sam asked.

"In the Barston family we wasn't raised to steal," Seth said. "It's a Christian family."

"But hang it boys! We got to have a cannon for the Fourth of July!"

"Got to have it enough to steal it?" Jared asked.

"Yes. It's only borrowin' it anyways, and it never cost 'em a thing to start with. Go and get it!"

"Shame, shame, Grampy Sam," Seth said, shaking his head. "I hope tonight before you go to bed you'll reflect on the sin in your heart and do your best to mend it."

"Oh you boys can both just . . ."

"No, Grampy Sam," Jared said, interrupting him. "If it'll make you feel better, Seth and me will go back out and see if we can't find a cannon to buy. We didn't have much luck the first time, but maybe there's one someplace that somebody just decided to sell. Maybe we'll find it."

"You know there ain't a chance you'll find a cannon anyplace to buy," Old Sam said.

"We can always hope," Seth said. "We can always try and hope for the best. It's the least we can do for you, Grampy Sam."

"You got that right," Old Sam said. "That is the least you can do — in a dead tie with just settin' and not doin' a blessed thing!"

Annie came into the room, caught Jared's eye, and waved to him.

"Here's Annie," Jared said. "She's takin' you home, or so she said. We will go out and see if we can't buy a cannon for you, Grampy Sam. If we can't find one, then maybe we'll just have Steve buy ninety-six dollars of powder. We'll set it under a stump and see if we can't blow the stump right over the top of Rattlesnake Hill. All you want is noise anyways. You don't need a cannon for that. All you need is some powder."

"Well, we can try to carry you back downstairs, Grampy Sam," Seth said. "But the sins in your heart now are so heavy that I ain't sure we can manage."

"I'll walk!" Old Sam thundered.

*****

Annie flicked the reins occasionally to keep the horse going. She was anxious to get Old Sam home and then go home herself. Sue could take care of the twins for a while, and she was good at it, but when the twins got hungry, there wasn't a thing she could do. She glanced over at Old Sam, who was slouched in the seat next to her.

"You look tired, Old Sam," she said. "I hope meetin' didn't wear you down to nothin'. Hope you had a good time there this afternoon."

"Yes. I'm pretty tired. No doubt about that. Ain't used to so many folks."

The sleigh glided over Tannery Bridge. Old Sam peered over at the canal.

"You know, Annie, that Mark Hosmer is an awful good man. Him and Charlie Porter both."

"Well, they are. There's a lot of good folks in the village."

"Wish I could do somethin' for 'em, but there ain't much an old man can do. Seems like babies and old folks can't do anythin'. Other folks have got to take care of 'em. I wish it wasn't that way, but it is."

"There's things you can still do, Old Sam, if you remember. For one thing you hardly gave Sue a glance today. She put on a dress special for town meetin' and did up her hair, and you didn't even notice. If you could of told her she looked good like she was, that would of made her happy. She don't feel comfortable tryin' to act like a woman. It's somethin' new for her. Prob'ly thinks the whole world's lookin' at her and laughin' at her."

"No, I didn't even notice. Guess I was thinkin' too much about my own troubles from bein' old."

"She's a lot quieter now too, so it's hard to figure what she's thinkin' or to know if she's happy or sad. I hate to see her settle back to the way she was when she first come to the village, but she might. Right now she prob'ly don't know whether she'll put on her dress tomorrow or her old britches and shirt — figures folks 'll make fun of her either way."

"Oh she'll grow out of it. You had some troubles when you was her age, and you managed just fine as I recall."

"Well, it surely helped to have you teasin' me so, Old Sam, about marryin' me and all. I don't s'pose I ever told you how much that meant. You was always awful good to me."

"You was special — that's why," Old Sam said. "And Sue's special too. Caught the fish with Malik for one thing and . . ."

"That's right," Annie interrupted. "And she was proud of it. Benjie and Foss and Tom couldn't make her their friend fast enough after that — first friends she ever had her own age. So she settled down to bein' one of the boys with 'em and figured she had to keep showin' 'em she could do anythin' they could. And that's just how all the folks in the village still think about her — that fish and runnin' around with that gang of boys. Problem is that now she's older, and she wants to change, but she's scared to death of tryin' to act like a woman. Likely she's afraid folks 'll laugh at her.

"Oh she was makin' me good and mad there for a while with her wild ways, but then I figured that maybe she was scared to act any other way. She ain't really made friends her age besides Benjie, Foss, and Tom. I think she's scared the three of 'em won't be her friends any more if she don't go along with all their pranks and games, so that makes it harder for her to change. She'll grow out of it all right, but it might take a while, and she could be miserable, scared, and alone while she's doin' it. I know I would of been when I was her age if you and other folks hadn't of helped me along. That's why I think it'd be good if maybe you could tease her some the way you used to do with me."

"Ha," Old Sam said. "Bein' old takes up so much time that I guess I didn't notice about Sue. Well, let me rest a day or two, and then I'll see if I can't think of somethin' for Sue. But right now I'm too tired. I just want to get home and go to bed."

"Almost there now, Old Sam."

Old Sam yawned and lapsed into silence. When the sleigh arrived at his house, Annie had to give him considerable help getting inside. She helped him off with his coat. Then he went to his desk and rummaged in a drawer for something before he sat down on his bed. Annie helped him get his shoes off."

"You all right, Old Sam? It ain't but about four o'clock."

"Just tired. I'll get a nap before Benjie comes back."

"Good. You get rested."

"Here," Old Sam said, holding out his hand as Annie was about to go.

"What is it?"

Old Sam dropped two dimes into her palm.

"Tell Sue I want her to get some ribbons for her hair."

Annie gave him a hug and settled him on his bed with a blanket and his coat. She left, telling him she had to hurry back to the twins.

Old Sam lay still on his bed thinking that if he hadn't pulled down the blankets from the windows it might be easier for him to fall asleep while it was still light out. Well, he'd had quite a time at town meeting. He smiled to think of Charlie Porter walking away with his mug and then returning it; of Mark Hosmer urging people to get a cannon any way they saw fit instead of buying one; pointing the way across the river to draw attention to Wheelock Village's cannon. Yes sir. Charlie and Mark had some stuffing in them. Jared and Seth were quite a disappointment in comparison. Well, Mark Hosmer was the village's best hope for a cannon. He wished him luck. Oh yes, he certainly was tired. Old Sam yawned and closed his eyes.

*****

When Benjie came in at supper time, he found Grampy Sam acting quite strange. For one thing he'd been asleep in bed until Benjie had started refilling the wood box. Then it seemed all he could talk about was Charlie Porter and Mark Hosmer and what good men they were and how he hoped that Benjie would amount to something. Benjie thought it was the strangest he'd seen Grampy Sam act all winter long.

Grampy Sam hadn't managed to eat more than a mouthful of supper, claiming that he just wasn't hungry. Then when it was time for bed, he'd insisted that Benjie leave a candle burning — not like him at all. Benjie had awakened during the night to discover that Grampy Sam was no longer in the room. After a few minutes Benjie had checked to see if he was in at the chamber pot, but he wasn't. In a panic Benjie had started across the road to rouse his parents. That was when he'd found Grampy Sam standing out in the middle of the road on the packed snow looking up at the stars.

"Remember this night, Benjie," Grampy Sam had said. "After I'm dead, you remember this night that the two of us stood out and looked at the stars together. I hope some night we can see the Roar Borallus together too, but if we don't, I want you to remember this night and the stars."

Well, Benjie wasn't likely to forget the night. He lay awake after they were back inside and the candle had been blown out and thought that maybe Grampy Sam knew he was going to die during the night and had just been trying to say goodby to him. When dawn came, however, Grampy Sam was still alive. Furthermore, he got right after Benjie to pick up the blankets and the strapping from the floor, to knock down the cobwebs all over the room, to straighten the bedding on the two beds, and to sweep the room from one end to the other. He was even threatening to have Benjie wash the windows. As he was sweeping, Benjie thought about how much easier it had been with the blankets over the windows and Grampy Sam just sitting in his rocking chair all day and not caring how the room looked.

XVII

The four horses trotted easily, their hoofbeats muted on the packed snow, as the pung glided along behind them. Charlie Porter snapped his whip occasionally to keep the horses on their pace. Mark Hosmer sat on the seat next to Charlie. George Ballard and Joe Reckford flanked the two of them, sitting just behind on boards set across on the forward corners of the pung box. The four men talked incessantly; had scarcely had a moment's quiet since they'd left Barston Falls four hours earlier. Periodically each would arch a brown streak of tobacco spit off to the side.

"Oh, what a day!" Mark said. "Just like spring. That sun feels awful good."

"And maybe we'll wish it was the middle of winter again if we run out of snow before we get down to Charlestown," Joe said.

"It's true a pung don't drag too good on mud," Charlie said. "But the three biggest men in Barston hitched in with the horses should be more'n enough to get us through. Likely you ain't got to worry though. There's plenty of snow between here and Charlestown."

"If there ain't, Charlie," George said, "you're the one that gets hitched in with the horses, and the three of us'll be the ones to drive."

"Ha!" Charlie said. "That ain't smart. I ain't but about half the size of any of you. That's how come you'll never make a teamster, George — just no notion of what can pull and what can't. That's how come you ain't ever goin' to be nothin' but a plain old ignorant blacksmith."

"With the three of us beatin' on you, Charlie," George said, "I bet we can get you to pull. Why get three of us tired and muddy when you're the only one that needs to?"

"If we run out of snow, we'll vote on it," Mark said.

"It don't much matter to me who pulls," Joe said, "but Annie won't want us to do anythin' that might wear down George's good looks 'fore we get to Charlestown. We got to have him happy and fresh, case there's a woman down there that might want him. Annie's always after me to keep my eye out for George so she can get him married off. It's embarrassin' for her to have a bachelor brother like that. He's so shy with the girls that if somebody don't help him along . . ."

"Oh, that's a good one, Joe," Charlie said. "And you so good with the girls that for months you thought Annie was George's wife!"

"No. That was just a plan to get her interested in . . ." Joe began.

"Give it a rest, Joe," George said. "Save your stories for when we run into somebody that might believe 'em. What I was thinkin' is that when the pung decides to start wallowin' in the mud, Mark's the one to help the horses along on account of what he said at town meetin' yesterday about everybody goin' right over to Wheelock Village and stealin' their cannon. About let our cat out of the bag yellin' that for all the town to hear — when we wanted to keep even the notion of stealin' a cannon just as quiet as we could."

"So how am I s'posed to know all your secrets?" Mark said. "Seth and Jared couldn't buy a cannon, and there wasn't a chance of gettin' one that anybody told me about. Nobody doin' a thing about gettin' a cannon, so I thought I might get somebody in the town interested."

"Oh, they're interested for sure," Charlie said. "And with all of 'em blabbin' about it so, if they did go over to

Wheelock Village and grab it, they'd have about as good a chance of keepin' it a secret who's got it as hidin' a candle flame in a powder keg. That's one good reason for why Steve Danforth ain't ridin' with us right now. We got to keep this a secret."

"And the reason we're goin' way down to Charlestown?" Joe said.

"That's right," Charlie said. "If Wheelock Village gets their cannon stole, where do you s'pose they'll look for it first? They know we want a cannon and that we can't find one to buy. If Charlestown gets their cannon stole . . . no, when Charlestown gets their cannon stole, they sure ain't goin' to look for it way up in Barston Falls — not so long as we keep our mouths shut about it they ain't. Besides, that Charlestown cannon is just achin' to get stole — right out in the open like it is. I think if we don't grab it fast, somebody else might, or maybe somebody down there might smarten up some and do a better job keepin' it safe from folks like us."

"I still can't quite figure how you can get the cannon into the pung easy as you say with just rollers and a block and tackle," Mark said. "Awful lot of weight to a cannon."

"You'll see how next time we stop," Charlie said. "We'll practice quite a bit before we get down there. That's how come we're carryin' that log. Must be close to dinner time now anyways. Guess we might as well stop at next water. Give the horses a rest and practice loadin' the log with the block and tackle. We got to get so's we can do it quick and in the dark. And George, you s'pose you could hop down and rummage in the hay in the corner under you and see if you can't come up with a jug? No sense stayin' both hungry and thirsty 'til we stop."

George found the jug, and it made the rounds. Only Joe didn't have any of its contents, saying he would wait until later. Charlie and Mark kept the jug between them on the seat.

"That's what temperance really is," Mark said. "Just not havin' so much, ain't it? Never did mean not to have any at all, but that's just exactly what it's comin' to mean. I guess you're the only true temperance man I know, Joe. Not like Deacon Russell and them."

Charlie handed the reins to Mark and took another drink from the jug.

"But you got to admit there's a lot of truth in what the deacon says," Charlie said. "Some awful things happen on account of rum. Killed my grandfather, for one thing. And that's a fact."

The other men didn't say anything, so Charlie continued.

"Course it was kind of unusual, the way he died."

"How was that?" Joe asked.

"Well, he fell into a vat of whiskey."

"Thought you said rum killed him?" Mark said.

"Whiskey, rum — all the same. Killed him dead anyways."

"That's awful," Joe said.

"Yes it was," Charlie said. "Four men tried to pull him out, but he fought 'em hard and whipped 'em all and went right back under."

"Oh you weasel," Mark muttered as he handed the reins back to Charlie and took the jug from him. Joe and George laughed.

"Well, there was an interestin' thing that did happen when I was a boy on account of rum," Charlie said. "Right up in Lancaster, where I grew up. Folks talked about it for years. There was an old farmer up there that seemed to have better luck with his crops and his livestock than anybody else for miles around. Everythin' he set his hand to in farmin' seemed to turn out right. Even if folks whispered behind his back that he drank too much rum, they had to admit . . ."

"Rum or whiskey?" Mark interrupted.

"Rum, you clown. Now let me tell this story, will you? Anyways this farmer started every day off with a two-quart pitcher of hard cider. That would hold him, generally, 'til the middle of the mornin'. Then he'd get the corncob stopple out of his rum jug and leave it out for the rest of the day and just whistle and sing his way through work.

"This same farmer had a favorite cow, and she was a real good milker. He thought so much of her that she was like a member of the family. And it was on account of this cow that folks talked for years and years. Awful strange, it was, what happened with that cow."

After a moment's silence Mark said, "All right. Who's goin' to ask him?"

"Guess it's my turn," George said. "But Joe's turn comes next. All right, Charlie. We might as well get it over with. What happened with that cow?"

"Oh come on, you jackasses. This really happened. You want to hear about it or not?"

"You sure you want to ask that, Charlie?" Mark asked.

"I want to know what happened with that cow," Joe said.

"All right," Charlie said. "I'm glad there's somebody around here that's half polite. I'll tell you, Joe, but these other two clods can put their hands over their ears if they want, or maybe they can get off and walk a couple rods behind us.

"Anyways, this farmer couldn't do enough for that cow — brushed her, petted her, gave her special food. Then at milkin' time one mornin', just for a treat, he dumped two quarts of hard cider into her water bucket. Well, you should of seen that cow then. Great big smile on her face. Nuzzlin' right up to him. She liked it so well that he left off his milkin' and went and got her another gallon. After that she just had to have her cider every mornin'. And the funny thing was that after she started drinkin' cider, she gave almost twice as much milk, and it had a lot more cream in it too. He'd been milkin' her twice a day, but after she started havin' her cider, her bag 'd be so full that he started milkin' her three times a day. He bragged about that quite a bit.

"Now the farmer couldn't leave well enough alone. Since he'd got such good results from that cow with his cider, he naturally started wonderin' how much better she might do with rum. One winter evenin' after milkin', when he'd been suckin' on his rum jug a little more 'n usual to stay warm, he decided to find out with the little bit that was left in the jug.

"Oh, she loved it. But when it was gone, she gave him a look that shook him up a bit — almost a threat. He went and got another jugful, dumped it all into her water bucket, and then closed up the barn for the night and went to bed. Her bellowin' kept him from fallin' asleep for a few hours and made him start to think that maybe it was a mistake to give her the rum, but after a while she stopped makin' such a racket and let him get to sleep.

"Next mornin' he found the barn door lyin' flat in the snow — kicked down — and his cow gone. Her tracks pointed straight up into the mountains. He was so worried on account of all the bears and catamounts and wolves in those parts that he grabbed his gun, his snowshoes, a couple blankets in case he had to spend a few nights out, and a packful of food and set right out. He went for miles followin' her tracks up into the mountains, and sure enough after a while he saw where the bears had got after her. But he began to worry about her a lot less after he found the third bear she'd kicked to death. And then . . ."

"Where I grew up," Mark interrupted, "some bears made it a habit to sleep all through the winter."

"Bears? Did I say bears?" Charlie asked. "I meant wolves, of course. Bears don't travel in a pack like that.

"Well, the wolves would of brought him some bounty money, but he walked right by them anyways and kept after the cow, and she kept on goin' higher up into the hills. Finally after three days he had followed her all the way up into those big hills up by the town of Dartmouth — that was before the name changed to Jefferson — and there she was way up on the side of one of those steep hills that's got a big rockslide on it, and she was right at the top of the rockslide. He spent quite a while climbin' up close enough to get a good view of her. She looked half asleep and pretty beat up, and there wasn't even a hint of a smile on her face. When the farmer got right beside her and called out her name, it startled her so that she gave a little lurch and lost her footin' and fell.

"Down and down and down she tumbled all the way to the bottom of the slide, rollin' and bouncin' just like a boulder. Such a joltin' and a jostlin' and a jouncin' — well it didn't seem like anythin' in creation could live through such a smashin' and a bashin' and a crashin'. Seemed like she fell forever before she finally stopped. He was sure she was dead, but when at last he got down to her, there she was on her feet still alive, but lookin' like one big bruise with a wicked headache. Took the farmer the best part of a week to limp her home."

"Lucky she was still alive after all that," Joe said.

"She was indeed," Charlie said. "And she stayed on the farm afterwards. The first mornin' she was back he tried to cheer her up with a bucket of his hard cider, but she was Temperance by then. She kicked the bucket over and then stomped it flat, and he never tried to give her cider again. And for months after she got back home she didn't give a drop of milk — not a drop. Her bag was full and tight and her teats all swole up, but he couldn't get any milk out of her. He thought she might of froze her bag because it was hard as a pumpkin, but after she got back into the barn with the other cows and it should of thawed out, it still stayed hard. Nice sunny spring days when she was back out on grass, it stayed the same. Warm to touch it, but still hard as a pumpkin. Stayed like that, Joe, all the way to the next July before he finally found out what the matter was."

"Well, what was it?" Joe asked. "How come she had that problem?"

"It was on the first really hot day of summer," Charlie went on. "The cow come back to the barn bellowin' in the middle of the day. She looked awful, like she was goin' to die — tears runnin' right down her face. Teats all swole up almost the size of her bag. The farmer started pattin' her and rubbin' her, and then he discovered that for the first time since her ramble into the mountains, her bag had lost its hardness. Right away he grabbed his milkin' bucket, knelt right down beside her, and started milkin'. And what do you s'pose happened, Joe?"

"What?" Joe asked.

"Out it come in one big chunk — weighed forty-two pounds! A great big lump of butter!"

"Butter! But I don't understand how a lump that big could fit out through . . ." Joe began.

"Oh come on, Joe!" George shouted. "Ain't you got better sense than to swallow down all Charlie's trash?"

"What's to swallow down?" Charlie asked. "How can you possibly doubt . . ."

"When are you goin' to learn, Joe?" Mark interrupted. "Only thing you need to know when you hear a story like that is if Charlie Porter is the one tellin' it. If you know that much, you can pretty much guess it ain't true, and you'll be right nine times out of ten. There might of been a place called Lancaster. There might of been a farmer there once that had a cow that used to give milk. All that might of been true. But beyond that, just remember that it was Charlie tellin' the story."

"Now don't you go spoilin' a good victim for me," Charlie said.

"It was all those years you spent alone, Joe," George said. "Wanderin' from place to place with just Sue, I mean, and not settlin' down or havin' much of anythin' to do with folks. That's how come you believe anythin' that Charlie tries to pass off on you. You just don't know better. But I'm guessin' that if Charlie keeps goin' on and on like this, we'll have you pretty well cured by the time we get home."

"Give me that jug," Joe said.

Joe drank and kept the jug until they stopped for dinner at a bridge with a small brook under it and some open water the current kept free of ice. The men stretched their legs and ate, and Charlie gave the horses a little water each out of a bucket he held for them.

"All right," Charlie announced. "We're carryin' that log in back so's we can practice with it. Time to haul her out and get to it. Ain't nearly the weight of a cannon, but I think it's about the same size as our cannon down in Charlestown, near as I can recall."

The four men lowered the ramp and unloaded the box of the pung: stretched out the canvas pung cover — which they had yet to use — on top of the snow, forked hay onto it, unloaded various tools, food, jugs, ropes, buckets, and blankets. While Mark and Joe unloaded the log from the back down the ramp and onto the snow, George and Charlie rigged the ropes for the block and tackle.

"Now pay attention here, and let me explain a few things," Charlie said. "The cannon down there in Charlestown is restin' on a couple stones and might be prob'ly two feet off of the ground — that's bare ground. I ain't sure how deep the snow is there now. What we need to do is get the pung backed up to it just as close as we can so that the ramp can still come down. Then we'll tie to it on the two carriage mount stubs that stick out on the side of the cannon, hook the block and tackle to that ring in the pung and to the cannon rope, slide some rollers under where we're goin' to haul the cannon, and just pull on the block and tackle rope 'til the cannon's settin' all the way aboard the pung. Then up goes the ramp, and we get away quick as we can. There really won't be much to it 'cept we'll be doin' all the work in the moonlight, so we got to have the block and tackle stretched out all the way, got to know right where we can lay our hands on the rollers, got to be careful the cannon don't run over somebody's foot."

The four men loaded and unloaded the log several times without any difficulty.

"There ain't anythin' hard about that," George said. "The rig works pretty good."

"It does," Charlie agreed. "But remember things ain't goin' to go so good when we got just the moonlight to work by. And we got to dump everythin' out of the back before we put the cannon in and then afterwards get it back in on top of the cannon."

"Still, it all seems too easy," Joe said. "Seems like there's a lot of other things we need to think about that can go wrong before and after we get the cannon up into the pung."

"Well, that's right," Charlie said. "But I tell you I thought about this plan for quite a while, and I think I got everythin' covered. Listen up, and see if I don't. We ain't goin' to stop at any taverns near Charlestown 'cause we don't want anybody to remember us. Since there's a few folks that know me down there from my freight business, when we go by the cannon tomorrow mornin' for a look, I'll hide in the back of the pung. I know nobody 'll recognize the pung on account of it's new. And after we get the cannon tomorrow night, we're goin' south to cross at Hale's bridge at Bellows' Falls before we head up to home. We'll let 'em know there, if anybody's at the toll gate, that we're goin' on down to Massachusetts just in case somebody comes along afterwards askin' which way did we go. That'll be good for us too if our tracks are headed south out of Charlestown from where the cannon was. We can go all night — two of us up here and two of us sleepin' on the hay on top of the cannon — and that should take care of the chance that there might be people chasin' out of Charlestown on all of the roads tryin' to catch whoever might of stole their cannon. By the time anybody has the time to catch up with us, I think we'll have the cannon home and hid.

"Long as we can grab it without gettin' caught, only troubles I can see we might have are if one of us don't keep quiet about stealin' the cannon after we got it, and the other one is if the snow melts. Either one of 'em 'll bring bad trouble on us. We can't do much about the snow, but I'll be surprised if it ain't still good for pungs and sleighs all the way down past Charlestown to Massachusetts and maybe even Connecticut, so I think we're all right there. But if Old Sam Barston is goin' to have his cannon for the Fourth of July, we sure can do somethin' about keepin' our mouths shut 'til then. And that means we ain't to tell a soul about it. Nobody at all."

"Got enough oil for your lanterns?" Mark asked.

"Plenty of oil. And I got two buckets of ashes to keep live coals in, so if the coals go dead in one of 'em we can still get a flame quick to light a lantern with. I brought along a couple of candle lanterns too."

"Got a good place to hide the cannon when we get back to Barston Falls?" George asked.

"I was thinkin' just to cover it with a load of slabwood," Charlie said. "We can talk that one out on the way home and see if we can do any better 'n that."

"You still plannin' to stop tonight just above Charlestown, the way you said?" Joe asked.

"That's right," Charlie said. "It's fifty miles give or take a couple between Barston Falls and Charlestown, and I was figurin' to do about forty-five of 'em today. Then tomorrow durin' the daylight we'll give the horses a easy time of it so's to rest 'em. I thought we'd go right past the cannon so's you three can look it over good and then stop a mile or two below for the rest of the day — someplace where nobody 'll notice us — and practice more with our log and get some sleep. Then we'll wait 'til the middle of the night, when everybody in Charlestown anyplace near the cannon is asleep, and go grab it. I was thinkin' to go to Bellows' Falls to cross, the way I said, and then keep goin' right through the night and get home I hope by suppertime with the cannon. Important thing is to give the horses a good rest durin' daylight tomorrow."

"Might shock you to hear me say it, Charlie," Mark said, "but I think you got everythin' figured out. You did a fine job on all this, and I don't mind sayin' it right out. Buildin' the special pung and all."

"Hope it works," Charlie said. "Now I think all that's left is to practice loadin' the log every now and then so we get just as good as we can at it. Blue sky like this means it'll cool off enough at night to freeze things up and give the horses easy haulin'. Good sugarin' weather is good weather for stealin' cannons at night. Now let's get back on our way. We can stop again in a couple hours to practice with the log and then practice some more when we stop for the night."

The four men kept the pung moving for the afternoon down along the east side of the Connecticut River. When they stopped briefly at mid afternoon to practice loading the log, they did it smoothly and quickly. The rest of the afternoon they laughed and joked and flung joyous insults at one another, the happiest and the most carefree any of them had felt for months.

They stopped early for the night about four miles above Charlestown, practiced loading the log, fed the horses, built a fire, cooked a big supper, passed a jug of rum around the fire for several hours after dark, and admired the beauty of the moon and stars and of the moonlight on the snow.

"You know," George commented, "I hope tomorrow night the moonlight ain't so bright that everybody in Charlestown can see us stealin' their cannon. I hope there's a cloud or two to help us along."

"Well let's hope for it," Charlie said. "If the moon is too bright tomorrow, then we just got to be extra quick and extra quiet."

Before he crawled into his blankets to sleep on the hay in the back of the pung, Joe Reckford noticed that he couldn't see any stars to the south. He didn't say anything to the others about it; thought little about it himself. Instead he thought of how good it was to be away from his brickyard, from Annie and Sue and the twins, from the sameness of the village; to be out on an adventure instead with three men who had become his good friends. There was freshness and exhilaration and freedom to traveling and to being able to sleep right in the back of the pung in the thick, soft hay.

Joe fell asleep thinking of the steps he had practiced, one after another, of setting up the block and tackle, spreading out the rollers to where they could help the most, and hauling a log (tomorrow night a cannon!) right up onto the bed of the pung. He looked forward to the next day and night more than he could say and thought about the kind of look he might see on Old Sam Barston's face on the Fourth of July when the old man realized that the town of Barston did indeed have a cannon to celebrate the day.

XVIII

Mark Hosmer awoke before first light, a habit with him since his boyhood years. His father had always insisted on having Mark up before dawn either to attend to farm chores or else to be in the woods and chopping trees just as early as he could see to work. On his wood-cutting days if he'd had to stumble around in the dark to find the work site and wait there until he could see well enough to chop, his father was well pleased, for it meant he wouldn't waste any of the daylight. Mark remembered well his boyhood labors and for years now had religiously avoided work in the early morning, and often much further into the day. However, his habit of rising before dawn persisted.

The snoring of the other three men in the pung kept Mark from getting back to sleep on this particular day when there was no need to rise early. He lay on his back and stared, trying to penetrate the blankness.

No stars and a lot warmer than when we went to bed. Awful damp, but it ain't rainin', so it must be mist. We prob'ly should of rigged the canvas over the top of the pung last night.

Mark stared and waited and thought. Twice short chokes of laughter escaped from him, interrupting the snoring of his friends, but failing to awaken them. The time passed slowly as he waited for dawn, but finally objects began to emerge from the vagueness. When he could see the men beside him, Mark eased out from beneath his blankets and descended the ramp to get a fire going. Afterwards he sat by the flames to chase away the chill of the mist and waited for the other men to get up. Before long he heard them talking. Then Charlie raised his voice to make himself heard beyond the side of the pung.

"Some folks can't do even a simple thing like gettin' a fire goin' without wakin' up half the world. Ever notice that?"

"Breakfast ready yet, Mark?" George's voice rang out.

"Was when it was time for you to get up," Mark shouted back. "But you boys slept so long I was afraid it'd rot, so I ate it."

The voices in the pung returned to indiscernible murmurs, broken by occasional laughter. Eventually Joe came out and knelt by the fire. Charlie and George followed him from the pung, yawning and stretching.

"Well, George," Joe said. "You was the one hopin' for a cloud or two so the moon won't be too bright tonight. Looks like you got only one cloud, but it's pretty good size."

"Ha!" Charlie said. "Just spring mist from warm air on the snow. Valley fog. Burn right off. Sun'll show through middle of the mornin'. I'm guessin' it'll be just as nice as yesterday, but a little warmer."

"We don't want it too warm," Mark said. "Don't want to wind up carryin' the pung — not with a cannon on it we don't."

"Oh don't worry about that," Charlie said. "We're fine. A week or so this warm and the packed roads might start to loosen up too much, but the ground's froze hard now, and we ain't got a thing to worry about. Takes quite a stretch of spring weather to wreck a hard-packed winter road so's you can't use it. We'll just set back today and enjoy the sun when it burns through and get rested up for grabbin' our cannon tonight.

"Now I don't s'pose I'd mind eatin' some breakfast. Then we'll head down through Charlestown so's you three can have a look at our cannon, and after that we'll go find a place to wait out the day."

The four men moved slowly as they got breakfast, shoved hay and blankets over to the side of the pung so they could load the log back in, banked hot coals in their two buckets of ashes, and fed the horses. The men were more subdued than they'd been the previous day. Each of them from time to time would gaze up at the sky, trying for a glimpse of the sun burning through the mist. However, there was no sign of the sun. If anything, the sky seemed to be growing darker.

Finally they harnessed the horses and got the pung moving again. As they approached Charlestown village, Charlie unfolded their canvas pung cover and wrapped himself in it as he stood on hay in one of the forward corners of the pung box. At both of the toll gates before they got to the village Charlie ducked his head under the canvas and waited until the pung was moving again and the other men told him it was safe. He ducked out of sight too whenever they passed anyone on the road. In the village itself he stayed under the canvas so that there wouldn't be even a small chance that anyone he did business with in Charlestown might see him.

"There's a yellow house on the left that we'll come to after a little," Charlie said from under the canvas. "Got a white door on it. Then maybe fifteen or twenty rods beyond it our cannon's settin' over on the left a little ways off the road. Won't harm things if you swing the pung right over by it, I shouldn't think, but don't stop. Keep the horses goin' so we don't draw any notice. Then go south 'til we find a good place to stop for the day. If you find one in the first mile past the cannon, that means we don't have to pay a toll further on."

"Another toll house!" George said. "Don't they never stop takin' tolls?"

"No, they don't," Charlie said. "There's even another beyond that one — four in all just for Charlestown."

"Pirates and thieves," Joe said.

"There's ways around some of the toll houses," Charlie said, "but when the toll takers learn how folks are gettin' by, they do their best to fix it so they can't."

"How about the toll gates tonight? What do we . . ."

"Oh, they only run the Charlestown tolls durin' the day," Charlie said. "At night they leave the gates up, and folks don't have to pay. I think they leave the gates up Sundays, too, for people goin' to church, but I ain't sure about that."

"Hey Charlie. Got any more room under there?" George asked. "It's rainin'."

"Oh couldn't be," Charlie said.

"Well, then the sun's wringin' out the mist while it's burnin' through, and it only looks like rain," George said.

"And feels like rain," Mark said.

"Just a sprinkle then. A clearin' shower. Won't last. Won't melt you away. Stay up there so's you can have a good look at our cannon."

George mumbled something that Charlie couldn't hear. He did hear, however, the light patter of what sounded like sleet falling on the canvas.

Joe announced a yellow house on the left. Charlie popped his head out from under the canvas, spat a stream of tobacco juice out to the side, spat the tobacco after it, and glanced at the house.

"That's the one," Charlie said as he ducked back under the canvas to escape the rain, which seemed to be falling harder. He heard George, Joe, and Mark speak occasionally, but the sound of the rain on the canvas kept him from understanding any of their words. It didn't seem as if they were speaking to him anyway. Charlie settled down onto the hay and wondered just how long the rain might last.

A few minutes later Charlie's canvas cover was rudely jerked away. He drew a breath to protest, but scarcely got a start before Mark and George were scrambling in beside him.

"Make room! Make room!" Mark shouted.

Mark stepped on one of Charlie's feet; George on the other. The three of them thrashed at the canvas together until it covered them.

"She's comin' down pretty good now," George said.

"Just valley fog," Mark said. "Burn right off."

"Oh shut up," Charlie said. "You see the cannon all right?"

"Sure did," George said. "It's ours. Nobody else has got to it yet."

"How'd it look?" Charlie asked.

"Wet," Mark said. "Heavy. Looks like a lot of weight to it, but with rollers and the block and tackle I'm pretty sure we can get it aboard and take it home. Long as the ring bolt don't break, we'll be all right."

"That bolt won't break," George said. "I know the feller that made it, and it ain't goin' to break. How you s'pose Joe's doin' in the rain?"

"Wet," Mark said. "Heavy. And prob'ly cleaner 'n he was a few minutes back. It is really comin' down now. Move over a little, will you? It's runnin' off the canvas and down my leg. Move enough so's I can get my leg over on this side of the log."

The three trod on one another trying to rearrange their legs. Just as they thought they were settled, the rain started falling in a downpour. The pung stopped, and Joe Reckford was suddenly clawing at the canvas. They held it tightly to them.

"Let me under!" Joe shouted as he continued to pull at the canvas. He managed to bunch it up enough so that Charlie's face and Mark's face were out in the rain. He dropped down against Mark, and eight hands pulled and wrestled with the canvas, alternately leaving each man out in the rain and giving him reason to pull at the canvas harder than the others.

"Hold it!" Charlie shouted. "This ain't workin' out." The tugging continued. "Hold it, I said!"

"We'll hold it when you're the one out in the rain," Joe said.

"Now wait!" Charlie shouted anew. "Here. Let's get the canvas rigged over the whole pung box the way it's s'posed to be. Then we'll all be out of the rain. Somebody go out and spread it and tie the corners. Who's wettest?"

"Who's driest?" Joe said. "Let's don't get the wettest one any wetter 'n he already is!"

"Well, are we goin' to argue over this 'til we're all just soakin' wet?" George said.

"I might," Joe said. "I ain't got all that much to lose."

"Which is why you should be the one to go out," Charlie said. "Besides, the rain's easin' up a little now."

"Well, I don't want to be drippin' wet," Joe said. "Just wet is good enough. Why should I get drippin' wet when one of you can get just wet the way I am now? You go, George, and I'll tell Annie how good you was."

"She knows that already, and she's only my sister, so what difference will that make?" George said. "You do it, Joe, and I'll tell her how good you was."

"Why do I want to get any wetter 'n I . . ."

"Don't do it then, and I'll tell her how bad you . . ."

"Shut up!" Mark shouted. "Everybody get out and grab a corner! Just do it!"

Mark's momentum with a corner of the canvas he gripped with both hands started to spread the canvas out. When he tripped on the log underfoot and tried to catch himself, he further loosened the grips of the others on the canvas. With considerable grumbling they mounted the sides of the pung and shouted conflicting directions at one another for straightening the twisted canvas, finally succeeded in spreading it flat, and each began tying down a corner.

Charlie shouted in disgust, being the first to realize that they'd need the ramp down before they could get underneath the canvas. He called out directions to George, who was at the other rear corner of the pung. The two men pulled the pins which held the ramp upright. It swung down on its hinges with a crash and sent slush flying. They finished tying their corners. Charlie shouted at George to move over to the loose tie-line on his side at the middle, and the two men stretched the canvas taut between them and over the wooden sides of the pung and tied it down. George dropped to the ground, ran around to the ramp, and all but dove inside to get out of the rain. Charlie hunched his shoulders and walked around front to look at the horses and was still swearing when he, as the last man in, finally got under the canvas. Puddling water in the tarp was already causing it to hang down in the middle.

"Find the slats under the hay, and get 'em up," Charlie said. "Otherwise we won't have any headroom."

The slats were sought and found; pushed up against the canvas and laid across the walls of the pung from side to side. In place of one large puddle in the tarp, there were now the beginnings of seven smaller ones.

"Too bad you didn't steam some ash bows to hold up the canvas the way I told you," George said. "Then the rain 'd run right off."

"Oh hush up," Charlie said. "Didn't have the time and didn't have anythin' that long to steam 'em in. Just like it's too bad you didn't make us a cannon at your forge and spare us this trip down here."

Suddenly Mark and Joe both groaned loudly and sank to their knees as each held a hand to his forehead. At the same moment they had stooped quickly for a jug of rum and had cracked heads. Charlie pulled their hands away, clucked and shook his head at how quickly the swellings had come up, and was drinking from the jug before either of them.

Five minutes later the four men sat on the wet hay near the back of the pung with their backs up against the sides, their legs sharply elevated by the mound of hay they'd spread over the log. They sat a pair to a side with a jug between each pair as they stared out in silence at raindrops drumming onto the ramp and obscuring the sodden landscape beyond. The rain rose to a steady downpour with occasional gusts of wind, chasing the men a yard further back from the ramp. They kept squirming in attempts to avoid the drips coming through the canvas. Joe Reckford shattered the silence with a tremendous sneeze, then rubbed his forearm across his nose.

"I wish it was a lot warmer or a lot colder," Joe said.

"How's that?" George said

"If it was a lot colder, this 'd all be snow, and I wouldn't be wet. If it was a lot warmer, I wouldn't be so cold."

"If it was a lot warmer, all our packed roadbed 'd disappear, and we'd wind up stuck in the mud with my pung," Charlie said.

"That's goin' to happen anyways," Mark said. "The rain's plenty warm enough, and it's fallin' just like a waterfall. It don't take long like that for it to melt away all the snow."

"Oh it'll be fine," Charlie said. "Good winter roads for a week yet. See if they ain't. You don't know what you're talkin' about."

"Oh I don't know what I'm talkin' about, is it?" Mark said. "Well I'm glad to get set straight on that. And I'm glad that it's almost the middle of the mornin' 'cause that's when this valley fog is goin' to burn right off and the sun's goin' to shine through, and that's when it's goin' to turn out just as nice as it was yesterday. Yes sir. I'm glad to learn that I'm the one that don't know what I'm talkin' about."

"Daft," Charlie said. "Must of banged your head too hard."

"I just wish you'd of made some ash bows or hired it done, Charlie," George said. "I thought I was doin' you a favor savin' you money when I talked you out of havin' me make you some iron ones. Be nicer havin' it just rain outside and not in here too. Or maybe if you'd of used new canvas instead of this leaky old stuff . . ."

"It is new canvas," Charlie said, "and it don't leak."

"That so?" George said, holding his palms upward. "Sure you didn't bang your head?"

"It don't leak from holes, I mean," Charlie said.

"Well, that's nice," George said. "And just how come we're gettin' all this rain in here if it ain't leakin'? That canvas is only borrowin' the rain before it sends it on down to us, and it ain't borrowin' it for very long. Course it leaks from holes."

"Oh you ignorant cuss," Charlie said. "Any canvas with water fallin' on it 'll shed the water just so long as you don't touch it underneath. But soon as you do, it draws the water through right where you touched it."

"That is just about the silliest notion I ever heard," George said. "I didn't see you bang your head, but you sure must of."

Charlie got to his feet and grabbed the canvas over George's head with both hands, rubbing and squeezing it. Then he sat back down, took the corncob stopple out of the jug at his side, and drank. All the men's eyes were on the spot where he had grabbed the canvas. Before long, drops of water beaded there, and a little later a regular dribble commenced.

"Now ain't that interestin'?" George said as he rose and grabbed the canvas over Charlie's head.

"Oh stop it, you two!" Joe said. "It ain't like we need any more water in here than we got already."

Before long the men were pulling out their blankets from wherever they'd been flung that morning and were wrapping them around their shoulders. Each of the men had two blankets; all of them at least damp and several wet enough to be wrung out. The men found that none of the hay in the pung could be called dry; that water was puddled in many places underneath the hay on the tight pung bed, which seemed impermeable. When Mark suggested that they turn the pung upside down so that the water would drain out through the canvas and no more could come in through the floor, no one laughed. Charlie told him to shut up.

The rain settled into a steady, warm drizzle. About mid day Charlie, who'd been waiting for the rain to ease off a little, decided that it wasn't going to. He swore brutally obscene oaths at the world in general, wore his blankets over his shoulders as he went out into the rain, and soon had the pung moving south along the road — the lowered ramp smoothing the slush it was dragged over better than any mason's trowel could have. In a few minutes he pulled off the road a short distance and stopped. George and Joe and Mark expected him to come right back in and join them, but he stayed out in the rain for a full quarter hour. When at last he did walk back up the ramp, he didn't say a word; grabbed a double armload of hay and went back out into the rain with it. He came back three more times for hay, leaving the whole back half of the pung bed bare to its boards and puddles except for part of the log and a few swatches of hay caught beneath it. At last he came in and sat down with a look of bitter disgust on his face. He wrung out his blankets and put them back around his shoulders; reached for the jug and drank.

"Horses got enough water, Charlie?" Mark asked.

"They do," Charlie said without a shred of humor in his voice.

Charlie rose to his feet, though just an instant earlier he had sat down. He pushed at the rounded canvas intrusions hanging down between the slats overhead and one after another drained the water from them over the sides of the pung or into the canvas between the adjacent slats. The final section he drained splashed in a torrent onto the ramp.

"Horses are cold," Charlie said. "I was thinkin' that we might rig 'em a shelter. We could maybe take this canvas that ain't keepin' us all that dry to begin with and . . ."

"Oh no," Mark said, "We ain't givin' up this canvas for the horses. They still got their winter coats on, and they can stand to get wet a lot better 'n I can."

"You think you know anythin' about horses?" Charlie said. "Anythin' at all?"

"Don't claim to and don't have to," Mark said. "I do claim to know somethin' about how cold I am now though, and I am claimin' that if I don't have at least this canvas over me, that I'm either goin' to die or else wish that I could. Fix your horses some way if you have to, but don't do it with the canvas."

Joe and George likewise refused to consider any idea that meant giving up the canvas. George complained that the canvas was starting to leak where Charlie had pushed up at it to drain it. Charlie ignored him and continued to wheedle and complain about the horses' misery out in the rain; the probability of sickness. Finally he succeeded in talking them into each giving up a blanket. With their three blankets and one of his own Charlie went back out into the rain to cover the horses. While he was out, he realized that the slush he was wading in went right down to the dirt.

"Never thought everythin' 'd melt so quick," he muttered. "Hope the ice on the road is still good."

Charlie looked at the runners of the pung before he got out of the rain. They lay so deep in the slush that he set to worrying about how much longer a pung might be able to travel over the road north. For the first time he recognized the possibility that the pung might spend the summer in Charlestown.

Back under the canvas he kept his worries to himself as the four men huddled together under their remaining blankets. The men said little; tried to sleep in an effort to pass the time. Warm rain continued to batter the canvas and leaked through in so many places that nearly everything underneath it was wet. Occasional gusts of wind blew in under the canvas with enough strength to raise it and dump out some of the accumulated rainwater. The men shivered in their sodden clothes and wet blankets and waited for the end of the longest afternoon in any of their lives. What few words they did speak to one another were subdued.

Late in the afternoon Mark asked Charlie, "Didn't you say you have plenty of oil for the lamps?"

"That's right."

"Well, let's get 'em lit. We can get enough warmth from 'em at least to warm our hands."

"Good idea," Charlie said.

One of the buckets held nothing but a slurry of ashes. The other was damp on top, but still held live coals. While Charlie went out to get the lanterns from the box under his driver's seat, the others coaxed out a flame by blowing on damp straw set on a live coal. Before long they had Charlie's two oil lamps going. Their hands hovered by the flames.

"That is better," George said. "And the light makes it a lot easier for me to see how miserable I am. Good idea, Mark. Just keep the lamps out from under the drips."

"Serious now, Charlie," Joe said. "There enough snow left for the pung to go on?"

"I don't know that, Joe," Charlie said slowly. "The warm rain took a lot, and it's still meltin' what's left. The pung's restin' right on the ground now. I ain't been over to the road to see how that is. It'll last longer on account of bein' packed down all winter, but prob'ly not too much longer. If it's just warm air on it, a winter road 'll last quite a spell, but warm rain 'll ruin it pretty quick."

"So . . ." Mark said. "Old Sam? The cannon?"

"It don't look good," Charlie said. "The horses might manage pullin' just the pung on a slush cover like now, but the weight of the cannon 'd likely drive the runners right down into the mud and stick us good. And the rain's makin' everythin' worse all the time. No sir. I don't think we're goin' home with Old Sam's cannon. If the rain keeps up, I know we ain't."

"Pah!" Joe said. "Bad luck for us. If the rain 'd held off just another day, we'd have the cannon for sure."

"Well, what do we do?" George asked.

"Wait, I guess," Charlie said. "I don't know any better 'n you boys. The blankets make a big difference for the horses so I think they'll be all right. I got 'em tied over under a big hemlock where they won't get rained on quite so hard. I'll give 'em extra hay, and that should keep 'em warm enough for the night. But I do know we ain't goin' anyplace tonight with the rain comin' down so hard. Driver 'd get soakin' wet and cold, and besides a rain this hard 'd prob'ly put the lamps right out."

"What if the horses can't pull the pung?" Mark asked.

"We'll dump out the log in the mornin' and see how they do," Charlie said. "If they can't pull the pung then, I guess we'll have to leave it down here. If I can find a good place to store it, I'll get it back next winter. Otherwise I'll have to see about hirin' a flatboat to take it up to Barston Falls after the spring run-off. A wagon ain't any better 'n a pung if the rain keeps on 'cause the wheels 'll stick in the mud, so there's no sense tryin' to borrow or hire one. I guess with four horses and four of us, we might as well just ride 'em home. Be a long ride I know. They're awful wide horses. Never was meant to ride. But we'll decide all that in the mornin'."

The men turned their hands by the lamps and rubbed the dampness from them. They breathed in the warm fumes of rancid whale oil and slouched down, silent and thoughtful.

"Too bad for Old Sam," George said. "I wanted . . . we all wanted to get him a cannon in the worst way. And you, Charlie — special pung, all your plans, everythin' that was set down perfect if it hadn't of been for the rain. You prob'ly couldn't of planned it out any better."

"Never thought I'd hear you say anythin' like that," Charlie said.

"Well enjoy whatever you thought you heard me say 'cause I won't say it again," George said.

For the rest of the afternoon the men carried hay out to the horses, cut head holes into their blankets so they could wear them, ate most of their remaining food, drank occasionally from their jugs, and waited. The wind began to rise at dusk, and it seemed colder. Charlie took more hay out to the horses.

After dark they decided they would keep the oil lamps going for the night. None of them expected to get much sleep, for all the blankets they had brought with them were now being worn either by the horses or themselves; all of them wet to one degree or another. They mounded up the remaining hay in the back of the pung to keep themselves off the wet floor and then sat in pairs back-to-back for warmth. They dozed, muttered in low voices about the wetness and the cold, cursed their bad luck with the weather, and spoke of warm stoves and dry beds at home. Time scarcely moved.

XIX

Joe Reckford sat in the pung, hugged his arms more tightly to his chest, and rubbed the stubble of his beard slowly back and forth against the damp blanket over his head. His eyes burned with fatigue. His hands were cold; his legs and feet very cold. He felt warm only where his back pressed against George's back. He thought of Annie and of their warm bed at home; wondered how much more misery he would have to endure before he got back to her again.

Joe straightened a little from his slouch so that more of his back pressed against George. He yawned, rubbed his face with his hands, found the hole he'd cut in his blanket, and poked his head outside. The air was cold on his face; his breath a thick cloud in the light of the two oil lamps. Yes. It was either a good deal colder, or else his body had ceased trying to warm itself since he'd sat back-to-back with George. Well, he hated to give up keeping at least his back warm, but he had to go out. He couldn't put it off any longer. He nudged George.

"Hey George. Wake up."

George mumbled and sat up straighter.

"Wake up, George. Don't fall over. I got to go out and pee. You awake?"

George sighed and then said, "All right."

Joe eased to his feet, feeling the stiffness in his muscles. He stretched and yawned anew and then started toward the ramp. Suddenly his feet flew out from under him, and he crashed down onto the bed of the pung, banging his arm against the log as he fell. He lay flat, groaning loudly.

"Can't you pee a little quieter, Joe?" George said.

Joe sat up, still groaning, and cupped his left elbow in his hand. The sound of the crash and Joe's persistent groans roused both Mark and Charlie.

"What happened?" Mark said.

"I fell down," Joe said. "Slipped on the floor."

"Well next time fall someplace you don't make so much noise," Charlie said, as he crawled over to where Joe sat. He paid no attention to Joe, however; felt the bed of the pung instead.

"Ice!" Charlie said. "I thought I felt too cold for just bein' wet."

Charlie grabbed one of the lanterns.

"Watch out, Joe. Don't move," Charlie said. He walked by Joe and then eased down the ramp. He was gone scarcely half a minute before he hurried back in.

"Snowin' hard as can be out," he said. "I know you clowns don't care a whit about the horses, but they got to be exercised right now to warm 'em up. And you know what the best exercise for 'em is?"

"Don't know and don't care," Mark said.

"It's to have 'em haul a pung with a cannon in it all the way back up to Barston Falls! So heave your carcasses up, and let's get to work! Old Sam Barston's waitin' for his cannon!"

Joe bounded to his feet, slipping and staggering a little and still holding his left elbow.

"You sure?" Joe said.

"I'm sure," Charlie said. "Everythin's froze up solid, and we're back in the cannon-stealin' business. Only we need Mark to chop the runners free from the ice. So get a move on. Mark, get your axe. Joe, go with him so you can hold the lantern. George, you come with me and help harness the horses. Let's go."

Charlie and George disappeared down the ramp with an oil lamp. Joe flexed and kneaded the elbow he'd banged and waited for Mark, who was rummaging around under the remaining hay. Joe's hand brushed at the rounded beads of ice on the underside of the canvas. When he pushed up with his fist, the canvas creaked with stiffness and held the new form he'd given it.

"Got it," Mark said as he turned with the lamp in one hand and the axe in the other. "Come on, and watch out for the ice on the ramp."

*****

The four men crowded one another severely on the seat as the pung went up the main street of Charlestown village. Joe and George sat on the outside, each with an oil lantern in hand. The twin orbs of light illuminated the men, the horses, the front half of the pung, and the falling snow.

"Don't push!" George hissed. "Set still, or you'll shove me right over the side!"

"Was right up here someplace," Charlie said.

As the horses kept the pung moving up the road, the men strained to see out to the limits of the lamplight. The snow wasn't falling nearly as heavily as it had been before.

"No sir," Charlie whispered. "Missed it. That stone post's at the turnoff to the yellow house. We got to turn around."

Charlie swung the horses in a broad arc in the unusually wide road of Charlestown village and went back the way they had come. The snow had nearly stopped by the time Charlie told them to look hard for the cannon. The horses kept on, scarcely making a sound as they dragged the pung through the light accumulation of newly fallen snow.

"There it is over there," Charlie whispered. "That long hump. Now all we got to do is keep quiet and grab the thing. Remember the practice we took with the block and tackle and the rollers, and do everythin' just the same as with the log."

"Oh, we forgot," Mark said. "We should of dumped out the log and got the block and tackle all ready. Should of done that before we set out."

"Yes," Charlie said. "We should of. Guess we wasn't thinkin' too sharp. Well, never mind. Won't take but a minute. Won't make a bit of difference long as we're quiet about it. Just don't go shoutin' back and forth. We don't want to wake anybody up. Take your time and whisper. Better for us to be slow and quiet than quick and noisy."

"Better to be quick and quiet than slow and noisy," Mark whispered.

"And watch out to see if anybody gets a light goin' in any of the houses," Charlie said. "Keep the lanterns down pretty low, and if we do see somebody with a light, let's get the lanterns back inside the pung and maybe hold a blanket over 'em 'til it's clear for us again."

Charlie guided the horses skillfully in a wide loop so that the pung stopped with its back end perhaps twenty yards from the cannon.

"Out you go boys," Charlie whispered. "I'm goin' to back her in, but the runners ain't flared up at the back much, so you hop out and give the horses a hand — just lift a little at the very back, and push on the side if you have to so we go back straight. One of you hold the lamps, and the other two lift. Shouldn't take much of a lift. And then stop me when I'm close enough, and get the ramp down quick. Mark's right for once. Quick and quiet is better 'n slow and noisy. Now down you go."

Charlie guided the horses to back in their traces. He twisted around in his seat in an attempt to see the other three men, but the box of the pung blocked his view. A few feet at a time he backed the pung toward the cannon. Finally George, carrying two lanterns, hurried back to stop him.

"That's good," George said.

"All right," Charlie whispered. "Get the ramp down, and dump out the log and anythin' else that's in the way. I'll be right there."

Charlie leaned way over and felt around under the seat in the dark for gloves to save his hands when he hauled on the block and tackle rope. Later he realized it was lucky he didn't find them easily, for if he had, he would have been back with the other men and might never have stopped the pung.

Charlie remembered the sequence clearly for the rest of his life; remembered it as if it had just happened the day before: standing halfway up out of the seat as he held the reins and worked his hands into the gloves; the chill air on his face; the stillness shattered abruptly by the sharp shout of "Catch it!"; the tremendous, whacking crash and its echoes from surrounding houses; the surge of the frightened horses which sent him spinning back to smash his head against the box of the pung; the scrambling to straighten the reins in the dark, bring the runaway horses under control, and keep the trickle of blood out of his eyes; the wild ride in the dark with the horses pulling in panic against his attempts to stop them — the horses pulling until their fright had worn itself out. He remembered finally stopping the pung slightly crossways on the wide, straight, main road of Charlestown and looking at the barely discernible glow of lanternlight way back in the distance. In later years he always swore that if he'd had a lantern with him then, he would have left the three men where they were and gone back to Barston Falls alone (particularly when he was swearing it in the presence of those three men).

Charlie eased the horses back toward the lantern light; eventually stopped beside George Ballard, who was still carrying both lanterns.

"Did it happen what I think happened?" Charlie said. "What in the devil kind of . . ."

"Hush, Charlie," George said. "You don't want to wake up folks in the village."

"Of all the miserable . . ."

"Shut up, Charlie," Mark said as he and Joe came up to flank George. "The ramp fell right down on the cannon, is all. If you hadn't of backed it up too far, that never would of happened. Now swing it around again to where you was before, but don't back up 'til we tell you 'cause the ramp's already down and we got to hold it up when you back. And stop when we tell you this time, can't you? Now we got to be quick about this."

Charlie fumed, more than ready to launch into a tirade against the three men, but they had disappeared quickly back towards the cannon. His muttered curses gave him no satisfaction because no one was there to hear them. In frustration he set the horses into motion and again maneuvered the pung into position. George reappeared to tell him when to back towards the cannon; stopped him when he had backed enough.

"George," Charlie said, as George started to go to the back of the pung.

"What?"

"I'm holdin' the horses here so they don't bolt. You three dump out the log and work the block and tackle and the rollers by yourselves. And be quick about it."

Charlie sat holding the reins, worked one of his gloves off, and felt the wound on his forehead. *Sore and swollen. More of a bruise than a cut though. Cut ain't very big at all, and I guess the bleedin' is over. It does sting.* He waited.

Charlie noted with a start the appearance of a light in the house over on the far side of the road, but George returned and quickly took his attention away from it.

"Can't work the block and tackle, Charlie," George said. "We're havin' a terrible time with it."

"Oh, what next?" Charlie said in disgust. "I'll have a look. Hold the horses up front, and keep hold of 'em, George. Leave me that light to take behind so we don't have it blazin' right out here, and you keep an eye on that light over across."

Charlie waited until he was certain George had hold of the harness for the lead horses. Then he climbed down from the seat, picked the lantern up from where George had set it down, and carried it around to the back. The log was out on the snow right next to the cannon. Joe and Mark were crouched down on the floor of the pung.

"What's wrong?" Charlie asked, easing up the icy ramp.

"It's the miserable block and tackle," Joe said. "Useless."

"How come?" Charlie asked.

"Rope got all sogged in the rain," Mark said. "Now it's froze so that it don't hardly bend. The rope's twisted every which way, and we can't use it. Won't slide through the blocks."

"Got to."

"Won't."

"Well, we'll see. Joe, you go and tie the short rope to the cannon — solid around the carriage mount stubs and with a wrap and snub by the muzzle so she'll drag straight. Do it now so we at least got that done. And tie a good loop in the free end so it's all set for the block hook when we get the rope squared away. And when that's done, get the rollers right where we can use 'em."

Joe took a lantern outside. Charlie grabbed at the rope strung through the two blocks and tried to flex it into suppleness. His mutterings grew louder and louder. Mark stood beside him holding a lantern.

"Useless," Mark said. "Rope's stiff as a fencepost. Most of it anyways."

"Miserable, worthless excuse for a . . ."

The clatter of the flung blocks against the pung wall and then down onto the floor drowned out a pair of Charlie's words, but he had more: "Go to all the trouble to set this rig up, and it comes down to absolutely nothin'! Comes down to a miserable rope that's froze! Nothin'!"

Mark set down the lantern he was holding and picked up the axe. He straightened the rope between the two blocks as best he could and then with two swings of the axe cut out a length of it.

"Now what are you doin' that for?" Charlie asked.

"Block and tackle won't work," Mark said. "There ain't nothin' left for us but to haul it up here by hand, and we need a rope long enough for us to get a good grip on."

"That cannon? You're crazy. Way too heavy."

"Well, likely you're right, Charlie, but we won't know for sure 'til we try. It's the last chance we got."

Joe came in for the rollers, noticed the cut rope and the disarray of the blocks, and asked why Charlie and Mark were making so much noise.

"We got to pull like oxen right now, Joe," Mark said. "We can't use the block and tackle, so we got to haul the cannon in here without it. Hope you're feelin' strong enough to give her a try."

"If that's all that's left for us, let's do it," Joe said. "I just tried heavin' on the rope and couldn't budge it, but that was only me. Sure we'll try."

Mark limbered one end of the cut rope enough to knot it to the short rope Joe had tied around the cannon. Joe and Charlie spaced several rollers between the ramp of the pung and the stone blocks the cannon rested on. Then the three men took their grips on the rope.

"Ready?" Mark said. "One, two, three, heave!"

The cannon didn't budge.

"There ain't any footin'," Joe said. "My feet just slip around. I can't get strength into the pull. It's just too slick."

"Ashes!" Mark said. "From the buckets for the coals. Scatter 'em here where we're steppin'."

Mark seized one of the ash buckets, but discovered that the ashes were frozen into it in a solid block. He flung it off into the darkness. With the second bucket he was more successful. As he began scattering ashes with live coals onto the snow between the cannon and the ramp, Charlie grabbed his arm and stopped him.

"Don't get any on the ramp," he said. "Leave it slick with the glaze ice. That'll help the cannon if we get it up that far. But do put some inside the pung where the floor's so slick in there. No! Just put 'em on the sides, and leave it icy in the middle. Quick! Quick!"

The ashes were scattered quickly by the light of the lamps; the empty bucket flung aside. In the snow the live coals hissed and died. On the bed of the pung, however, many of the coals continued to glow — an eerie sight as the men glanced in. Without further delay Joe and Mark and Charlie set themselves for a pull and heaved against the rope as hard as they could. There was no perceptible movement of the cannon.

"I think we moved her a little," Joe said. "We got to get George and . . ."

As if in anticipation of Joe's thoughts, George appeared beside the ramp.

"There's two lights on now in that one house!" he said, "and one in the house next to it!"

"Well, all right," Charlie said. "We got to get out of here right away. Have to chance it with the horses boltin' and give the cannon one more try with all four of us."

"What's . . ." George began.

"Shut up and grab the rope," Charlie said. "We got to pull it up by hand or else go home without.

"All right. Listen to me. This is the last chance we got. Get a good grip on the rope, and brace your feet, and pull harder 'n you ever pulled before in your life! Pull harder 'n you can, and if you can't do that any more, then push! One chance, the last one we got. Two of you down there and one of you up in the pung with me."

"All right," Joe murmured. "This is for Old Sam. This is Old Sam Barston's cannon, and it's goin' home to him. For Old Sam. Please, for Old Sam."

"Yes sir," Mark said. "Breathe deep boys, and get set. For Old Sam Barston."

Joe and George went to stand next to the cannon. They set their feet against one of the rocks the cannon rested on and started drawing deep breaths. Mark flexed his hands and then grabbed the rope. He braced a foot against a vertical timber on the wall of the pung right by the ramp. Charlie was further back with just the flat bed of the pung for his footing.

"Get set, boys," Charlie said, speaking in a whisper which gradually rose to a shout. "For Old Sam. You're the three strongest cusses I know, and if you can't haul this cannon for him, then it can't be hauled. Get set. One, two, three, heave! Heave! Heave! Heave!"

"Old Sam! Old Sam!" George rumbled through clenched teeth as he jolted against the rope. Mark and Joe bellowed wordless roars.

The cannon barely nudged forward from its perch on the two rocks, but it kept moving. It teetered on the forward rock and then nosed down onto the rollers, skewing them out of position, but still the cannon kept moving; dropped down hard from the rocks and sank the rollers deeply into the snow. The cannon muzzle touched the ice on the ramp and started sliding upward. It paused slightly, but George and Joe grabbed the trunnions and jerked in short heaves as they shouted out together. The cannon nudged up the ramp an inch at a time, teetered at the top, and then thudded down onto the bed of the pung, stopping dead. Charlie quickly flung off his gloves, ran the rope in his hands through the ring bolt at the front end of the pung bed, and drew the line taut.

"Just a little more!" he shouted. "Heave it in! Heave it in! Heave! Heave!"

The cannon slid all the way past the ramp and came to a halt. Charlie knotted the rope tightly to the ring bolt.

"Flop up the ramp, and let's get out of here!" Charlie shouted.

He ran past the others, crashed down hard on the icy ramp, sprang to his feet immediately, and stormed out of sight back towards the front of the pung. He lurched and banged and groped his way up onto the seat, in a panic of motion until the reins were back in his hands. Lights were on in four houses that he could see, and even as he watched, one of the house doors opened, and a lantern began easing tentatively toward the pung.

"Quick! Quick! Quick!" he shouted, his voice drowning out the clattering in the back of the pung.

A second lantern came out of a different doorway. The lanterns converged and began approaching the pung more quickly. Just then Joe, George, and Mark ascended the seat in a confusion of arms and legs and hooting and laughter. The two lanterns they carried swung wildly. Charlie endured the crashing momentum of the three bodies as best he could and urged the horses forward. As the pung moved south at an increasing pace, Charlie bellowed.

"Springfield! Springfield! Springfield!"

The other three took up the cry. They shouted and whooped and laughed and quickly left the village behind.

Charlie didn't slacken the pace until he was several miles out of Charlestown. When he did, it was to hand the reins to George and ask the men to give him room enough to rummage under the seat. He fussed there for what seemed a considerable amount of time, but at last came up with something in his hand.

"What's that?" Joe asked.

"What I been savin' for three months for us for after we got the cannon," Charlie said. "Seegars, boys! Give me that lantern."

Charlie leaned into the lantern and lighted a cigar, puffed the end of it into a glow, and handed a handful of cigars to the others. Though all three of them smoked pipes, none of them had used cigars before.

"You got to bite the tip off or you won't get the smoke to draw through," Charlie said. "Light 'em up, boys, and let's celebrate. Old Sam is goin' to be mighty surprised and proud of you next Fourth of July."

"We got it," George said. He spat out the tip of his cigar, lighted it from the lantern, and puffed smoke out toward the stars emerging from the breaking clouds. "And when the Charlestown boys get done lookin' for their cannon in Springfield, Vermont, and can't find it and then go down to Springfield, Massachusetts, and can't find it and then maybe go all the way over to Springfield, New Hampshire, where do you s'pose they'll look next? That was good thinkin', Charlie."

"Yes sir," Mark said. "Not too bad, Charlie. Your scrawny old carcass was handy for us too."

"Ha! You ornery cusses!" Charlie chortled. "Didn't even need the block and tackle with the three of you along! Just wait 'til Old Sam hears his cannon this Fourth of July! But remember what we said. We got to keep our mouths shut.

The one thing left that can trip us up is if somebody starts blabbin' just like Steve Danforth. When we get home, we can't start mouthin' away about how good we was grabbin' this cannon. That's the only chance left I can see that might keep Old Sam Barston from hearin' his cannon-thunder for the Fourth of July. So we all got to shut up about this 'til the Fourth of July. Not one word! Not to nobody! You understand?"

"That's right," George said.

"Sure," Joe said.

"Yes," Mark said. "If we need to brag about this, let's get together and brag. Think about Old Sam if you catch yourself wantin' to tell somebody else. We got to keep this a secret. We ain't to say a word."

"I'll see about gettin' us a keg or two of powder," Charlie said, "so we got somethin' to make a little noise with on the Fourth of July. Leave that up to me. I'll get it someplace away when I'm out with a freight wagon this spring. I think pung season might be just about over. What do you boys think?"

"I think it's just valley fog," George said. "Burn off by the middle of the mornin'. Now hold up that lantern, and let me see whose face is smashed up the worst. Yes sir. Looks like you, Charlie."

The men were well up the Vermont side of the river, and it was almost dawn before their euphoria had worn off, they had finished their last cigar, they had begun to fret about how crowded they were on the seat, and each had pledged silently to himself not to have cigars or rum or whiskey for a long time.

A thorough chill had settled into them by the time the sun rose and had begun to draw forth a more or less regular chorus of coughs and sneezes. They had talked about stopping long enough to build a big fire to warm themselves, to dry out their clothes, and to cook the last of their food, but suddenly there was no need. Somehow the remaining hay in the back of the pung had caught fire. In spite of the four men's efforts to fight the fire, it had blazed up so quickly and so hot that even the sodden pung covering had burned down to a few charred scraps of canvas. The heat had popped the corncob stoppers out of the remaining jugs of whiskey, and all their liquor had burned up along with just about everything else that had been in the back of the pung. They managed to make headway against the fire only after all the hay had burned. The cannon didn't seem affected a bit. The pung bore the fire scars all the years Charlie Porter used it. He told several different stories to explain why the wood happened to be charred.

The men were warmer and drier after they had fought the pung fire, but this relative comfort, such as it was, didn't last long. Soon enough, as they were continuing back up to Barston Falls with the cannon for Old Sam, they were sneezing and shivering and coughing again.

All of them took to their sickbeds after they arrived home. It was nearly two weeks before they were healthy again.

XX

Old Sam finished sticking a worm onto his hook. Then, twisting in the chair set down beside the brook, he looked back over his shoulder and watched until Elizabeth — Jared's wife — had driven the wagon out of sight.

Awful silly notion. Dump me off in the forenoon with no more 'n about two hours 'til dinner. Then expect me to set in a chair and fish the same pool for two hours. That woman surely don't know fishin'.

Old Sam gave a final glance down towards where the wagon had disappeared. Satisfied, he put his bait firkin into his creel, slung the creel over his shoulder, and got up out of the chair. With his pole in one hand and his cane in the other, he started making his way up alongside the brook toward the good fishing spots above. Soon he was panting hard from the effort.

*****

An hour and a half later Old Sam returned carrying his bait firkin in the same hand with his pole. He was glad for the anomaly of the brookside chair; let his cane drop and clatter into stillness as he sat down. He set the pole and the firkin onto the ground, eased the strap of the creel over his head, and set the creel down carefully.

Well, I am tired, but here's another day's fishin' that didn't kill me. I surely can't get around the way I used to, but it is better than lyin' in the graveyard or in my bed and not doin' a blessed thing.

Old Sam felt twinges in his chest. His hands eased up to cover his heart, and he braced himself for an onslaught of pain. As his breathing slowed, however, the twinges disappeared. He rested his hands on his lap.

Got to happen sometime. Might be any day. But I never expected to set foot out of the house this year, and I did, and I never expected to catch another trout, and here it is May and I'm catchin' 'em every single day. Any one of 'em could be the last trout I ever catch.

"June," he said aloud. "If I can make it through June, then I can make it to the Fourth of July."

Old Sam reached into his pocket and picked out the last of the half dozen nubs of tobacco he had cut from a plug at home, not wanting to carry the whole plug and see if his teeth were still good enough to bite off a lump. He put it into his mouth, stretched out his legs, and began to think about the Fourth of July.

Seth and Jared's attempts to get a cannon for the village had been pathetic, but Old Sam had been disgusted with them for so long that he really hadn't expected them to get one. Why, they were going about getting a cannon just as if they expected some peddler to drive into the village one day with a wagon full of cannons and ask if anybody wanted to buy one! Worthless. Mark Hosmer, however, had been the real disappointment. From what he'd said at town meeting, Old Sam had expected that Mark himself would lead a raid over to Wheelock Village and grab the cannon there for the town. Unfortunately, the talk at town meeting had just been hot air: nothing to it at all. Mark, when Old Sam had talked to him in recent weeks, had seemed embarrassed that he'd ever opened his mouth at town meeting. Some of the other men Old Sam had thought might have some gumption weren't doing any more than Jared and Seth. They kept saying that they hoped Barston Falls could find a cannon somewhere, but they, too, seemed to be waiting for that peddler with his wagonload of cannons.

If I was thirty years younger, I know for a fact that we'd have Wheelock Village's cannon over here right now. Twenty years younger and we'd have it — maybe even ten years. We need a cannon in the village — got to have one. But there don't seem to be even one man with stuffin' enough in him to take Wheelock Village's cannon. It surely ain't like the old days. Why, I could name you twenty men in the graveyard that would of been over across the river in half a shake to grab that cannon. Maybe it is true that all the good men either died off or went west.

"Have I got to do this all by myself?" Old Sam said.

And just how would you go about gettin' that cannon all by yourself, Old Sam Barston? You're prob'ly just about strong enough to look at it and listen to it get shot off. How would you steal that cannon all by yourself?

Old Sam spat toward the water and shook his head.

"Ha!" he said. "You ain't even strong enough to spit all the way to the water. Think you can get a cannon, do you?"

Old Sam turned toward the sound of the approaching horse and wagon. It was Sue, as he had expected, but she was earlier than she was most days. He smiled to see that she was wearing a dress again and wore a blue ribbon in her hair. It had now been more than a week since he'd seen her in her old britches. She got down from the wagon, tied the horse, and carried a basket over towards Old Sam.

"How's my best girl today?" Old Sam called out. "I thought I saw the prettiest a girl in Barston could be yesterday when you had that green ribbon, but I guess I was wrong — now that I see you with the blue one."

"Oh you and your teasin', Grampy Sam," Sue said. "I thought I might bring your dinner to you today instead of bringin' you to your dinner."

"That's fine," Old Sam said. "Long as you still set where

I can see you while I eat. What good is food without a pretty girl to watch?"

Sue set her basket down and lifted the lid on Old Sam's creel. The creel was half full of trout.

"Well, you done it again," Sue said. "I don't see how anybody can catch so many trout."

"First thing is you put a worm on your hook and put it in the water," Old Sam said. "Anybody that does that every day is bound to get some fish. If you want somethin', you got to try for it. Course these ain't but shadows of the big trout we used to catch in the old days, but still they're good to eat. There was quite a pile of 'em here in this pool today — must of sneaked in last night. Anybody could of caught 'em. But there's still one in here that no matter how hard I try, I can't catch him. Pulls the bait off the hook every time. I just ain't good enough to catch him. Course you might be. Why don't you give it a try while I'm eatin'? I don't think you can catch him, but you might. I know I can't."

Old Sam took the tobacco from his mouth and put it into his pocket before he helped himself to food in Sue's basket. Then he settled back in the chair, chewing slowly and watching Sue fish. When Sue concentrated on fishing, she had a way of sticking her tongue out the side of her mouth that he thought was funny.

Hang it all. Now even Sue's gettin' old on me. Seems like yesterday she wasn't but thirteen years old, and now she's a grown woman. And seems like the day before yesterday Annie was her age, and now Annie's got two sons. And I remember the day Annie was born just like it was last week or last month. Where do the years go?

Sue let out a short yelp as she launched a trout into an arc over her head. She dropped Old Sam's pole and scurried back to pounce on the fish as it thrashed on the ground.

"It is embarrassin' to me, Sue, to see how good you are at fishin'. That one just drove me crazy for must of been a half an hour, and I couldn't catch it, but it seems you no more 'n just get the hook in the water, and you got him. Yes, it is embarrassin', but at least I know for a fact that's the last trout in this pool."

Old Sam feigned open-mouthed astonishment as Sue caught two more trout and added them to the ones already in the creel. Then she sat on the ground beside him and ate.

"Tell me about the old days," Sue said. "I want to know if you really could catch big trout then any day, the way everybody claims."

"Oh yes," Old Sam said. "Every brook was full of 'em. Whatever ones the otters and minks and eagles and fish hawks couldn't catch used to die of old age. Oh, you should of seen it in the early days, Sue. Huge trout in the brooks and huge salmon in the river. And such trees that you can't even imagine 'em. Why, you could go end to end in the town of Barston on a clear day and scarcely ever see the sun on account of how thick the old trees grew. I tell you none of us back then could guess what the valley would grow to here in 1826, and it just ain't as good as it was. Everybody's so crowded together now, and so much of the old woods are cleared for sheep pasture that it don't seem like there's any place to get away to these days the way there used to be. Everythin's just too opened up, and seems like there's way too much noise all the time anyplace you turn. It wasn't like that at all in the old days. Course then, at the beginnin', we wanted more neighbors. Fact we used to get desperate lonely just to see somebody that wasn't in our family. But even so, sometimes now I'd give about any-thin' to be back in those times again.

"And it's awful hard to get old. I used to have so much fun when I was young, and I thought it would never end. Back then I used to be pretty proud of how strong I was.

And I was big too. I can't remember that I ever met a man stronger than me. I used to love the loggin' and the river drivin', and it was wonderful to work year after year buildin' up this town from what was only a wilderness before. And the best part was to be young and have a wife and a family and to think that all my work was for them. Would of been too, but my children for some reason or another didn't stick to the valley and all headed out to the west. Now I don't even know for sure how many grandchildren I got or if there might be any great-grandchildren yet.

"I guess I might of been a little younger 'n you are now when our family moved onto the land and started clearin' it. Come up from Connecticut. What year was you born, Sue?"

"Eighteen-hundred-and-aught-nine."

"Well, I s'pose I can cipher that close enough," Old Sam said. "When I was your age, I never thought I'd get old, but here I am. You're young now, Sue, and you're meant to enjoy it. But never forget how fast the years go and how much of a sin it is to waste any of 'em. When you get to be my age — think of that, Sue, 'cause you will — it'll be around eighteen-hundred-and-ninety. Seems like a long time off, but it'll come. If you live to be 'specially old, you might make it all the way to nineteen-hundred. When I was young, I couldn't imagine the valley the way it is now, and I guess it'll be the same for you. I expect that by the year nineteen-hundred, sheep 'll cover just about every inch of ground and that all the houses and barns 'll either be on ledges or else on docks over the river and ponds so they won't take up valuable pastureland. But I guess it's for you to wait and see how it turns out.

"Now I s'pose all my blabbin' away has let you eat up the rest of the food."

"No, Grampy Sam. There's still plenty, but I do need to get back and help Annie."

"I guess Amos and Aaron are keepin' the both of you busy from the sounds of it. Well, we'll go when you want. I won't eat any more. Had enough already. You can use these trout today, can't you? Only right for you to take 'em since you caught half of 'em anyways."

"I only caught the three," Sue said. "But sure we'll eat 'em. Now, you got to stop at home today? Or can we go right down to the warehouse?"

"Go straight down, I guess. No reason to stop at home any day 'cept to eat dinner with you, and here you've brought it out to me today."

They left the chair where it was and left Old Sam's pole leaning up against its usual tree; put the firkin, cane, and creel into the back of the wagon. Then they headed down along the road by Tannery Brook towards the village.

Old Sam was quiet on the way down. Sue thought he seemed more tired than on the days when she took him to his own home and fed him dinner there. Perhaps it had tired him more to eat by the brook. Well, for the next few days at least she'd take him to his home for dinner before she took him into the village. Old Sam stayed quiet until the wagon rattled across the planking of the bridge over the canal.

"Made it through another day of fishin' I guess, Sue. Some day I might not. I've said it before, and likely I'll say it again: if you come out to get me some day and find me dead, you remember the times I told you that's just the way I wanted to die — out fishin'. You open my creel and see what I caught for my last trout, and then you go and tell Tom or Seth or Jared that I'm gone. And you remember that I was happy when I died."

"Yes," Sue said. "Just like you said before."

"That's right. Don't forget."

Sue took the wagon down to the lower warehouse, at the foot of the canal. Jared came over to the wagon and handed Old Sam his usual mug of rum before Old Sam even had a chance to get down from the wagon. Jared admired the trout for the short time it took Old Sam to drink the rum. Then he helped Old Sam down from the wagon, handed him his cane, and walked beside him into the warehouse. Old Sam lay down on the bed in the back corner, where for the past month he'd been taking his afternoon naps, and pulled the blanket up to his neck.

"See you after your rest, Grampy Sam," Jared said.

Old Sam nodded and closed his eyes.

Oh, that's just right. Fishin' and food and rum and then a nap and then friends to talk to this afternoon. Yes. That's just right if any one of these days turns out to be my last one.

XXI

As he rocked in the chair with the sun warm on his face and gazed out over the big eddy of the Connecticut below the falls, Old Sam smiled to himself.

"Now this really ain't too bad," he said.

At the far end of the dock he watched Benjie, Foss, Tom, and a fourth boy he didn't know as they plodded through the very tedious labor of loading a flatboat with lumber. Back and forth they moved between the flatboat and a mountain of stacked boards up beside the warehouse. Each trip down they carried one or two boards, took them to the piles of same-length boards slowly rising on the flatboat, stacked them neatly, paused, and then went back for more. The only variation in the work came when a layer in one of the stacks was completed and the boys had to put down stickers to rest the next layer on. Old Sam laughed, knowing that when he'd been in his prime he could have loaded the lumber faster by himself than the four boys could working together. In his prime, too, he would have made it into some sort of game; never would have drudged through the work as the boys were doing. He tried in vain to remember what he'd been like at sixteen or seventeen, the age of these boys; if he'd been as skinny or as slow. Well, no matter. Likely Jared wasn't paying them any more than they were worth.

Old Sam yawned, still feeling drugged from his nap. It would be nice later on to have someone to talk with, but for the time being he was content simply to sit in the sun and gaze at the river. The Connecticut had been an important part of his life, and he savored the luxury of being able now, in his final days, to think back over all those years.

Jared came out briefly to hand Old Sam his rum and his telescope. He checked on the boys and then went back to work inside the warehouse. As Old Sam drank, he noticed a flatboat way down the Connecticut slowly working its way up the river. Through the old brass telescope he could see men poling along the sides of its deck. As the flatboat covered the last of the distance to where the bay widened out, it stayed well over by the west bank. It slowed perceptibly right there at the neck, where Old Sam knew the current was strongest, but before long the polemen had heaved the flatboat free from the grip of the current and had gained the eddy. Then all the poles came up, and the men rode the eddy around towards where Old Sam was sitting.

Company after all. Wonder where these boys are from and where they're headed.

As the flatboat neared the dock in the swing of the eddy, the steersman leaned hard against the tiller, and the polemen got back to work. Old Sam noticed that the flatboat wasn't carrying any cargo and that the men weren't very skilled with the poles. They took quite a while to get the flatboat over against the dock, near where he was sitting. Two of the polemen jumped out onto the dock — in a panic, Old Sam thought, to tie up before the boat could get away. The steersman stepped onto the dock right by Old Sam.

"Well, old sir, nice day for it," the steersman said. "Tell me how I can get a job like yours."

"Got to be born handsome to start with," Old Sam said, "and then you got to earn it. Takes eighty years or so. Where are you boys from?"

"Charlestown. Down the river. Ever hear of it?"

"I have, and it's heard of me, but not for quite a few years. I used to run masts and sawlogs down the river when I was younger and, if you can believe it, even handsomer than I am now. And my pa was down there at Fort No. 4 for a while back in the French and Injun days. Later on he was one of Rogers' Rangers — and two of my brothers too. Yes sir. I have heard of Charlestown, and it's a fine, fine town."

"Well thank you for sayin' it."

"Easy to say it," Old Sam said. "You stoppin' here, or headed further up?"

"Goin' up a little further. Up to Wheelock. How far's that?"

"Oh you're practically there now. Some of it's right across the river, but it's a couple miles more above the canal before you get to where there's many folks. Now why on earth would anybody want to go to Wheelock?"

"Got some business there."

"East Wheelock? Haulin' sheep from the Robertsons over in East Wheelock?"

"No. Right in Wheelock Village, I guess — wherever that is."

"Well, Wheelock Village is in the west part of the old Wheelock township — the part that's still called just Wheelock. The whole east half of the old township they now call East Wheelock. What kind of business?"

"Oh . . . that ain't exactly arranged yet. Maybe you can help us. Can you tell me about Wheelock Village and maybe some of the people there? Nobody in particular — just the people in general."

"A few good folks there," Old Sam said. "Very few. Rest of 'em are a bunch of pirates."

"How come?"

"Oh, they never help us any. Didn't so much as lift a hand when Barston Falls burned down years ago, and we surely could of used help then. And now they tell us they're in favor of a bridge across the Connecticut, long as we're willin' to pay for it. They won't give a penny towards it, or timbers, or work — nothin'."

"Not the best of neighbors then."

"No they ain't," Old Sam said. "They just ain't neighborly: not to us; not even to folks in their own town."

"Can you tell me more about 'em?"

"Course I can," Old Sam said. "I can fill your ears with stories about 'em if you got the time. You in a hurry?"

"Well, not a big hurry. I'd like to hear . . ."

"Fine," Old Sam interrupted. "Give a yell when you need to get away. Prob'ly the story of the Robertsons and of how East Wheelock got split off of Wheelock is the best way to tell you about 'em. Ever hear that story?"

"Can't say I have."

"Well, the first settlement in the township was all in the west half. Folks let the east half pretty much alone on account of it was so rugged. Hackmatack Ridge runs prob'ly half the length of town with Catamount Ridge and Mount Wheelock north of it stretchin' right up to the Piermont line and with another hump south of it so that to get from the east half of the town to the west half you practically got to go all the way down to the Orford line. That's the only good way on account of the hills. Catamounts and bears and wolves stayed in there for quite a spell after they left everyplace else, and they might be there yet if the Robertsons hadn't of hunted 'em so hard.

"A few folks tried settlin' in the east half of town, but they all failed and moved away. William Robertson was the first to settle there and stay. He came down from Canada to Ryegate just before the Revolution. Then he moved over to Wheelock. He was young and poor and wanted land, and he wanted to be left alone, so he wound up back over there by what we now call Robertson's Pond. Got the land from my brother Israel. It wasn't 'til after the Revolution was over that anybody else to speak of settled in the east half of town. There was a number of poor families after cheap land. They'd make a start and fail and move away. Nobody stuck for long except for William Robertson.

"Might of been twenty families over there at one time or another and all of 'em so poor and their land so worthless that they didn't pay much in taxes to the town. All the same, they had a right to a district schoolhouse and schoolteacher and to a kept-up road and kept-up bridges like the rest of the town. But the Wheelock selectmen, with plenty of help from other folks in town, decided that they just wouldn't go to much expense for that poor half of town; said they wanted folks over there to pull their own weight and not be a drag on everybody else. Folks in the east half of town that wanted to work off their taxes doin' roadwork generally found themselves workin' on the roads in the west half of town. It got bad. The poor folks in the east half had to petition with warrant items at town meetin' just to try and have their one road kept up and have a school and a schoolteacher of their own. But the folks in the west half of the town voted 'em down just about every time. There was a lot of name callin' back and forth that went on for a few years. Then, finally, somebody got the idea to make separate towns out of the east half and the west half. Not many voted against the idea at town meetin', so they got together a committee and worked up a petition to the General Court so they could split off East Wheelock, and just about everybody in the rest of Wheelock said 'good riddance' when the General Court approved the split. East Wheelock lost more people that moved away. Then William Robertson's brother came over from Scotland and took over one of the failed farms. Both of the brothers had big families and put their children to work clearin' land, killin' varmints, and raisin' sheep. They've made somethin' of East Wheelock. But no thanks to the folks in Wheelock Village or any place else in Wheelock.

"So there you have it. The folks in Wheelock Village as good as kicked the poor folks out of their town and made 'em struggle along by themselves. They should of been helpin' 'em like good neighbors, but they turned their backs on' em instead. That's the kind of folks that live in Wheelock Village. Me, I don't like 'em much. Sometimes I think it's a mistake even to have a ferry between the two towns."

"Sounds like I might be on the right track then. Not all that nice a bunch of folks up there."

"It ain't."

"Well, let me put it to you plain. Think they'd go and steal a cannon on us? Think they're the kind of folks that'd do that?"

"Steal a cannon? Whatever do you mean?"

"Here, let me show you," the man said as he fumbled with the button on a pocket of his shirt. "We got our own cannon down in Charlestown — or used to. It was a nice thing to make a little noise with every now and then when we felt like it, and I guess everybody in town was proud to have it. Then a while back somebody went and stole it on us. Some thought it might be folks in Springfield, but it didn't seem like anybody there knew a thing about it. Then here . . ." He pulled a piece of paper from his pocket and began unfolding it. "Last week our town clerk got this letter. We didn't know whether to believe it or not, but then we figured we should. Here, read it if you want."

Old Sam took the paper, smoothed it, and held it out as far as he could.

"See what she says," Old Sam began. His lips moved as he read the scrawled message to himself:

> If you ain't got your canon, try looking in
> Wheelock Village New Hamshire for it.
>
> A frend.

"Stealin' a cannon!" Old Sam said. "What 'll those Wheelock Village folks be up to next?"

"Think there's anythin' to it? We come up special to get it back."

"Well . . . I . . . kind of hard to steal a cannon — so big and all."

"S'pose they could of? They're the kind of folks that might, ain't they?"

"Could of, I s'pose," Old Sam said.

"Wouldn't know where they might keep somethin' like that, would you?"

"No sir. No idea."

"Well thanks anyways. From what you say about the folks up there, my bet is that they done it, and we're aimin' to get our cannon back. Now, can you tell me who I need to see about gettin' up through the canal?"

"See Jared," Old Sam said. "Up in the warehouse someplace. Just go up and give a shout."

The man nodded and went up towards the warehouse.

The devil if I'll let 'em do that. They can't steal Wheelock Village's cannon. That cannon belongs to us to steal. If Wheelock Village went out and stole another one, then that's ours to steal too. No sir. I can't let these Charlestown boys go up there and steal our cannon.

Old Sam glanced out at the polemen. Every single one of them was lying down on the flatboat with his eyes closed. Old Sam got to his feet thinking that sixty years earlier it had been the same: polemen with a little time free during their workday always seemed to grab some sleep. He stumped along the dock with his cane, passed the flatboat with the sleeping polemen, and went all the way to the end of the dock, where the boys were loading the lumber. He caught Benjie just as the boy was headed up towards the lumber pile for another load.

"What is it, Grampy Sam?"

"I need you this afternoon, Benjie. I hate to drag you away from the fun of loadin' lumber, but I need you to drive a wagon for me. Why don't you run home and harness up Brownie and bring the wagon back on down here? I'll square it with your pa. You just run on home, and get back here quick as you can. I'm in a hurry for it, you know, so don't dawdle. I don't expect it'll take more 'n a few hours."

Benjie never explained to the other three boys where he was going; left in a hurry for home. Old Sam didn't explain to them either. He headed back to his rocking chair. Shortly after he sat down again, Jared and the man from Charlestown came out of the warehouse. They walked down to the dock, next to Old Sam. Jared shouted to the boys to come to him. The Charlestown man went to awaken the polemen.

"Now where's Benjie off to?" Jared said.

"He's off doin' an errand for me," Old Sam said. "You charge me for his time, Jared. Hear?"

"He goin' to be gone long?"

"Couple hours maybe," Old Sam said.

"Pah, Grampy Sam. I was goin' to send two of the boys up through with the flatboat and have two of 'em stay here and keep loadin' lumber. Guess now I'll send three boys up. That 'll kill the lumber loadin' for a little, but I guess I won't hear the boys complain about that."

Old Sam watched the three boys as Jared talked to them; saw how grateful they were to leave off loading lumber. As the polemen were roused to their feet, two of the boys hopped aboard the flatboat to ride up into the lower lock. The third boy went to get the team to pull the flatboat up through the canal. By the time Benjie returned with the horse and wagon, the flatboat was already up in the middle lock.

*****

Benjie and Old Sam sat in the wagon as Tom Goldthwait, the ferryman, heaved against the rope anchored to an elm on the west side of the Connecticut and to a huge silver maple on the east side. Thus he moved the ferry. The rope was tied higher in the elm to allow for river traffic to pass underneath. The ferry moved slowly across the Connecticut.

"He's got big arms, Grampy Sam," Benjie said. "Biggest ones I ever saw."

"You would too, Benjie, if you did this for a livin'. You want to see how strong Tom is, you watch him when we get more 'n half way across and he's pullin' the ferry up against the current. That's what takes the strength."

Benjie watched Tom as the ferry gained the east side of the Connecticut. Old Sam paid the passage fee, and Benjie set Brownie into motion again off the end of the ferry and up along the road towards Wheelock Village.

"Course I had a ferry back about there myself when I was young," Old Sam said. "Ever hear about that?"

"No, Grampy Sam."

"It was when it was just one family of Barstons and one family of Parkers in the whole of Barston and not much but blazed trees for a path. It was a raft I made, I guess out of pine logs, and it wasn't much. I poled it across, and I don't s'pose I made as many as a half a dozen crossings before I lost it."

"What happened?"

"Oh, I was comin' across with Eli Parker. We'd got some grain ground up in North Haverhill and was comin' back with the flour, and I talked Eli into savin' the cost of ferry passage at Stone's up above by comin' down to my own ferry. Problem was I had a fir pole with dry rot in it, and the thing broke out in the middle of the river. Nothin' to do then but swim for it if we didn't want to ride over the falls. Our flour got good and wet, and the raft kept right on down the river. Never saw a scrap of it again. Ma made about twenty loaves of bread that night, and that's all we ate for days. My brothers sure let me hear about that again and again over the years. It put me right out of the ferry business, I can tell you that. Except when we used to go huntin' for moose and bears over by Mount Wheelock we had another raft, but that was just for huntin', and the rafts never lasted from year to year. Oh it was rugged livin' then, Benjie, but I wouldn't of traded those years for anythin'."

"I wish I could of lived back then," Benjie said. "I know the fishin' and huntin' was a lot better 'n it is now."

"Oh, it was. A lot of things seemed better. Funny thing is that we never appreciated it enough at the time. Seems like I spent my first thirty years in Barston tryin' to cut trees and build houses and get more people to come to the town and seems like I been spendin' the rest of the time wishin' there wasn't so many people or so much cleared land and that we hadn't shot off so many animals and caught so many big fish. Sometime there in the middle there must of been a year or two when I should of been happy with the way things set, but I'll be hanged if I can remember it. The best part of the early years, Benjie, was bein' young and strong and havin' plenty of things to use my strength on. It was a good life, and I surely have loved this valley, but my turn is just about done now, and it's close to time to turn it over to somebody else. You'll have your turn now, Benjie. You're growin' right into the best years of your life here. Main thing you got to decide is if you'll spend the time near the Connecticut River or if the itch to go west will claim you the way it claimed every one of my children. Abby, I s'pose might of stayed if she'd of had her way, but she went and married a man that couldn't bear the thought of stayin' in the valley; couldn't wait to leave it behind and get out west to see if there was any truth to the stories about the farmland out there."

"I want to stay in the valley, I guess," Benjie said. "If you get back away from the river, there's still wild land in the hills — up north anyways. Me and Foss and Tom want to have our own flatboat too — have fun goin' up and down the river and get rich at the same time."

"Well, you're the one that's got to decide how to spend your life, Benjie. Just make sure you don't waste any of the years. They go so quick you won't believe it. Get out and live just as hard as you can so that, when you're an old man, you can look back and be glad you did just exactly what you wanted with your life."

The wagon kept on through the May countryside; through the warmth and clean greenery of new growth. Sheep grazed behind the fences on both sides of the road: ewes with newly born lambs. The youngest of the lambs waggled long tails as they nursed. The tails of the others had already been docked and tarred. In the fields fenced off from the sheep the grass was long enough to stir with the breeze. Old Sam spoke of the lambing and shearing and the first haying that would all be completed within the next month and told Benjie he could be glad at this season of the year that his last name didn't happen to be Robertson. Finally the wagon rattled over the bridge at Robertson's Brook, near where it flowed into the Connecticut, and entered Wheelock Village.

"Built it here on account of the mill power, such as it is," Old Sam said. "Robertson's Brook here and Moose Brook, of course, up at the north side of the village."

"Oh, I know all that, Grampy Sam."

"Good. Well, pull over there in front of Barlowe's store, and we'll go in."

The sign on the store claimed Chester Barlowe as its proprietor, though in fact his son, Danny, had been running the store for the past several years. Half a dozen men dangled their legs over the edge of the porch and dark-

ened the first dust of the season with their tobacco spit. They all stared at Benjie and Old Sam as the two got down from the wagon — stares sullenly acknowledging their presence, but without the slightest nod of greeting. The two escaped the stares as they opened the door and went inside the store.

"Shut the door or you'll let in all the flies!" a voice shouted at them.

Benjie shut the door. A fat, red-faced man waddled towards them.

"What do you want?" he demanded.

"Danny," Old Sam said. "Ain't you?"

"I am. Who are you?"

"Sam Barston. From across. I know your pa."

"You want to buy somethin'?"

"Not today. What I need to tell you is there's a gang of men from Charlestown that'll be here pretty quick with a flatboat. They're aimin' to steal your cannon. Thought I'd warn you."

"That so?"

"It is."

"How do you know that?" Danny Barlowe asked.

"Heard 'em talkin' at the canal just before they headed up through. Best do somethin' pretty quick."

"I guess I'll decide that," Danny said.

"Suit yourself," Old Sam said. He nodded his head towards Benjie to get the boy started back out through the door. "Thought I'd just tell you."

"Well, I'll think about it."

"You do that," Old Sam said as he followed Benjie out the door. Old Sam left the door open.

As Old Sam was climbing back up into the wagon seat with a boost from Benjie, one of the sitting men spoke loudly to the others.

"Must be hell to be that old. Glad I ain't."

"Must be hell to be that young," another added.

"Must be hell to have a horse that ugly," a third said.

A long and loud belch from a fourth man set all of them laughing. Old Sam whispered for Benjie to get the wagon started.

"See you in church on Sunday, Reverend," Old Sam called over his shoulder. "I hope your voice recovers in time."

"Don't hurry back, old man!" someone shouted. "Have a nice funeral!"

Old Sam kept Benjie from turning around and heading back toward Barston Falls. Instead he directed him to go to the north end of the village.

"I s'pose if I was older, I would of got in a fight back there," Benjie said. "Folks here ain't very nice."

"Never have been," said Old Sam. "That fat man's pa never was much politer than his boy, but I could of counted on him to do somethin' when I went and warned him like that. So we'll go up and tell Cy Clifford. He's a selectman for Wheelock, and I know I can count on him a lot more than on those boys back there."

Just before they got to the bridge over Moose Brook, Old Sam had Benjie turn to the right and follow a road up along the brook for about a quarter mile. Then he made him stop at a particular house. A gray-haired man of about fifty came out the door.

"Hello, Cy," Old Sam said.

"Well, Sam. Sam Barston. I thought it was you, but I couldn't be sure. Heard you was quite sick."

"I ain't well. You can see I lost a lot of weight, but I ain't quite dead yet. I found out somethin' down below and thought maybe I needed to come up and warn you. I told the fat feller down at the store, but I think he might of forgot about it already."

"About what? What's the warnin'?" Cy Clifford asked.

"Some boys from Charlestown goin' up through the canal. I heard 'em talkin', and they mean to steal your cannon. Thought I might warn you so you could hide it or get ready for 'em. I figured if I didn't come up and warn you, tomorrow mornin' you might wake up and find out you don't have your cannon anymore."

"Well, I will do somethin' about it and right now," Cy said. "And if nobody down at the store thanked you, I'll thank you right now, Sam Barston. And who's this with you?"

"Benjie. Jared's oldest boy."

"Thanks to both of you then."

"You're welcome," Old Sam said. "I thought I'd be a good neighbor. That's all. Now we need to get back home, and I s'pose you need to run around and tell a few folks. The Charlestown boys might be here only an hour or so from now."

"Thank you, Sam. Yes, I do need to run around right away. Thanks specially for comin' up when you ain't feelin' all that good."

Old Sam nodded. Cy Clifford hurried inside his house.

"Well, at least he's polite," Benjie said.

"Cy's the one man that keeps me from hatin' the whole town," Old Sam said.

"That was nice of you to warn him too," Benjie said.

"Yes. It was very nice of me, wasn't it? Now let's get on home, Benjie. You got some lumber to stack."

XXII

Seth Barston ambled in to see his brother in the small room inside the lower warehouse. Jared was slouched back in a chair with his arms folded.

"How's everythin'?" Seth asked.

"Slow today. How 're things up above?"

"Prob'ly slower," Seth said. "Grampy Sam feelin' all right?"

"Didn't you see him on your way in?"

"He's asleep," Seth said. "Still breathin'. I checked."

"He's fine," Jared said. "He just fished too long this mornin', and he's still recoverin' from when he had Benjie take him out for that long ride in the wagon. In fact he's so much better from the way he was last winter that he's gettin' to be a pain in the neck. He keeps after me to get a cannon, but I guess we'll just let him stew. It's good to see him worked up about somethin' again."

"Yes it is," Seth said. "Speakin' of cannons, we got another letter from Sewall today."

"What's he got to say?"

"Oh, I wrote him that folks in the village want him back teachin' here next winter, but I guess it's too early for him to decide about that. And he answered about when it might be good for us to visit Dartmouth College if we got any business down around there."

"I know there's some old iron down there by the Tontine that might count as business some day," Jared said.

"Well, Sewall claims that all of Dartmouth College goes on vacation for two and a half weeks startin' on the Thursday before the last Wednesday in May. So that makes it 'til about the middle of June that they're away. He said to come before or after that."

"So we go down and grab the iron cannon when everybody's gone?" Jared said.

"No. Got to be later. Got to be towards the end of June, when the moon's better for us. We got to take the cannon at night, and we don't want any lanterns burnin' when we do."

"But all the Dartmouth boys 'll be there then," Jared said. "How 're you plannin' to get it away from them? They'll be after us like hornets."

"Oh, we'll smoke the hornets just like they was bees," Seth said. "Anyways we need the Dartmouth boys there to haul the cannon for us."

"And how exactly are you goin' to get 'em to do that?"

"Don't you worry, Jared. I got everythin' planned. All you got to do is about the middle of June free yourself for a week so's we can go get the iron cannon. We'll take one of our flatboats down to Hanover — just the two of us; see a few things on the way down and a few more on the way back and have a good time. And when we come home, we'll be carryin' the cannon on board with us, and the Dartmouth boys 'll be tryin' to decide where their cannon went."

"Just like that?" Jared said. "Tell me how in the world you think we can . . ."

"No. You just come along and be surprised. I planned all this out for a long time, and there ain't a thing I missed. Everythin' is perfect. Trust me. Just be ready to go about the middle of June."

"I still wish you'd tell me how . . ."

"No," Seth said. "Not 'til we get down to Hanover. And don't you let on to a soul we're even thinkin' about grabbin' a cannon. We got to keep this quiet."

"I'm already keepin' one quiet, Seth, case you forgot. But I was thinkin' if Grampy Sam don't live to the Fourth of July it might be a comfort to him right now to know what we're plannin'. He ain't too pleased with us that we won't run over and grab Wheelock Village's cannon."

"Oh let him fuss. That and the fishin' are prob'ly keepin' him alive. And the more he bothers us about not gettin' a cannon, the better the joke on him 'll be when he hears us shoot off two cannons on the Fourth of July. I hope that'll make him feel good and foolish."

"Right now it ain't two cannons," Jared said. "It ain't but about half a cannon if that little brass one gets counted fair. You sure you got everythin' planned out right to get the big iron cannon? Don't want me to think over your plan with you at all?"

"No. Come along and be surprised," Seth said. "Stealin' that little brass one was just for practice. Now I'm ready for somethin' bigger. There is one thing you might help me think about though."

"What's that, Seth?"

"Grabbin' that Zebra. I ain't got a good way to do that yet."

*****

The four men gathered at Reckford's brickyard at dusk, the only people there.

"All right," Charlie said. "Who was it? Had to be one of you three. They said the Charlestown boys was crawlin' all over Wheelock Village lookin' for their cannon, and the only way they would of been up here in the first place is if one of you couldn't keep your mouth shut. One of you three got 'em thinkin' about this part of the valley for their cannon — and after all the trouble we took to make 'em look south for it. Could of ruined the whole thing. Who was it?"

"Guess it was me," George said. "Wrote 'em a letter, but I didn't sign any name to it. Told 'em to look in

Wheelock Village. I sent it to their town clerk from up in Haverhill Corner with a teamster that was goin' through Charlestown and told him that somebody else gave it to me to send along, so there ain't much chance they'll guess where it come from."

"But why get the Charlestown boys up here in the first place, George?" Charlie asked. "If they'd of stole Wheelock Village's cannon, then the Wheelock boys would of guessed it was us, and they would of come right over here lookin' to get it back. And they'd prob'ly keep comin' over here and pokin' around 'til they did get ours. Why stir things up when it's better not to do anythin'? That was pretty foolish."

"Maybe it was," George said. "I wasn't thinkin' about that. All I was thinkin' about was gettin' even with Wheelock Village, and I thought it'd be a good joke on 'em if they got their cannon stole. See, they owe me for some iron work — some tie braces for the rafters in their town hall to keep the roof from spreadin' on account of the buildin' wasn't put together very good to start with. I made the braces over a year ago, and every time I ask somebody over there to pay me for 'em, they just laugh. I wanted to get even."

"I think we're lucky there's no harm done," Joe said.

"I guess I don't like the Wheelock Village folks any better 'n you do, George," Mark said. "I think it'd be fine if they got their cannon stole, but Charlie's right about where they'll look first if they do lose it. Forget about Wheelock Village's cannon, and think about ours and about what we have to do if we want to still have it on the Fourth of July. No talkin' about it except to each other is what we agreed on before, you know. Maybe we need to add on to that agreement that we'll leave Wheelock Village and their cannon alone."

"All right," George said. "I'm sorry. I won't do anythin' like this again."

"Good," Charlie said. "Joe's right that there's no harm done, and maybe I'm makin' too much of it, but I just don't want to do anythin' that might make us lose that cannon after all we went through to get it. You boys do remember that little pung trip, don't you?"

Mark laughed. "I remember it, Charlie, no matter how hard I try to forget. And I think it might be the Fourth of July before I finally thaw out. I'll always remember when you threw the block and tackle against the pung wall and made all that racket and we had to haul the cannon in just by heavin' on the rope."

"Racket?" Charlie said. "The racket I remember is when you clowns let the ramp fall right on the cannon, and it sounded like you'd shot the thing off. If you think I'm lyin', you just ask the horses. They still get spooked when they even think about the three of you."

"I remember how wet and cold and miserable I got," George said. "Worst I ever felt in my life, waitin' there that night in the rain and thinkin' about ridin' a draft horse all the way back home in the mornin'. And then when we did grab the cannon and got out of there and had the Seegars — oh that was fine."

"Yes it was," Joe said. "It was awful there for a time, but then it sure was good to come home with the cannon. On the Fourth of July when we shoot it off and get to see what Old Sam Barston thinks of that, well I guess that's goin' to be the best I felt for a long time. So George, no more letters. And everybody leave Wheelock Village alone, and keep quiet about our cannon. All right?"

The men all agreed.

*****

Benjie came through the door shortly after dark and found Old Sam sitting in his rocking chair with all the windows of the room open. June bugs and moths bombarded the two lighted candles. Smoke from the open door of the stove filled the room: Old Sam's apparently effective measure to smudge biting insects into docility.

"How are things across?" Old Sam asked.

"Good," Benjie said. His wandering gaze paused here and there on large bits of dirt, bark, and dust — readily visible even by candlelight. "I'm sorry I ain't swept out for a while, Grampy Sam. I'll get to it tomorrow. I really will."

"Oh that can wait 'til you need a shovel, for all I care," Old Sam said. "Sit down for a little, Benjie. I got important things to talk to you about. A little bit of the outdoors on the floor never was worth fussin' over, no matter what some folks might of told you. Sit down, and get out of the smoke."

Benjie sat, gazing at the erratic arcs of moths in their staggered flights around the candles.

"I guess I'll say it to you plain, Benjie," Old Sam began. "You know I'll likely die one of these days, don't you? Don't you, Benjie?"

"I guess so, Grampy Sam, but you could go on for quite a while yet."

Old Sam laughed.

"Oh that's what everybody says to old men who don't have much time left. Old men die, Benjie, and they got to expect to — same as young men got to expect they'll get old some day. I know my time is about up, and that's just the natural way of the world. Anybody that is lucky enough to get born has got to die sometime.

"What I wanted to tell you, Benjie, is that I don't want to just set in this rockin' chair and turn into a hunk of old gristle and hair that happens to keep breathin'. I don't want to just rock back and forth waitin' to die. I want you to understand that. Doc Willard tells me that if I keep goin' out fishin' every day that it's goin' to kill me, and I tell him that I can't think of a better way to go — doin' somethin' that I've loved all my life. I saw too many old folks in my day, Benjie, that was actin' just like they was already dead when they still had a few years of life left in 'em, and I don't ever want to be like that. I don't want to set here in this room day after day feelin' sorry for myself and waitin' to die. I want to have some fun in the last days of my life — even in the last hour of my life — and if I die doin' somethin' that I like to do, I want you to know that's a good way to die. You understand that, boy?"

"I s'pose so, Grampy Sam."

"Main thing, Benjie, is not to feel sad when I do die. I want you to feel happy that I was havin' a pretty good time right up 'til I died, and I want you to remember me for that. Promise you will?"

"Sure I promise, Grampy Sam."

"Good boy. And if there's somethin' you can help me with so I can have a little more fun with my last days, you'll help me, won't you? Somethin' that'll be fun for you to do at the same time. I promise."

"Of course, Grampy Sam."

"Fine, 'cause there's somethin' I got in mind. There's maybe one last prank I want to pull so I can die happy. One last prank that's goin' to be good and embarrassin' to our friends over in Wheelock Village. And since I'll likely do it at night, I'll need help from you and from some of your friends that like to roam around at night."

"I ain't sure I know what you're talkin' about."

"Course not, Benjie. It's down that old ash tree, ain't it?"

"I ain't sure what you mean."

"That's how you sneak out of your room, and that's how you sneak back in after you do whatever you set out after. We left that ash there when we built the house, and I knew then that some boy might find a use for it one day. I sure would of when I was young if I'd of had a room of my own with a window right next to a tree like that and if I'd of had a place to go when I did get out. Problem was that I didn't have anythin' that I could go out and tar and feather except for maybe catamounts and wolves and bears. Course you don't know a thing about puttin' tar and feathers on anythin' now, do you?"

Old Sam laughed at Benjie's stuttering embarrassment.

"Oh don't fret, Benjie. We'll keep your tar and feather days secret. Fact is, I'm proud of havin' somebody with the last name of Barston show so much promise for his age. But you still got a few things to learn, Benjie, that I might teach you and your friends when we go out. You will go out with me, won't you? If we get caught when I take you over to Wheelock Village, I'll tell Jared and Elizabeth that I made you go with me because any number of things can happen to an old man like me wanderin' around alone at night. I got to have you come and keep an eye on me — you and some of your friends."

"All right, Grampy Sam. But when are we goin', and what exactly will we do?"

"I can't tell you yet, Benjie. I got to think about it a lot more. All I know is that we'll go, but I won't tell you more 'til I figure out just how to do what I want."

A June bug hit the wick of one of the candles hard enough to put out the flame. Benjie relit it with the other candle.

"How'd you find out about what you think you know about me and tar and feathers, Grampy Sam?"

Old Sam laughed.

"I'll tell you some night when we're over in Wheelock Village. You ask me then, Benjie."

XXIII

The flatboat drifted with the faint current down through the valley. Seth leaned on the steering oar, but whether to give the flatboat direction or to keep himself upright could only be guessed. His eyes opened into a half squint as he gazed languorously across the valley. The early summer level of the river kept him down too low for a view of the fields just beyond the riverbanks, but he saw many pastures sprawled out over the low hills, most of them holding the small, moving dots which were newly shorn ewes and their lambs. A light breeze ruffled the water, throwing constantly changing reflections of the sunlight in all directions. In spite of the breeze, Seth felt the heat.

"Hey Jared, wake up!" Seth called.

Jared stirred from where he'd been lying asleep in the sun on a pile of lumber.

"What is it? We there?"

"No, not yet. But I'm tired of workin' my fingers to the bone while you sleep. You steer for a while."

Without waiting for any response, Seth stood and walked between two barrels to the edge of the flatboat, shedding his shirt as he went. He paused long enough to drop his britches onto the deck and then hopped over the side. A moment later Jared splashed in beside him. The brothers swam a few strokes, and then each put a hand onto the edge of the deck and drifted with the boat.

"Oh, it's brutal work," Seth said. "If it wasn't for wantin' to get a big cannon for Grampy Sam so bad, I don't know as I could stand the pain."

"Hope he appreciates it," Jared said. "Hope your secret plan is more than just hot air, and we do go back home with the iron cannon."

"Don't you worry about that, Jared. You just stand back and watch, and see if things don't come out just the way I'm plannin'."

"I know that can't miss," Jared said. "Since you ain't told me a thing, all you got to do is claim that however things come out, that was part of your plan. There are two ways I'll know you're lyin' though, Seth."

"What's that?"

"Well, I know you're plannin' to get the Tontine cannon, and I hope I know you ain't plannin' to sink this boat. So if we don't get the cannon or we do sink the boat, I'll figure your plan didn't work. Those are a couple things you can't lie your way out of."

"I hope I ain't got to try," Seth said.

"How far down you figure we are now?" Jared asked.

"Well, I ain't been payin' close attention," Seth said. "Near as I can guess, though, we'll get down to Hanover a little before dark. We'll want to have the smudge goin' pretty good before we tie up for the night so's the bugs 'll have to go chew on somebody else.

"Now I s'pose we need to get back to work."

Seth pulled himself up onto the flatboat and got back into his clothes.

By the time they reached Hanover and tied up for the night, Seth and Jared had already cooked and eaten supper and had built up a fairly respectable cloud of smoke from their smudge fire in the box of sand on the deck of the flatboat. They talked for a while before they wrapped themselves in their blankets and went to sleep.

*****

At first light the next morning Seth shook his brother awake. Jared argued the hour to no avail and, under the threat of a soaking with a bucket of water, reluctantly arose. In the light, which Jared claimed was more from the moon than from the sun, they set out walking down along the riverbank. Seth carried a mysterious sack over his shoulder, refusing to tell Jared what was in it.

"Don't know why we got to get up so early," Jared complained. "At home you ain't ever out of bed much before the middle of the mornin', are you Seth?"

"There's times I been known to stay abed," Seth said. "But I always make it a habit to get up early when I'm out stealin' a cannon."

By the time the light was indisputably from the sun rather than from the moon, Seth and Jared had gotten down as far as the toll bridge between Hanover and Norwich. At such an early hour there was no one yet in the toll house, which stood next to the east end of the bridge, and the toll gate was still up. As Seth and Jared stood on the New Hampshire side of the bridge, a teamster taking advantage of the night passage without charge drove a team and wagon past them over towards Vermont. He nodded to the brothers and kept on his way.

"All right now, Jared," Seth said as he shifted the sack he was carrying from one shoulder to the other. "I need you to study the New Hampshire bank down from the bridge, but not too far from it and pick out for me the best place you can see for us to run the flatboat in and drag aboard a cannon that'll be settin' right on the bank."

"What are we goin' to drag it on with?" Jared asked.

"Our capstan, of course," Seth said. "And a ramp. Rollers if we need 'em. Crank it right aboard. But you ain't to worry about that 'til tonight. You got to pick what you think is the best place and see if I pick the same one. Let's go walk along the bank and have a close look."

"How 're you goin' to talk anybody into draggin' it right to the bank?" Jared asked as they left the bridge.

"Too many questions," Seth said. "You just watch, and when we get up to town, you just watch up there too, and don't go sayin' things that might let anybody guess what we're up to. Understand that, Jared?"

"All right."

"Just pick out the easiest place to load a cannon from."

The brothers walked down the bank a few rods more. Jared stopped.

"Right here, Seth, or maybe back a little where it's flat."

"Good," Seth said. "I vote for back there too because it'll be easier for 'em to drag a cannon to it."

"Who's goin' to drag it?" Jared asked.

"Too many questions again, Jared. You just watch, and don't plague me with 'em. Just do what I say, and things 'll come out fine. A few minutes more and we can head back to sleep as late as you want."

The brothers started walking back up along the bank. Every few yards Seth slowed his steps, looked back, and then looked forward. They were perhaps half a dozen rods north of the bridge when Seth stopped.

"This is it," Seth said. "Got a good view from the toll house. Right here is perfect."

Seth upended the sack he'd been carrying and dumped a mound of clothing onto the ground.

"All right, Jared. Get busy, and sort the clothes out quick with me. Two piles. Shoes and stockin's on the bottom. Underwear on top. Quick in case somebody comes over the bridge."

"There's . . . there's a woman's things here!"

"That's right," Seth snapped. "Two piles: one for a woman and one for a man, and make sure you get the clothes in the right piles."

"Ain't these Sarah's shoes?"

"Not any more, but she'll be happy to give 'em when she sees how good the plan works. I'm even givin' up a pair of my own shoes, even if they are fallin' apart."

"And the clothes?"

"Deacon Russell's clothesline," Seth said. "Where else would I get 'em? He's always buyin' new clothes anyways. Now stop your questions 'til we're done here and out of sight of the bridge. Hurry, Jared!"

They quickly laid out the clothes. Seth all the while kept an eye on the bridge, but no one passed over it. Just before they left the spot, Seth scuffed out the tracks the two of them had made. Then he picked up the sack and led Jared back up to the flatboat.

"Now Jared," Seth said as he dumped more wet, rotted wood onto their smudge fire, "you just forget about all your questions. We're goin' back to sleep, and when we wake up, we'll cook breakfast. Then we're headed up into town to look around for a while, visit Sewall, and have a good time. And don't let on that we ever set foot in The College before. If we both kind of hang back and keep pretty quiet, there's less chance we'll make some mistake."

"And the cannon?" Jared said.

"We'll get it aboard tonight. Just hope that the moonlight's good," Seth said. "Now hush up, and let me get some sleep."

*****

At the end of the morning the brothers paused at the top of the hill, where the road up from the bridge joined the main street of Hanover. The heart of the village lay down to their right. They glanced across at the Dartmouth Hotel and let their attention linger down the street to the right of it on the massive brick building known as the Tontine.

"Want to go down now and see if we can find where they keep the cannon?" Jared asked.

"No. That ain't in the plan," Seth said. "Fact it 'd prob'ly be better not to go look for it at all. We'll try and find Sewall at The College first off and see how he is."

They gazed at the green, which lay between them and The College, and started across it. A well-rutted cart track snaked over towards its northeast corner. To either side of that track half a dozen cows found enough grass among the rotten stumps to interest them. They were surprisingly active in their feeding, considering the heat then at the end of the morning. Seth kicked at the remains of an enormous stump.

"Boy they had some pretty good pines in here," he said. "I could lie right across this one!"

As they were admiring the stump, a bell pealed three times from the tower in The College. The brothers' attention was immediately drawn to an outpouring of boys from the middle door of The College. Then another jostling mob emerged from the door on the right; a moment later a similar group from the door on the left. The three mobs converged at the east edge of the green and then halted as a loud chant was taken up. The words were drawn out slowly.

"Freshhh-mennn! Cowwwwww reeves!"

The chanters stood with their arms crossed in exaggerated postures of impatience as the freshmen ran toward the cows. At the commencement of the chant the cows had abruptly left off cropping the grass and had begun to sidle off toward the village. The tempo of the sidling had increased to a full-fledged gallop by the time the fastest boys had caught up to the cows and, with gleeful shouts and loud whacks of their open palms on the cows' rumps, chased them off the green.

"Juniors hike!" was the next shout, but a simple repetition of individual voices rather than a chant. Another group of students separated from the original mob and with swaggering nonchalance walked toward Seth and Jared. When they were about two-thirds of the way over, they merged with the freshmen cow reeves and turned to face back toward The College. Then a ball the size of a small pumpkin flew through the air, and every Dartmouth boy on the green set himself into motion trying to kick it.

Seth and Jared were fascinated with the masses of moving Dartmouth boys as they ranged all over the field. Though the central part of the green was almost completely free of stumps, there were still quite a few on the edges. The southeast corner of the green was thick with stumps and looked swampy. Whenever the boys were after the ball over there, many of them fell down.

As Seth and Jared were watching the spirited scuffle, a man of about thirty came across the green towards them carrying a pair of books in one hand. A long kick sent the ball rolling towards his back. When he was only a few feet from Jared and Seth, he turned toward the noise of the Dartmouth boys thundering behind him. A thrashing confusion of quickly moving legs and elbows ensued among the members of the mob before another long kick sent the ball to the south with the boys after it.

"Say," Seth said. "You a teacher here?"

"Why yes," the man said. "I instruct in Latin and Greek. William Chamberlain is my name."

"Oh, we're Barstons. I'm Seth, and this here is Jared."

"Pleased to meet you, of course," Chamberlain said.

"What are the boys doin'?" Seth asked.

"It's football. The boys sport at it every day after morning recitation for perhaps a half hour before their dinners. The freshmen and juniors try to kick the ball towards The College. The sophomores and seniors endeavor to kick it away from The College. Some of them are quite skilled, and of course it's a harmless enough diversion. I'm jealous, naturally, because we never had it when I was a student here ten years ago."

"How come you didn't?" Jared asked.

"There were, I suppose, four times as many stumps then, and it simply wasn't practical. Every class in those days was supposed to extract one stump of the largest of the old trees and as many of the smaller ones as it could. All of the smaller variety have, I believe, let go their grips on the land and have been extracted, but as you can see, many of the largest yet remain even after more than half a century of their having been cut down. Virtually indestructible apparently, but one of these years none will remain to remind us of the beginnings of Dartmouth College in the wilderness."

"You know Sewall Tenney?" Jared asked. "He's a friend of ours, and we're lookin' for him."

"Oh . . . from . . . what is it? Chester?"

"That's where he's from," Seth said. "But we're from Barston Falls, where he was teachin' our village school this winter. Best teacher we had for years."

"I imagine he would be good," Chamberlain said. "There's a maturity to him, of course, and he would find it easy to maintain order."

"Sewall pretty smart?" Jared asked. "Good student?"

"Solid," Chamberlain said. "Diligent and thorough, but not the best I've had the pleasure of teaching. That honor I accord to Alpheus Crosby, who is brilliant in the classical languages."

"Where's Sewall live?" Seth asked. "We ain't been at Dartmouth College before."

"Easy question to answer," Chamberlain said. "Everyone at Dartmouth knows where Sewall lives by virtue of his being the bell-ringer this year. Number ten in The College."

"Where's that?" Seth asked.

"Oh, pardon me. Dartmouth and Hanover are so in-grained in me now from my undergraduate years, teaching at Moor's School, and now as a professor that I frequently assume a knowledge among strangers of things I simply take for granted. Pardon my clumsiness. The College is the main building there across. Number ten is on the third floor. You can get to it through the door on the left or the one on the right, and then follow the stairs up."

"Can you tell us what the other buildin's near by it are?" Jared asked.

"Easily done," Chamberlain said. "To the left of The College and closer to us is New Commons Hall, built originally to feed students in, but currently used solely as a dormitory. Beyond it is Brown Hall, a privately owned building where students rent rooms. Kimball's is next — a private home — and behind it, right on the ridge, is the building known as the Acropolis — built by Eleazar Wheelock, Junior, about forty years ago and now with rooms rented to students and others. The structure there to the right of The College and closer to us is Chapel and to the right of that is Eleazar Wheelock's mansion, now a private home. Eleazar Wheelock was the founder of Dartmouth College and of Moor's School."

"Moor's School was the one for Injuns wasn't it?" Seth asked.

"Yes. That was correct. Right there," Chamberlain said, as he gestured to a building behind them and slightly to the north. "Though now it prepares white youths as well for Dartmouth. Sewall Tenney himself prepared there."

"Two schools so close," Jared said.

"Three," Chamberlain said. "The Medical School is just a short way up College Street from The College."

"Well, much obliged for the information," Seth said.

"You're more than welcome," Chamberlain said. "Sewall may be somewhere in the mob out there, though not everyone plays at football. If you don't find him on the green, let me suggest his room. If he doesn't happen to be there now, he will be eventually, for he'll need to ring the bell. Now I need myself to run along. Very pleased to have met you, Seth and Jared."

Chamberlain nodded to the brothers and left.

"What did he say his name was?" Jared asked.

"Don't know," Seth said. "Didn't catch it. Friendly cuss, but he talks kind of funny. Don't he, Jared?"

XXIV

Sewall Tenney was eating oatmeal porridge from a small, cast-iron pot when Seth and Jared appeared at his door.

"Well, Seth and Jared!" Sewall exclaimed. "What are you doing here? You should have written to me that you were coming."

"Just seein' the sights mostly," Seth said. "Thought I'd get out from underfoot at home, and so didn't Jared. We drifted down on one of our flatboats with a few things aboard so we can pretend we're tradin' if we get the urge to. It's fun idlin' down the river enjoyin' how pretty the valley is this time of year, but I guess here is about as far as we go. We'll stay up above White River Falls. Don't want to run the expense of canal passages — down and back — if we ain't really makin' any money on business. Long as we're down here, we thought we'd poke in and see you and then see if there's any cargo we might take upriver before we hire a pole crew and go home."

"Well, I'm glad you stopped in. Had I known you were coming, I would have had some decent food. What I eat these days is pretty plain and coarse."

"We already ate," Jared said.

"Sure did," Seth added. "Kind of lazied around on the flatboat this mornin' after we got up late. Then we had breakfast and dinner both at the same time. Should hold us 'til supper, and we brought plenty of food along with us anyways."

"Where's your flatboat tied?"

"Down a ways from where an old rope ferry used to be, from the looks of it," Jared said. "Down from where a brook flows into the river."

"So, you came up Rope Ferry Road?"

"No," Seth said. "Where's that? We walked down to the bridge and then come up from there."

"Rope Ferry Road is shorter, if you're anywhere near the mouth of Girl Brook," Sewall said. "Just head out on the road there at the northwest corner of the green and follow it down."

"We're closer to the bridge than we are to the brook, but we'll try that road when we go back down," Seth said. "Didn't even know it was there."

"Let me show you around Bedbug Alley," Sewall said as he set down his oatmeal pot. "I've taken to eating right after morning recitations so as to have more time to myself at noontime. This rope is, of course, the bell rope. I suppose I've rung the bell thousands of times by now. As you can see, our rooms don't amount to much. But come. I'll show you the museum I told you about."

Sewall led them out into the corridor and through the shattered wall of the museum, pointing out to them the damage wrought by a cannon years earlier. Inside the museum Seth and Jared made a credible show of being impressed by assorted curiosities, particularly the zebra. Seth eyed the cages full of chickens and flared his nostrils.

"Don't the air get kind of thick in here sometimes?" Seth asked. "I'd think that after a while you boys might get tired of havin' the chickens up here."

"Oh, a lot of that smell is from the bats up in the attic and from the boys living down below," Sewall said. "We don't allow anyone in Bedbug Alley to butcher chickens anywhere on the third floor or leave feathers or legs or heads or innards lying around the way they do downstairs. It does indeed stink down there most horribly at times, but we've come to expect it from them. Surely a more uncouth bunch of louts has never lived in The College as the students on the second floor. We caught them stealing our firewood last autumn. And when we came back from our winter vacation — when I arrived here from Barston Falls — the boys on the second floor were actually burning the flooring in their stoves! Imagine that! Our floor down by the other end of the hall was just a gaping hole — waiting for one of us to fall through — with their axe marks everywhere around the edges. We even caught them in the act of chopping their own floor down below. They tried to lie their way out of it to President Tyler that someone else had chopped the holes first and that they were merely neatening up around the edges! It was a wonder that no one was killed trying to walk through the halls at night. President Tyler made the students go buy their own planking to cover the holes. Well, the holes are covered now so no one will fall through, but no attempt was made to fit the planking to the old floor. The boards were simply laid over the holes and their ends nailed to the boards beneath — no effort even to aim for the floor joists. It looks as bad as the walls of this museum, and probably that's the way it will look for decades, Dartmouth's finances being what they are. Really inexcusable behavior to chop the holes in the first place and insufficient amends for their crime to do such slovenly work when they were ordered to repair the flooring they had destroyed."

"It makes you wonder what kind of homes the boys come from," Seth said, shaking his head. "It must make it hard for your president to run Dartmouth College."

"I imagine it does," Sewall said.

Jared and Seth were poking around at the remaining shelves of the museum, occasionally holding up one thing or another for Sewall to identify, when suddenly someone down the hall began shouting Sewall's name.

"In here! In the museum!" Sewall shouted back.

A boy ducked through the hole in the museum wall. He was panting and sweating.

"President Tyler wants you to ring the bell, Sewall! There's been a drowning!"

"Oh no," Sewall whispered, then spoke aloud. "A student? Anybody we know?"

"Nobody said. President Tyler wants you to ring the bell to get everybody to meet out beside Chapel."

"All right. Right away," Sewall said.

He quickly went through the hole in the wall with the other student right after him. Seth and Jared followed, but without haste. By the time they got back near Sewall's room the first peals of the bell could be heard, but sounding strangely distant to the brothers. Jared commented on it.

"It's on account of the attic is between us and the bell," Seth said. "Muffles it, and you hear more of it through the windows than you do through the attic."

As they entered Sewall's room, Sewall abruptly grabbed the bell rope as high as he could and dragged at it with his full weight. He rode the rope down and then part way back up as the rope rose again.

"I hope it wasn't someone I know," Sewall said as he again threw his weight onto the rope. "Everybody likes to go swimming down there. I think all were present at our recitation this morning, but I don't know about the other classes. Oh, that would be terrible!"

"Look, Sewall," Seth said. "If you want to go down below and find out, we can ring the bell for you. Just tell us how long we should ring it."

"Oh, would you? Here. Ring this next one. Grab it high, and pull down hard. Don't let the rope burn your hands when it goes back up."

Seth rang the bell once and then a second time.

"Fine," Sewall said. "Keep it going for about five minutes — or perhaps sixty rings would be a better gauge."

Sewall left the room at a run.

"I hope it ain't one of Sewall's friends," Jared said.

"I don't believe it was," Seth said. "Here Jared. You do this a few times. This is prob'ly the only time in our life we're goin' to get to ring a big bell like this. Enjoy it 'til we finish, and then we'll go down below and see how the excitement is workin' out."

The brothers finished the sixty count of ringing the bell before they headed down the stairs.

*****

When the Barstons went out through the northernmost door on the west side of The College, the whole green was deserted except for a pair of dogs over on the far side and half a dozen cows cautiously working their ways back onto the green over by the swampy southeast corner.

"Where'd everybody disappear to?" Jared asked. "Thought they was s'posed to be out beside the Chapel."

"I imagine we'll find 'em down in the village," Seth said. "We're headed down there anyways on account of I'm gettin' thirsty."

"How do you figure they're down . . ."

"Too many questions now, Jared," Seth said. "Just don't say much, and keep your eyes open the next hour or so, and everythin' 'll likely come clear to you."

When they neared the southwest corner of the green, a mob of Dartmouth boys charged up the middle of the main street towards them. As the boys drew closer, Jared saw that those in the center pulled a rope. The mob turned abruptly down the hill towards the bridge, gathering speed. At the end of the rope an iron cannon plowed a continuous furrow in the dust of the road, rolled and tumbled slightly as it rounded the corner, and then jerked back into a straight course as it followed the boys down the hill.

"Well, what do you know about that?" Jared murmured as he watched the scatterings of students and townspeople following the procession.

"That's better, Jared," Seth said. "I was sure you was goin' to ask me a question, but you didn't. You just keep right on watchin'. Now we'll go on down to the Union House and see if we can't find a little rum. Then we might go down to the river."

They walked against the thinning traffic on the main street, passed the Tontine, and continued on down to the Union House. Inside they saw no one. Their shouts raised no response.

"Maybe they don't want our business," Seth said. "Well then, they'll have our business, but they ain't goin' to have our money."

Seth went into the taproom and filled two mugs of rum from a keg. He handed one to Jared, and the brothers sat. Jared started to talk, but Seth interrupted him.

"Hush now, Jared. Just drink, and keep still or we might not hear Grampy Sam's thunder."

They were down nearly to the bottoms of their mugs when they heard the dull, insistent thud and its echoes.

"Sounds like somebody's shootin' off a cannon down by the river," Seth said. "We might go down and have a look. But first we need to find somethin' to carry away some rum in. Have a look, Jared."

A few minutes later they left the Union House with a jug of rum in a sack and sauntered down the middle of the street without seeing a soul. As they turned the corner towards the river, they heard the roar of the cannon down below.

*****

A tremendous crowd lined the upstream railing on the New Hampshire side of the bridge and stretched around up along the riverbank to where the cannon lay and beyond it as well. Seth and Jared passed the toll gate, which had prudently been raised. When they were halfway across the river — over the thirty-foot-square, stone pier which supported the bridge — they spotted Sewall standing by the railing. They shouldered their way in next to him, and Seth tugged at his sleeve.

"Oh hello," Sewall said. "Thank you for ringing the bell."

"That was easy," Seth said. "What's goin' on? I hope it wasn't one of your friends."

"No. I don't believe it was," Sewall said. "Nobody seemed to recognize the clothes. But what do you think? It was two that drowned — a man and a woman! They found the clothes right next to each other!"

"You don't say!" Seth exclaimed. "A man and a woman swimmin' together with no clothes on? Oh my!"

"Evidently," Sewall said. "And oh yes it caused quite a stir, as you can imagine. Everyone got a good look at the clothes until someone from the village came down and said it wasn't decent for the Dartmouth boys to gawk at a woman's things like that and took the clothes away."

"How come they're shootin' off the cannon?" Seth asked.

"I thought everyone knew that," Sewall said in surprise. "If a cannon is fired over a body in the river, it will cause the body to rise to the surface. Have you not heard of that before?"

"Can't say that I have," Seth said. "But growin' up in Barston Falls there's a lot of things I guess I never heard about."

"I'm not certain of the physical principle involved," Sewall continued. "But everyone I've spoken to about it knows that it works, so empirically it must be true. There is also some sentiment about floating a loaf of bread with quicksilver in it and the accompanying claim that the loaf will stop directly over the body, but that, I am convinced, is mere superstition. But the cannon is different. Some force in the concussion of the blast over the water will stir a corpse to the surface. Now watch out! They're about to fire again! You'll want your hands over your ears."

Seth lowered the sack and the jug to the bridge planking and covered his ears. He distinctly felt the concussion of the air on his skin when the cannon fired. As the echoes rumbled down to silence, men and women crowded the edge of the bridge and stared eagerly here and there at the water.

"Don't shove! Don't shove!" someone shouted. "The railing's not all that strong, you know!"

Seth took his sack further over towards the Vermont side to a section of the bridge where no one was crowding. He made a show of perusing the river for a glimpse of a corpse floating up, but really spent his time studying the railings on both sides of the bridge and the posts which supported them.

The cannon fired three more times before a mob of men and boys dragged it two rods south along the riverbank. As they were jostling it into position to reload it, Seth led Jared back through the crowd on the bridge, and then worked up along the riverbank until the two of them had managed to get close to the cannon.

"Now maybe we'll learn a few things about loadin' and firin' our cannon, Jared," Seth whispered. "Pay attention."

The cannon muzzle rested on a low mound of shoveled dirt. A heavy, bald-headed man standing beside the cannon took a cigar from his mouth and shouted, "Stand clear!" People behind the cannon and off to its sides pressed back away from it. The bald-headed man puffed hard on the cigar as he held it to a punk stick lashed to the end of a pole about ten feet long. "Here she goes!" he called loudly, stretched his arms out to full length, and brought the smoldering punk stick down onto the touchhole of the cannon. With a flash and thundering roar the cannon jerked backward in a skewed somersault amid thick smoke. Before the smoke had cleared, a crew of Dartmouth boys scrambled forward to haul the cannon back into place.

"Aim her a little more to the left this time," the bald-headed man said as he squinted out over the river and smoked the cigar.

Seth nudged Jared over until the brothers stood next to the man. They glanced at his huge belly, which hung well over the top of the frayed and patched trousers of some ancient military uniform. He wore an equally ancient, but impressively outlandish, military jacket festooned with faded ribbons and tarnished gilt. Only at the top of the man's chest did its buttons meet the buttonholes. Further down they were linked by short lengths of cord, which themselves were taut under the strain of containing so large a mass.

The two Barstons watched as a crew of Dartmouth boys shoved a dripping rag tied onto the end of a stick all the way down the cannon muzzle, twisted it several times, and then brought it back out.

"How come you wet it inside?" Seth asked the bald man.

The man took the cigar from his mouth and spat to the side. For a moment he studied Seth and Jared and the shape of the sack Seth carried. Then he took another puff on his cigar.

"A lot don't bother swabbin' it out after they shoot it off," the man said as he drew his shoulders up. "Some of 'em ain't got but one arm now . . . or one eye . . . or one headstone. Sometimes if the charcoal in the powder ain't ground fine enough, a chunk of it'll hold fire down in the muzzle after the cannon's got shot off. It don't happen often, but it don't have to happen but once. When the folks go to reload powder, the cannon generally sends their ramrod a quarter mile or so with a hand or arm or head followin' along after it. Me, I always swab, and I still got all my parts."

"Sounds pretty dangerous shootin' off a cannon," Seth said.

"It ain't if you know what you're doin'," the man continued. "But every now and then some ignorant cuss gets killed, and it's always the same reasons."

"What are some of 'em?" Seth asked.

"Oh, they don't swab, like I said. Or if they got a cannon like this one with no carriage for it, they stand behind it or just to the side and get mashed to mincemeat when it jumps so quick. Sometimes they get to drinkin' and keep puttin' in a bigger and bigger charge each time to make more noise, and the cannon finally explodes and sends chunks of it all over the countryside and right through anybody that might be standin' in the wrong place. Or if the touchhole has got spiked a lot, every time they pry the spike out it makes the touchhole a little bigger 'til the cannon tries to shoot out the touchhole and the muzzle at the same time and explodes the cannon."

"I never thought there was so many things that could go wrong firin' off a cannon," Seth said. "I'd be afraid to try it. You must of been a soldier to do it so handy."

"Well, I was. And I know artillery. Know it well. Captain Ben's what folks call me. Experience is what you need. The right kind of confidence comes with experience. The wrong kind comes with ignorance, and that's the kind that gets men killed."

"The town's lucky you're here to show folks how to shoot off the cannon," Jared said.

"Waddin' can give you trouble sometimes too," Captain Ben continued. "Rags or heavy paper are best for a real fight, if you're usin' grapeshot or anythin' else besides a cannon ball that fits perfect into the cannon bore. If you're shootin' off a single ball like that, you don't really need waddin', but otherwise you should use it, or the cannon won't shoot as good as it should. For shootin' it off like we're doin' right now, dry straw or hay is good enough. I say dry because sometimes people run out of good waddin' and jam in green grass. That don't come out quite so fast as other waddin' — catches on the sides a little — and if it's a old cannon or one that's got a touchhole that's gettin' too big or one that somebody loaded up too heavy with powder, then just that little bit of green grass can be enough to blow the cannon all to flinders and kill a whole crowd of people. If we did that right here with this crowd refusin' to get back enough, I bet we could give a dozen gravediggers the lumbago with the crop we'd harvest with this old cannon."

"Ha!" Seth said. "I had no idea. Thanks to you General, now I know I never want to fire off a cannon. Just too many dangers to it."

"Not dangers so much as just rules. That's why you're touchin' off this round, soldier."

"Me? But I wouldn't know . . ."

"That's an order, soldier," Captain Ben said. "Besides, it's safe. I'll stand right by you to prove it."

"Well, all right, General. If you put it like that, I guess there ain't a way around it. But of course you'll help me lighten my burden here." Seth held up the sack.

"What is it?" Captain Ben asked.

"Some throat and belly swab, General."

They passed the jug as they watched the Dartmouth boys dump a ladle measure of powder deep into the muzzle, jam in a wad of hay, and tamp it tight with a ramrod.

"Dump in some small rocks this time," Captain Ben called over to the Dartmouth boys, "and then tamp some more hay in on top of that. Prime the touchhole last thing."

They watched the Dartmouth boys work. Captain Ben at last called for everyone to stand clear. He renewed the smolder on the punk stick with his cigar, shouted out, "Here she goes! Stand back!," and handed the punk stick to Seth. Seth leaned as far away from the cannon as he could and brought the punk stick down onto the touchhole.

The cannon leapt back with a roar. Out on the river, water exploded skyward in a towering column as bits of hay drifted down. The splash startled the people on the bridge, who tripped over one another as they shrank back from the railing. Many of those on shore laughed at them as the smoke thinned to nothing.

"All right boys," Captain Ben called over to the Dartmouth students surrounding the cannon. "Move her down a ways more. If we didn't raise the corpses with that one, then they've drifted further down."

Captain Ben helped himself to a few swallows from Seth's jug and then carried it with him as he moved down the riverbank with the crowd to point out where he wanted the cannon dragged. Jared started to follow, but Seth stopped him with a hand on his arm.

"No reason to stay longer, Jared," Seth said in a low voice. "We need to get back up to the flatboat and get some sleep this afternoon. I got a few things I need to fuss around with anyways. We got a long night ahead of us, and we best be rested for it. We'll come back about sunset to look things over."

"All right," Jared said. "I s'pose there ain't much of a chance they'll find the corpses this afternoon anyways."

"No. Not much of a chance at all," Seth said.

XXV

Seth, to make certain he wouldn't sleep through the night, had drunk close to half a gallon of water before he'd gone to bed. Each time he got up, he drank more water. Now he awoke again and walked over to the side of the flatboat.

The moon had yet to rise into view over the edge of the Hanover plain, but nonetheless now gave enough light so that Seth knew he should be underway.

"Wish us luck, Grampy Sam," Seth said. He bit off a chunk of tobacco from his plug, walked back to where Jared slept, and shook his brother's shoulder.

"Wake up, Jared. It's time."

*****

Moonlight illuminated the tops of the Vermont hills as the flatboat began to drift along the east bank of the Connecticut, buried in the shadows of the steep slope rising to the Hanover plain. Only the stirrings of the summer insects, the occasional hooting of a distant barred owl, and the very faint barking of a Vermont dog broke the stillness. The brothers drifted in silence until finally Seth whispered.

"I wish they hadn't of left the cannon down so far, Jared. We went to all that trouble to pick out the right spot for 'em, and then they left it too far down. That means more work gettin' the boat back up above after we got the cannon aboard."

"I hope you don't mean polin'," Jared said.

"No. We'd never move her that way with just the two

of us, even against that little bit of a current. We got to tie to trees along the bank or sink a deadman where there ain't trees and crank our way back up with the capstan. That's the only part of the plan I couldn't figure out a way around the hard work. We could of brought more folks with us from home, but that'd mean more mouths to keep shut after we got it. The best way is the way we're doin' it, but it does mean more work for us."

"I guess that before the night's done we'll feel like we earned our rest," Jared whispered. "But at least we didn't have to haul the cannon down here to begin with. That plan with the clothes . . . Wait! Up ahead, Seth. Lights! Look at 'em!"

Seth stared in disgust at the half dozen lanterns moving along the riverbank down below the bridge.

"Now why would they want to go and keep lookin' for bodies at night?" Seth said. "They can't be expectin' to find 'em — can't see much past their own feet. It don't make a bit of sense."

"We can't get the cannon with 'em down there," Jared said. "What are we goin' to do?"

"Pole her over against the bank and wait, I guess," Seth said. "Ain't much else we can do. I'm tellin' you right out, Jared, that this ain't in my plan. Why are they lookin' at night? It just don't make sense."

After the light crunch and lurch as the flatboat touched the bank, Jared stepped over the side and tied the flatboat to a tree. The brothers waited perhaps fifteen rods above the bridge and watched in frustration as the distant lanterns went up and down the riverbank below the bridge.

"I hope they get tired of it pretty quick, Jared," Seth whispered. "We got a lot of work yet to do tonight."

They waited more than an hour as the moon rose higher, though still the flatboat lay in the shadows. The activity of the people carrying the lanterns never ceased.

"You'd think they might get tired of the bugs," Jared said as he put more rotted wood onto their smudge fire.

The brothers watched the moonlight touch the west bank of the Connecticut. Then Seth nudged Jared and drew his attention to three more lanterns coming down the hill from the village.

"Might as well give it up, Jared," Seth whispered. "It don't matter if they get tired. They got more comin' anyways. Guess we might as well get some sleep."

The three lanterns reached the bottom of the hill, moved out past the toll house and onto the bridge, and then stopped. A drone of low murmurs and light laughter reached the brothers; then a few moments later several sharp whoops followed immediately by loud splashes.

"Swimmin' off of the bridge," Seth said.

They listened to the light banter of the swimmers as it came to them clearly off the water; heard them splash up onto the riverbank and complain about the mosquitoes as they climbed back onto the bridge. The lanterns moved a few feet on the bridge and then evidently were set down again. The other lanterns continued to move along the shore down below the bridge, but further down than they had been before. Then a few shouts began to come from those on the bridge.

"Hey sawbones! Give it a rest!"

"What's the matter, sawbones? Not enough supper tonight?"

"Leave 'em alone, or they'll come back and haunt you!"

Seth muttered. "So that's what it is."

"What?" Jared asked.

"It's the medical school boys down below with the lanterns. They're tryin' to rob the grave before the bodies even get buried. What do you know about that?"

"Never fresher," Jared said. "And never cleaner. Well

that's kind of a kick in the head. Grave robbers! I hope they don't find the bodies. This all part of your plan, Seth?"

"Shut up," Seth said.

The boys on the bridge continued to shout out "Sawbones!" Their shouts turned into a chant, long and drawn out on the first syllable: "Saaawwwww-bones!" After a few minutes they tired of the chant and began singing out the word, harmonizing with endless variation, creating quite a din with their voices and echoes. They kept it up for a long time.

The sudden explosion of a gunshot startled both Seth and Jared and ended the singing abruptly. The brothers leapt up from where they'd been sitting and jerked their attention over to the Vermont side of the river. There by the water's edge they saw three lanterns. Even as they watched, they saw the fiery illumination of a second gunshot. A moment later the report reached them. The three lanterns on the bridge winked out one right after another. Down below the bridge there were only half as many lanterns burning as before. At the third gunshot the remaining lights disappeared from the New Hampshire side of the river. A loud drawl from the bridge reached Jared and Seth.

"Well, I feel clean enough. I think I might go home."

A few moments of giggling and a complaint about someone having put on the wrong pair of pants and then a fading murmur of voices ended the noise from the bridge. A second volley of three shots followed.

"Now that might discourage the body snatchin' some," Seth said.

The three lanterns on the Vermont side of the river moved up to the bridge and then came across. Seth and Jared saw the men clearly: lantern in one hand and gun in the other. They carried the lanterns over to the New Hampshire side, circled the toll house looking in through the windows, and moved down along the riverbank, where the other lanterns had been burning earlier. Then they returned, re-crossed the bridge, and finally disappeared.

"All part of the plan, Jared," Seth said. "We'll wait a little more for the moon to light up the cannon and for the shooters to get to sleep. Then we'll go grab it for Grampy Sam."

Half an hour later with no further human sounds from either side of the river, Seth and Jared untied the flatboat and drifted slowly down to the bridge, underneath it, and down along the riverbank below. The moonlight showed them the cannon clearly. Maneuvering with their poles, they put the bow of the flatboat against the riverbank directly in front of the cannon.

"Tie us up to somethin' so we don't drift off, Jared," Seth said. "This part of the plan I know pretty good."

Jared tied the flatboat. Next he and Seth wrestled a ramp of heavy planking into place over the bow and onto the bank. Then they secured the capstan rope around the trunnions on the cannon.

"Just a downhill haul," Jared said.

"Part of the plan," Seth said.

The brothers put a pair of poles into the drumhead of the flatboat's capstan. Each grabbed one and put a severe bow into it as he slowly trudged around the capstan, stepping over the rope with each circuit. The pull on the capstan drew the flatboat further up onto the riverbank, but then the boat stopped moving, and the cannon began to inch down the bank and onto the ramp.

"It ain't goin' to roll on us, is it Jared?" Seth asked.

"I don't know if that part is in the plan or not," Jared said. "Shouldn't roll much with the iron stubs on the barrel sides, but if it does, get out of the way."

They leaned harder into the poles and kept winding the rope around the capstan, inching the cannon down the ramp. They paused once as Seth straightened the rope windings and pulled out the slack. Then they heaved anew and before long had the cannon down off the ramp and onto the deck of the flatboat almost up to the capstan.

"Well, didn't that work slick?" Jared said.

"All part of the plan," Seth said. "But we ain't anywhere near done yet. We won't get the boat off of the riverbank 'til we have the cannon weight right back by the boardpile, so don't quit yet. Just let me reset."

Seth loosened the rope from the capstan. Back by the boardpile he fixed a single block to a cleat on the deck, ran the rope through it, and took it back to wrap around the capstan. He and Jared pulled the ramp aboard and then heaved against the poles in the capstan as hard as they could. When the cannon was at last up by the block, both men collapsed onto their knees, sweating and panting hard. Seth recovered first.

"No time for lazyin' around, Jared. We got to get away now. Gettin' the cannon on board ain't but about half of it."

The brothers unlashed the capstan rope from the cannon and tied a much longer rope to the freed end, running it through an eye-bolt at the front of the flatboat on the right side. Seth sent Jared up along the riverbank, paying out the long rope to him as he went. Jared tied it and returned. Then the two of them shoved the flatboat out from the riverbank and began the first of their many pitches of tying the long rope up along the riverbank and cranking on the capstan bars until all the rope had been retrieved. In four such pitches they reached the bridge. Three more put them up far enough above to ease Seth's mind about being found out.

"We need a rest now, Jared. I got a lot of things to get to down by where we grabbed the cannon and then on the bridge — things that'll likely come clear to you tomorrow. And you got a board pile to stack."

Seth showed Jared what he wanted done: restacking the lumber to hide the cannon with long boards beside it and short boards at its butt and muzzle to give the impression of a solid pile of lumber.

"Just get the cannon out of sight for now if you get tired," Seth said. "Before dawn we still got to crank ourselves back up to where we set out from, and we could finish stackin' first thing tomorrow mornin', but it'd be better if we could finish all the stackin' tonight. See how the plan works, Jared?"

"How's that?"

"I mean just the part that there's only the two of us, and we don't have a pole crew tonight to take us back up against the current. No sir. The way things set now nobody's goin' to give half a thought about us havin' anythin' to do with takin' the cannon, but after I fix a few things down below the way I want 'em, nobody's goin' to give it any thought at all."

"I know," Jared said. "I ain't to ask questions, and then tomorrow I'll be good and surprised."

"Now you're learnin'," Seth said.

"We goin' home tomorrow?" Jared asked.

"No, we ain't," Seth said. "We'll stick around a few days. If we run off for home right after the cannon disappears, somebody might get to thinkin' about that. We stay a few days, and nobody in the world is goin' to suspect us. Besides, I'm still tryin' to think of a way we might get that Zebra."

Jared paused in his lumber-stacking to stare after Seth and wonder about the crowbar, hoe, and bulky sack he took with him as he walked down towards the bridge in the moonlight. Then Jared got back to work and kept at it steadily until the cannon was completely hidden with long and short boards. The rest of the stack yet remained to be moved on top of the hidden cannon, but Jared left it for later and stretched out between the two lumber piles, pulled his blanket over him, and went to sleep.

Later, when Seth returned, he roused Jared. The brothers set back to work. By then the moon was in the western sky and gave them good light all the way back to their earlier mooring site. Then, in spite of Jared's protests that they put the work off until the morning, they finished moving the pile of lumber over on top of the cannon. Before they finally went to sleep, Seth insisted that they rise early the next morning, get up into the village, and return to the river with the first surge of a crowd. Before he went to bed, he drank a great deal of water.

XXVI

As Seth and Jared were preparing to leave the flatboat early the next morning, they heard the rising bell up at The College. It rang ten times. Seth led the way from the flatboat straight up the steep riverbank, telling Jared it was a short-cut up to Rope Ferry Road. Twenty minutes later, after they had left Rope Ferry Road behind and were approaching the Dartmouth green, the bell began ringing for morning chapel.

"Well, Sewall's right at it," Jared said.

For six minutes each morning the bell rang for chapel. It habitually roused the vast majority of Dartmouth undergraduates from a dead sleep (the rising bell being an irrelevant annoyance), drew them stumbling from their beds and into their clothes, and set them into motion towards the chapel as they wondered what portion of the six minutes remained to them before the doors would slam shut.

From the northwest corner of the green the brothers stood and watched the stream of college boys enter the chapel. The bell ceased ringing, and all was still. A moment later a single figure emerged from The College and walked without haste into the chapel. Seth guessed it was Sewall.

"Now there's somethin' I didn't think about," Seth said. "The teachers likely won't let the Dartmouth boys just drop everythin' and look for the bodies down in the river. Maybe they won't be free but a little part of today."

"That's right," Jared said. "It'll be the folks from the town that go down first. Be best maybe if we wait over by the hotel for 'em."

"Prob'ly don't matter all that much when we get there," Seth said. "But I'd like it if you're there when they discover all the little things I worked up last night."

"I want to see that too," Jared said. "Unless maybe you'll just tell me about 'em instead."

"No," Seth said. "You got to see for yourself."

The brothers walked down by the southwest corner of the green and sat waiting across the road from the Dartmouth Hotel.

*****

Two hours later scatterings of activity through the village focussed into a procession down towards the river. The rallying point was a horse and wagon carrying a keg of powder and an assortment of materials for cannon wadding. Its driver was Captain Ben, who was puffing on a cigar as he readied himself for another day of firing the cannon. Since the day before, he had added a rather unusual hat to his military attire. Seth studied it and then wondered aloud if that day they should perhaps call him "Admiral" rather than "General." The brothers fell in at the rear of the procession and followed it down the hill. Jared wanted to catch up with the crowd, but Seth held him back.

"Don't get too anxious now, Jared," Seth said. "We'll just follow along behind and keep quiet and watch and listen."

"All right," Jared said.

They left the road at the approach to the bridge, where the toll gate was now down. Beside the gate the toll collector sat in a chair that was tilted back against the toll house. Seth and Jared passed Captain Ben's horse and wagon and went south along the east bank. People ahead had just left off studying the spot where the cannon had been the night before, and the brothers met the crowd returning. Captain Ben was in the lead, directing everyone's attention to the ground as he proceeded with a monologue. Jared and Seth stepped out of the way and then walked alongside the group, listening.

". . . right along through here even if everybody did walk all over the drag track. Now keep your eyes out for hoof marks down here, 'cause if there ain't hoof marks to be found, it means there was quite a crowd of thieves to take it. Had to be on account of that cannon drags pretty hard — a dozen anyways and maybe a score."

The group stopped when they were almost back to the horse and wagon.

"Right here now. Yes sir. The drag mark stops. And there! See it right there? Wheel tracks, so they loaded it on a wagon right here. Now where would they go? Think about it. Not likely up the hill with all that weight and the chance somebody up in the middle of town might see 'em and not with the toll gate open at night so they could haul it straight over to Norwich. But follow the tracks now. Pick 'em out from under all the footprints."

The group inched its way to the bridge approach, following the wheel marks Captain Ben had pointed out to them. He called a halt, however, before the group went out onto the bridge.

"Well, that can't be right," Captain Ben said. "Wheel marks don't look to be the same distance apart. What in the devil . . ."

Captain Ben stepped off the distance between the two wheel marks and found it to be nine of his foot lengths; stepped it off again back two rods and found it was only eight. He puzzled aloud about the discrepancy as the crowd began buzzing at the phenomenon.

"Hoe," Seth whispered to Jared. "Hard to get it even all

along the way with just the moonlight, but keep quiet, and let's see how this turns out."

Someone out on the bridge shouted excitedly to the group and got its attention. Everyone ignored the continuing protests of the toll collector, ducked under the toll gate, and went out to the spot where a section of the railing was missing from between two posts. Amid the buzzing and the murmuring several of the men picked up small pieces of wood lying on the bridge planking. The wood was quickly identified as fragments of wheel spokes and one section of a wooden rim.

"Ha! Their wheel busted!" Captain Ben proclaimed. "Well, that explains it. The weight of the cannon likely bent the axle and made the track wider, and then it got up to here before it busted their wheel all apart."

The murmurs of agreement abruptly halted as Captain Ben's voice boomed out again.

"Any gouge marks in the plankin' up there like a cannon was dragged over it?"

"No, there ain't," several voices came back.

"Then they didn't drag it beyond here. Now whoever found the busted spokes, tell me how close to the edge you found 'em."

"Right next to it — leastwise the one I picked up was," one man said.

"One I found was too," another man said.

"Well then, she's clear boys," Captain Ben said. "I ain't a tracker if that wheel didn't bust, and the cannon didn't carry the wagon right through the railin'. The cannon's right down below on the bottom. There might be a wagon with it, or the wagon might of drifted down the river. Depends on how they landed in the water and if the cannon was tied down to the wagon. That's how I read her anyways. Anybody think any different?"

Seth bent his head to Jared's ear.

"Watch this part," he whispered. "I hope they get this part right."

Most of the men fell to talking, trying to decide with their mouths if the wagon had indeed plunged through the railing and fallen into the river. Two or three of them, however, went right to the section of missing railing and gave the area a close scrutiny. After several minutes one of them called out loudly.

"Oh look at this! Look right here!"

The crowd's attention turned to the man so quickly that he squatted by the post he'd been standing next to and put his arm around it to keep himself from being crowded right off the bridge.

"It's a chunk of hide that the post tore right off of a horse!"

"Cow," Seth whispered to Jared.

The fragment of hide with hair on it was held aloft, the tiniest of trophy scalps. It authenticated Captain Ben's explanation and set off an uproar of speculation about the fate of the horse or horses, the wagon, its driver, and any passengers. Many of the men in the crowd stood on the edge of the bridge and scanned the water below for a sign of anything besides water.

"These boys are good trackers," Seth whispered to Jared. "They got every part just right — even the part I got wrong they turned it into a bent axle. Yes sir, they're good trackers."

Captain Ben decided that before anyone went diving to search the bottom that a thorough inspection should be made of both riverbanks down below to find any possible evidence of horses scrambling out of the river and up onto dry land. Two small groups left on that mission. It was acknowledged that the Dartmouth boys probably were better divers anyway and that they couldn't be expected at the river before their morning recitations had finished. Consequently the crowd on the bridge spread out into small groups, most of them migrating over to the New Hampshire side. People stationed themselves to intercept latecomers from Hanover and lead them on tours of the marks where the cannon had been dragged, where it had been loaded onto a wagon, where the axle had bent, where the wheel had broken to pieces, and where the post had gouged a chunk out of a horse as the cannon, wagon, and team had plunged through the railing and into the river.

Jared and Seth were among the few people not completely wrapped up in speculations about where the "dozen or score" of men needed for dragging the cannon to the wagon had come from, about whether the cannon now anchored a wagon and drowned team to the bottom of the Connecticut, about whether any men had been killed when the wagon went off the bridge, and about what kind of effort would be needed to retrieve the cannon. Both brothers felt their lack of sleep from the night before. They decided that they could best use their time by returning to the flatboat and sleeping. Before long they had worked their way to the fringes of the scattered groups of people and then had eased away up along the riverbank.

Back on the flatboat they ate. Then they smoked their pipes and talked for a while, built up their smudge fire anew, and lay down to sleep.

*****

The heat of mid day and the light breeze made the smudge fire unnecessary, its only valid function being to keep smoldering until it would be needed later on. The light clapping of waves against the side of the flatboat encouraged the brothers to renew their naps each time they stirred enough to open their eyes. They had slept for hours, but had yet to pay off the debt of sleep lost and muscles over-taxed during the previous night. Each lay in placid comfort as the afternoon barely moved along.

The sudden boom and thundering echoes of a cannon jerked both brothers upright; left them sitting in confusion and turning their heads this way and that.

"Well?" Jared said.

"Ain't ours they shot off," Seth said.

"We best have a look down there," Jared said.

"Guess so," Seth said. "One more thing to keep us from our rest."

"Rum before we go?"

"No, Jared. I'm sick of it. Don't know as I can stand even the thought of it 'til I've got good and rested and have about three good meals in me."

"Kind of tired of it myself, come to think of it," Jared said. "I s'pose that's how folks get to takin' the temperance pledge. They go out and steal a cannon and don't get enough sleep, and then somebody asks 'em do they want to sign a temperance pledge, and they go right ahead and sign. Well, we'll give the jug a rest."

The brothers limped in stiffness down along the riverbank, passed the bridge after pausing to watch the Dartmouth boys diving by the missing section of railing, and kept on down towards the crowd in the distance. A cannon blast drew their attention to a brass cannon mounted on a carriage with crowds of people up and down the riverbank from it.

"Well, well, well," Seth said. "Now that one must be the militia's cannon. 'On a gun carriage' and 'brass' was what Sewall told us last winter. We'll go have a look. What do you know about that?"

They walked closer; admired the bright reflections of sunlight from the heavily burnished brass.

"Ain't she a beauty?" Jared said. "Wouldn't Grampy Sam . . ."

"Hush up now, Jared," Seth interrupted. "Quite a few folks around with ears. Don't go gettin' into any bad habits."

They stood where they were long enough to watch men finish loading the cannon and fire it again. Then as they approached, a crowd of men started moving it along further down the riverbank. Seth and Jared followed slowly so that they never were quite close enough to be invited to help pull with the rest of the men. When the cannon stopped and men began reloading it anew, Seth and Jared passed by it and kept walking. They stopped at a point right where a brook flowed into the Connecticut, faced toward the cannon and the men, and every now and then glanced up the brook and down the river to make sure that they still were alone.

"She is a beauty," Seth said. "There ain't a doubt about that. Moon tonight ain't goin' to be much different from what she was last night — hour later is all. What do you think?"

"Flatboat's big enough," Jared said. "I know that. And with a gun carriage this one 'd roll right aboard without hardly any work at all. Only problem I see is hidin' it afterwards. Be a shame to get rid of that gun carriage, but we'd have to on account of we just ain't got anythin' to hide it with. Don't even have anythin' we can use to hide the cannon without the gun carriage."

"We could buy more lumber," Seth said.

"Have to buy it today and get it aboard before dark," Jared said. "And then we'd have to be up again most of tonight. And what are we goin' to buy the lumber with? I ain't got enough money with me."

"No. I ain't either, come to think of it," Seth said. "Have to get somebody to trust us for it. Never thought we'd need much money this trip. We brought along our own board pile and food and drink and didn't have to worry about payin' a pole crew 'til they got us home. I never thought the folks in Hanover 'd leave cannons layin' around every day for us. I thought we was goin' to get just the one — not goin' to have the chance to lay in a real supply."

"I hate to say it, Seth, but I think we ain't got enough time left today to go find somebody to let us have a pile of boards we can pay 'em for later and get somebody to load 'em on a wagon and unload 'em on our flatboat. Even if we had the money to pay, we ain't got the time. And if the folks that sell lumber and hire out wagons are down here with the rest of Hanover lookin' for drownded bodies and horses and wagons and cannons in the river that ain't there, then that wouldn't help us even if we had sacks of money. No sir. We just ain't got the time today — or the money — to get ourselves ready for takin' that brass cannon tonight. Who knows if they'll leave it where we can run the flatboat right to it anyways? And it's goin' to be a lot farther down the riverbank than ours was last night."

"Oh, I guess you're right, Jared. It's a bother and a temptation for 'em to have a shiny brass cannon like that to start with. That's the one they should of hauled down here yesterday for us to take instead of the old iron one. All right. Let's give it a rest tonight — give ourselves a rest — and see if we can't find some boards first thing tomorrow mornin'. Then we can grab the cannon tomorrow night, that is if they still got the cannon down here to look for the drownded folks. We got two hours less moonlight, but maybe we can manage if we don't have to wait for body snatchers and swimmers to get shot at and go home. Sure, let's do it that way."

"Want to help look for drownded bodies this afternoon?" Jared said.

"No sir. I'm goin' to sleep this afternoon, and then I'm goin' to cook us a good supper. After that we can come down and see how they leave the cannon for the night. Then tomorrow we'll get more boards. Might even see if we can't arrange to get enough to hide our Zebra under. But this afternoon I'm goin' to sleep."

The cannon fired again. People on shore and in boats stared hard at the water for any sign of a body floating up. They saw nothing. Jared and Seth walked up by the cannon on their way back to the flatboat, where they would try to sleep away the afternoon in spite of the cannon fire rumbling across the low hills.

Late in the afternoon Seth bolted upright with an idea which ended any remaining chance for daytime rest and threatened to keep them from sleep for much of the night as well. He explained to Jared that they didn't need to buy more lumber after all. They would grab the brass cannon that night and sink it in the Connecticut where they could find it again. Then just before the Fourth of July they could come back with a large crew of Barston Falls men, haul the cannon aboard, and return home in triumph. Using a large crew would mean less of a surprise for the village on the Fourth of July, but Seth told Jared that they could still surprise everyone with the iron cannon and the small brass one.

Jared agreed it was a good idea. However, inwardly he groaned in anticipation of another sleepless and muscle-wearying night.

After their supper and almost until dark that evening the brothers watched the firing of the cannon. Then without comment they saw the cannon hauled back towards the bridge and hitched to a team of horses to pull it up to the Hanover plain. They listened, again without comment, to an announcement to the world in general that the cannon would spend the night in a barn with members of the militia sleeping beside it. As long as the search for the drowned bodies continued, it would be thus protected at night. Somehow the surprise never did transform itself into disappointment for the brothers. Both were quietly relieved to lose the chance of stealing another cannon.

"Besides," Seth later rationalized, "we don't want to rob all the cannons out of Hanover. It'll be nice to think that Sewall can hear a cannon firin' on the fiftieth celebration of the United States of America. We're already goin' to make plenty of cannon noise ourselves up at Barston Falls. No need for us to be a pig about it."

They spent three more enjoyable days in Hanover — days they would reminisce about for the rest of their lives. They watched the firing of the brass cannon over the Connecticut in its unsuccessful attempt to raise corpses to the surface. They watched Dartmouth boys dive from the bridge repeatedly in a fruitless search for an iron cannon with or without a wagon and a team of drowned horses — one of them with a missing chunk of hide and hair. On their final evening they had a supper on the flatboat for Sewall and half a dozen of his friends. The boys sat on and leaned against the pile of lumber — at times scant inches from the iron cannon — and drank most of the rum Seth and Jared had left; stayed until it was time for Sewall to get back to ring the nine o'clock bell summoning all students to return to their rooms for the night.

The next morning the crew of polemen Seth and Jared had hired began poling them up the river. All the way back home Seth tried to think of a way to steal the zebra for Old Sam, but decided grudgingly that there was no good way.

XXVII

Old Sam rocked hard in his chair on the dock at the lower warehouse, stopped abruptly and spat into the Connecticut, and then continued haranguing Jared.

"Embarrassin' is what it is," Old Sam said. "I never thought anybody with the last name of Barston would just set and do nothin' when his clear duty for his town and his family is to get folks over and grab that Wheelock Village cannon. Like talkin' to a post tryin' to get anybody in this town to do anythin' about the Fourth of July. Don't it mean anythin' to you, Jared, that it's the fiftieth celebration of our country — fifty years after the Declaration of Independence? Don't it mean anythin' to you that it ain't but ten days from now?"

"I know I ain't said it since yesterday, Grampy Sam," Jared said, "but that cannon don't belong to us. We tried to buy a cannon for you, but nobody wants to sell us one. How would you feel if we had a cannon over here all set to use for the Fourth of July and the Wheelock Village boys snuck over here and stole it from us? What would you think if . . ."

"Oh rubbish, Jared. It's Wheelock Village! Ain't like it was widows and orphans. Unfriendliest bunch of thieves and liars and lazy pinchpennies in the whole Connecticut Valley. They need their cannon stole — earned the right to get it stole. And if there was half a man anyplace in Barston Falls, they would have it stole. But I guess there ain't, so they won't."

Seth had come down the ramp onto the dock; stood behind Old Sam's chair, listening.

"If we did that to them, Grampy Sam," Jared said, "then they'd come right back and do somethin' to us, and who knows where all that would end? Now don't you think it'd be better if we just left 'em alone? We'll get some powder and blow a stump or two for you on the Fourth of July. That'll make just as much noise as any cannon ever could."

"Ha!" Old Sam said. "You got about as much gumption as a rotten fish. You're young and healthy, and it wouldn't take much for you to get a few friends together and go over some night and bring that cannon home. If you was even half a man, you would. But you ain't. And Seth ain't a bit better. And Steve and Mark and George and Joe and that feller Stowell and Charlie Porter. All of it was just a lot of talk from a bunch of old women."

Seth walked around and stood beside Old Sam.

"Oh we never should of let go of the old days, Grampy Sam," Seth said. "A man was a man back then, and it's just disgustin' what they've sunk down to since that time. It's embarrassin' for me even to breathe these days, and I tremble every time I think back to when all the men in Barston Falls stood twelve foot tall."

"Yes sir!" Old Sam said. "You got that right, Seth. And you and Jared — the both of you, one standin' on the other one's shoulders — come up to just about eight inches tall compared to what there was around here in the old days. Now how come the two of you boys can't get together and take a few friends over to Wheelock Village some night when it's good and dark and grab that cannon for us?"

"I'm scared of the dark, for one thing," Seth said. "And I thought I explained to you before, Grampy Sam, that it just ain't Christian to go out and take somethin' that don't belong to you. Do unto others . . ."

"Pah," Old Sam said as he spat again into the Connecticut. "That ain't a Christian concern. It's your excuse for settin' at home like a scared old grandmother and not doin' a thing. If you had half a pound of gumption . . ."

"Careful, Grampy Sam," Seth said. "You hurt my feelin's too much and I'll break right down and cry."

"Wouldn't surprise me one bit!" Old Sam said. "The way the both of you are actin', I think that, old and crippled as I am, I could lick the two of you together."

"Well, let's not find that one out," Seth said as he reached into his pocket. "Got a letter from Sewall today, Jared."

"Oh, what's he got to say?"

"Quite a bit, and Grampy Sam needs to hear parts of it on account of it's about cannons and it shows that the Dartmouth College boys have got the gumption that you and I ain't.

"The boys on the boat Benjie and Foss took up through this mornin' dropped this off," Seth continued as he was unfolding the letter. "But here — you'll like this part, Grampy Sam. The Dartmouth College boys got their cannon stole a while back, and somebody dumped it in the river off of the bridge for 'em — least that's near as they could guess. But Sewall says that the divers can't find any trace of it, and now folks are figurin' that whoever stole it only pretended to dump it in the river and got away clean with it. Now here's the part that made him write the letter. He says that there's rumors around that Wheelock Village has been stealin' cannons, and he wants to know if we think maybe they stole the one that belongs to Dartmouth College."

"Oh, wouldn't that be just like 'em?" Jared said.

"But they already got a cannon," Old Sam said.

"Course they do," Seth said. "But don't it sound just like 'em to go out and steal somebody else's cannon even if they don't need it? They just ain't good Christians over there in Wheelock Village. I wouldn't put it past 'em. But see what else Sewall says here. He says that if we think

Wheelock Village might have Dartmouth's cannon, that there's a crowd of boys down there — especially seniors — that want to come up and take it back. He says that quite a few 'd come up to Wheelock Village and take it by force if they had to. They just want it back."

"Oh there ain't a bit of doubt about it," Jared said. "Course it was Wheelock Village that stole their cannon. And I hope for the sake of Wheelock Village that the Dartmouth boys get their cannon back because if they come all the way up to get it back and can't find it, why they might tear Wheelock Village apart lookin' for it! Wouldn't that be awful?"

"Certainly would," Seth said. "Who's goin' downriver next do you s'pose that could carry a letter down to Sewall?"

"I don't know," Jared said. "But we need to find somebody quick to take a letter right down to him so that the Dartmouth boys can get their cannon back in time for the Fourth of July. Course it was Wheelock Village that stole their cannon."

"But it ain't!" Old Sam protested. "Nobody'd go all the way down from Wheelock Village to Dartmouth College to steal a cannon. Wheelock Village has already got one anyways. And besides, the Dartmouth boys 'll come up and grab Wheelock Village's own cannon if you tell 'em Wheelock Village stole theirs."

"Now what'd be wrong with that, Grampy Sam?" Seth asked. "What I hear about the folks over in Wheelock Village is that they're thieves and liars and need to get their cannon stole. That's what somebody was tellin' me anyways not five minutes back."

"Course they need it stole," Old Sam said, "but they need it stole by us — not by somebody from way down the river! That ain't the Dartmouth boys' cannon to steal! You let them take it, and it won't be here for us to take!"

"But we ain't goin' to take it, Grampy Sam," Seth said. "You know, Jared, sometimes I think that maybe Grampy Sam ain't saved. And he drinks too."

"I pray for him every day," Jared said. "You?"

"Twice a day most always," Seth said. "But sometimes I don't think any amount 'd be enough. It's goin' to be such a struggle to save him from his evil ways."

"Oh you miserable, worthless, no accounts!" Old Sam blustered.

"You goin' to write to Sewall, or should I?" Jared asked.

"Let's both do it," Seth said. "Let's do it right now if you ain't got anythin' else to do and send it down first chance we can. Sewall's got to know about those thieves over in Wheelock Village."

"Oh go ahead! Go ahead!" Old Sam said. "But first, one of you get me a mug of rum, and the other one find Benjie for me. I got to get away from the both of you this afternoon."

"Sure, Grampy Sam," Seth said. "I'll go up, and, just as soon as I'm done prayin' for you, I'll get you some rum."

*****

Brownie pulled the light wagon towards the bridge over Robertson's Brook on the outskirts of Wheelock Village.

". . . and your uncle Seth was named after my pa. Let's see. He'd of been your great-great grandfather. My pa and my brothers Caleb and James all went up to St. Francis with Major Rogers and killed a lot of Injuns there. That's what made it safe for everybody to move up into this country in the first place. Pa got wounded at St. Francis and got blood poisonin' from it, but kept on runnin' from the Injuns 'til he got down this far and died right over where he's buried now at the Barston Boulder. That was back in 1759, Benjie. Far as anybody knows, he was the first white man buried in the town. That's how come Ma and Caleb dragged us up here to settle — 'cause it's where Pa was buried."

"I know all that, Grampy Sam," Benjie said. "I heard it all before."

"Well then, here's somethin' I bet you ain't heard before because the family's kept it pretty quiet: that same trip back from St. Francis was what made my brother James a crazy man. Maybe it was somethin' about killin' the Injuns at St. Francis or havin' so many Injuns chasin' him and the other Rangers afterwards, or maybe it was just havin' Pa die, but anyways he was crazy the rest of his days, and a lot of the time we had to keep him locked up in a cage. Ain't somethin' families brag about, but you're old enough to know now. And you're old enough to know that finally he went and hanged himself."

"No!" Benjie said. "I didn't know that!"

"Well now you do," Old Sam said. "Nothin' more to it than he was crazy, and finally the pain of it got too much for him, so he ended his life. We buried him up by Pa, and Ma's buried up there too. So you see, Benjie, you got your roots deep in Barston. The Barstons and Parkers settled first, and it was a few years before anybody moved in over here in Wheelock. We used to come over every year to hunt. Oh it was wild country then, Benjie."

The wagon crossed Robertson's Brook and kept on until Barlowe's Store, where Old Sam had Benjie stop. The same loungers, apparently, of more than a month before dangled their legs over the side of the porch and spat tobacco juice. This time, however, Danny Barlowe's fat figure was among them.

"Well now," Old Sam called out to them. "That looks like a slow way to wet down the dust. If you boys was to get a few buckets, you could soak everythin' down in no time. But the way you're goin' at it, it's dryin' out faster 'n you can spit."

"Anybody ever see a uglier horse than that?" one of the loungers asked.

"Only if one of the critters up there on the seat is a horse," another said. "But I can't tell for sure just what they might be."

"Now don't waste too much time flatterin' me," Old Sam said, "'cause I'm over here to do you boys a favor."

"What's that?" Danny Barlowe asked.

"Just to tell you again that somebody's goin' to come up and try and grab your cannon. Any point tellin' you boys, or should I run on up and see Cy Clifford?"

"Oh let 'em try and get the cannon," one of the loungers said. "Be the last time they try somethin' like that."

"Sure," another said. "We ain't had a good fight for a while anyways. Let 'em come."

"We don't need no warnin'," Danny Barlowe said. "Nobody's goin' to haul our cannon off quicker 'n we can catch 'em. We don't need but about three minutes from ringin' the church bell to have a whole pile of folks here ready to punch a few faces. Do whatever you want, old man, but you're just pokin' your nose in where it ain't needed. We don't need your help."

"Sounds like you don't," Old Sam said. "And sounds like it must be a challenge goin' to Sunday meetin' here. Well, I s'pose I'll run up and see Cy anyways, long as I'm up this far. Good luck keepin' the dust down this afternoon, boys."

Old Sam nodded to Benjie to urge Brownie forward. The inevitable loud belch and coarse laughter followed them. Old Sam gazed at the village church as they approached it and turned to stare back at it after they had passed.

"Well, those boys on the porch ain't improved since last time," Old Sam said.

"No," Benjie said. "It sure makes me wish I was a lot bigger and a lot stronger."

"I'm glad you ain't," Old Sam said. "I was in my share of fights over the years, when I was workin' on the mast drives and runnin' sawlogs down the river. There's times when that's just the right thing to do, but the problem with fightin' all the time is that it keeps you from thinkin' about better ways to go at things. I learned some of that from Eli Parker. Eli was about as poor a fighter as I ever met, but he was smart, and a lot of times he could just think his way out of a bad spot. When his thinkin' didn't work, of course he was glad to have me close by because I was a strong man when I was young, but other times he saved me from a few fights by thinkin' of a way to stop 'em before they got started. Nowadays my thinkin' is pretty feeble, but it's better 'n my muscles, so that's what I got to use. If I want to teach the boys on the porch back there some better manners, I know I ain't goin' to do it with my fists. And you ain't either 'til you got two or three more growin' years behind you."

"You got a way to teach 'em better manners, Grampy Sam?"

"Not yet, Benjie, but I'm thinkin' about it. Leave me in peace for a little, and I might come up with somethin'. Now take us up to Cy Clifford's. You already know the way."

They found Cy Clifford at his home beside Moose Brook. He invited them into his house, but Old Sam said they couldn't spare the time.

"Just needed to tell you, Cy, that there's a bunch of folks from down the river — Dartmouth boys — that I think are goin' to try and steal your cannon sometime in the next week or so — somethin' I overheard down by our canal. So, I think you want to make good and sure you got it in a safe place."

"We're obliged to you a second time, Sam," Cy Clifford said. "How's it happen that you're always the one that hears these things?"

"It's because I set there on the dock at the lower warehouse every afternoon, and I ain't got much else to do but talk and listen. And when I hear somethin' about folks after your cannon, it gives me an excuse to have Benjie take me out for a ride."

"Well, thank you, Sam."

As Benjie drove the wagon back down towards Barston Falls, Old Sam kept quiet — trying to "think of things," as he explained. After Tom Goldthwait had pulled them across the river on his rope ferry, they continued down towards Barston Falls. Then, as they were approaching the bridge over Tannery Brook, Old Sam had Benjie stop the wagon over by the side of the road.

"Now Benjie, you think I been pretty nice to warn everybody in Wheelock Village about folks that might take their cannon, don't you?"

"Yes sir."

"And you know I don't much like the folks over there, so you might think it's strange for me to warn 'em, first about the Charlestown boys and now about the Dartmouth College boys."

"It does sound strange, Grampy Sam."

"I hope you been wonderin' a little about that promise I had you make about helpin' me with somethin' over in Wheelock Village sometime. I need you to keep your mouth shut about this, Benjie, but I know you're just the man I need, and I know it more on account of your last name is Barston. The reason we keep savin' Wheelock Village's cannon for 'em is that we're goin' to steal it ourselves. You and me, Benjie."

"Oh, Grampy Sam!" Benjie said, his eyes and whole face lighting with pleasure.

"You and me are goin' to embarrass a lot of grown up men, Benjie. Today's trip was just to make sure we still got a cannon to steal when we finally go after it. And since the Dartmouth boys 'll come up here anyways — on account of your pa and uncle — we might as well use 'em. So when we get home, Benjie, you write a letter for me to that teacher of yours down at Dartmouth College. We won't say who it's from, and you'll write it with your left hand so nobody can ever tell who might of wrote it."

"All right," Benjie said. "What are we goin' to tell Teacher Tenney?"

"Just a couple things to make everythin' come out right for us. First you're goin' to tell him that the Dartmouth boys have got to take the clapper out of the bell in Wheelock Village church soon as they get up there, and they're to have a bunch of boys waitin' by the bell rope to grab anybody that comes to ring it for an alarm. And then you're goin' to tell him to make sure they bring shovels and crowbars because they got to do some diggin' to get the cannon up from where it's buried."

"But we ain't got any idea where it's buried or if it's buried, do we Grampy Sam?"

"No, Benjie. But if you think hard enough, you'll know right where we want 'em to dig for it."

"Well, I don't know where you mean," Benjie said.

"You write him, Benjie, that the cannon is buried three feet down under the porch of Barlowe's store. And tell him they got to bring enough short ropes to tie up a few folks with so they can go about their porch-wreckin' and diggin' in peace."

"Oh, that's good, Grampy Sam."

"It is pretty good, ain't it?" Old Sam said. "A lot better than us gettin' into a fight. You remember that, Benjie. Well, Cy Clifford 'll likely see to it that the Dartmouth boys don't steal our cannon. And even if diggin' up everythin' under the porch don't teach the lazy loudmouths at Barlowe's better manners, at least it'll make 'em roost someplace else. With a bunch that lazy, I can't see 'em buildin' the porch back on any too quick. Now get us on home, Benjie. You got to write that letter right away, and we got to get it down to Hanover about as quick as the letter from your pa and uncle. We don't want to waste a chance like this by havin' the Dartmouth boys start up here before they get our letter. If we're too slow, then Danny Barlowe ain't goin' to lose his porch, and he needs to lose it bad."

"But how are we goin' to get the cannon?" Benjie asked. "We don't even know where it is."

"You just leave that to me, Benjie. But if you want, you might start pokin' around to see if you can't find us a team of horses strong enough to drag a cannon a pretty good ways. We're goin' to need to have a flatboat in the river too most of the way up towards Wheelock Village so's we can get the cannon across, and I was thinkin' if we got the thing aboard we might just as well keep right on and come down through the canal. And if we got it aboard and we're comin' right down through the village anyways, I guess it might as well be the Fourth of July when folks notice we got a cannon with us, so we'll go up and grab it the night before and float down through the canal and shoot the cannon off to wake everybody up for fifty years of the United States of America — the Fourth of July in eighteen-hundred-and-twenty-six. We'll likely need Foss and Tom and maybe some others too, Benjie, to help us that night, but most of the haul work 'll be with horses, so get us a strong team — four horses 'd be better 'n two. Get your friends interested in helpin', but don't let 'em know too much. The more that know, the worse chance we got that somebody 'll say the wrong thing and let the Wheelock Village folks know we're after their cannon. Oh we got a lot of thinkin' and plannin' and runnin' around to do still."

"If we get the cannon for this Fourth of July, Grampy Sam, then that'll be the best day of my life."

"I hope it's just the best day so far," Old Sam said. "And you remember this, Benjie, because I told you to remember it — if I die chasin' after that cannon, that was a good way for me to die, and I was happy doin' it. You remember that. Promise me you'll remember that."

"Yes sir. I will."

"Now get us on home, and be quick about it. We got a letter to write."

XXVIII

Annie felt particularly tired when she finally sat down to supper with Joe and Sue. The twins crawled among a scattering of carved maple blocks over in one corner and, for the time being at least, neither needed her nor seemed on the verge of hurting themselves. Annie had been up before first light that morning baking pies for the Fourth of July celebration in the village square the next day. Since then she'd been so busy that she'd scarcely had time to sit down. Even during the afternoon hours, when Sue usually watched Aaron and Amos, Annie had had to work on making the pies and had missed the time for a rest she generally found necessary to help her through the day. As Joe finished saying a short blessing over the food, she let out a deep sigh.

"I am surely glad that this Fourth of July ain't goin' to come again," Annie said. "What with all the bakin' and the twins fussin' so, I don't think I ever felt so tired before."

"Seems like you must of baked a pie for everybody in the village," Joe said. "But just think of the day it's goin' to be — the fifty year celebration. Fifty years that we been free of England, even if we did have to remind 'em again. This is a day to remember. And if we live an extra long time, maybe we'll even see the hundred year celebration."

"That'll be the one Amos and Aaron remember," Annie said. "I'm too tired to live another fifty years."

The three of them fell into silence as they ate. After a while Joe spoke.

"Looks like Old Sam Barston will make it to the Fourth of July after all," he said. "Who would of guessed that last winter or even last fall? He kept havin' those spells, and everybody was sure he'd die. Then everybody was surprised to see him still alive at town meetin', and tomorrow I hope everybody's goin' to be surprised again."

"I'm glad of that," Annie said. "We made a special pie just for him, didn't we Sue?"

"That's right," Sue said.

The twins tired of playing with the maple blocks and crawled over to the table. Amos and then Aaron pulled themselves upright on Annie's dress and stood leaning against her thigh.

"Oh just look at 'em," Joe said. "They'll be walkin' any day now. Think of that!"

"I'm tryin' not to," Annie said. "They're enough trouble right now just crawlin' everyplace. When they start walkin', I don't know what I'll do. Maybe just send 'em down to the brickyard to help you, Joe, and remind you that you're their father."

"Now what's that s'posed to mean?" Joe asked.

"Only that you don't spend much time with 'em," Annie said.

"Well, how am I s'posed to do that? I got a livin' to make down at the brickyard for one thing. And what am I s'posed to do with 'em now anyways? I can't feed 'em, can I?"

"You could feed 'em mush if you wanted," Annie said. "They're takin' some of that now. Or you could just set in a rockin' chair and hold 'em every now and then."

"That's a woman's work to take care of 'em when they're so small," Joe said. "I'll spend more time with 'em when they're big enough to go out and do things. They wouldn't even appreciate it if I did set with 'em and rock."

"Well, I might appreciate it!" Annie snapped. "Ever think of that, Joe?"

"Now, now, now," Joe said, glancing uneasily at Sue. "Let's not get cranked into that just now."

Annie followed Joe's glances to Sue and gazed at her for a moment. They finished their supper scarcely saying a word. The twins crawled off into the next room. Annie checked on them and then brought a pie over to the table.

"I guess Old Sam didn't get the cannon he wanted," Annie said. "Too bad."

"It is," Joe said, quickly reaching for the pie. "Seth and Jared looked all over for one to buy, but nobody had one to sell. They said they might blow up a stump or two, though, to make some noise for the Fourth of July."

The twins started crying, and Annie left the room to attend to them. The sounds of their fussing and the low murmurs of Annie's voice drifted through the downstairs. Joe finished a piece of pie and helped himself to another.

"You're awful quiet these days, Sue," Joe said. "I guess I been so busy down at the brickyard that I ain't had much time to spend with you or the twins. But for the first time in my life I got a business to build, and that takes time. I ain't just workin' for wages any more. And if you're thinkin' I don't spend enough time with you, Sue, I promise I'll make it up later. Things 'll likely ease off some by the end of the summer, and then we can all go out and do things together."

"That'll be nice, Pa."

"You're growin' to be a real woman now, Sue, and it scares me sometimes to think how quick the years go by. Seems like just yesterday you was a little girl. And now, whether you know it or not, well . . . you might break a few boys' hearts before you're settled down. Let me tell you how pretty I think you look wearin' a dress these days. You're startin' to look a lot like your ma, Sue — 'specially when you smile — and she was a pretty woman."

"Thank you, Pa. Annie's pretty too."

"Yes, she is. Another pretty woman that I ain't spendin' enough time with. And she's got a kind heart, too, and she's a good worker. I been a lucky man with both of my wives.

No man's any luckier than me with my wives and with my daughter."

Annie returned with a son in each arm; handed one to Sue before she sat down.

"Oh, have they been a bother today," Annie said. "Fussin' right through the day except for their nap and a little while after playin' with the blocks, but now they're right back at it."

"Maybe they're gettin' their teeth," Joe said. "Sue fussed a lot when hers started comin' in."

"They already got some if you ain't noticed," Annie said.

"When did that happen?" Joe asked.

"Been a while now, Joe," Annie said. "You'd know that if you spent more time with 'em."

Joe got up from the table and went over to sit in his rocking chair. Annie and Sue kept an eye on the twins and cleaned up from supper. When Annie spoke to Joe and got no response, she discovered that he'd fallen asleep. Thereafter she and Sue whispered. They finished cleaning up and then put the twins to bed. When they came back downstairs, Joe was still asleep in the chair.

"I guess he does work pretty hard in the brickyard, Sue," Annie said. "Prob'ly I shouldn't be so hard on him for not spendin' more time with us."

Annie put her hand on Joe's shoulder.

"Wake up, Joe. Wake up so you can go to bed."

"Oh," Joe said in momentary confusion. "I must of fell asleep."

"Must of," Annie said as she leaned down and kissed him. "Think you're ready for bed yet?"

Joe got to his feet, yawned, and stretched.

"Like to, Annie, but I got to go out for a little."

"What?" Annie flared. "This time of night?"

"Afraid so," Joe said.

"What in the world could be so important to get you out at this time of night?"

"I can't really tell you, Annie. Just some kind of business."

"Why, Joe Reckford . . ." Annie commenced. Her voice trailed off, however, as she glanced sideways at Sue. "Sue, do you think . . ."

"Think I'll go up to bed," Sue said. She kissed Joe and then Annie, went up the stairs, and paused at the door of her room to listen to the voices downstairs. Annie started right in.

"So you're goin' out now after dark and won't tell me where?"

"That's right," Joe said. "I'm just goin' out and . . ."

"When will you be back?"

"I can't say for sure. Don't wait up for me. Might be all night for what I know."

Anger flashed into Annie's voice. "You ain't got time to spend with me or the twins or Sue, but you got time to go out in the middle of the night for what you call 'business' and won't tell me what it is?"

"It's just somethin' I got to do," Joe said, himself starting to anger. "And no, I ain't goin' to tell you what it is. Can't a man just . . ."

"It's a woman, ain't it Joe? I let it slide by when you went away for those days after town meetin' and you wouldn't tell me where you went, but I won't let it pass this time, Joe Reckford! You ain't goin' out in the middle of the night and expect that I'll . . ."

"I am goin' out!" Joe said. "I'm goin' out right now!"

"It's a woman, ain't it Joe? I just know it's another woman!"

"That ain't a bad idea, Annie! I'll see what I can find!"

Sue heard the door slam. She listened to Annie's low muttering and then to what might have been a brief moment of crying. At the sound of Annie's slow footsteps on the stairs, Sue shrank back into her room and quickly lay down on her bed. Annie passed by the door and went down the hallway. Sue heard her murmuring something to the twins and heard her blow her nose several times. Then all was quiet in the house.

For a long time Sue lay in purposely uncomfortable positions so that she wouldn't fall asleep. She pinched herself occasionally. Finally, after what seemed hours, she eased off the bed as quietly as she could. She tiptoed over to where her old clothes hung from pegs on the wall, shed her dress, and got into her britches and shirt. Then she stood still and listened hard for any sounds of Annie. There were none.

The floorboards creaked as she stepped into the hallway. She froze; listened for a moment before she resumed her slow stalk in the dark towards the stairs. The rattle of a door latch stopped her dead. An instant later candlelight flooded the hallway.

"Now what in the world are you up to, Sue?" Annie demanded. "Sneakin' out of the house, ain't you?"

"Just goin' out for a while," Sue said.

One of the twins began crying.

"Oh, what next?" Annie said. "Come help me with the twins. They just don't want to sleep tonight. I got to talk to you, Sue."

Sue followed Annie sheepishly as the second twin started crying, had Aaron thrust into her arms as soon as she had entered Annie's bedroom, and sat down on the bed as Annie had told her to.

Annie lifted Amos from his cradle and soon stopped his howling with her breast.

"Oh, give me Aaron too," Annie said over his crying.

Soon enough the twins' noise subsided to the quiet sounds of suckling.

"Now you and me have got to talk," Annie said. "I'm about at the end of my rope between the twins and your pa. And now you sneakin' out is about the last thing I need. Got your same old clothes and your same old tricks, ain't you Sue?"

"I heard you and Pa," Sue said. "And you're wrong if you think he's out after a woman. He ain't that kind of a man, Annie. It's just been you and my ma he ever cared about. If he tells you he's got some kind of business, then he's got some kind of business, and you ain't to worry."

"I guess I know that deep down," Annie said. "But he got me so awful mad when he wouldn't tell me where he was goin' or just why he had to go off in the middle of the night. I guess he'll come back when he's good and ready, but I wish he wouldn't be so pig-headed about it. But you're the one I'm worried about now, Sue. I told you before that if you keep goin' out at night and drinkin' and runnin' around with the boys, then some day you'll get in bad trouble. It's because I care about you that I don't want you to go out. It ain't like I'm a witch to you for no good reason. Now is it all that important for you to sneak out of here tonight? Can't you just stay at home and get a good night's sleep and stay out of trouble?"

"Yes. It is important for me to go out tonight, Annie."

"Anythin' you can tell me, or is it just 'some kind of business'?"

"Well, I ain't s'posed to tell anybody. S'posed to keep it a secret. I'll tell you, Annie, but I don't want you to tell anybody else or do anythin' to stop him — Grampy Sam, I mean."

"What about Old Sam?" Annie asked.

"You know how he's wanted a cannon for so long, don't you Annie? Well, nobody in the village could get him one for the Fourth of July, so he's goin' out tonight to steal one himself."

"Old Sam? He can't do that. He'll kill himself runnin' around like that at night."

"He knows that, Annie, and all he says about it is that it's a better way to die than just settin' around at home and waitin'. He wants to do it and claims he's got some plan for stealin' Wheelock Village's cannon. He ain't to be talked out of it. He was so tired today he didn't even go fishin', but still he's goin' out tonight. I don't much care if he gets that cannon or not, but I know somebody has got to go along just to take care of him while they try to grab the cannon."

"At his age. Old Sam," Annie said, shaking her head. "Who else is goin' to get the cannon with him? Joe — your pa — in it by any chance?"

"No he ain't, Annie. It's Benjie, Foss, and Tom."

"Just that bunch of 'em like that, I don't know how they expect they'll get a cannon."

"I don't know either," Sue said. "But I'm just goin' along to take care of Grampy Sam. I got to, Annie."

Annie very awkwardly began to lean towards Sue, but gave it up.

"Kiss me, Sue. I can't move."

Sue kissed her.

"Course you're goin', Sue. You got to. We can't count on the boys to take good care of Old Sam. You got to go right now?"

"Benjie said to meet a couple hours after dark. He was goin' to have a wagon and a team just past the bridge over Tannery Brook. We're goin' to meet there and then ride up."

"How 're you s'posed to get across the river?"

"I don't know any more about the plan," Sue said.

"Ha!" Annie said. "Old Sam up to his tricks just like the old days. Who ever would of thought it? And you're goin' along to take care of him. You know, Sue, you make me proud to be a Reckford woman."

Annie rocked three times in the rocking chair and then stopped abruptly.

"I'm goin' with you," she said. "Maybe the both of us together might keep Old Sam out of trouble. Don't you waste time arguin' about it, Sue, 'cause I got to go, same as you."

"But what about Amos and Aaron? We can't take 'em, Annie. You ain't goin' to leave 'em here alone, are you?"

"No," Annie said. "We can't take 'em, and I won't ever go off and leave 'em alone. George don't know it yet, but he's just about to find out what it means to be an uncle and have a couple nephews livin' so close. He's likely goin' to learn too how to cook mush in the middle of the night just the way his nephews like it. Let's get ready, Sue, and go surprise him."

Ten minutes later Sue and Annie, each carrying a baby, made their way to George Ballard's house by the light of a candle lantern. Sue carried the lantern. Annie carried a basket of things her brother would need for taking care of the twins.

XXIX

The reflectors on the lanterns mounted to each side of the wagon seat badly needed polishing. They cast dim beacons onto the outside flanks of the team harnessed in front and illuminated the roadway so short a distance ahead that the two horses pulling the wagon were kept at a walk. A second pair, already in harness and tethered behind, had as yet been taxed with no chore other than following the wagon. The sound of their hooves was a surer confirmation of their presence than their shadowy forms. The five people riding on the wagon glimpsed many stars overhead; saw increasing numbers the longer they kept their gazes averted from the lamplight. They talked to counter the so porific clap of hooves.

"How much farther you figure it is to where we cross?" Annie asked no one in particular.

"I ain't sure," Benjie said, "but I think it might be a half a mile or so. Foss said he'll have a lantern burnin' on the boat for us, so keep your eye out."

"Just how was it you found out where the cannon was hid, Old Sam?" Tom Beasley asked. "Seems like somethin' they'd never tell to somebody that didn't live in Wheelock Village."

"It's on account of my good character, Tom," Old Sam said. "There was some Charlestown fellers that wanted to grab the cannon, so I warned the Wheelock Village folks. Then there was some Dartmouth boys that wanted to get it, so I warned the Village folks again. So the third time I went up to warn 'em, folks in Wheelock Village was ready to listen on account of I already saved their cannon for 'em twice. What I did day before yesterday was tell Cy Clifford — he's one of the selectmen — that I thought some of our Barston Falls boys had grabbed the cannon already. I figured Cy might know where it was hid, and sure enough he did. He took me right to it and showed me it was still there. So now I know where it is, all we got to do is sneak in and drag it away."

"Where is it?" Annie asked.

"Under some loose floorboards in the gristmill a little ways up Robertson's Brook. Perfect for us because it's maybe twenty rods from the nearest house, and the sound of the brook 'll cover up a lot of noise. If we don't make a real crash and clatter takin' the cannon, we should get away with it and not wake anybody up."

"How come you didn't bring me along that last time, Grampy Sam?" Benjie asked. "Tired you out so not havin' me to help you. If you'd of brought me along, you wouldn't of had to drive Brownie all that way. You could of just slouched back and rested. And then when you did get home, you wouldn't tell me a thing about your trip 'cept that Danny Barlowe's porch was gone. I would of kept my mouth shut about where the cannon was hid."

"I know that, Benjie. But I thought we'd have a better chance gettin' the cannon if Cy Clifford thought I was the only one outside of Wheelock Village to know where they hid it. If he had to worry about you knowin' too, then it might of made him nervous. The way it sets now is best on account of Cy trusts me. I never thought I'd get so tired goin' up alone, but that was the best way, and I am recoverin' from it, and it was worth the effort."

"And I thought you was sick the last couple days," Sue said.

"Just about the same thing when you get old as me," Old Sam said. "And I'll be tired again tomorrow for the Fourth of July, but it'll be worth every ache and pain because we'll have a cannon to celebrate the day with. And if Jared and Seth are nice to me, I might even let 'em run their stump-blowin' powder through my cannon."

"How are we goin' to get the cannon out of the mill?" Benjie asked.

"I was figurin' we could lever up one end of it with the planks that are hidin' it," Old Sam said. "Then the horses can either drag it out together with a long rope, or maybe we can take one of 'em right to it and haul it out that way — ain't really wide enough in there for two horses from what I remember. We'll see how that goes when we get to the mill."

"And then we drag it down to the boat the way you said," Tom added, "and bring it home for the Fourth of July."

"That's about the plan," Old Sam said, "except that the cannon's too heavy just to drag. That's what that one-axle wheel rig on the flatboat is for. It's a little like the huge rigs we used to use for gettin' mast pines to the river in the summer. The cannon goes underneath the axle, not on top, with most of the weight held up off of the ground with chains. The end of the cannon that drags shouldn't be too tough on the horses. We'll get it aboard the flatboat and drift on home. And just in case somebody up in Wheelock Village smartens up and chases after us, one of you three boys will take the wagon down the New Hampshire side of the river with a drag mark behind you so they think it's a cannon. There's a log on the flatboat right now we'll use. Or maybe two of you 'll do it — one for the team with the wheel-rig and one for drivin' the wagon. We'll decide that later on. Anyways, you'll drag the log all the way down by the bridge between Orford and Fairlee and then maybe dump it in the river and come back up the Vermont side to Barston Falls. You need to meet us up at the head of the canal with one of the teams and take the flatboat down through to the lower warehouse. Tomorrow mornin' I plan to embarrass Seth and Jared just as much as I can, and we'll make some noise for the Fourth of July with their stump-blowin' powder, and I won't let 'em forget the day for the rest of my life. Think how ashamed they'll be when they find out how two women, three boys, and a old man went and stole Wheelock Village's cannon when all the men in Barston Falls couldn't do a thing. Yes sir. That'll make the work tonight worth all the pain. This 'll be a Fourth of July every one of us can remember 'til the day we die. Count on that."

"I'll remember it even if we don't get a cannon," Annie said.

"We'll get the cannon," Old Sam said. "I did all the work to make sure we get it, and I promise you it's ours."

"Is that the light up there?" Tom asked.

"Sure is," Benjie said. "There's Foss and the boat."

*****

The wagon moved at its slow pace up along the New Hampshire side of the river. The looming masses of Rattlesnake Hill a mile or more to the southwest and of Hackmatack Ridge off to the east left noticeable voids in an otherwise starry sky. The six people in the wagon — Old Sam, Annie, Sue, Benjie, Foss, and Tom — made little effort to hush their voices, for they were still a good half mile south of Wheelock Village. The land on both sides of the road was cleared and separated by fences into hayfields and sheep pastures; the occasional farm buildings set back well beyond lantern-range, nearly all the way over to the eastern edges of the clearings, where even the most extreme floodwaters of the Connecticut would never reach them.

"Oh I hope Amos and Aaron are all right," Annie said.

"I ain't worried about them," Old Sam said. "The one I'm worried about is poor old George."

"Me too," Sue said. "I bet right now they're both howlin' away, and George is up tryin' to get a fire goin' so 's he can cook 'em some mush. He did look kind of puzzled when we left the twins with him, and he was dressed up almost like he was plannin' to go out someplace — even if he didn't look very awake."

"Too bad if he was plannin' to cat around after some woman tonight 'cause he don't do enough of that," Annie said. "But the twins 'll keep him from thinkin' about it too much. The way they're fussin' lately they'll make him glad to get any sleep at all. Yes, I guess you're right, Sue — about he was plannin' to go out someplace. Well, if we kept him at home tonight when he wanted to go out, that's too bad. I'll have to do somethin' nice for him later on."

"Wicked stars tonight," Benjie said. "Hundreds of 'em."

"Thousands," Foss said.

"At least a million when you look high and low," Tom said. "But hold on! What's that light up there to the right."

"Where?" Sue, Annie, Foss, and Benjie asked at the same time.

"There to the right a little," Tom said.

"I see somethin'," Sue said. "Sure. Right there. Oh, now it's gone. And it moved. I'm sure I saw it move."

"Didn't see a thing," Benjie said.

"Looked like a lantern," Tom said. "Maybe some farmer out lookin' after his sheep or maybe . . ."

"Fireflies," Foss said.

"Sure looked like a lantern to me," Tom said.

"Me too," Sue said. "Up here a little ways more. I'm sure it wasn't fireflies."

The wagon continued on and ascended a low knoll, where the road passed by the hewn stone walls and iron gate of the village cemetery. The poor light of the carriage lanterns gave the dark slate stones a weirdly sinister aura. The few marble stones rose like ghosts among them.

"Right up here someplace was where I saw a light," Sue said.

"I think it was over farther," Tom said.

"Just spirits out lookin' for the next folks to drag down under," Foss said. "If you're the one that sees the spirit lights, they say you're the next one that gets dragged down under. Glad it wasn't me that saw 'em."

"Foss," Annie said. "This really ain't the time."

"Go and say all you want," Old Sam said. "It don't matter who thought they saw lights in the graveyard 'cause it ain't your turn next. It's my turn next, and the rest of you have just got to get in line and wait."

"Oh, you'll last for years yet, Grampy Sam," Benjie said. "And it was just fireflies. No ghost lights or lanterns or anythin' else."

"Well now," Old Sam said. "None of that's important. Ain't worth your breath. I'm only plannin' to live for the rest of my life anyways and then have done with it. Only important thing is to get our cannon for the fifty year celebration tomorrow — the Fourth of July of eighteen-hundred-and-twenty-six. Now up past the cemetery the houses are closer together and ain't so far from the road, so we best just whisper. We want all the village folks to sleep right through the night. Things might get pretty hot if they don't, so keep as quiet as you can."

Thereafter their voices dropped to murmurs and whispers blending readily into the general background somnolence of the summer night. The slow and muted drumming of the horses' hooves and the creakings of the wagon barely rose above the sounds of the night insects. The most violent activity was that of the moths in their frenzied, erratic arcs around the two carriage lanterns. None of the six people spoke as they approached Robertson's Brook and crossed the bridge. They turned right and followed the brook up on the barely sloping plain. They came to the mill right where the land began to rise more abruptly.

"This is the place," Old Sam said. "One of you — Foss — you wait here, and keep hold of the reins. Last thing we want now is for the horses to wander off or get scared off or get stole, so you stay here and watch 'em while the rest of us go in and decide how we can best set up to have the horses haul the cannon out. And get your lantern down and out of sight just in case somebody over in the village can't sleep and looks out the wrong window. Let's go. And bring along some ropes."

Old Sam moved very slowly after they had helped him down from the wagon. He made no objection when Annie and Sue each took hold of an arm and helped him towards the mill.

"Feels like I died and went to heaven," Old Sam said. "A pretty woman holdin' me on each side. Maybe I need to go out and steal a cannon more often."

"You just take it slow, Old Sam," Annie said. "We got a lot more night ahead of us, so you take it slow and don't wear yourself out all at once."

Benjie carried one of the carriage lanterns, led the way to the doorway of the mill, lifted the latch, and opened the door. The five of them entered the mill.

"Where's it hid, Grampy Sam?" Benjie whispered as he aimed the reflected beam of the lantern here and there through the mill.

"Over there," Old Sam said. "Well, under all the barrels and sacks. Didn't have 'em there when Cy showed me the cannon. Got to move 'em, but I'll leave that to you folks."

Old Sam leaned against the wall and watched Benjie and Tom and Sue and Annie move a small mound of full flour sacks and barrels. The lantern sat on the floor as they worked, its light casting wild shadows onto the upper walls of the mill.

"Oh, I been waitin' for this for quite a while," Old Sam said as the other four moved the last of the obstructions aside.

"There's three loose planks there in the middle," Old Sam said. "They ain't nailed down or pegged down. Cy just pulled some little wedges out from between the boards, and they come right up. Wedged in hard against each other, so get the wedges out first thing."

"There," Annie said. "Got it." She threw aside a small piece of wood and then felt for a grip between two of the planks. She and Sue rattled one of the planks loose, lifted it enough to work their fingers underneath, and then pulled it up from the floor.

"Don't hit each other with the plankin'," Old Sam said.

Two more planks rose from the floor and were set quietly aside.

"Get the lamp, and bring it over here," Benjie said.

Old Sam crowded up behind Annie as she aimed the lantern beam into the gap in the planking. He was eager for another glimpse of the cannon he had seen there two days earlier. With a sudden shock, however, he realized something was wrong.

"Nothin' in here, Grampy Sam," Benjie said. "You sure this is where . . . no. Wait. There is somethin' in here."

Benjie lay flat and reached down and then brought up an earthenware jug. A rolled paper had been thrust through its handle and tied into place with a cord.

"But where's the cannon?" Tom asked.

"Let me have a look at that paper, Benjie," Old Sam said. "And, Annie, bring that light closer."

With weak hands Old Sam pulled the rolled paper through the loop of cord around it, unrolled it, and held it top and bottom out at arms' length.

"From Cy Clifford," Old Sam said.

"What's it say?" Sue asked.

"Let me read it here," Old Sam said. "A little closer with that light, Annie. Well, here it is:

Dear Sam Barston,

    Good try, but you been known to play tricks before, so I thought we best hide the cannon some-place safe. The jug is to thank you for your help before with the Charlestown boys and the Dartmouth College boys and to ease you through your disappointment. Come back on the Fourth of July if you want to hear a cannon. We'll haul it out about noon time.

                                       Cy

"Ha," Old Sam said as he broke the lingering silence. "So much for gettin' us a cannon."

"We could decorate the mill pretty good with all this flour, Grampy Sam," Benjie said.

"No, Benjie. I won't have it," Old Sam said. "It's a sin to waste food and another one to cost a man the earnin's of his labor. No. Leave it alone. We got beat fair and square, and that's the end of it. Cy Clifford. And I never thought he was all that smart. He beat me on the cannon, and just look how he beat me with the jug. If it was only a note he left, then we would of put the note right back the way it was, put all the sacks and barrels back, and left pretendin' we was never here. But add a jug to it, and he's got me. He knows I'll take the jug, and that'll give him the satisfaction of knowin' that he beat me. Smart man. Well, we'll take the jug. And we might as well leave the floorin' up too. Come on now. We'll go home."

Annie put an arm around Old Sam and gave him a hug. "I'm sorry," she said.

"We gave it a good try, didn't we?" Old Sam said. "Only ones in Barston Falls that did, and I think it come pretty close to workin'. I guess this is a little comeuppance to me for gettin' away with so many other things over the years. One thing it's hard to do is change a reputation that's got built up in one place for sixty-odd years. Let that be a lesson to me."

Benjie carried the jug as they went back out to the wagon and told Foss of their failure. All of them were deeply disappointed.

"Pretty good joke on us, ain't it?" Old Sam said. "I thought I had that cannon right in my pocket, but it turned out way too big for my pocket. Well, let's go. The horses likely won't mind if they don't have to drag a cannon."

They remounted the lanterns onto the wagon. The three boys climbed into the back, leaving the seat for Old Sam, Annie, and Sue. Annie drove the wagon back down along Robertson's Brook. Though the jug several times made the rounds among the six people, it seemed that only Old Sam drank from it. Then he told the boys to keep it back with them. Whispered conversations slowed and then ceased.

XXX

The wagon left Robertson's Brook and Wheelock Village behind. In the lateness of the hour and the light chill, the night sounds of insects had faded almost to obscurity.

"Must be long after midnight," Old Sam said, breaking the silence. "Guess I lived to the Fourth of July after all, but I didn't get my cannon for the village."

"Sorry you didn't," Annie said.

"Well, I had fun tonight, Grampy Sam," Sue said. "I'll remember this night when I get to be an old lady."

"It was kind of fun," Old Sam said. "But it ain't the same as haulin' a cannon home and shootin' it off and havin' everybody make a fuss over us. Kind of like that big fish you caught with Malik, Sue. You can have some fun plannin' how you're goin' to get it, but then at the end if you don't get it, you can't surprise folks with it, and it just ain't so good. Ain't nearly so good."

"You rest now, Old Sam," Annie said. "Don't think about it too much."

"I was just a silly old man, I s'pose, with one last chance to play another good trick after years and years of 'em. I wanted this last one to come out right, so maybe I could believe I wasn't a worthless old man after all, but Cy Clifford outsmarted me.

"One of you boys want to pass me that jug?"

Sue spoke after a moment's silence.

"They're all asleep, Grampy Sam. I can climb over and find it."

"No. Don't bother," Old Sam said. "I don't need it that bad. Let the boys alone. They didn't get any sleep tonight, and I had 'em runnin' around most of last night too arrangin' things for gettin' the cannon. Can't have you steppin' on 'em and wakin' 'em up just so's an old man can have a little rum that he don't need anyways. They need their rest."

They kept on in a silence broken only by the footfalls of the horses and by the light creaks and rattles of the wagon. Old Sam at last spoke.

"I can't see so good as I once could," he said. "Maybe one of you pretty-eyed women could look down there to the left and tell me if you don't see a light."

"Nothin' wrong with your eyes, Old Sam," Annie said. "That's a light all right."

"That's where it was before, I think," Sue said. "Right in the graveyard, ain't it?"

"Sounds like a good guess to me," Old Sam said, his voice dropping off to a whisper. "About the right place for it. If that's one of Foss's spirit lights, then the three of us are in big trouble. Keep it pretty quiet."

The wagon hadn't moved much further before Old Sam told Annie to stop.

"Well, it is in the graveyard," he whispered. "Now generally anybody that's in a graveyard at night with a lantern ain't up to much good. Sue, you and Tom saw the light before, but whoever it was heard us comin' and hid it, so we know he ain't up to any good."

"A grave robber, Grampy Sam?" Sue asked.

"Might be. Cy didn't say anythin' about anybody dyin' in the village when I was up day before yesterday, but then again a lot of folks ain't comfortable tellin' an old man about somebody else dyin'. Or somebody might of died after I left, and they planted the body quick as they could in the hot weather."

"Should we get somebody from Wheelock Village?" Annie asked.

"Let's find out for sure what he's up to first," Old Sam said. "If it's a grave robber, then he's been here a while already and might be done and gone by the time we could get back with somebody."

"I'll wake up the boys," Sue said.

"No. Leave 'em alone for now," Old Sam said. "We'll sneak in there — the three of us — and spy out what's goin' on first. If we need the boys, one of you can come back and get 'em or you can scream for 'em, but for now we'll go in a lot quieter without 'em. And the lanterns stay here. Now help me down, but first both of you pick up a few throwin' rocks to carry along if you can find any. Might need 'em if somebody starts chasin' us."

In response to Old Sam's hushed directions, Sue and Annie tied the horses and hung the carriage lanterns over on the side of the wagon away from the cemetery. They stooped to pick up a few stones in the lanternlight before they helped Old Sam down from the wagon. Then the three of them started groping their way toward the light in the cemetery. As they neared the hewn stone walls surrounding the cemetery, Annie made them stop.

"It's two lanterns," she whispered.

"So it is," Old Sam said. "Well, be careful sneakin' in. Stay low, and use the gravestones to hide behind, and I think we can get pretty close. And remember we can see a lot better than whoever is by the lanterns. The light blinds 'em from seein' much of anythin' that ain't right in the brightness. Slow now. And don't get in too close."

Sue and Annie together lifted Old Sam over the wall and then guided him among the gravestones as the three of them drew closer to the lanterns. Old Sam had to stop to rest. As his breathing slowed, they listened to the irregular, metallic bangings and rattlings of what they took to be shoveling. Those sounds were of short duration, however. Periodically they were replaced by lengthy murmurings of indiscernible words, which lasted much longer than the sounds of shoveling.

"Awful lot of talk and not a lot of shovelin'," Old Sam said. "These boys ain't much for work if they been at it like that since we passed 'em on the way up. Well, let's get closer. Both of you got those throwin' rocks handy?"

They said they did.

"All right," Old Sam whispered. "We'll go in close and then sit and listen. Keep as quiet as you can, and don't do anythin' 'til I tell you."

They drew to within perhaps fifty feet of the lanterns before they stopped. They saw clearly the two lanterns resting on the ground — one a perforated metal candle lantern and the other a glass chimney oil lamp — and the partially illuminated back of a man standing between the lanterns as he leaned on a shovel. A second man stood waist high in a hole in front of the first and every now and then stooped over and threw out another shovelful of dirt.

"This is getting to be real work," the man in the hole said. "I'm not used to it. But at least we have all night."

"It may very well take all night if you don't start flinging a little more of the bottom of the hole up here. Simply work as swiftly as you can. Then, when you get tired, we'll shift positions until I tire myself out."

"'Slow and steady wins the race,' as they say."

"That is true, but slowness alone doesn't win a thing."

"Perhaps you'd like to start digging right now."

"I would except that it doesn't seem you've had a proper turn down there yet."

"Ha! When you were last down here, I didn't exactly see the dirt fly. You took . . . Did you hear that?"

For a moment all was still. Then the other man spoke.

"No. You're hearing your own imagination. You're hearing your own procrastinations. You're hearing everything but the proper sounds of shoveling."

Five or six cascades of dirt came leaping out of the hole one after another. They landed close enough to the shovel-leaner to make him move back. Then, however, the shoveling rate settled back into its more familiar, sporadic pace before it ceased altogether.

"It shouldn't be too much deeper," the man in the hole said as he climbed out. "As soon as the shovel strikes wood, we'll be virtually finished."

Old Sam whispered to Sue and Annie. "I wonder how many days they been diggin' this hole."

The former shovel-leaner descended into the hole and set to work shoveling at a measured pace. The former shoveler leaned on his shovel as he held the oil lamp, surveyed the shoveling effort, and busied himself making judgements. The steady pace of the shoveling didn't last. The moving shovel stopped.

"What's your guess?" the man in the hole asked. "Man, woman, or child?"

"The flesh will all be gone at the rate you're getting down to it. You'll have to identify it from its skeleton. Do you think you're capable of that, you charlatan?"

"Fully as capable as the quack with the question. Now if you'll excuse me from this conversation, I have shoveling to do."

The shoveling recommenced and continued for a relatively impressive interval. Then the shovel clanged hard several times, followed by a drawn-out, metallic scraping.

"Here it is," the man in the hole said. "The coffin appears to have a metal lid, however. Could you hold a lantern for me?"

Old Sam whispered to Sue and Annie.

"Get your throwin' rocks ready. I want you to throw a couple so they land beyond the men. Throw 'em at the same time, and then duck down quick, and stay down. Get ready now. All right."

Sue and Annie leaned away from Old Sam and threw. One of the rocks made a sharp clack as it hit a gravestone beyond the two men. The lantern bearer jerked his attention and the light of the oil lantern away from the hole and over toward where the stones had landed.

"Down here," the man in the hole called out. "This happens to be where I happen to need the light in order to work."

"I heard something," the other man said. "Someone might be here!"

The man in the hole stood upright. For a moment both men listened in silence.

"I can't hear it now, but it sounded as if something moved."

"Some small animal, perhaps. Never mind about it unless it recurs. Just hold the lantern so I can see to work."

The man with the lantern directed its light back to the hole, but continued to turn his head this way and that as he gazed out across the cemetery.

Old Sam whispered again.

"Now see if you can't land a rock right in the grave."

Sue and Annie threw again, failing to duck back down.

The man holding the lantern gave an abrupt cry of pain, and the lantern jerked into the air. It landed with a crash and immediate flare as Old Sam commenced a staccato of wordless shouts, more beastlike than human. The other man shot out of the grave and sprawled against his partner. Just before they bolted in panic, one of them grabbed the candle lantern. When its light began dodging among the tombstones, away from the blazing oil at the grave, Old Sam started shouting.

"Bring the guns up! Quick boys, bring the guns up! Kill 'em! Kill 'em!"

Benjie's shout rang out from back at the wagon. "What's goin' on? You all right, Grampy?"

Over past the far side of the cemetery the candle lantern paused briefly in its flight and twitched in a tight frenzy. Then it moved with renewed swiftness off to the south to the accompanying clatter of a moving horse and wagon.

Sue, Annie, and Old Sam stood in the cemetery and watched the light from the candle lantern disappear. Then, finally, even the sounds of the retreat faded to obscurity. The flames by the grave burned low.

"We sure scared 'em off," Annie said. "Saved the grave from gettin' robbed."

"Yes, we did," Old Sam said. "And there they go runnin' back down to Hanover. Dartmouth slime. Run right home to the medical school, or I miss my guess. They go out durin' the day and tour the countryside for fresh graves and then come back at night and dig 'em up. Well, if they steal my body after I die, I want the both of you to go down to Hanover and burn that medical school right to the ground."

"I'll do that myself," Annie said. "I promise."

"Good girl," Old Sam said. "And say, that was quite a throw to hit the man with the lantern. Whose was that?"

"Wasn't me," Sue said. "I was aimin' for the hole."

"Wasn't me either," Annie giggled. "I was aimin' for the hole too."

Old Sam laughed.

"Good work anyways, however it got done."

"Here come the boys with the lanterns," Sue said. "I guess they can help shovel the grave back in."

"Ha!" Old Sam said. "We might not shovel it back in at all."

"What do you mean?" Sue asked.

"Well, I don't want to get your hopes up, but I think there's a chance that if we hadn't of been here those body snatchers wouldn't of got their body anyways."

"Course they would of," Annie said. "They was right

down to the coffin when we scared 'em off."

"And when was there ever metal-top coffins used around here? Unless I miss my guess, I think we scared those two off from findin' out right where the Wheelock Village boys went and hid our cannon.

"Over here with those lanterns, boys!"

*****

It was indeed Wheelock Village's cannon that the six of them gazed at in the lantern beams as Benjie finished digging with one of the abandoned shovels. Though immediately it began to assume its new identity as Barston Falls' cannon, both thought and work were needed to strengthen title to it. It still had to be raised from the grave and be started on its way down towards Barston Falls.

Old Sam made them wait until he was sure that the loud disturbances in the cemetery hadn't roused anyone up in the village. Thereafter he kept an eye out for approaching lights. However, his caution proved unnecessary.

It took two horses pulling ropes in opposite directions to raise the cannon; a snub line around a tombstone to hold it from settling back down while the ropes were tied for a new purchase to haul it clear of the grave. Snaking the cannon out to the road from among the tombstones proved equally challenging, but the work was accomplished. The boys, under Old Sam's direction, slung most of the weight of the cannon under the one-axle wheel rig, using the two horses to raise it up to where it could be chained, and then harnessed them to haul it. The cannon muzzle dragged on the ground but lightly enough so that the horses wouldn't have hard pulling. Old Sam took a last drink of rum from the jug before he gave it to Benjie to leave at the bottom of the cannon grave.

"Only right to give Cy Clifford a present and give him

a chance to say a few words to the folks of Wheelock Village," Old Sam said. "Now it's their problem to try and figure out how to steal it back, ain't it?"

During the next hour Sue and Annie kept trying unsuccessfully to calm down Old Sam, who bubbled over with joy as the horses took the cannon down along the river. It wasn't until the cannon was aboard the flatboat, however, that they could persuade him to rest. By then the team that had been pulling the cannon had been hitched to a log to counterfeit a drag trail. Foss and Tom rode together in the wagon so they could take turns sleeping. The team dragging the log was tethered behind the wagon.

Benjie, Sue, Annie, and Old Sam drifted down the Connecticut on the flatboat in those very earliest hours of the Fourth of July in 1826. Although Old Sam sat back in comfort and fatigue on the flatboat, sleep was the furthest thing from his mind. He talked endlessly as the other three fought to stay awake; recounted the events and pranks and joys of a lifetime in the Connecticut River valley. He spoke of occasions six decades earlier as if they had happened only the week before. All his talk was of the past; an old man having progressed as far as was possible through the experiences of life and now having set his back firmly against the future, as if it were a locked door he would never have the key to.

"After this day is done, I can die happy any time," Old Sam said several times without being aware he was repeating himself.

Just before dawn there were lapses into silence and sleep for those not charged with a turn at steering the flatboat. Old Sam, however, never fell asleep; regarded sleep that night almost as he regarded death and did not want to interrupt with unconsciousness — either temporary or permanent — the successes of the day, the memories of his long past, and the images of the river valley at night.

At the coming of first light Old Sam's fatigue felt bone-deep, something from which mere rest would not allow him to recover. He roused the sleepers as the flatboat drifted towards the slot between Rattlesnake Hill on the east and Barston Hill on the west. Annie and Benjie poled them closer to the western bank of the Connecticut. Then they drifted down toward the village of Barston Falls. They glimpsed the brickyard, the mouth of Tannery Brook, and the upper warehouse. The canal began right beside the upper warehouse. When they got close enough, they saw Tom and Foss waiting with a team.

XXXI

Old Sam's thoughts, in his extreme fatigue, rode with the mist rising in wisps from the canal and from the Connecticut River. Dawn by the lightly veiled river set him musing about the timelessness of the scene. On countless July mornings long before he'd been born, mist had risen from that part of the Connecticut in just the same way. On summer mornings centuries into the future, the top of Barston Hill would still catch the first sunlight just as it was now doing, and shadows would linger on the slopes of Rattlesnake Hill well into the morning. Every summer dawn perhaps until the end of time the river would continue to tumble through the gap between Barston Hill and Rattlesnake Hill.

He had come as a young man onto the land, which had then all been wilderness, and had spent most of his life less than a mile from the falls. His family had given the township its name and had built the village. His parents and his four brothers were buried here. His wife was buried here, waiting for him. All his friends from the early years had died; now lay in cemeteries within half a day's travel. Before long, he knew, his own life would end. People were born, skittered like water striders over the brief years of their existences, and then left everything behind: love, wealth, power, vanity, arrogance, and occasional good deeds. The best they could hope for in their meager gleanings was to be remembered with fondness for a few years and to have children to continue the skittering. The river, the sunrises, the mist, and the hills all endured. In the sweep of time a man was very poor indeed.

Old Sam's thoughts returned to the special day that was dawning. He stood between Sue and Annie by the idle steering oar and glanced at the boys, who were all off the flatboat. Tom held the team. Benjie and Foss waited for the upper lock to drain so they could open the gates and continue the flatboat's passage down through the canal. From the settling boat he looked out over what he could see of the village.

Bats fluttered among the buildings, which were vague in the mist. No longer did they swoop after bugs, but instead sought the familiar niches where they rested during the heat of the day. One by one they returned from their night wanderings, circled for a time with the throng, and at last squeezed in under the eaves of the mill buildings, the belfries of the Methodist and Congregational churches, the attic of the Eagle Hotel, and into attics of homes, dark corners of sheds, and lofts of barns wherever even slight openings permitted them passage. Old Sam watched the thinning flurry of bats over by the upper warehouse.

You ain't the only ones that was up all night. Don't get too comfortable now if you expect to sleep today. This is the Fourth of July of eighteen-hundred-and-twenty-six. Fifty years it is since we called ourselves free of England, and this is goin' to be a day when my cannon will make a little noise. Nobody can stay abed while we have our celebration, so you might as well stay up and enjoy it. Fair warnin'.

"How are you feelin', Old Sam?" Annie asked.

"Tired," Old Sam said. "As tired as I ever was. But I ain't dead yet, and I'm plannin' to live right up to the minute I die. And I'll do a little crowin' today on account of here it is the Fourth of July, and here we are with a cannon for the village."

"I got to go to George's and get my babies. Think he'll fight much about givin' 'em back? Sue can . . . well, the two of you can keep each other company while I'm gone."

"Yes, we will," Sue said. She gave Annie a boost up over the canal wall as the flatboat was settling lower into the lock. Then she went back and sat next to Old Sam, who continued to stand.

"We did it, Sue," Old Sam said after Annie had left. "Three boys and two women and one old man went out and got a cannon for the village. I hope you live to be a hundred years old and remember this day all your life."

"I ain't likely to forget last night, Grampy Sam," Sue said. "I don't see how the day can be any better."

"I'll borrow some powder from the lower warehouse and show you," Old Sam said. "We're goin' to wake up everybody in the whole village, and we won't let even one of 'em forget this day for years. Just wait 'til you hear the echoes! That's what the Fourth of July of eighteen hundred-and-twenty-six means. When you're an old woman, Sue, in eighteen-hundred-and-seventy-six, I'm expectin' you to tell all the young folks then how they need to go about celebratin' the Fourth of July."

"Yes, Grampy Sam. I already promised you that before. And if the Wheelock Village folks steal the cannon back, I'll go right out and steal it from 'em again."

"Good girl."

A spasm shuddered through Old Sam's body. Both his hands clutched at his chest, and his knees supported him so poorly that he began to sink backwards. Sue bolted to her feet, wrapped her arms around his shoulders, and eased him to sit down.

"You all right?" she asked.

"No. I ain't," Old Sam said as he labored to breathe. "Oh, I can't go and die now when we're so close. Please, God, don't let me die now. Don't you want to see how the cannon-shootin' is goin' to come out? Don't let me die now."

"Breathe deep, and set back, and rest," Sue said.

Sue kept an arm around Old Sam's shoulders. Benjie and Foss climbed down onto the flatboat as Tom began to urge the team forward to pull the flatboat through the long stretch to the middle lock and lower lock.

"You all right, Grampy Sam?" Benjie asked.

"I don't think so, Benjie. It's the twinges again, but this one hit me sudden. Mostly I can tell when they're comin', but this one didn't give me a warnin'."

"Should I go get somebody?" Benjie asked.

"No. I can't see what good that might do. You just get this boat down to Jared's warehouse, and then you find us some powder to feed into our cannon, Benjie. That's what I need."

Sue continued to hold Old Sam as the flatboat moved down the canal. Benjie and Foss looked on with concern. At the end of the long, flat stretch through the village — after the flatboat had entered the middle lock and was settling down to the level of the lower lock — Annie appeared on the eastern bank of the canal. Foss, already there to work the gates of the locks, gave her a hand to climb down into the flatboat. Annie was breathing hard and sweating.

"They ain't there," she said to Sue and Old Sam. "George ain't there, and the twins ain't there. Oh, what could of happened to 'em? I hope they ain't . . . you all right, Old Sam? You look kind of pale."

"I was just havin' a little spell," Old Sam said. "It ain't so bad as it was. Sue's takin' good care of me."

"You sure you're all right?" Annie asked.

"Course I ain't sure," Old Sam said. "Only thing I know for sure is that we stole Wheelock Village's cannon from 'em last night and that, soon as we can get some powder from the lower warehouse, nobody in this village is goin' to sleep late this mornin', and everybody is goin' to find out pretty quick just who it was that stole a cannon for 'em for the Fourth of July. And if the cannon fire ain't loud enough to bust a few windows, that ain't my fault. Now what about the twins?"

"They ain't at George's, and he ain't either. I'm worried about 'em."

"Don't worry about 'em," Old Sam said. "Just go find 'em wherever they are. You checked at home?"

"No."

"That's where they are then. George got tired of 'em, if you can imagine that. You said Joe went out, wasn't it? And you was good and mad at him 'cause he wouldn't tell where he was goin'?"

"Yes. That's right."

"Well, Joe's back, and George took the boys to him. That's where you'll find the whole pack of 'em, and like as not they're worried to death about you and Sue — couple women out cattin' around at night and no idea what you're up to. You run on home, Annie, and find 'em and set 'em at ease. Hear me?"

Annie leaned over and gave Old Sam a kiss.

"You take care of this good man, Sue," Annie said.

"I will, Annie."

Annie called up to Foss. He helped her up from the flatboat in the nearly drained lock, and she hurried off towards home. Benjie and Foss opened the gates between the middle lock and the lower lock and closed them again after the team had pulled the flatboat into the lower lock. Tom untied the tow line from the team and started leading the horses over towards the lower warehouse. Then Benjie and Foss began draining the lower lock to settle the flatboat to the level of the bay below the falls.

"Your color looks a little better, Grampy Sam," Sue said.

"Well, I feel better," Old Sam said. "Didn't mean to scare you with that spell. If it wasn't the Fourth of July, I might go home and go to bed. But it is the Fourth of July, so I won't. We got to steal a little powder from the lower warehouse, Sue, and run a few rounds through our cannon to get folks in the village up and movin'."

"And then I'll fix you a breakfast, Grampy Sam," Sue said. "I'll get a breakfast for all of us, and we can brag to Pa about last night."

Benjie and Foss eased open the last gates of the canal and whistled for Tom as they climbed back down onto the flatboat and picked up their raft poles. Tom joined them. As soon as the flatboat had cleared the lower lock, the three boys began maneuvering towards the dock of the lower warehouse. Soon enough, however, Benjie abruptly ceased poling as his attention fixed itself on the far end of the dock.

"It's Pa!" he called out. "And Uncle Seth is with him!"

Tom and Foss kept the flatboat moving over toward the near end of the dock. Jared and Seth strode the length of the dock to meet it.

"Well, well, well," Seth said as the flatboat touched the dock. "We was wonderin' who might be cheatin' us out of canal fare sneakin' down like that. I was under the misimpression that a cranky old man like you, Grampy Sam, needs all the rest you can get and that you might be abed at such an hour."

"Wrong again, Seth," Old Sam said. "Gettin' to be a regular habit with you, ain't it?"

"Is this the old misleadin' the young, or the other way around?" Jared said. "What are you doin' up so early this mornin'?"

"Up late or up early," Old Sam said. "It's all the same. We ain't been to bed tonight."

"Out cattin' around for a boat ride all night, Grampy Sam?" Seth said. "At your age? What in the devil is ailin' you?"

Old Sam stabbed his forefinger alternately towards Seth and Jared as he spoke.

"Oh you ignorant, lamb-hearted, lard-butted, poor ex-cuses for grand-nephews. Somebody had to go out and make sure we could do more for the Fourth of July than set around and eat things. It wasn't goin' to be the two of you, so I got a good crew together, and we went up and stole Wheelock Village's cannon! Now what do you think about that?"

"No!" Jared said.

"Uncover that thing, Sue, and let's see if these two worthless excuses for Barstons can't recognize a cannon after they been told right out that's what it is."

Sue pulled the sailcloth tarp from the cannon. First Seth and then Jared started to laugh.

"You ornery old cuss," Seth said. "I ain't even goin' to ask. At your age, Grampy Sam, I can't do anythin' but shake my head and be proud to be a Barston. If it wouldn't swell up your head so, I might even say you're still quite a man, but it'd swell your head so bad that I ain't goin' to say it."

"Well, don't you forget it anyways, even if you won't say it — the both of you," Old Sam said. "Now the least you can do is run get me a little of your stump-blowin' powder and a coal to touch her off with."

"No sir," Seth said. "The least we can do is nothin' — or so I heard it said before. Truth is, Grampy Sam, we was about to blow a couple stumps at the other end of the dock, so we got the powder and a punk coal already. You come along and have a look, Grampy Sam. Sue, you and the boys bring the boat up to the other end by the boardpile, and we'll unload the cannon there. You ain't to fire it loose like that on one of our flatboats. Come along, Grampy Sam."

Jared and Seth steadied Old Sam on either side as he trudged the length of the dock.

"Now you can see we're better grand-nephews than you thought, Grampy Sam," Jared said. "If you want to eat a flock of crows for the things you said about us, go right ahead. Just see how we went out and stole you a little cannon for the Fourth of July. We got it a while back, but we wanted to keep quiet about it so we could surprise you today. Look!"

Old Sam squinted at the near side of the board pile as he moved closer, gave a start, and shook his head for a moment before he spoke.

"Call that a cannon, do you?" Old Sam said. "No wonder you wanted to keep quiet about it. That thing ain't but a toy. Hardly even a cannon. Looks like an old fowlin' piece that somebody forgot to make a stock for. Just a little popgun."

"She'll make enough noise, Grampy Sam," Seth said as he kept Old Sam moving past the little cannon. "Maybe almost as much noise as you. But if that ain't to your likin', then step around to the other side of the board pile. We stole the little one for practice. And we stole this other one for you, Grampy Sam, so you could hear it thunder and echo for the Fourth of July. This is your cannon now — both of 'em, I mean — from us so you can have a proper fifty year celebration this year. Happy Fourth of July, Grampy Sam."

Old Sam stopped with his mouth open for a moment as he gazed down on the full-sized cannon lying on the dock next to the board pile.

"Oh you miserable, sneaky, little liars!" Old Sam roared. "Plaguin' an old man like that — teasin' me so and makin' any number of excuses when I wanted you to go help me grab Wheelock Village's cannon! You had these all along, ain't you?"

"We wanted to surprise you with 'em today, Grampy Sam," Jared said. "We got the little one before town meetin', and we got the big one when we went away a couple weeks back."

"You surprised me with this all right," Old Sam said. "And tortured me too! You miserable cusses got any idea how much sufferin' I went through to steal a cannon? If I'd of known you was thinkin' about gettin' one yourselves, it would of saved me no end of pain. If you'd of only told me, I wouldn't of chased around so gettin' one myself. I could of at least got some sleep last night."

"Hah!" Seth said. "And on account of we didn't tell you, all of Wheelock Village is blushin' right down to their toes 'cause it was you stole their cannon. And on account of we didn't tell you, I'm goin' to brag to everybody in Vermont and New Hampshire that my great-uncle, Old Sam Barston, is still up to his tricks and still might be the best man in the whole Connecticut River valley. Oh, don't you waste your breath tellin' tales, Grampy Sam. You loved stealin' that cannon last night. And now you're goin' to love havin' everybody find out about it. If you hadn't of gone out last night and stole that cannon, then you wouldn't have even half as good a time today as you will."

"Yes sir, Grampy Sam," Jared said. "You set back today and enjoy folks fussin' over you because you stole Wheelock Village's cannon and because we stole two more for you so we can have a little noise. Today is your day. Today is Old Sam Barston day in Barston Falls. And the two cannons ain't the only surprise we got for you. Seth has somethin' else too, but you ain't to have it yet. You got to wait for that part. We'll make a little noise with your cannons today, Grampy Sam, and if there's one thing I'll try to do when folks come down to gawk, it's to see if I can't out-brag Seth about you."

"Oh you boys!" Old Sam said. "I should of known the Barston name still means somethin' — should of known you two wasn't nearly so worthless as you was pretendin'. Makes me proud enough almost to just set right down and cry."

"Course you can if you want," Seth said. "But while you're settin' there blubberin' away, all the folks in the village will still be sleepin', and Jared and me was thinkin' that they prob'ly already slept too long. You can't let 'em settle into bad habits on the celebration day of the fiftieth year of our country just so's you can have a good cry like some old maid peelin' onions. No sir. Some of us men that are still proud of the Barston family name don't want some snifflin' old goat draggin' it right down when instead he needs to be braggin' about it. We got some powder to load and some cannons to touch off and a whole village of folks to wake up."

Old Sam started laughing.

"Well get to it, boys! How you want to do this anyways?"

"It's your day, General," Seth said. "You tell us how we need to do it. Only we ain't shootin' it off on the flatboat 'cause it'll either bust up some of the boat or hop off into the river or do both things at the same time."

"All right then," Old Sam said. "Get the boardpile out of here. We'll line up the three cannons and touch 'em off one right after the other — little one first so's we can gentle folks awake and then the two big ones right after. That's the way to start off this Fourth of July."

"There is another thing, Grampy Sam," Jared said. "We need to aim the cannons straight out over the river, at least to start with."

"How come?" Old Sam asked.

"It's on account of the waddin' we got," Jared said. "A lot of it is right off of Deacon Russell's clothesline, and we already cut it up. If we can use all that up before everybody starts gatherin' around, then he won't know where his clothes disappeared to. If we aim the cannons the right way, the waddin' 'll land in the river and all drift away."

"Good," Old Sam said. "Line 'em up side by side on the dock then, and point 'em over the river, and let's get to it."

Sue and the boys made a considerable fuss over the other two cannons, but were quickly at work nonetheless offloading Wheelock Village's cannon to the dock with Seth and Jared and a team of horses. They moved the boardpile off the dock from between Seth and Jared's two cannons, spaced the three cannons about ten yards apart and under Seth's direction ladled powder into their bores, jammed cloth in on top of the powder, and tamped down the wadding and charges as best they could with a raft pole. Seth primed the touchholes of the cannons.

"Sometimes folks have Seegars goin' to hold fire," Seth said, "but we ain't got Seegars. We got a bucket of coals and long punk sticks instead. Long sticks on account of when I was learnin' how to go about shootin' off cannons, they told me to be careful of cannons that ain't mounted on carriages. You don't want to be anyplace behind 'em. Now seein' as how this is Old Sam Barston Day in Barston Falls, I think that maybe you need to shoot off the first round, Grampy Sam. Just stand off to the side and touch the punk stick to the touchhole, and we'll start off this Fourth of July celebration."

"All right," Old Sam said. "I'll do it, and we'll get a few folks out of bed. Get me a punk stick, one of you boys."

"You need to give us a speech, Grampy Sam," Jared said. "That way we'll start this day off right. A short speech."

Foss Richardson handed Old Sam a smoldering punk stick. Old Sam held it like a staff as wisps of smoke curled and disappeared around his head.

"Fifty years ago today," Old Sam began, "we went about our business here in the town and didn't know a thing about the Declaration of Independence. The village of Barston Falls was just startin' out. My brother Israel had a carry business around the falls and a store, and all the buildin's in town was wood — not brick like today. My brother Caleb went off to help General Washington get us free of England

and have a separate country of the United States of America. But most of us before then just went about livin' as settlers in the New Hampshire Grants and didn't pay much attention to the Allen brothers and to the folks down in Massachusetts that was stirrin' things up. John Wentworth was chased out as Royal Governor by then, but a lot of us in the valley still thought highly of him. It wasn't 'til later when most folks started to appreciate what it meant to be a whole new country, the United States of Amer — "

A whistling shriek overhead abruptly cut off Old Sam's words and flattened everyone but Old Sam right down onto the dock. He himself glanced up, but then almost immediately turned his gaze out to the eddy, where, in half a dozen scattered jolts, water erupted in huge columns. Before the splashings had settled, a tremendous roar from behind jerked the attention of prone and upright alike up towards Barston Hill. Mouths agape, all those prone on the dock were beginning to rise when another roar from out over the river slammed and flattened them anew. Thereafter roaring re-echoes from Barston Hill and Rattlesnake Hill merged into increasing disorder. The rumbles filled every inch of the valley before they faded, eventually, to a silence broken first by Old Sam's laughter.

"Wicked, wicked, wicked," Benjie murmured as a smile contorted his face.

"What in the devil was that?" Seth shouted loudly enough to vent some of his fright. He got to his feet slowly.

"A cannon," Jared said, shaking his head without taking his eyes off the three cannons on the dock. "And it wasn't one of ours. A loaded cannon."

"A cannon!" Old Sam chortled. "Four cannons for the village!"

"Four so far," Jared said.

"Well, that's what comes of wastin' time givin' speeches," Old Sam said. He turned towards Barston Hill and shouted. "Cannon number four! You might of beat us wakin' up the village, but we ain't about to let you roar louder than us! No more speeches, so stand back! Hooray for the United States of America!"

Old Sam lowered the punk stick toward the small cannon and fumbled for a moment around the touchhole. The cannon leaped back with a roar as fire shot from the muzzle and smoke wreathed the dock. The others stood amid dissipating smoke, listening to Old Sam's whoops and laughter punctuated by the echoes and re-echoes of cannon fire. Long before the rumbles had had a chance to die, he had stepped over to the nearer of the large cannons and had again lowered the punk stick. A second explosion — far louder than the first — set Old Sam chortling with glee. He stumbled through the smoke and with some difficulty succeeded in finding the third touchhole with the punk stick. At the third explosion he flung the stick into the air and lurched towards the others, hugging each one of them and laughing with an intensity bordering on hysteria. All were cheering loudly and continued to cheer after the cannon rumbles had ceased.

Seth directed the others in hauling the cannons back into place, swabbing down their bores with a wet rag on a stick, and reloading them. While they were at work, another blast from the direction of Barston Hill surprised them as it again flooded the valley with drawn-out rumblings. This time they all managed to stay on their feet. Jared noted a disturbance of cascading debris on the steep slopes of Rattlesnake Hill, pointed it out to the others, and swore it had been caused by a cannonball shot from hill to hill. They all puzzled aloud about who else in the village might have a cannon, but then, because of their urgent need to fire another round from their own cannons, gave up guessing. Seth and Jared and Sue each fired a cannon during that second round, and the boys were promised their turns next.

Joe and Annie Reckford came walking down onto the dock hand-in-hand. Each carried a son. Joe shook his head as he looked at the three cannons and approached Old Sam.

"That was Joe's cannon, Old Sam!" Annie said as she stared hard at the three cannons. "That cannon up above was what Joe stole for you! But you got a whole flock of 'em now!"

"It wasn't just me, Old Sam," Joe said. "It was Charlie Porter mainly. George and Mark went along with us there right after town meetin', and I tell you we had quite a time gettin' it. You see, Old Sam, we wanted to do somethin' special for you this Fourth of July. You mean a lot to all of us, and we wanted to surprise you. Seems like a lot of folks around here had cannon secrets, but I hope you don't think our cannon for you means any less on account of it. I'd like it, Old Sam, if you can come up with us and see the cannon we got for you. Had to go all the way to Charlestown for it."

"Hah!" Old Sam said. "So the Charlestown boys did have a reason to be up here after all."

"Well," Joe began. "George was a little mad at the Wheelock Village folks, and he . . ."

"That don't matter," Annie interrupted. "All that matters, Old Sam, is that a lot of people in this village tried to get you what you wanted this Fourth of July. And just on account of it's you, Barston Falls has now got four cannons. Four at last count, anyways."

Annie handed Amos to Joe and gave Old Sam a long hug. Meanwhile Seth had directed the boys through the reloading of the cannons, which stood charged and primed. He nodded to the boys and, as the rest of them watched, the boys took their turns firing the cannons.

"You boys keep shootin' off the cannons for a while," Seth said. "You know how. Just swab 'em out every time before you reload, and don't overload 'em. I got another cannon to go see. You, Jared?"

"Yes," Jared said. "I think we might have a few cannon-stealin' stories to trade around. You boys mind what Seth says now about the cannons. Hear me?"

"Yes sir," Benjie said. "Don't you worry, Pa. You ain't the only man in this village that knows how to steal a cannon or what to do with it afterwards. I don't want to get killed or crippled today. All I want is to make some noise for the Fourth of July and hear the wicked, wicked echoes."

"Good boy, Benjie," Old Sam said.

"You boys keep firin' 'til all the waddin' is used up," Seth said. "Then go on over to the village square 'cause I'll have somethin' there you might want to see. And if anybody wants to know how we got all the cannons, you tell 'em we bought 'em down in Boston. All but Grampy Sam's. You tell 'em how Grampy Sam stole his from Wheelock Village."

"We got a wagon and team so you can ride up to Joe's cannon with us, Old Sam," Annie said. "How are you feelin' now?"

"No more twinges anyways, Annie, and this is the happiest I been for a long, long time. This is a Fourth of July everybody in the town can be proud of, and I'm goin' to enjoy every minute of it."

Sue stayed with the boys to help fire the cannons. The others rode up to the cemetery, where they found Charlie, Mark, and George firing off their cannon. Seth right away impressed on them the need to swab out the cannon between firings. Soon enough a jug began circulating, and the cannon thieves began trading severely embellished accounts of how the cannons had been stolen. As soon as other villagers began to gather around, however — drawn by the noise — all of the cannons had suddenly been "bought down in Boston," except, of course, for Old Sam's.

Old Sam, in spite of his extreme fatigue and in spite of occasional, recurring twinges in his chest, insisted on staying awake all day to celebrate the fiftieth anniversary of the country. He dreaded the return to home and to his bed almost as he dreaded the grave and, indeed, feared that it would be the same thing. Each moment seemed distilled for him. People remarked throughout the day how alert he was and how he seemed to savor each event and each contact with friends.

The four cannons remained where they were that day. A great deal of powder was run through them. Seth Barston left the group gathered around the cannon by the cemetery and hinted at a mysterious surprise half an hour hence down in the village square. Curiosity ran at a moderate level, and a small crowd was there at the appointed time. Seth arrived in a wagon with a tarp covering the cargo he was carrying. With a dramatic flourish he unveiled a strange-looking, preserved beast: the size and shape of a horse, but with black and white stripes all over its body. In response to the many questions he was asked about where he had gotten it, he replied only that the beast had come from Africa, a place on the other side of the world. Taken from the wagon and set down on the ground in the exact center of the village square, the beast was a continuing sensation. Every man, woman, and child in the village touched it at some point during the day. Joe and Annie Reckford remembered it with special fondness because it was under and around the beast that Amos and Aaron took their first unassisted steps, repeatedly staggering from front legs to back legs of the creature and from back legs to front and clutching at each accomplished goal so that they could remain standing. After they were both grown, they remembered the memories of others about the day they first walked almost as if the memories were their own — swearing, in fact, that they could remember the occasion.

The cannons fired sporadically throughout the day, each time rumbling long echoes and re-echoes between Barston Hill and Rattlesnake Hill. Great multitudes of townspeople gathered in the village square to celebrate. Mountains of food were consumed — more than at any town meeting day. Many speeches were given, honoring in nearly equal proportion Old Sam Barston and the United States of America. Some men of the village became as drunk — and as sick from drinking — as they had ever been in their lives and by their bad examples did their part to further the growing sentiment for temperance. The Methodists made a few converts that day and were clear winners over the Congregationalists.

Old Sam himself drank very little. He bubbled over with happiness throughout the morning, the noon hour, and well into the afternoon. Towards the end of the afternoon, however, he could no longer ignore his extreme fatigue. He resigned himself to returning home and going to bed, but first insisted on saying what he thought might be his final farewells to many friends. At last Seth and Jared got him into a wagon and circled the village square twice as Old Sam waved to people. Then they took him home and put him to bed.

Old Sam awoke the next morning feeling weak and miserable. It was more than a week before he felt up to dressing and going outside; nearly the middle of August before he returned to late morning fishing in Tannery Brook and afternoon chair-rocking on the dock at the lower warehouse. When rumor and then eventual confirmation reached Barston Falls of the deaths of both Thomas Jefferson and John Adams on the Fourth of July in 1826, Old Sam was vaguely envious of both men.

Old Sam Barston surprised everyone by living for nearly two more years, dying at last in his bed on a May night in 1828. Although he did not get his wish of dying while he was out fishing for trout, he had in fact caught trout from Tannery Brook on the day before his death.

Benjie came forward with explicit, written directions Old Sam had left for his funeral, and without dissent from any of the Barston relatives they were carried out to the very letter of his wishes. He was laid out in a plain, pine coffin. His fish pole was cut into three sections and laid on his chest; his creel set in beside him. Old Sam had written clearly how he had felt about having his body ride to burial in a hearse, so the hearse was left behind in its shed. Old Sam's pall bearers were to be "any that bore the last name of Barston and any that helped get cannons for the Fourth of July in 1826, and don't you dare drop me!" The pall bearers carried his coffin from his home over to the cemetery on the side of Barston Hill. Sue and Annie Reckford were particularly proud to have a turn at helping carry the coffin.

At the cemetery the pall bearers lowered Old Sam's coffin into the grave beside that of his wife, Amanda. Reverend Harper preached what everyone acknowledged was the shortest and best sermon of his life; filled with joy and hope and humor. Then various members of the Barston family said a few words over the grave and invited anyone else to speak who wanted to. A barrel of rum was tapped; people encouraged to help themselves. As a gesture of respect for Old Sam Barston, many of the extreme temperance advocates in the village drank token swallows of the rum.

A single shovel was passed from hand to hand, and the grave was slowly filled. When the task was done, Seth Barston stood over the grave and rang a bell loudly. A moment later a cannon blast roared down at the lower warehouse, followed almost immediately by a second one. The echoes rumbled and faded as people smiled with approval at the appropriateness of the cannon fire: "some farewell thunder for Old Sam." The supply of cannons in the village by 1828 had unfortunately dwindled to two. Some arrogant young thieves from Dartmouth College during the previous spring had stolen the small cannon and one of the big ones. In addition, they had stolen Seth Barston's extremely valuable African beast. As a result, the popularity of Dartmouth College was low in the village. There was talk among some citizens of finding teachers for the winter school from some place other than Dartmouth College until such time as the Dartmouth boys repented and returned the stolen items.

People stood by the grave and the keg of rum and reminisced about Old Sam as the cannons were loaded and fired three more times. Then the crowd gradually thinned away. The keg of rum was left beside the grave, according to Old Sam's wishes: "until the rum's all gone and my curse on anybody that carries any off. Drink it all right by the grave." It was a week later that Seth finally carried off the empty keg. Benjie likely drank a great deal of that rum, for he took it upon himself to sleep by the grave at night because of his concern about body snatchers from the Dartmouth medical school. He continued to sleep his nights there for nearly a fortnight after Seth had taken away the empty keg.

On that Fourth of July in 1828 Old Sam Barston's headstone was set over his grave. The slate stone bore his name, the years of his birth and death, and then two carvings — one of a cannon and one of a trout.

The tradition of firing at least one cannon in the village of Barston Falls each Fourth of July persisted throughout the lifetimes of all who had been present at the 1826 celebration. It wasn't always the same cannon or cannons each year, however, for the Barston Falls cannons were stolen from time to time by the men of Wheelock and other towns in the valley. Though the men of Barston Falls weren't always able to steal back the right cannon, they generally were able to steal at least some cannon, and in only a handful of years were they forced to do without one completely.

It was always a soul-stirring thrill for the people of the village to hear a cannon fired. Barston Hill and Rattlesnake Hill seized the initial roar and flung it back and forth across the Connecticut River in a long series of rolling, rumbling, and thudding reverberations which seemed to shake people — and satisfy them — to the very marrow of their bones.

When people who had been born in the village too late ever to have met Old Sam Barston had themselves reached old age, they still spoke of "Old Sam's thunder" every time a cannon was fired in the village, and they honored his memory with their smiles.

About the Author

Jack Noon lives and writes in Sutton, New Hampshire, his base for forays – in fiction and non-fiction – into northern New England's past.

About the Artist

Walt Cudnohufsky resides in Ashfield, Massachusetts, fully immersed in the rural New England scenes that are his regular inspiration. He finds tranquility in his surroundings and, with realistic pencil and watercolor works, captures the spirit of the rapidly disappearing landscape.

For those who enjoyed

Old Sam's Thunder . . .

The Big Fish
of Barston Falls

by Jack Noon

In the summer of 1822 twelve-year-old Sue
Reckford and Malik, an old man and one of the
few Abenakis left in the Connecticut River valley,
fish together in the river at the Vermont village of
Barston Falls. They catch perch every day and
trade them in the village square.

In response to a teasing bet from Old Sam
Barston about the size of the fish, Malik sets out
to catch something bigger. He and Sue start fishing out in the big eddy below the falls and there
make **an astounding discovery** . . .

Some responses to

The Big Fish
of Barston Falls

Jack Noon

"A classic fish story with a delightful climax! When I finished it, this fisherman couldn't help looking for Barston Falls on the map."

Willem Lange, author of
Tales From the Edge of the Woods

". . . an adventure tale about a girl and a man who match their combined strength and wits with a worthy opponent, the big fish of Barston Falls. It's *The Old Man and the Sea* on the Connecticut, only the Old Man happens to be Abenaki with a smart and sensible girl to help him. *The Big Fish of Barston Falls* is a yarn and a half, by God."

Rebecca Rule
The Sunday Telegraph

"Jack Noon writes historic stories of the Upper Connecticut River and the Valley. This is a story of the old canal days when rafts and flat boats went down the river, and it is an exciting tale of a fish big enough to satisfy the imagination of any angler!"

William S. Morse, author of
A Mix of Years & *A Country Life*

"This book has something for everyone. Mystery lovers will be intrigued by the big fish, history lovers will be charmed by the detailed descriptions of New England life in 1822, fishing enthusiasts will be fascinated and ecologists will be pleased. There's even a romantic sub-plot, with a surprising twist at the end. *The Big Fish* is destined to become a coming-of-age classic in the tradition of *Huckleberry Finn* and *Tom Sawyer*."

Hope Jordon
Ex Libris

❄   ❄   ❄

An excerpt from
The Big Fish of Barston Falls

Reuben White sat in a chair hanging from ropes tied to Colonel Hale's bridge across the Connecticut. He was deeply content as he held his salmon spear ready and kept an eye on the water rushing inches beneath his dangling feet. The river, though down from its earlier spring levels, still surged over the ledges with tremendous force. A fall from the chair would have been certain death, but Reuben wasn't concerned. The chair hung from four new ropes and was itself so tightly overlaced with cord that even if every wooden part in it broke, it would still hold together. In addition a separate rope knotted around Reuben's chest was tied to the bridge timbers above. Finally, his brother and two cousins waited up on the bridge to give whatever help he might need. Reuben felt so secure that he didn't worry even about getting wet. He thought only of spearing salmon.

He remembered stories his father and Uncle Douglas frequently told of how plentiful salmon had been nearly thirty years earlier, when they had been boys. They hadn't had Hale's bridge to spear from then and had worked from the ledges on the Vermont side of the river or from rafts anchored out in the eddy below the fast water. Tremendous numbers of salmon had come up the river then, they said, and shad had been even more plentiful than salmon. Shad couldn't ascend the fast water; never got further up the Connecticut than the huge eddy below the falls, where they were netted easily. Though it had been common for several hundred people to be fishing at the Great Falls, as Bellows' Falls had then been called, there had always been plenty of salmon and shad for everyone. But over the years Reuben's father and uncle had grumbled increasingly about the worsening fishing, blaming the greed of those people down in Massachusetts and Connecticut who weren't content simply with catching enough fish to last their families through the year, but who instead wanted to get rich selling fish. There was a sure market in the West Indies for all smoked or pickled fish: food for slaves on the sugar plantations. Massachusetts and Connecticut fishermen, Reuben's uncle claimed, wanted every single fish; would never be happy as long as anyone up the Connecticut in Vermont or New Hampshire was still catching any. There were far fewer salmon now, his uncle said, and they were a lot smaller than they had been in the early days. When Uncle Douglas's own sister, Reuben's Aunt Molly, was sixteen, hadn't she speared one herself from the ledges that had weighed forty-eight pounds on the flour scales in the Whites' gristmill? And in recent years a fish half that size had been thought an unusual catch.

A salmon arched out of the water fifty feet down below Reuben. Instantly his hand tightened on the spear shaft. He scanned the water below his feet carefully, waiting. Then the salmon appeared over to his left, but out of range. Reuben muttered at it.

A few minutes later a salmon struggled up against the current and headed directly towards the hanging chair. Reuben plunged the prongs of the spear down hard over the salmon's back. The salmon tore the spear from Reuben's grasp, but he quickly pulled it back with the long cord tied between the chair and the end of the spear. He wrestled in the salmon hand-over-hand until he could grab its gills. Then he shouted for his brother and his cousins. He shouted repeatedly to make himself heard over the roar of the water. Finally one of his cousins looked down from the railing of the bridge. Then Reuben's brother and his other cousin appeared. They lowered the end of a rope to him. Carefully he threaded the rope through the salmon's gills and knotted it. Then he freed the prongs of the spear and motioned for some-one to haul the salmon up. Fifteen pounds, he guessed as he turned his attention back to the river.

A moment later a jug hanging beside his elbow gave him a start. He looked up to see his brother laughing. Reuben let the spear drag in the current as he drank three long swallows of rum. He waved to his brother and put the stopper back into the jug, which then rose up and disappeared over the railing. There were no salmon for the next half hour. Occasionally Reuben's brother or his two cousins glanced over the bridge railing and gave the river down below a look to see if they could spot any salmon for Reuben, but then they lost interest. They sat leaning against the railing, drinking rum, and watching the bridge traffic pass.

Reuben himself all but lost interest in the fishing. His swallows of rum had made him feel good inside for a little while as he continued to watch for salmon. However, as the minutes passed and he saw no more salmon, he grew bored and then sleepy. He shook his head to ward off the sleepiness and yawned repeatedly. He shut one eye and let the other droop until it was nearly shut. Several times as his chin fell down onto his chest he lurched back into being half awake, but his drowsiness gave every promise of having him fall asleep in the chair.

Then, without knowing why, he was suddenly wide awake and staring hard at the river. He was scarcely breathing, his heart was beating wildly, his hand clenched the spear hard, and still he didn't know why. He looked right and left and straight at the river down below him, ready for any salmon.

Reuben jerked his head hard to the left and caught only the shortest glimpse of an enormous dark shape.

"A log. Had to be a log," he said to himself, but confusion flooded over him. The shape had been too big to have been anything but a log. His eyes had been tricked, however, into thinking that it had been headed up the river and, as he gazed down below to where the current would have carried a log, it hadn't risen again. He couldn't explain why he kept looking for the log long after it would have washed down into the eddy below. Nor could he explain the prickly feeling on the back of his neck and his overwhelming anxiety.

Then fifty yards below he saw a dark back roll up out of the water and disappear. Reuben gasped at the size, then felt foolish that he had let his eyes trick him into believing he had seen something bigger than a man and ten times the size of any salmon. He took a deep breath, trying to calm himself. Suddenly, twenty yards below, the broad back rolled up again out of the white water, right in the heart of the current. All the air rushed out of Reuben's lungs in a moan. His spear dragged on the surface of the swift water, and he found himself standing in the chair and trying to claw and thrash his way up the ropes, which were too thin to get a good grip on. He held himself in the air above the chair, both hands clenched around three ropes bunched together; the fists one on top of the other right at his chin and the ropes pressed against his cheek. Just beneath him he saw the dark, wide, scaleless back roll again — the back larger than Reuben himself — and then an enormous sickle tail rise and disappear beneath the white froth of current. An uncontrollable moan rattled in his throat — continuous except for Reuben's sharp gasps for air. His whole body clenched tight. Then, in a quickly moving procession, he saw four more of the great backs and sickle tails rise and fall in and out of sight down below, right beneath him, and then up above the bridge. Finally they were gone, and Reuben was shrieking hysterically. He didn't stop until his brother and cousins had pulled him and the chair up onto Hale's bridge.

No one believed Reuben, and after a few days he himself doubted what he thought he had seen. Nonetheless he never again tried to spear salmon from the hanging chair. It was over a year before he had another drink of rum. His brother, cousins, and others he later regretted telling his fish story to teased him mercilessly. It wasn't until he mocked himself better than the others did — shaking his head and laughing and using the story to caution others about drinking too much rum — that the teasing eased.

Secretly Reuben hoped that someone else fishing from Hale's bridge might see what he thought he had seen. It had seemed so real to him that he always kept a picture in his mind of the backs and the tails of the fish. If two or three other people could see the same sight, that would prove it hadn't been just a rum hallucination. Other men that spring and early summer hung in the salmon chair and speared fish, but they saw nothing but salmon. The following year the chair was used briefly, but then never again because there were no more salmon coming up the river. Someone had built a dam down in Massachusetts, and the salmon couldn't get by it. Young salmon, trapped up above the dam, lingered for a few years and were caught on baited hooks, but they were never of any size. They were no bigger than trout. The big salmon were gone from the Connecticut. Most people thought they'd be gone forever.

Nearly thirty years later Reuben chanced to read something in a newspaper that caused him to think hard remembering that last day he had speared salmon from the hanging chair.

To order books from

Moose Country
Press

Call us
TOLL FREE

1-800-34-MOOSE
(1-800-346-6673)

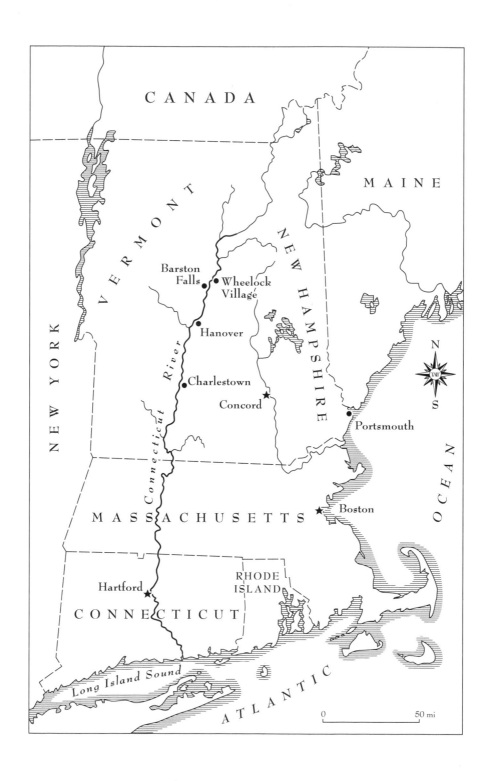

CANADA

MAINE

VERMONT

NEW HAMPSHIRE

NEW YORK

Barston
Falls

Wheelock
Village

Hanover

Connecticut River

Charlestown

Concord

Portsmouth

MASSACHUSETTS

Boston

RHODE
ISLAND

Hartford

CONNECTICUT

Long Island Sound

ATLANTIC

OCEAN

N
S

0   50 mi